The Wolf and the Lion

Mason Origins Book One

by

REX HOLLOWAY

First published by Rex Holloway 2024

First edition

ISBN: 979-8-9906572-3-6

Contents

1

The Two Paths to Hell

July 1994
Montreal, Quebec, Canada

Two boys, ages 12 and 14, hid in the shadows near a chain-link fence, just outside the yellow cone of a streetlight. It was closer to sunrise than sunset, and the alley, which ran through Saint-Henri like a seam through a grimy patchwork blanket, was dark and still. The backs of each row house were as different from each other as possible. Some were made of brick and covered in graffiti. Others were of decaying wood and crusted paint. Some had ramshackle garages, while others had fenced backyards. In the distance, a dog barked incessantly.

"Arrête de respirer si fort," the older boy, Raison, snarled to the younger in French. "Stop breathing so hard. You sound like a horse."

He was an average sized boy, with shaggy brown hair and blue eyes. His cheeks and frame were lean, but his shoulders were broad, and he was wearing black jeans and a black T-shirt.

The younger boy, Rage, frowned. "Tu es celui qui est bruyant," he whispered back. "You're the loud one." Dressed in all black and with light brown hair, he was much smaller than his older brother.

"Shut up!" Raison hissed.

They were squatting in the shadows, listening, waiting. Cicadas chirped all around. Raison fumbled in his pants pocket and pulled out a pack of cigarettes. Cupping his hand close to his chest, he lit one.

"What the fuck, Raison? You're gonna smoke now?" Rage gawked.

"Shut up, punk," Raison said. "Just keep an eye out."

The boys were huddled together in the shadows. Rage glanced around anxiously.

"Let me hit it," he said.

"No, you don't need it," Raison spat.

"You don't need it either," Rage growled back.

"Yeah, I do. I need it for my nerves. You don't know yet," Raison dismissed him.

"You better let me hit it, or I can go home right now," Rage said and started to stand.

"OK! Shit! Here," Raison said, grabbing his younger brother by the arm and pulling him back down. He passed Rage the cigarette, and they sat smoking for a moment.

"It makes me dizzy," Rage said, leaning his head between his knees.

"I fucking told you," Raison snapped, snatching the cigarette from his brother's hand. "You're so fucking stupid sometimes."

"You're fucking stupid," Rage lashed out with a punch to Raison's head, which the taller boy easily dodged.

"Ostie tu m'énerve!" Raison spat. "Fuck, you're getting on my nerves! Cut the bullshit, and let's do this."

"Come on then," Rage snapped. "You're the one acting like a scared little pussy."

"Fuck you," Raison said, shoving Rage's head. He extinguished the cigarette with his shoe. "Stop talking shit and do what I told you. Go to the front and create the diversion. Here, take these."

Raison handed his little brother the lighter, then he picked up a glass bottle filled with liquid from the ground, a piece of cloth hanging from its neck.

"Remember, go fast and count to 20. When you get to 20, light it, throw it, and run back here as fast as you can. And don't get it on you or you'll catch on fire, too. Got it?"

"I've got it," Rage said, reaching out to take the lighter and the Molotov cocktail.

"OK," Raison said, standing up. He lifted his shirt and retrieved a flathead screwdriver and a hammer from his waistband. Sweat beaded on Raison's face, and his hands trembled. "Are you ready?"

Holding the firebomb and the lighter, Rage looked up and down the alley, smiling, his eyes twinkling in the streetlight. "I said I was ready."

"Go!" Raison urged, and Rage darted across the alley to a gap between a chain-link fence and a dilapidated garage. He wriggled his thin ribcage between the galvanized post and the rotting wood, and then he was gone in the darkness between the houses.

"One...two...three..." Raison whispered as he trotted to the fence, placed one hand on the top rail, and climbed over. He cleared it easily, landing gently on the dusty backyard.

He crouched and listened. The yard was silent, and the house ahead dark. He slinked through the shadows toward the rear of the home.

"...eight...nine...ten..." he counted as he carefully placed each foot, avoiding sticks and empty cans. The yard was filled with junked engines, rotting tires, and empty jugs of motor oil. He paused in a puddle of mud, just behind a rusty burn barrel, the smell of charred paper and burned plastic mixing with the stench of wet garbage and gasoline.

"...fourteen...fifteen...sixteen..."

He peaked around the barrel to the driveway next to the home, and there it was, parked next to the house, a 1991 Harley-Davidson Fat Boy. It had a wide gas tank painted glossy black, plenty of chrome, and solid billet wheels. Black saddle bags hung from the rear fender, and a braided leather get back whip over three feet long hung from the throttle grip.

Raison crouched and waited.

"...eighteen ... nineteen...twenty."

There was a clank and a crash from the front of the house, then a whoosh and a flash of light that spilled out into the neighbor's yards, orange and dancing. Instantly, Raison darted across the dirt and onto the driveway, straight for the motorcycle. As he slid to a stop at the bike, a motion-activated flood light popped on, bathing the yard in halogen rays.

Panicked, using the flathead screwdriver and hammer, Raison went to work on the ignition lock. His jaw clenched rhythmically as he focused on the task. He'd almost defeated the lock just as he heard a man shout from the front yard.

"Que diable se passe-t-il?" the voice boomed. "What the hell is going on?"

Then, "Feu! Feu!" the man shouted. "Fire! Fire!"

Raison flinched at the thunderous bark of a dog from the front yard, and his heart caught in his throat. He heard footsteps thumping rapidly inside the home as occupants scrambled. The orange glow from the front grew brighter, and the scent of burning wood wafted to him.

Then Raison heard a scream, his brother's, first in fear, then in pain. Jolted, Raison dropped the screwdriver, and it clanged against the bike before smacking the concrete and rolling under the Fat Boy's wide frame.

"Merde!" he muttered, then fell to his shaking knees and felt around for the lost tool.

From the front, Rage's cries turned from pain to terror. Raison's heart thudded in his chest, and his arms felt weak. He found the screwdriver and quickly went back to work on the ignition.

"Raison! Aide-moi!" his brother screamed for help over and over.

Raison squinted his eyes and worked as fast as he could until, finally, the lock broke. With the ignition lock defeated, he turned his attention to the fork lock. Placing the tip of the screwdriver exactly right, he smacked it with the hammer until it broke, the loud banging lost in the shouts and barks from the front. With both locks defeated, Raison mounted the bike, kicked up the stand, flipped the run switch, and pushed the start button.

The hefty motorcycle roared to life, exhaust billowing from its exhaust pipes, the powerful V-Twin engine rumbling and shaking his thin frame. Raison kicked the bike into gear, eased off the clutch, and it lurched forward. The tools fell from Raison's grasp, clanking to the concrete as the bike rushed down the driveway toward the front yard mayhem.

Raison skidded the bike to a stop at the front of the house, his eyes bulging in shock. The entire front porch was engulfed in flames. A man was running around frantically dressed in white briefs, dragging a garden hose and yelling about the fire department. When he saw Raison, the man slipped and fell in the grass, staring in surprise. Then realization struck him, and he jumped up in a rage.

Raison looked around. Everywhere was chaos. The flames cast flickering lights and shadows across the small yard, and he could feel the heat and hear the crackle of the growing blaze. He forced himself to focus, to listen, and in a flash, heard his brother crying and begging for help from the shadows.

"Descendez de ma moto!" the furious man shouted, charging at Raison. "Get off my bike!"

Raison cranked the throttle and drove straight at him. Mouth gaping, the man jumped out of the way as Raison barreled across the yard, bumping over stones and a sidewalk as he raced to the sound of his screaming brother.

Rage was on the ground, curled in a ball. His pale face was scrunched in anguish as a huge dog with thick, dark hair like a wolf thrashed about him, growling and whipping its head furiously. The dog's powerful jaws were clamped onto Rage's hand, its feet were dug in, and it was yanking hard at the appendage. Blood ran freely between its yellow teeth.

In the last second, as Raison crossed the yard, he flicked on the headlight. The dog flinched and looked up, but too late. The front tire of the motorcycle struck the hound broadside, sending the beast sliding across the grass. Raison slammed the brakes and slid to a stop. His adrenaline raging, he reached down, grabbed his brother's shirt, and heaved him onto the back of the bike.

"Hold on!" he yelled.

Rage pressed his face onto his brother's back and held tightly to his waist. The dog scampered to its feet, then charged them, a blur of teeth and fury. Raison grabbed the leather whip attached to the right grip and swung it at the dog. The whip's end, weighted with a billiard ball, smacked the dog soundly on the shoulder. It yelped and recoiled away. Raison cranked the throttle and sent a shower of dirt and grass into the air as the bike fishtailed out of the yard and onto the blacktop road. He opened the throttle. The engine howled, and the two brothers took off on the stolen motorcycle, leaving a barking, shouting, blazing inferno behind them.

Block after block passed, and Raison didn't stop. He could feel Rage behind him, leaning against his back, sobbing and shaking. Raison's heart pounded and his eyes stung, but he kept going.

"Stop! Please!" Rage cried, his voice breaking. "Please, Raison, stop!"

Raison pulled the bike to the curb. The front of his jeans were soaked with warm liquid. For a moment, he feared he had wet himself. He touched it. It was blood.

"Ah! Raison! Ah!" his brother bawled behind him, so he jumped off the bike to look. Rage was hunched over his hand, holding it tightly.

"Let me see," Raison said.

Rage tipped his head back and howled into the night, gripping his arm closely.

"Rage! Let me see it," Raison demanded, grabbing his brother's arm firmly.

Rage tried to pull away, but Raison was stronger. Gripping him by the biceps, he yanked Rage's hand free and held it up to the streetlight.

Only three fingers remained. The hand was split longways into three parts, as if someone had torn it between the fingers and metacarpals. His middle finger was hanging from ripped flesh, and blood was pulsing and streaming from the mangled stump.

Raison ripped his sweatshirt over his head and quickly wrapped his brother's hand with it. Rage whimpered and pleaded, too hoarse and weak to scream anymore.

"Maman! S'il te plaît, emmène-moi chez maman," he pleaded, over and over. "Mom! Please, take me to mom."

"I'm taking you," Raison assured as he remounted the bike. "Just hold on to me!"

Clenching his teeth, Raison gunned the engine, roaring off into the night, his injured brother behind him, the wind streaking his tears away.

2

Buddies

July 2014
  Denver, Colorado, USA

A Denver Police Chevrolet Tahoe, white with a blue shield on the door, drove along the freshly poured concrete drive through a pristine suburban development, past newly constructed two-story American castles of brick and vinyl siding, each surrounded by tiny estates of freshly laid sod and shrubs still baring nursery tags. The flowerbeds cooked in the afternoon sun, and the air smelled of mulch and manure. Winding streets of completed homes blended into even newer streets lined with the skeletal frames of homes still under construction. Stick framed structures, some with insulation or house wrap and some with exposed studs, marched into the distance. The yards were bare dirt, and the mud-caked curbs were lined with work trucks and vans with ladders on their roofs. The police Tahoe continued to the end of a cul-de-sac where it stopped at a construction site swarming with workers.

  Within seconds of the police cruiser stopping, the sounds of hammering and sawing ceased. The door to the Tahoe opened, and a uniformed Denver police officer stepped out. He was stocky, with a swarthy face and black hair with buzzed sides and a razor part. He wore a black uniform and his patent leather boots glinted in the sun. He looked around under dark sunglasses as he walked up the driveway, past a sawhorse and sacks of concrete. A laborer wearing muddy rubber boots walked quickly, head down, toward the back of the house. The officer strolled casually up to the gaping front entry where he stopped and shouted inside, "Yo!"

From the shadowy interior appeared an obese, sweaty man with thick glasses, shaggy brown hair, and a belly barely tucked under his T-shirt.

"Afternoon, officer," the man said, wiping his hands together. "I'm Morty Jones, the superintendent on this site. What can I do for you?"

"Mr. Jones, I am Benito Mendez. I was in the area and stopped by to see an old friend. He's expecting me. Mason?"

"Oh," Morty said, releasing a chestful of air. "Yeah, uh, no problem. If you want to come inside, I'll have to ask you to wear a hard hat. Or he can come outside. Your call, boss."

"Outside is good," Officer Benito Mendez said. "If you could tell him I'm here, I'd appreciate it."

Morty waddled back into the partially constructed home. The walls were exposed studs with some wiring and electrical boxes installed, and the floor was bare concrete. He walked through the dining room, down a hallway, and into the main suite. He passed through the roughed-in doorway of the main bathroom and looked up into the rafters.

"Mason! Your cop buddy is out front scaring the shit out of the wetbacks. Fucking shit, like I need this right now. We are already a week behind. Would you get him the fuck out of here so the Mexican roofers can get back to work? Jesus Christ!" Morty blurted. Spit flew and his face turned purple.

Above him, high in the rafters, was perched a tall, wiry man wearing dirty cargo shorts, hiking boots, and a blue bandana as a headband. He was shirtless and had brown hair down to his shoulders and a thick brown beard that hung to his chest. He was tanned and covered in sawdust. A leather tool belt hung about his waist, and he was holding a tape measure. He looked down at Morty through black sunglasses.

"Guatemalan," Mason said. He reached down and used a ceiling joist like a chin-up bar to lower himself to the floor. "The roofers are all Guatemalan.

The plumbers are mostly Mexican, except Javi, who is Venezuelan. And I hate to tell you, but whoever framed this bathroom should have read the plans, because they forgot to account for the skylight."

"Listen, I don't care about sky lights. Just get the cop out of here. Me and you are the only two U.S. citizens on this fucking job site."

Mason dropped his tool belt on the floor and shouldered past the obese supervisor, slapping sawdust off himself as he went. He passed through a hall lined with regularly spaced wooden studs, like ribs lining the gut of some massive whale. At the front of the house, Mason stepped through the opening of the front door and into the sun.

"Mason!" Benito shouted, a grin spreading across his face.

Mason smiled as he crossed the yard. "Benito, you old Devil Dog! What are you up to?"

The two men clasped hands in a firm handshake.

"Just making my rounds," Benito replied, his eyes scanning the construction site. "Thought I'd swing by and see how you're holding up in the civilian world."

Mason chuckled, wiping his brow with the back of his hand. "You know me, staying busy."

"Bro, it's weird seeing you work like this. From Delta Force operator to construction worker," Benito shook his head and smiled. "Every day I picture us back in Fallujah, especially that night you saved my ass."

"Yeah, man, that was one hell of a cluster fuck," Mason agreed. "How's life on the force?"

Benito's expression was a mix of pride and weariness. "Thanks, man. Eh, every day is a new adventure, Mason. I can't complain. All I really know is a uniform and a gun, so it works for me, you know? How about you? Is this working for you?"

Mason didn't respond immediately. He looked around, back at the house he was working on, then at the many other homes, each on their symmetrical lots, each built precisely to code.

"After seeing all those buildings blown up and leveled overseas, it feels good to build something from the ground up," he replied.

"I get that, bro," Benito said, nodding. "Change of subject. So, you know they're legalizing marijuana in this state, right?"

"Yeah, I saw that," Mason said. "How does that affect you at your job?"

"Bro, honestly, nobody knows," Benito replied, hooking his thumbs into his duty belt. "The entire department is like 'What the hell?' Where's your probable cause to search a vehicle if everyone smells like weed? How do you prove DUI? Bro, it's a mess. But honestly, I don't care. I say legalize it all. And that's really why I'm here to see you."

Mason looked up and cocked an eyebrow. "Oh?" he asked.

"Yeah, bro. Check it out. Not everyone knows this yet, so I wanted to come tell you myself. The chief of police—everybody calls him The Colonel—quit the force to start a new security company specializing in the legal cannabis sector."

"Really? Why do they call him 'The Colonel?'" Mason asked.

"Because he was a colonel in the Marine Corps. In fact, he was commander of our regiment during Operation Phantom Fury. Colonel Mack Radford. In fact, I'm leaving the force, too, and joining his new company."

"Wait, so you served under him in Iraq, then again here on Denver PD, and now you're leaving the department to work for him in the private sector?"

"What can I say? Let's be real," Benito said. "The risk is less, the money is better, and the hours are regular. I am done with overtime, bro. Plus, he's a good boss. Things have been going pretty good so far, so I figured why not just stick with the winning team?"

"Well, damn. Aren't you loyal?" Mason said.

"As a dog," Benito laughed. He looked around, picked up a nail from the street, and flung it into the yard. "I know you say you're happy here, but The Colonel is offering top pay at this new company. He wants guys with combat experience. Like you, Mason. You'd be perfect. Former Delta Force operator, decorated war hero."

"Last time I listened to a recruiter," Mason replied, "I ended up freezing my ass off in the mountains of Afghanistan and getting shot at. A lot. And for not enough money."

"Ah, man," Benito brushed him off, "it's nothing like that. It's basically armed transport. The dispensaries can't put their money in the banks because weed isn't legal federally. So, The Colonel had the idea of collecting the cash from the dispensaries in armored vehicles and storing it himself in a safe house."

"He wants to start his own bank?" Mason asked.

"Not exactly. More like just a storage vault. Armored transport and safe storage, that's what he told me. He already has a building figured out and all that. Now he's looking for drivers and guards, and he wants the best of the best."

"I'm not licensed to do security work," Mason said.

"It's nothing," said Benito, waving him off again. "It's just a city license. There's no state security guard license in Colorado. Piece of cake, bro."

Mason looked into the distance quietly.

"Look, the reason I came to see you is to tell you that tomorrow, The Colonel is meeting with a bunch of recruits at the gun range. He rented out the entire place, and he wants to see everyone go through drills."

"I thought you said it wasn't a shooting kind of job," Mason objected.

"The Colonel says he can tell all he needs to know about a man by how he shoots. And I bet he's never seen anyone shoot like you," Benito replied.

"Eh," Mason said, waving him off.

"Look," Benito stepped closer, "at least come and hang out with me. If you want to shoot, then shoot. If not, at least it'll be cool to be at the range. Don't tell me you're going to be out here climbing around in rafters on a Saturday. Come, hang with your homie."

Mason thought a moment longer. "Sure, man, I'll come shoot. Just text me the details."

"Hell, yeah!" Benito said, punching Mason in the arm.

"Damn, chill out. I need that arm today," Mason said, laughing and pulling away.

"Cool, Mason. I've got to take off, but I'm glad you're coming," Benito said, reaching out to shake Mason's hand goodbye.

"It's good to see you, too, Mendez," Mason said.

With a toothy smile, Benito strolled back to his cruiser. "You better bring your good eyes because I've been practicing. I might be able to out-shoot you."

"We'll see," Mason said, watching his friend leave. Just as Benito opened the driver's door, Mason called out. "Hey, what's the name of the new company?"

"Green Zone Defense," Benito called back.

"Oh, great," Mason grumbled. "Green Zone, like in Iraq."

"Yeah, but with less bombs and more bongs," Benito said, holding his pinched fingers to his lips to mimic smoking a joint.

Mason laughed and waved. He watched his friend drive away, then turned and walked back into the job site.

The gun range was a well-maintained, expansive outdoor facility on the outskirts of Denver. It was bordered by a towering dirt berm designed to absorb bullets. The range was segmented into several lanes, each marked by weathered wooden stands and tables where shooters could prepare their firearms and gear. The parking lot was made of dirt and gravel.

Mason pulled into the lot in his lifted 1986 Ford Bronco in Desert Tan Metallic, a few spots of rust showing around the chrome trim. The air was alive with the sharp reports of gunfire, each shot resonating crisply in the open air.

He opened the tailgate of the Bronco and slid a rigid black rifle case and an olive drab canvas duffle from the rear of the vehicle. He was wearing a worn blue ball cap, a gray T-shirt, and jeans. Black sunglasses covered his face, and the tails of his beard and hair blew in the breeze as he carried his gear into the staging area. As he was checking in with the range master, Benito, who had been engaged in a discussion with a group of fellow officers, spotted him. With a broad smile, he approached Mason, extending his hand.

"Mason! Glad you could make it," Benito exclaimed, his voice carrying over the noise of the range. He was wearing tan cargo pants and a black Denver Police T-shirt.

Mason returned the handshake firmly. They walked together through the staging area. Men wearing shooting glasses and ear protection were scattered around, about 50 in total. Some were already at stations shooting. Others were loading magazines or checking their weapons.

"Can't miss a range day," Mason replied.

"Oh, yeah? You still keep your skills sharp?" Benito asked.

"I do what I can," Mason said, setting his gear bags on an open table.

"Good deal," Benito said. "Everybody out here today can shoot. You've got Denver PD, sheriff's department, SWAT, everybody. I see one former SEAL right now."

Glancing at Mason's gear bags, Benito asked, "What toys did you bring?"

"Oh, nothing major," Mason said, clicking open the clasps on the rifle case. He lifted the case's lid, revealing a short-barreled FN 15 semiautomatic rifle. It had a three-point sling, vertical fore-grip, and Trijicon holographic site. It was scratched, and in many areas, the black finish was worn to the shiny metal underneath.

"Nice, old faithful" Benito said. "The instructors have some different drills planned. I'm not really sure. I know there will be pistol and carbine drills, but they're talking about some vehicle work, too."

Mason unzipped his canvas gear bag and pulled out a tactical belt set up with a holster, pouches for extra magazines, and other gadgets. He pulled a SIG Sauer P226 MK25 pistol from the bag and racked the slide to verify the chamber was empty. He slid the pistol into the holster and dug around for magazines.

"I'll be ready," Mason said.

"Cool, I'll let you do your thing," Benito said. "I'm glad you made it, bro."

His friend walked away, and Mason continued preparing himself and his gear. Once his rifle, pistol, and magazines were ready, he retrieved a pair of shooting glasses and protective ear muffs from the bag, then stood waiting for instructions.

Just then, a man with a blonde flattop and wrap-around sunglasses wearing black cargo pants and a black T-shirt with "SWAT" across the front called for everyone's attention. The chatter died down.

"Listen up! Let me get all eyes on me, please. My name is Sergeant Matt Anderson. I am a training officer with Denver PD, and I will be the officer in charge today. We are still getting a few things squared away, and we will get started shortly. The main thing I want to stress right now is safety. Let's keep those weapons clear and on safe when not on the firing line, OK? Get geared up. In a few minutes, we're going to divide you into groups and assign team leaders to walk you through the drills. OK, guys?"

A few minutes later, five team leaders wearing matching black SWAT T-shirts spread out in front of the shooting lanes, and once again, Matt Anderson addressed the crowd.

"Listen for your names. When I call out a team leader's name, they will raise their hand. If I call your name after that, line up on the leader with their hand raised. Here we go."

Matt Anderson read down the list, and the men divided themselves into five groups of ten. Mason found himself on Charlie Team, shooting third after Alpha and Bravo. The team leaders called out drills and provided instructions to their teams.

Just as Alpha Team took their stations to start the pistol drills, Mason noticed a group of three men standing to one side who were not dressed to shoot. Two of them were older and one younger, and all three wore civilian clothing. The two older men had pistols in leather holsters on their hips. One was short but powerfully built with a salt-and-pepper flat top. He wore blue slacks and a blazer. The other older man was tall, balding, and dressed like a cowboy in jeans and a straw cowboy hat. The younger man, wearing jeans and a T-shirt, looked a bit like the first man with the salt-and-pepper Marine haircut, but about half the age. All three wore dark sunglasses and watched the proceedings intently, occasionally chatting amongst themselves.

When it was Charlie Team's turn, Mason took his position at the firing line and aligned his stance. He took a few deep breaths and focused his mind. The team leader, a large, baby-faced man with a barrel chest, stood behind them, a whistle hanging from his neck. The other participants took their places at the shooting line, each awaiting instructions for the drill.

"First drill, rapid engagement!" called out the team leader, his voice cutting through the air. "Draw. Present. Take two shots per target, hit all three targets as quickly as possible! On my mark!"

Mason's stance tightened. The whistle blew and instantly, Mason's pistol was up and firing. His movements were a blur — two shots rang out, hitting the first target dead center. Without hesitation, he pivoted, firing two more shots at the second target, and then swiftly to the third. The rhythm of his shots was precise, and the steel disks rang out like dinner bells six times.

"Transition drill!" the team leader barked next. "Engage right, center, left—two shots each, move!"

Mason's transitions were fluid, his body turning smoothly as he engaged each target in succession. His shots were deliberate, each one finding its mark with a mechanical consistency.

The team leader then upped the challenge. "Movement drill! Advance towards targets, engage with two shots each as you move. Go!"

Mason advanced, his steps measured and controlled. He fired as he moved, keeping a steady aim. The targets had no chance against his unerring precision, even in motion. Then, he repeated the drill in reverse, moving backward with the same level of accuracy and control.

As the drills concluded, the team leader blew the whistle, signaling the end of the session. The other participants were visibly impressed, some shaking their heads in disbelief at Mason's display of shooting prowess.

After completion of the pistol drills, the Charlie Team leader waved for the team to move down to the rifle section of the range. Mason, along with the others, prepared for the next phase of their evaluation. He carried his FN 15, a familiar weight settling comfortably into his grasp.

The team leader called out the first drill. "Multiple target engagement! Start close, move to long range. Two shots each!"

Mason's stance shifted as he raised the carbine, his eyes focusing intently through the sight. The first burst of fire from his FN 15 was crisp and precise, the rounds punctuating the air as they hit the set of close-range targets dead center. Without missing a beat, Mason advanced to the next position, engaging the longer-range targets with the same pinpoint accuracy.

"Transition drill!" the team leader shouted next. "Engage, switch shoulders, move to the next target!"

Mason fluidly transitioned the carbine from one shoulder to the other, a maneuver that allowed him to keep a steady line of sight and fire as he moved between targets. He flowed through the course, adapting to different shooting positions with ease. Standing, kneeling, through doorways, windows, partially obscured targets, reactive targets—anything the range offered—Mason peppered with bullets easily.

Interspersed between the bursts of fire were Mason's swift and seamless magazine changes. He ejected each spent magazine and loaded a fresh one with an economy of motion that was almost balletic. While he was shooting, some of the other men stopped to watch.

As the carbine drills ended, the baby-faced team leader nodded approvingly at Mason's performance. "Outstanding work, Mason! You've done this before."

The final drill was shooting from a stationary vehicle. Mason positioned himself in the driver's seat of a parked Chevrolet Suburban, his weapon ready. At the signal, he rolled down the window, leaning out to engage targets positioned at various angles and distances. His control of his pistol and rifle were masterful, his shots precise and effective. He demonstrated various techniques—shooting with one hand, transitioning to the passenger side, and exiting the vehicle to engage targets. He executed every move flawlessly.

As Benito watched, the tall, older cowboy from the group of three observers quietly made his way to his side.

"Mendez. Who's the hotshot?" the cowboy asked.

"Captain Frazier, how are you?" Benito asked. He turned toward Mason and smiled. "That, sir, is my buddy Mason, former Delta Force operator, and real-life bad ass. He saved my life in Fallujah. The Ba'athists had a fifty-thousand-dollar tag on his head. After the war, we always stayed in touch. Then we both ended up moving here."

Captain Frazier stood watching for a moment. "What's he doing with all that hair? Is he a cop?"

"No, sir," Benito laughed. "He's a builder."

Captain Frazier harrumphed. "The Colonel wants to talk to him."

Benito grinned even broader. "I bet he does, sir. I bet he does."

Mason walked over, breathing hard, his rifle slung over his back, sweat dripping down his face and soaking his shirt.

"Good shit, Mason," Benito said as they bumped fists. "You got the brass all hot and bothered."

"Oh, yeah?" Mason replied, glancing around for the three men he had seen watching, but he couldn't spot them.

"Nice shooting," another man said, walking up and offering his hand. He was young, Asian American, athletically built, and had the good looks of an actor or model. "I'm Park Min-kyu, but everybody calls me 'Mink.'"

"Because he's so soft," Benito said, dragging his fingers tenderly down Mink's cheek. He quickly brushed Benito's hand away.

Mason chuckled and shook Mink's hand. "Thank you. I take it you're with Denver PD, too?"

"Yeah, yeah. Grew up in San Diego. Was supposed to go to college but joined the Marines instead. Ended up getting married and dumping the Corps. My wife and I moved here about 5 years ago. What about you? Where are you from, Mason?"

"Texas, mainly," he replied.

"I did advanced infantry training at MRTC, but I haven't seen anybody shoot, move, and reload like you just did. I heard somebody say you were Delta Force. Is that right?"

"Mmmmm," Mason replied, fidgeting with his gear and looking around.

Mink nodded. "Cool, man. I know you can't really talk about it. But the training shows. Are you applying for a job at The Colonel's new security company? GZD, I think they're calling it?"

"Man, I really just came to knock the cobwebs off my trigger finger," Mason replied.

"Este vato," Benito laughed. "Don't even bother trying, Mink. He's always like this. He's Mr. Freeze when he's around a lot of people, but in a firefight, bro, he's the one you want."

"I bet," Mink said. "Well, it was good to meet you, Mason. Benito, you need help."

Mink feigned a punch at Benito's face as he walked away.

Benito flinched. "Hey, watch it, pendejo. I know judo."

Mason finished packing his rifle into its case when he saw them coming. The three men he had seen together earlier stepped up to his table. The shorter man with the dark high-and-tight haircut spoke without removing his sunglasses.

"That was some damn impressive shooting," he said, extending his hand. "Mack Radford. Colleagues tend to call me 'The Colonel.'"

Mason shook his hand. "Thank you, sir. Pleasure to meet you. I'm Mason."

"Mason? First or last name?" The Colonel asked.

"Last," Mason replied, and The Colonel nodded.

The Colonel gestured to a young man standing beside him. "This is my son, Caleb. Just starting as a licensed security officer."

Caleb shook Mason's hand enthusiastically. "Nice to meet you, sir."

"And this is Doug Frazier. Doug is a captain with Denver PD, where I used to work," The Colonel said, and the tall cowboy reached out his hand for Mason to shake.

"They tell me you were a military man of the highest caliber. I recently resigned from my post as police chief and have decided to take my 40 years of combat and tactical experience to the private sector. Recent changes in laws and societal norms have created a unique opportunity for men like us. A chance to blaze new trails. I am guessing your buddy Sergeant Mendez has mentioned Green Zone Defense to you?"

"Yes, sir, he gave me a general briefing," Mason replied.

"And what are your thoughts on that, Mason?" The Colonel asked. "Your skills are valuable in the private sector. Hell, you can do pretty well these days just instructing. Have you ever thought about having your own business training others how to shoot?"

Mason stood tall, blinking, looking around. He ran his hand through his beard and stammered, "Well, no. No sir, I have never given it much thought."

"Where do you work now, Mason?" The Colonel asked.

"I subcontract as a carpenter. Framing, mostly, but sometimes I do trim work or custom cabinets."

"A carpenter, huh? Well, that's a valuable skill, too," The Colonel said. "Listen, I won't keep you. But if you get tired of wondering where your next paycheck is coming from, we are well-financed and ready to move. We'll have an application process set up soon. Segreant Mendez can keep you updated. I would love to see your application come across my desk. Understood?"

"Yes sir," Mason replied. "Thank you for letting me come shoot today."

The Colonel smiled and clapped Mason's shoulder. "The pleasure is all mine."

Mason packed his gear, shouldered his bags, and carried them back to his Ford Bronco, the thunder of the range fading behind him. Benito waved goodbye after promising to keep in touch. After loading his bags in the back, Mason slammed the tailgate and climbed into the driver's seat.

He cranked the V8 and sat behind the tinted windows, letting the engine rumble. He stared ahead, then removed his sunglasses and rubbed his temples. His head was spinning. His ears rang and whistled, his teeth were clenched, and his fists were balled into knots. He forced himself to take deep breaths, to relax his muscles, starting with his feet, then his calves, then his thighs. Little by little, he fought down the wave of anxiety.

Reaching under the seat, Mason pulled out a bottle of Tito's vodka. He unscrewed the cap and took a mouthful, feeling the warm burn as it slid down his throat, the tension in his gut releasing.

As he sat there, the muffled sounds of gunfire continued to resonate in his head. Mason reached for the Bronco's radio. He turned the dial, the speakers coming to life with the abrasive, thundering double bass and screaming guitars of thrash metal. The intense, pounding rhythms and aggressive guitar riffs filled the vehicle, drowning out everything.

With the music blaring, Mason didn't stop or bother looking back as he barreled out of the driveway, the bottle of vodka sloshing in his lap. He took the blacktop road out of town, trying not to think about anything.

3

Fight

Inside the octagon, a glob of bloody spit splattered across the referee's black shoes just before Matheo and Ramon crashed to the canvas. The crowd inside the Cabaret du Casino de Montreal jumped to their feet and roared. Grunting and straining, sweat running down his bald head, Matheo took the top position, hooking his legs under Ramon's and wrestling to control his arms. Ramon wrenched his arms free and unleashed a flurry of elbow slashes to the side of Matheo's head. Forced to retreat, Matheo released his clinch and stood up. Standing at 5-feet 6-inches, wearing red and black trunks, Matheo was the shorter of the two combatants. He was white, bald, clean shaven, and covered with tattoos. With his square jaw, heavy brow, and swollen, scarred ears, he looked like he was chiseled from granite. Blood mixed with sweat trickled from a cut on his eyebrow, and his chest heaved with each breath.

Ramon, a Dominican boxer and jiu-jitsu expert, stood, and the two fighters squared off in the center of the ring. Matheo darted in and landed a kick to Ramon's lead leg with a resounding smack. The fighters exchanged punches, kicks, and elbows, crashing into the cage and struggling for dominance.

The Cabaret was bathed in a soft, red glow. In the center of the room, an octagon of black chain-link fence had been erected on a platform. Every seat in the theater was filled with 600 mostly French-Canadian fans. A raucous crowd, they shouted encouragements to Matheo, the hometown hero, and jeered Ramon in Quebecois French.

Loudest of all was a group of burly, leather-clad bikers in the front row nearest to Matheo's corner. They ranged from tall to short, thin to massive. There were women mixed amongst them, wives and girlfriends with bleached blonde hair, wearing minidresses and cropped leather jackets. One biker had the swarthy complexion and traditional hairstyle of the Mohawk people. The sides of his head were shaved bald, leaving only a narrow strip of black hair down the center. A strand of black and red beads hung from his neck, along with a gold chain.

"Leg kicks, Matheo! Work the leg kicks!" he shouted.

The other bikers around him cheered and pumped their fists, sloshing beer from plastic cups and banging metal chairs on the ground. Each of them wore a black leather vest, or "cut", covered in patches, though some had more patches than others. Large patches covered the backs of most of their cuts, featuring a menacing wolf's head with blood-streaked fangs flanked by mechanical gears. The top banner, or "rocker", read "Dead Wolves," and the bottom rocker read "Montreal." A black, diamond-shaped "1%" patch was displayed to the left of the wolf's head, and on the right, a patch bearing "MC" completed the design.

At the front of the group, an older biker with long brown hair and a mostly gray beard raised a plastic cup in the air and bellowed. A patch on his right breast read "Max", while a similar patch on his left breast read "President". He wore a black T-shirt under his cut that revealed tanned, wiry arms covered in faded tattoos. His face was sundried, and his eyes were surrounded by wrinkles.

To his right, a tall man with long brown hair and a reddish goatee stood drinking heartily from a pint of foamy beer and smiling widely. He whistled and cheered with the rest. His chest patches read "Wild Bill" and "Vice President." He wore a red bandana around his neck and had large rings on every finger.

To Max's left, a younger but larger member of the Dead Wolves MC stood, his thumbs hooked in his belt loops. He watched the fight with a furrowed brow. Unlike the others, he barely cheered. He had short brown hair and a square jaw covered in stubble. His intense blue eyes sometimes stared into the distance for a moment before snapping back to the present. He wore a white T-shirt under his cut that revealed the muscular and tattooed arms of a weightlifter. On the front of his vest, one patch read "Raison" while the other read "Sgt. at Arms."

Wild Bill clapped Raison on the back. "He's going to get this asshole!" he shouted.

In the octagon, the fighters were clenched against the cage, trading knee and elbow strikes. Matheo almost secured an arm lock just as the bell dinged for the end of the round. The crowd cheered and clapped.

"Only one round left," Raison said. "Matheo should go for the knockout."

"Nah, the Dominican is an excellent boxer, and he's got reach on our boy," Wild Bill said. "He's doing the right thing going for the submission."

"Matheo is submitting this guy this round, guaranteed," said another biker as he stepped up to Raison and clapped him on the shoulder. He was in his early 20s and had long, unkempt brown hair and a curly brown beard. Three teardrop tattoos ran down his left cheek. He wore black jeans and a long-sleeved black shirt under his cut. He rested his rigid, flesh-colored prosthetic left hand on Raison's shoulder with a grin.

"Your brother doubts Matheo's boxing skills, too, it seems," Wild Bill said.

"You both assume he will use his hands. But you forget, Matheo studied Savate. He will win with his feet, not his hands," Raison replied.

A cocktail server came by, and the men ordered a round of drinks. Across the room, also in the front row, another group of about twenty bikers and their women congregated. Most of them were sitting casually, but several of the biggest men, hulking beasts covered in prison tattoos and wearing dark sunglasses, stood as bodyguards. Their cuts all bore the red, white, and black colors of the Big Machine Motorcycle Club. Their back patch, or "colors", featured a grinning skeleton riding a massive V-twin motorcycle. The top rocker said "Big Machine" in red on a white field. Below the main patch, some of their bottom rockers read "Toronto" while others read "Nomads". To the left of the chopper-riding skeleton was a diamond-shaped patch with

"1%" written in red.

One of the Big Machine members sat smoking a cigar, one ankle crossed over his knee. A tall, thin man in his fifties, his long blonde hair and beard fell wildly around the collar of the Western shirt he wore under his cut. Unlike the others, his cut was made of denim. He wore tight blue jeans, brown ostrich skin cowboy boots, and a big belt buckle like a bull rider. His chest patches read "Tommy Boy" and "President".

On the Dead Wolve's side, Raison leaned down and said to the club president, Max, "Big Machine is over there. Looks like Tommy Boy from the Toronto chapter and a few Nomads, too."

Max kept smiling. "I see them," he said. "We're good until I see a Montreal or Quebec rocker underneath a motorcycle-riding skeleton. They can pass through Quebec. They can even visit Montreal. But if we ever see Big Machine *claiming* Montreal or Quebec, then we have a problem. Do you get it?"

Raison inclined his head but did not respond. "We've been seeing them more and more in the city," he said. "They're probably offering local clubs the chance to patch over and join them. Bruno said he saw them hanging with a new club in town the other night, which could mean they're setting up dummy clubs here to recruit."

"Raison, you don't have to tell me how Big Machine operates," Max growled. "I've been riding since before you were some poor mom's biggest mistake. I can't stop another club from patching over if they choose, but if Big Machine is setting up dummy clubs in Quebec, then they're looking for war. And just because they're the biggest, doesn't mean they're the baddest. We're a vicious pack of wolves. This is our turf and always will be."

Max spit on the floor and glared at the group of Big Machine bikers through squinted, wrinkled lids. Raison stood quietly.

The bell dinged to start the final round of the match. The fighters met once more in the center of the ring. Matheo's face was bruised and bloodied, and his torso shone with sweat in the flashing lights. He reached out his glove to tap Ramon's in a show of sportsmanship, but the Dominican refused. Matheo grinned and beckoned the taller fighter to come closer. Ramon launched a quick left-right combo at Matheo's head, which he easily avoided. Matheo slipped left, through a left hook which caught Ramon in the chin, then an overhand right that caught him on the side of the head. The Dominican fighter wobbled, and the crowd leaped to their feet cheering. The Dead Wolves MC members roared.

"Get him, Matheo! Finish him!"

Matheo unleashed a barrage of punches, driving Ramon across the ring. He bounced off the cage, his footing uncertain. Matheo unleashed a snapping front kick followed by a spinning, jumping back kick. His heel crashed into Ramon's cheek, and the Dominican dropped to the mat. Matheo dove onto the collapsed man and reined hammer blows to his head. The black-shirted referee dove between the fighters to stop the carnage, and Matheo jumped up, screaming and beating his chest in victory. The Dead Wolves were on their feet, hugging and shouting. Some of them left the stands, climbed the steps of the raised platform, and forced their way into the ring. Nobody tried to stop the triumphal bikers as they lifted Matheo onto their shoulders.

"That's my boy!" Max cheered. "That is one vicious son of a bitch."

Raison did not join his brothers in the ring. Instead, his eyes never left the group of Big Machine bikers, all of whom had risen and were clapping and whistling to support Matheo. The blonde-haired cowboy in the group, Tommy Boy, looked across the room at Raison. Both men held each other's gaze for a moment.

After the fight, the Dead Wolves, shouting and whooping with excitement, made their way to the casino's main bar, le Roi de Pique. The bar was a lavish and opulent space. Circular balconies lined with ornate wrought-iron railings rose above the casino floor, creating a multi-tiered oasis of entertainment. The bar itself was a masterpiece of dark mahogany, polished to a high sheen, which stretched along the curved wall of the circular room. Overhead, a grand chandelier bathed the space in a warm, golden glow. Plush leather stools lined the bar, and bartenders in crisp white shirts and black vests expertly mixed cocktails. The sound of clinking glasses and animated conversations filled the air as guests celebrated their victories or commiserated their losses.

Around the circular room, small tables were arranged with plush velvet chairs. Richly adorned curtains in deep burgundy framed tall openings offering a panoramic view of the bustling casino floor below. In one corner, a jazz trio played smooth tunes on a small stage. The rhythmic beats of the drums, the sultry notes of the saxophone, and the skillful strokes of the piano keys supplied the perfect backdrop for the evening. The Dead Wolves lined up at the bar where Max ordered a round. They raised their glasses in a toast to Matheo's victory.

"May we never go to hell, but always be on our way," Max shouted, holding his glass high.

The men cheered. They downed their drinks, clapping and shouting.

Next to him, and in stark contrast to Wild Bill's seasoned appearance, Marky was a younger member of the Dead Wolves in his late teens. He had long sandy blonde hair that flowed freely down his shoulders, and a wispy mustache adorned his upper lip. Marky was tall and slender, with arms almost devoid of muscle. Like the others, he wore the black leather cut and vicious wolf's head patch of the MC.

Wild Bill stepped over, a warm smile on his face, and clapped Marky on the back. "How about that, eh, my boy? He did it!"

Marky grinned. "Hey, Dad. Yeah, great fight. Epic finish!"

Wild Bill chuckled, taking a sip of his beer. "Damn right it was. But it ain't just about the fight, son. It's about brotherhood and family. You're part of something special here."

Marky nodded, his hair falling across his forehead. "I know, Dad. Being a Dead Wolf means a lot to me."

Wild Bill smiled. "To the pack."

Marky raised his glass and clinked it against his father's. "To the pack."

Amid the jubilant celebration at le Roi de Pique, as the Dead Wolves basked in the glory of Matheo's victory, Tommy Boy, the President of the Big Machine MC's Toronto chapter, along with a group of his brothers, made their way through the crowd towards Wild Bill and Max. Raison, ever watchful, remained nearby.

The mob of Big Machine bikers stopped at the bar and waited as Tommy Boy's bodyguard and Sergeant at Arms approached Raison. He was a 6-foot

6-inch, 400-pound brute named Jester. He had a ring through his septum, long greasy brown hair, and an equally greasy beard he kept bunched together with green rubber bands. He had a massive gut, and his forearm featured a tattoo of Elvis receiving a sex act from a nun. He wore his leather cut over a black Rush concert T-shirt. On his left breast, under his name patch, there was a red and black patch featuring the word "Mechanic" with several rows of screw patches underneath, one screw for each kill he'd committed for the club.

"What's up, Raison? Your bro can definitely scrap," Jester said.

The two men shook hands.

"Thank you, Jester. We appreciate that," Raison responded.

"Tommy Boy wants to congratulate Max and Wild Bill," Jester said.

Raison nodded. "I'll go ask," he said, and strolled over to Max.

He leaned into Max's ear and said, "Tommy Boy wants to speak with you. Say congratulations and shit," Raison said.

Max looked up at Raison, then over to Tommy Boy. He thought for a moment, then said, "Ok."

Max went back to his conversation as Raison returned to where Jester was waiting.

"He said it's cool, man. Come on over," Raison said.

Jester walked to where Tommy Boy was at the bar, drinking and laughing with his brothers. Jester whispered in his ear. Tommy Boy turned and walked across the bar to Max, his hand out, a big smile on his face.

"Impressive win out there, Max. Your boy Matheo's got some serious skills," he said as the men shook hands.

"We appreciate the compliment, Tommy, but you didn't come over here to talk about the fight, did you?" Max responded.

Wild Bill, standing beside Max, crossed his arms over his chest and regarded Tommy Boy with a stern expression. "We know how your club operates, Tommy Boy, and we've got no interest in playing along. We've done great business over the years, but Montreal is and always will be Dead Wolves territory."

Tommy Boy's demeanor remained calm, despite the tension in the air. "I understand your reservations but hear me out. Big Machine is expanding, and we've been looking to build alliances, not rivalries. Quebec is a big place, and there's room enough for both our clubs to thrive."

Max's temper flared, and he stepped closer. "You think we'll just roll over and let Big Machine muscle in on our turf? You've got some nerve, Tommy Boy."

Raison watched intently from a few feet away.

Tommy Boy sighed. "Max, all I'm saying is let's sit down, talk about the future, and find a way for our clubs to coexist peacefully. No one wants a war, especially not in our own city."

Max's eyes narrowed, and he leaned even closer to Tommy Boy. "*Our* city? I'll tell you this once more, and I won't say it again. This is Dead Wolves' territory. We don't need your alliances, and we sure as hell don't need your peace talks. Now, if you don't want trouble, you better back off."

Raison continued to watch, silent but vigilant, as the tension between the two clubs hung in the air. The charged atmosphere in the bar simmered as Tommy Boy and his Big Machine companions turned to leave. As Tommy Boy passed Raison, they held each other's eyes once again. Then the Big Machine members trailed out of the bar and vanished into the casino.

Raison realized the bar had gone silent with everyone watching, but as soon as Tommy Boy and his goons left, the mood within le Roi de Pique picked back up.

Matheo wandered into the bar wearing a blue tracksuit, his face swollen and battered. Despite bruises and a piece of tape holding his eyebrow together, his smile was broad, his eyes shining with the thrill of triumph. As he approached his fellow Dead Wolves, a chorus of cheers and backslaps greeted him.

Bruno, a seasoned member of the Dead Wolves in his 50s, cut an imposing figure. His square jawline and hawkish nose gave him a rugged appearance. A salt and pepper goatee framed his lips. He had a long ponytail cascading down his back, and his dark eyebrows complemented his intense gaze.

"Look at the champ," Bruno exclaimed, his voice booming over the chatter as he wrapped Matheo in a bear hug. "You made us proud tonight."

Matheo smiled, wincing slightly at his bruised ribs. "Thanks, Bruno. It feels good to win, especially with you all here."

Raison, who had been quiet for most of the night, raised his glass towards Matheo. "You fought like a wolf out there. Fierce and relentless."

"Couldn't have done it without the pack's support," Matheo replied, clinking his glass with Raison's.

Marky, standing nearby, piped up with youthful enthusiasm. "Man, you should have seen the look on Ramon's face when you landed that kick. Priceless!"

The group laughed, the sound mingling with the smooth jazz playing in the background.

Max, observing the scene, clapped Matheo on the back. "You did more than win a fight tonight. You reminded everyone here why we ride together."

Matheo nodded. "Thanks, Max. Means a lot coming from you."

Nearby, Wild Bill and a giant biker named Moose were chatting up a table of women who laughed and blushed at the bikers' antics while the jazz band riffed on a Duke Ellington tune.

After a while, Wild Bill excused himself from the group. "I'll be back in a minute. Just need to find the bathroom." He navigated through the crowd, disappearing from sight as he headed towards the restroom.

Max ordered a round of shots from the bar, and everyone raised their glasses in another toast.

"Tonight, we witnessed greatness," Max said, raising his glass. "Our brother, Matheo, has secured himself a shot at the title belt. But most importantly, he showed those who would take what is ours that the Dead Wolves are fearless!"

"Wolves, what do we say?" Raison shouted, lifting his drink higher.

"Roulez comme si vous étiez déjà mort!" they shouted in unison. "Ride like you're already dead!"

The men cheered and downed their drinks.

As Wild Bill stood at the urinal in the relatively quiet casino bathroom just outside le Roi de Pique, smooth jazz playing softly, he chuckled at an internal joke. The celebratory mood had somewhat loosened the tight grip of caution he usually maintained.

Suddenly, the bathroom door swung open, but Wild Bill paid no atten-tion, assuming it was another patron. Then the sound of heavy footsteps approaching with urgency made him look. He glanced up, catching a dark reflection in the polished metal surface above the urinal.

Behind him, a figure dressed in black riding leathers and wearing a motorcycle helmet with a tinted visor pulled down closed the distance. He raised a gloved fist, a black pistol in his grip. Wild Bill saw a flash of orange as the killer squeezed the trigger just feet away, then blasted shot after shot into Bill's back and ribs as he floundered and fell. The booms were deafening inside the tiled bathroom. Wild Bill hardly had a moment to react. His body jerked and blood splattered onto the porcelain urinal as he collapsed to the floor, lifeless under the fluorescent light. The assassin took a moment to study the dead body before dashing from the bathroom, its swinging door slamming loudly against the wall as he fled.

At the bar, patrons flinched at the muted sounds of popping coming from somewhere nearby. Most continued smiling, while others looked about uneasily. Bruno glanced around, his forehead wrinkled.

"Are they supposed to have fireworks tonight?" he asked the biker next to him.

Just then, a man rushed into the bar wearing black leather riding gear and a helmet, holding a sawed-off pump shotgun. A woman screamed. A man at the bar flinched, grabbed his wife by the blouse, and shoved her hard out of the way.

"Gun!" Bruno yelled as he drew a shiny stainless steel 1911 from the back of his belt.

Max was standing at a high-top table talking to the ladies from the bachelorette party. The first shotgun blast hit him in the ribs, knocking him sideways as if he'd been kicked by a mule. The second shot hit him in the stomach. One of the Dead Wolves shouted in primal rage and anger. Doubled over, Max staggered back, his body slamming against the balcony railing. The third blast hit him in the head, sending the Dead Wolve's leader flipping over the balcony. He fell thirty feet and crashed onto the main casino floor's stage, landing directly on the drum set, sending cymbals, drums, and hardware scattering. The band ducked and ran from the sudden falling object, and screams erupted from the casino like tornado sirens.

Bruno drew a bead on the black clad shooter and fired. The rounds hit the killer's back, but he ducked and dove behind the bar. Bruno wondered if the assassin was wearing body armor just as the black helmet appeared over the bar, followed by a blast from the shotgun. The pellets went wild past Bruno's head, causing him to duck. He waited a second under a table before popping up and letting off three rounds into the bar where the shotgun-wielding killer had been. Then he noticed movement from the right of his vision just in time to see the killer running full speed from the room.

The casino erupted into a frenzy of confusion and alarm. As patrons scattered and screams echoed through the opulent halls, Raison's instincts kicked in. His eyes locked onto the shooter making his way quickly through the panicked crowd, and he bolted after. His powerful strides carried him swiftly through the casino's flashing lights, weaving between startled gamblers and overturned chairs at slot machines.

The shooter quickened his pace, pushing gamblers aside and knocking over chairs. As they neared the entrance, the bright lights of the casino's facade spilled into the dimly lit interior, casting long shadows that flickered with the movement of the fleeing figure. Raison's breath came in heavy gasps, his focus on the retreating shooter.

Bursting through the doors, the humid night air hit them. The shooter made a beeline for a motorcycle idling at the curb, where an accomplice waited, engine running. Raison burst out just in time to see the shooter leap onto the motorcycle's back. The bike lurched forward and sped off into the night.

Raison stood, panting, his hands clenched into fists. The taillight of the motorcycle disappeared into the distance. The roar of the engine still echoed in his ears as he turned back to face the chaos inside.

Three days later, under a leaden sky, the surviving members of the Dead

Wolves Motorcycle Club congregated in the hallowed stillness of the cemetery. They stood alongside friends and family, and the air was thick with a somber reverence. The cemetery was dotted with rows of headstones standing as silent sentinels over the departed. Amidst this backdrop, the twin black caskets of Wild Bill and Max lay side by side. Each casket bore the snarling wolf's head of the Dead Wolves MC.

Raison stood stoically. His eyes, usually sharp and commanding, held a depth of sadness as he gazed upon the caskets. Beside him, Bruno, his features etched with grief, stood in quiet solidarity. The air was filled with the muted sounds of weeping and whispered condolences as those gathered paid their respects.

Finally, Raison turned to Bruno, his expression grave. "We need to talk," he began, his voice low.

Bruno's eyes stayed fixed on the caskets. "What's on your mind, Raison?"

"Tommy Boy called me this morning. He knows who's behind Max and Bill's deaths."

Bruno's eyes narrowed, a mix of surprise and skepticism crossing his weathered face. "Big Machine Tommy Boy called you? Shit, of course, he knows who killed them. Big Machine killed them, right? He probably ordered it himself."

Raison shook his head. "He said it wasn't Big Machine. He said it was some Middle Eastern dope dealers trying to move into Montreal. But he's got his ear to the ground. Big Machine has connections and information we don't. If anyone knows who's behind this, it's them."

Bruno continued staring at the caskets. "Are you saying you believe this guy?" he asked.

"I am saying maybe it was Big Machine, but maybe it wasn't. We've got beef with fifty other gangs, clubs, and cliques across Canada, but we've never had beef with them. Tommy Boy was just there partying with us and congratulating us for Matheo's win."

"Yeah, and Max told him to fuck off," Bruno cut in.

"He did," agreed Raison. "So, I guess we decide right now rather to blame Big Machine and start a war with the biggest outlaw motorcycle club on earth with no evidence, or we go hear what Tommy Boy has to say."

Bruno sucked his teeth and spit. He breathed out hard and thought for a while. Finally, he said, "You know, my dad was in the Corsican mafia. He was a close associate of Paul Mondoloni, one of the French Connection guys. They were some of the first big time dealers to bring smack to Canada. They had to build the distribution from scratch. So, here's my dad, an Old World mafioso who speaks Italian and French. He comes to Quebec to meet with the local bosses and convince them to buy their dope from him. The trouble is, the guys he's trying to sell to speak Quebecois French, while my dad speaks Corsican French, and they have all kinds of misunderstandings. One time, he was trying to convince this old French-Canadian gangster that they should do business, and the old gangster told him 'Tire toi une buche' or 'take a log', which is something a French-Canadian says when they mean 'Sit down. Let's talk about it.' But my dad thinks it's some kind of Canadian insult, like 'Go take a shit' or something. Anyway, my dad gets offended, and the guns come out. I don't know, maybe he was having a bad day, but he was convinced the guy was telling him to fuck off and he didn't like it, so he shot the guy. The Canadian boss's bodyguard shot back, hitting my dad in the stomach. He survived, but with bullet fragments all inside him. Those fragments caused him pain for the rest of his life. It really slowed him down. So, anytime I would have a problem with a guy or didn't like someone, my dad would say, 'You can always tell a guy to go fuck himself tomorrow.' He would always say that. What he meant was, if he had given the guy the benefit of the doubt, or even waited to ask somebody else what the guy meant by 'Tire toi une buche', he wouldn't have had to suffer the rest of his life with bullets in his belly."

Raison waited for him to finish. "I think I got from that story that you are down to meet with Tommy Boy. Something about we can listen to them now and still tell them to fuck off tomorrow. Am I right?"

Bruno sighed. "It's probably the fastest way to figure out whether Big Machine is behind the killings of Max and Bill or not. So yeah, I'll go with you to meet Tommy Boy. But we better not tell the others. It won't look good. Most of them think Big Machine is behind this."

"I know," Raison replied. "But we're in the dark here. We need answers, and we need them fast. This isn't just about retribution. It's about survival. If there's a threat to the club, we need to know what we're up against."

Bruno sighed. "All right, Raison. But we better watch our backs. I feel the crosshairs on me now."

Raison nodded in agreement, his jaw set in determination. "We'll do it right, Bruno. For Max, for Bill, and for the pack."

As the funeral service continued, Raison and Bruno stood side by side, watching the ceremony, both deep in their thoughts.

In the back room of The Rusty Hub, a biker bar on the outskirts of Ottawa, Raison and Bruno sat at an old wooden table scarred with knife carvings and graffiti. They faced Tommy Boy, president of Big Machine MC's Toronto chapter, who sat smoking a cigar, sunglasses pushed up on his head. His golden hair and beard appeared weathered, like fall leaves. Jester, Tommy Boy's mountainous bodyguard, was at a pool table nearby with three other Big Machine members, smoking and drinking.

Tommy Boy broke the silence, his voice steady and deliberate. "I speak for myself and for our club when I say we are all real sorry for your loss. Max and Bill were legends. True outlaws. It's sad to see them go."

He took a drink from a longneck. "The streets talk, and we listen. But before I tell you what I know, I have a proposition."

Bruno's eyes narrowed. Raison remained stoic but alert.

"The landscape's changing," Tommy Boy continued. "It's time for what our boss, Pop, calls 'strategic alliances.' Everyone is coming to Canada now. We've got Turks, Moroccans, Iraqis—everyone—bringing product into our country. They want to take over, to push us old one-percenters out. We knew they were moving into Montreal. In fact, we've been watching them already, right in your city. That's why I came to the fight, to warn Max and Bill and to offer our support. We didn't realize the invaders were planning to move that night, or we would have stayed and protected you guys, even if Max and Bill didn't want our help."

Tommy Boy took a drag off his cigar as Bruno and Raison listened in silence, their faces unmoving.

"Why would Big Machine care if Max and Bill, or any of us, get smoked?" Raison asked.

"If we let the Pakistanis and Afghanis and the rest take control of the supply, they will soon replace all Canadian dealers with their own people. We didn't always see eye-to-eye with Max and Bill, but we always did good business. I've supplied the Dead Wolves with primo weed for the last decade, and we've made a lot of money together. Max and I never had an issue until he got it in his head that we wanted to push the Wolves out of Montreal. But nothing could be further from the truth. We know your club has always proudly claimed Montreal. We respect that. You're some mean sons of bitches, and we'd rather be on the same side with you than fight against you. We have product by the ton. Anything you want, anything you can move. Coke, crystal, smack, guns. And you know we have the finest weed on the planet, grown right here in Canada and distributed across the globe. When you ride with us, you get the best deals on the best shit. Plus, when the foreigners come to push you out, you have an army behind you. I'm offering the Dead Wolves a chance to patch over, to trade in your wolf's heads and join Big Machine. I never came to offer you war. We would see that as a major loss."

Bruno spoke first. "And what about our autonomy? The Dead Wolves have their own history, their own code."

Tommy Boy leaned back and grinned. "You'd keep your autonomy, to an extent. But think bigger. Think of the resources, the protection. You know how the world works. It's about power, and together, we have more of it."

"You said you know who killed Max and Bill," Raison cut in. "Do you have names? Locations?"

Tommy Boy nodded. "We do. But this information comes with the understanding that we're moving towards a partnership."

Bruno rubbed his chin. Raison's gaze remained fixed on Tommy Boy.

"Bruno and I can't make a deal to patch over," Raison said. "A decision like that has to be made by vote of the active club members. You know that."

"Of course," Tommy Boy said. "But before I tell you what we found, I need to know: Am I helping friends tonight, or am I walking away from rivals?"

Bruno and Raison sat watching the smoke drift in front of Tommy's face.

Broken blood vessels crisscrossed his nose and cheeks, and his mustache was yellowed from tobacco.

"We have to discuss this with the rest of the Dead Wolves," Raison finally said. "And we're mourning our loss. But we see no reason to have bad blood with Big Machine. Like you said, you're our biggest and best supplier."

Tommy Boy smiled, revealing stained teeth. He reached into his pocket and pulled out an envelope. Laying it on the table, he said, "Good. The assholes who killed your bosses are a Pakistani family. It's a bunch of brothers and cousins and shit. They move a lot of weight in Toronto, but a few months ago we caught one of their uncles and made him talk. He told us they were also in Montreal. Lately, they've been using the same three women to move the dope by passenger train from Toronto. We have photos of all three. Plus, we know their typical schedule and the location of their Montreal stash house. It's all in the envelope."

Raison took the envelope and slid it into his jacket pocket.

Tommy Boy stood up, extending his hand. "The invaders are coming for your club and your territory. I am sorry we didn't know ahead of time what they had planned. We had a great deal of respect for Max and Bill."

With that, Tommy Boy walked away to join Jester and the others at the pool tables.

Outside the bar, the night air was crisp, carrying with it the faint sounds of the city. Raison and Bruno walked to where their motorcycles were parked.

Bruno glanced over at Raison, his expression serious. "This won't be easy, you know. Convincing the club to patch over, it's a big ask."

Raison nodded, his face set in a grim line. "I know. Especially Rage. He's Dead Wolves through and through."

"Yeah, your brother takes the club to heart," Bruno replied. "But we need to think about the future. Big Machine's offer could give us the edge we need, especially now that Max and Bill are gone."

Raison sighed, a hand running over the handlebars of his bike. "It's not just about power. We've got a responsibility to our brothers. To keep everyone safe."

Bruno mounted his motorcycle, his eyes meeting Raison's. "We'll lay it out for them, every detail. They need to understand why this might be our best move."

Raison swung his leg over his bike, the engine roaring to life under him. "We'll make them see. For the club, for Max, for Bill. We owe them that much."

Both men kicked their bikes into gear. The engines growled, a powerful symphony that echoed off the nearby buildings as they rode off into the night.

The Dead Wolves MC's clubhouse stood in a forgotten corner of the Saint-Henri neighborhood in Montreal, on a street bearing scars of neglect. Asphalt, cracked and uneven, weaved between the looming shadows of old, derelict buildings. Graffiti sprawled across their brick facades, telling tales of turf wars and forgotten dreams in vibrant hues. Abandoned cars, their once-glossy paint now faded and peeling, sat on deflated tires. The air held a stagnant smell, a mix of old trash and exhaust with none of the hope other recently gentrified streets in Saint-Henri exuded.

The three-story row house looked like any other, with its aged brick facade and sturdy wooden door. Painted on a black background above the door was the snarling wolf's head of the Dead Wolves MC. Inside, the clubhouse was dim. Most light came from neon beer signs over the worn pool table. Stale beer, cigarette smoke, and the scent of leather conditioner permeated the space. Aged stools and mismatched chairs were scattered about. An old bar with a collection of bottles stretched along one wall, next to a basic kitchen with worn appliances.

That night, the Dead Wolves gathered under the dim lights of the main room. The air was somber, with a heavy mix of grief and anger. Most sat in wooden chairs, while Raison stood at the front. His eyes scanned the gathered members. Bruno was there, wearing all black and a pensive expression. Matheo was there, his face still bruised and cut from the fight. Next to him sat Okwaho, their Mohawk brother, who wore beads around his neck and three upright feathers in his hair. Behind them sat Moose, the powerlifter. Next to Moose sat Marky, Wild Bill's son. The thin young man was pale, his eyes swollen with dark circles. He sat staring at the floor.

Leaning against the wall was Raison's younger brother, Rage. Tall and lean, his long hair hung limp and oily around his collar, and his beard was curly and tangled. His cheeks, lean and sunken, sported three tear-drop tattoos. He wore black jeans, cowboy boots, and a dirty T-shirt under his black leather cut. He was smoking a cigarette with his right hand, the thumb of his prosthetic left hand hooked in his pocket.

"Loups! Écoutez," Raison began. "Wolves! Listen up."

He waited a moment for the room to quiet down.

"This is now a club business meeting. Any disruptions won't be tolerated," he said. "In the wake of the cowardly assassinations of our President, Max, and Vice President, Wild Bill, it is time to choose new club leadership. As sergeant at arms, I am the highest-ranking member alive, so I will conduct this vote. We should start with the highest position. Do I hear any nominations for club president?"

"I nominate you, Raison," said Moose in his deep, booming voice.

"Ok, I accept," Raison nodded. "Any other nominations?"

"I nominate Bruno. He's the oldest," said Okwaho.

Bruno sat up straight and blinked. Murmurs arose amongst the club members.

"Ok, Bruno, do you accept the nomination?" Raison asked.

"Boys, I think I'll have to decline. I am honored though," Bruno said, clapping Okwaho's hand.

"Ok, Bruno declines. Are there any other nominations?"

The group sat quietly.

"I nominate Rage as president," Matheo said.

Murmurs broke out again. Raison looked at his brother leaning against the wall, smoking.

"Well, brother, do you accept the nomination?" he asked.

Rage smoked. Raison waited.

"Well?" Raison asked.

Rage continued to smoke. The whispering amongst the men died down, and they waited in silence.

"Hell, why not?" he finally said.

"Why not what?" Raison growled through gritted teeth. "Was that an acceptance?"

"Yeah, fuck it, count me in," Rage said.

"Anyone else?" Raison asked.

The room was silent.

"Ok, then we vote for club president. There are two nominees: Raison and Rage. If you vote for Raison as president, say 'Aye!'"

Many "Ayes!" rang out around the room.

"If you vote for Rage as club president, say 'Aye!'"

Matheo was the sole vote.

"The vote carries, and I accept the position as president of this club," Raison said. "Now for the position of vice president. I will now accept nominations. I nominate Rage for VP."

A few eyebrows lifted amongst the men, but otherwise, the room was dead silent.

"Do you accept," Raison asked.

From his place on the wall, Rage chuckled.

"Yeah, I accept," he said.

"Good. Any other nominations?"

Silence again. Raison scanned the men's faces.

"Anyone?" he asked again. "No? Ok. With just one nominee and nothing barring you from serving, the VP position is yours, Rage."

Rage made an elaborate bow, then held up his beer. "Many thanks to the men and women of the Academy of Motion Pictures for this lovely evening and this fine award," he joked.

The men chuckled, and Raison sighed quietly.

"That leaves one open officer's position: Sergeant at Arms. Rage, I propose we give it to Bruno. What do you think?"

Rage looked at the older Corsican man.

"Absolutely," Rage said.

"That means this is yours," Raison said as he removed his cut and laid it on the podium. He pulled a shiny hunting knife from a leather sheath on his belt and cut the "Sgt. at Arms" patch from his vest. He handed it to Bruno as he stood.

"You know the job. I don't have to tell you. Do it well, brother."

Bruno held the patch and flipped it around it in his hand, studying it.

"I will," he said, his face like stone. "I am honored."

"These are trying times for us. We've lost brothers, and now we face decisions that will shape our future. But together, as Dead Wolves, we'll ride through any storm. We'll honor the memory of those we've lost by keeping this club strong and united."

The room erupted in a chorus of agreement.

"First order of business: We destroy the assholes who killed Max and Bill."

The men cheered and stomped their boots on the wooden floor. Raison reached into his pocket and removed the envelope Tommy Boy had given him.

"We know exactly who and where they are," he said, holding the envelope up.

The room erupted in cheers. Bruno clapped but said nothing. Raison stood at the podium. He looked toward Rage, but he was already walking out the door.

4

Bust

Inside the bustling Denver Police Department's District 3 substation, an African American woman in her mid-thirties sat at her desk inside a cubicle typing rapidly at a computer. She wore black slacks, a black blouse, and a leather belt that carried her badge, a holstered Glock 17, handcuffs, and two extra magazines. Her hair was pulled into a neat, tight ponytail, and she wore minimal makeup. Her brows were arched, and her eyes were tilted in a cat-like manner. The name plate outside her cubicle read "Det. Kim Wright."

In the cubicle across from her sat a middle-aged white man with bifocals perched on his red nose. He was bald and had a thick gray mustache. He wore a navy suit that hung loosely on his overweight frame. His name plate read "Det. Harold Clarke."

Unlike Kim's desk, which was virtually devoid of paper, Harold's was piled high with stacks of files.

"I don't know about this new generation," Harold began, "but it takes some real balls to sit there with not one case file on your desk. In the old days, if brass walked by and saw a narcotics detective with no cases to work, they'd make them go outside and do hand-to-hands with the street thugs. They really loved to make rookies do that kind of thing in the dead of winter. If there was a hard freeze coming, you did not want to be sitting at your desk slacking."

Without looking up, Kim Wright rolled her eyes.

"Luckily," she said, "not everyone is as old as you, Fred Flintstone. Some people understand that paper files on a desk don't mean you're getting any work done. We both know you haven't opened all those files you pulled just to make yourself look busy. That stack has looked the exact same for three months."

Harold laughed. "I don't need to open them. I've been a detective so long I can lay my hand on them and know exactly what they say."

"Ha!" Kim exclaimed. "Now you're a psychic? Too bad you can't lay your hand on your computer and learn how it works."

"I don't know how you did it in the Air Force Security Forces, but I can tell you that narcotics cases aren't won with computers. This isn't forensic accounting or check fraud. Narcotics detectives bust drug dealers by catching them with drugs in their cars or homes or in their pockets. That's what we do. Nearly 40 years with a badge and I never saw a dealer hide his dope in a computer."

"So, you think a drug bust can't be made with a computer?" Kim asked, swiveling in her chair to face the older man.

"As soon as they sell heroin on eBay, I guess we can get a bust, but until then, no," Harold said.

"Ok, Harold," Detective Wright said, her eyes sparkling as she leaned forward. "I bet you I can make a bust today, using nothing but the internet."

The older detective raised an eyebrow, his interest piqued. "Just the internet? No informants, no stakeouts, no rip and run?" he asked.

"Exactly," she replied with a grin. "Technology has changed the game. I don't need to pound the pavement like the old days. I can set up a bust sitting right here."

Intrigued and amused, the older detective leaned back in his chair, crossing his arms. "OK, Wright, you're on. But let's make it interesting. If you pull it off, I'll do your paperwork for a week. But if you fail, you buy me lunch for a week."

Detective Wright's smile widened. "Deal," she said. "I'm about to give you a master class in modern policing."

"We'll see," Harold replied.

Kim slid open her bottom desk drawer. Inside was a shoebox filled with cell phones. Reaching in, she chose a touchscreen model. She plugged it into a charger on her desk and booted it up. Once the screen illuminated, she tapped an icon to open a dating app. She checked the profile. The photo was of a pretty young girl of college age with blonde hair wearing a bikini on a beach. There were several other photos of the same young woman wearing tight or revealing clothing at bars, nightclubs, and parties. The profile read, "From Arizona! In Denver visiting friends! Looking for a plug." The words were followed by an emoji of a green tree, a snowflake, a wall plug, and a puff of smoke. The account had 1,589 notifications and scores of unread messages. Kim tapped to open the messages folder. The first dozen were from eager men offering to supply any drug, often for discounted rates, sometimes even for free.

Kim chose a message received earlier that day. It was from a young man appearing to be of Indian descent. In his profile photo, he wore a hooded sweatshirt from the University of Colorado Boulder. In his message, he offered "White, Molly, Lucy, and green in many flavors for the best prices."

"Oh, yeah. Get ready, Harold. This won't take long," Kim said out loud. Harold waved her off and returned to reading.

Kim messaged the boy, "Need green and molly. When can you meet?"

Before she could set the phone down, the boy messaged back, "Right now. What do you need?"

"What's the molly like?" she typed back.

"Fire! Pinkest I've seen," he texted back with flame emojis.

"It's for me and my friends. We're going to a music festival this weekend. Whoop whoop! How much for 5g of molly and two zips of green?"

The boy took a moment to respond.

"It's $350 for the first part. For the green, depends on what you're trying to spend?"

Kim went back and forth with the dealer a few more times before she exclaimed, "Boom! Done. Let's go, Harold."

The older man looked up from his desk and removed his glasses.

"Go where, Wright?" he asked.

"To the Shell station at Federal and West Florida to make a bust," she replied as she put on her jacket.

Harold sat looking at her incredulously. "Are you serious?"

"Come on, grandpa. I've got a bet to win," she said.

The two detectives walked through the substation and out to the parking lot where Harold offered to drive. As they walked toward his personal vehicle, a light blue Chevrolet Caprice Classic, Kim laughed.

"Harold, you drive an unmarked police car as your personal vehicle?"

"Hey," Harold snapped back, "I spent 30 years driving one of these around. I can't be switching from cruiser to minivan then back to cruiser every day like some of these cops. I like to have the same car in my driveway as I drive at work. Switching cars back and forth everyday just leads to stress and ulcers."

"You are too much," Kim said, laughing as they climbed in.

Harold pulled the blue sedan out of the precinct parking lot and drove south on University Boulevard. After a few blocks, he turned right onto Evans Avenue.

"So, how do you like civilian policing?" Harold asked as they drove.

"I like it," Kim replied, looking out the window through black sunglasses. "Being an Air Force cop was fun, but I had enough of the military's 'hurry and wait.'"

"You're a real go-getter, huh?" the older man asked. "What made you leave the Air Force?"

Kim looked out the passenger window.

"In 2010, I was sent to Bagram Air Base in Afghanistan. My unit was tasked with interdicting narcotics trafficking, especially any of our own service members tempted to send Afghan heroin or hash back to the States on one of the C-17s. I was only supposed to be there for 90 days, then I was going to cycle back here to Schriever Air Base. While I was at Bagram, early on May 19, we came under attack by the Taliban. They sent about 40 suicide bombers at our perimeter. They had vests covered in grenades, AKs, RPGs, and mortars. Some made it through the wire. Four of them were dressed in American uniforms. They were trying to make it into a tent or mess hall to inflict mass casualties. I just remember waking up to explosions and running to a bunker. After that day, I realized that, more than anything, I wanted a life of peace. Especially as a mother. I wanted to wake up every day to a normal, calm, safe world. And there is nothing normal, calm, or safe about war. I had over ten years in the service, and my husband, Mike, had already retired and was finishing civilian flight school, so I requested a separation once we cycled back. I took a year off to travel and see the world, then I moved here and joined Denver PD."

"So, you think being a civilian cop is—what did you call it?—'Normal, calm, and safe?' Let me tell you, you never know what you'll come across in these streets," Harold said.

"I know," Kim replied as she stared out the window at the passing city, "but this is my home. My family is here. If I am going to risk my life, it should be here."

At the intersection of Federal and West Florida, Harold pulled his Chevrolet sedan into the parking lot of a Super Save station directly across from the Shell they were scheduled to meet the dealer at. Harold parked the car so they had a full view of the station's parking lot. The Shell station was a small, one-story red brick building with glass windows covered in steel bars. Four white, red, and yellow gas pumps stood under a yellow trimmed canopy. It was mid-afternoon, and the intersection was busy with cars and pedestrians.

"OK, detective," Harold said as he put the car into park. "We're here. Where's your guy?"

"Let's see," she said as she tapped to open the cell phone.

"OTW, what are you driving?" she typed to the dealer.

He didn't immediately respond. After a minute, Kim put the phone on her lap.

"What's wrong? Is he not coming?" Harold seemed pleased.

"Just relax," she soothed him.

After a few minutes of silence, the phone buzzed, and Kim checked it.

"Says he's driving. Be there in 10. Purple Nissan Altima," she said.

"Purple, huh? This just keeps getting better," Harold chuckled.

The two sat in silence.

"Were you in the service, Harold?" Kim asked.

"Army," he said. "After Nam. Spent a lot of time staring at North Korean border guards through a scope, but never saw combat. Finished my contract, got out, became a cop."

"Have you liked being a cop?"

"I've been a cop my whole life. At this point, if I don't like being a cop, it doesn't even matter," he said.

Kim thought for a moment. "I guess not," she said, and they went back to watching the intersection in silence.

After almost a half hour passed, a dirty purple Nissan Altima pulled slowly into the Shell station, hesitated, then parked.

"Boom," Kim said. "Purple Altima."

"This guy has dope on him now? And he told you he was going to sell it to you on that phone?" Harold asked.

"I have the texts, his phone number, his account details, car description, and profile photos right here," she replied, wagging the phone side-to-side at Harold.

"Ok, it's your show. Better call for backup," he said.

Kim pulled her personal cell phone from her jacket pocket and dialed the division dispatcher. After requesting uniformed assistance, she checked her decoy phone again.

"He's asking where we are," she said out loud as she typed. "I'm telling him we're almost there."

She hit send on her message, and almost at once got a response.

"He said, 'Cool, hurry,'" she read to Harold.

He chuckled. "Don't get in too big of a hurry there, ace. You aren't going to like where you're headed."

Kim's personal cell phone buzzed, and she answered, "Detective Wright." She listened for a moment.

"Sergeant," she told the uniformed officer on the other end of the line, "we're looking to make an arrest on a male suspect approximately 25, black hair, brown skin, possibly Middle Eastern or Hispanic, for possession with intent. He is driving a purple Nissan Altima that is now in the parking lot of the Shell station at Federal and West Florida. Detective Clarke and I are across the street observing the suspect from an unmarked blue Caprice. We already have enough cause to search the vehicle, so I want you to roll up on him and detain him. Sound good?"

She thanked the sergeant and clicked off the phone.

She picked up the other cell phone and texted the dealer, "5 minutes."

"Uniforms are almost here," she told Harold.

"Too bad we didn't bring popcorn, right?" he responded.

Five minutes later, a white Chevrolet Tahoe with a black steel bumper guard and a blue Denver PD shield on the door pulled into the Shell station, turned on its overhead lights, and stopped behind the purple Altima, blocking its retreat. A large white police officer in a black uniform climbed out of the SUV and took position overlooking the car. Within seconds, two more Denver PD Tahoes pulled into the station parking lot, and soon uniformed officers had the car surrounded.

"The fellow in that purple car just pooped himself," Harold said, and Kim laughed.

Harold put this Caprice in gear and slowly drove across the intersection and into the Shell parking lot. They parked, got out, and waved to the officers as they approached. The uniformed officers already had the driver out of the vehicle and spreadeagled on the hood. The would-be dealer was smaller than he appeared in his photos. His hair was shaggy and in need of a haircut. He was wearing sandals, swim shorts, and a Phish concert T-shirt. One officer frisked him while others opened his car doors and peaked around inside with flashlights.

"What the hell, man?" the dealer said. "I was just sitting in my car."

"Oh, yeah? Why were you sitting at a location known for drug transactions?" the officer frisking him asked. He pulled the young Indian dealer's wallet from his back pocket and tossed it onto the car. He then emptied the dealer's other pockets onto the hood. There were several lighters, a cell phone, a vape, and a wad of cash bound with a rubber band.

"Whoa!" Kim exclaimed, thumbing through the cash. "We've got a big-time dope dealer here. Who are you? El Chapo's nephew?"

"My last name is Patel," the dealer exclaimed. "Ashok Patel. My family is from Mumbai. How could I be related to a Mexican drug lord?"

"You sell his dope, though, don't you?" Kim asked.

"I don't know anything, and further, I don't consent to this search..." Ashok started to speak when one officer searching the purple Altima shouted. He pulled a black canvas duffle bag from the backseat and set it on the hood. Kim Wright unzipped the bag and tipped it forward to show it was filled with plastic bags of green marijuana.

"Are you licensed to have this much cannabis, Mr. Patel?" she asked. "The law says an individual can possess up to one ounce of marijuana at a time. This is four or five pounds."

"But cannabis is..." Ashok began when once again an officer searching the Nissan's front seat shouted. This time, the officer came out with a Ziplock baggy of crystalline powder. He walked over and set it on the car hood. Kim Wright put on blue latex gloves and picked up the baggy.

"What is this, meth?" she asked.

"That's federal prison time," Harold piped in. "And a lot of it. Did you know the feds don't even have parole? They give you twenty years, you serve all twenty years."

"Hey wait..." Ashok stammered. His thin arms were shaking, and he couldn't keep his mouth shut.

"Just have a seat right there, Mr. Patel," Kim said, and the uniformed officer pushed him down to the curb.

"Should I book you for possession of methamphetamine with intent to sell to an undercover cop, of are you going to tell me what this is?" Kim asked, holding up the baggy.

Ashok took a deep breath, then looked at his feet.

"Molly," he mumbled.

"What did you say? Speak up?" Kim instructed.

"It's not meth, it's just MDMA. It's no big deal," Ashok said a little louder.

"For you it's a big deal. It's getting you sent to jail," Kim said.

"Stand up," she motioned to Ashok, and a uniformed officer pulled him up by the armpit.

"Sergeant," she continued, "please place Mr. Patel under arrest for possession with intent to distribute."

"OK, Mr. Patel, I am now placing you under arrest..." the officer said as he handcuffed Ashok.

Kim and Harold turned back to the black duffle bag of marijuana on the hood.

"So, I guess this is how it will be from now on," Harold said. "My generation had to police the streets, but your generation has to police the internet."

"That's right," Kim agreed.

"Well, you promised a master class, and I was not disappointed. That was the easiest bust I've ever seen. I can't believe anybody would be dumb enough to sell drugs to a complete stranger over the internet."

"Embrace the new ways, Harold. Like you said, easiest bust ever."

The uniformed sergeant organized the transfer of the suspect and evidence back to the District 3 substation. Ashok was fingerprinted and photographed, then left in a holding cell. Harold tested a sample of the crystalline powder with a reagent testing kit, which turned deep purple.

"MDMA it is," Harold said, packing the evidence away in official bags.

"Let's see what else we can get from the kid," he said. The two walked over to the jailer and asked him to move the suspect to an interview room.

The interrogation room was stark and utilitarian, a setting designed for unvarnished truths. Kim and Harold sat across from the young college student. Ashok, visibly anxious, shifted uncomfortably in his chair.

"Ashok," Kim began, "we tested the substance in the baggy, and it came back as MDMA. We weighed it and the marijuana in the black bag, and all together you are looking at felony possession with intent to distribute. Since it was me you were messaging on the dating app, we, of course, have a record of the intended transaction."

Ashok sat looking at his hands.

"You're a student at UC Boulder, right?" she asked.

"Yes," Ashok said in an almost whisper.

"What year?"

"I'll be a senior next semester. I graduate next May."

"You mean, you were supposed to graduate next May, before you tried to sell dope to a cop," Harold said gruffly.

"A conviction for drug dealing and time in jail won't help you finish your degree, will it?" Kim asked more calmly.

"But it's not even real drugs. It's just party supplies. It's not like it's crack," Ashok protested.

"You're right," Kim said, "and you're not El Chapo's nephew. You're a good kid, about to finish college and make his family proud. But you made a bad choice, and now you have to face it."

Ashok looked at his hands again.

"Now, I've talked with my partner," Kim continued, "and we don't want to see you go down for this and throw away all that you've worked for. We don't want to see you disappoint your family. Not over a little weed and some molly. But to help you, you're going to have to help us."

Ashok fidgeted with his fingers.

"One thing I noticed is the labels on the marijuana packaging. They're from a dispensary. How did you get bulk cannabis from a dispensary?"

Ashok sat quietly.

"Which dispensary did the weed come from?" Harold asked.

Ashok sighed. "I didn't get it from a dispensary. I got it from the Dark Web."

Harold stared blankly at the boy while Kim smiled knowingly.

"So how did that go down?" she asked.

"I go on a site where you can buy anything. Guns, identities, all kinds of drugs. People have stuff to sell, and you can just buy it with crypto. It's like eBay for black market goods. I order what I want, and they send it to me," he said.

"How? Through the mail?" she asked.

"Sometimes, but not with this guy. He advertised as local. He actually dropped the order off and gave me coordinates to pick it up."

"Where was that?" Kim asked.

"At Barr Lake State Park, just outside of town," he said.

"So, the supplier sells weed on the Dark Web because it's anonymous, but then he meets you in public to deliver the goods? Defeats the purpose, doesn't it?"

"No," Ashok replied. "He sent me the coordinates, and I found the weed in the black bag under a bush in the park."

"How did you pay the guy?" Harold asked skeptically.

"With Bitcoin. You pay through the website, and they hold it in escrow until you confirm you received the product," Ashok explained.

"So, you're saying you never met the supplier?" Kim asked.

"Never," Ashok said. "Nobody sells drugs in person anymore."

"You did," Harold replied, and Ashok looked down at his hands again.

"Are you really going to charge me with delivery? What about simple possession?" Ashok pleaded.

"That's between you and the DA," Kim said, and she and Harold stood up and walked out. After Harold closed the interview room door, he turned to Kim Wright.

"So, is that it?" he asked.

"No," she said as she tapped her fingers against her leg. "The packaging is local, and he claims the delivery was local. If a dispensary is selling on the Dark Web, that's against the law. I am going to see if I can track this packaging to the source. We'll see what's up."

"Sounds good," Harold said. "Impressive work, Detective. You taught this old dog some new tricks today."

"It's been my pleasure," Kim said, patting Harold on the back. "But since I won that bet and you owe me a week of paperwork, you can get started by filling out the reports for the arrest of Mr. Patel."

"I knew that was coming," Harold laughed as he turned to walk to his cubicle. "Let me know if you find anything else."

Kim smiled and returned to the table where the black canvas duffle bag of cannabis and other evidence was laid out. She took photos of the plastic bags containing the green buds, capturing the logos, dates, and other markings on the labels. She paid special attention to a greenish rectangular tag printed with a bar code and a long identification number. When she was done photographing, she placed the contraband into a plastic tub, labeled it with the suspect's name, and walked back to her cubicle.

At her desk, she hung her jacket over the back of her chair and sat down. Within moments, she had emailed the photos of the cannabis packaging to the police liaison at the Colorado Marijuana Enforcement Division, requesting identification of the legal owner. Within minutes, she received an email back with the name and address of the dispensary associated with the RFID inventory tag.

"I've got the dispensary where the weed came from," Kim said to Harold, who was at his desk hunched over the keyboard. "Do you want to come?"

"Hell, Wright. You can't save the world in one day. I haven't even had lunch yet."

"Come on. We can get something on the way," Kim said as she walked away.

The dispensary was on the south side of town. It was a storefront in a shopping center that also had a tailor, a pho noodle shop, and a tax preparation service. They parked Harold's Caprice and entered through the glass door. Inside, they were greeted by a young security guard.

"Detectives Wright and Clarke, Denver PD," Harold said. "Is there an owner or manager here today?"

The guard pointed them towards a tall man of about 40 with long hair and a tie-dyed shirt standing at the register. Kim and Harold walked through the shop toward the man. It smelled of marijuana smoke and incense. As they approached, the man looked up from his cell phone.

"Officers," he said. "What can I do for you?"

"Are you the manager?" Kim asked.

"I am the owner," he replied. "Along with my wife. Allen Randall, but everyone calls me 'Moon Dog.'"

"Mr. Randall," Kim held up her cell phone. "Do you recognize these RFID tags?"

Moon Dog squinted and looked closer. The pungent stench of cannabis radiated from him.

"I mean, that's definitely an RFID tag. They all look like that," he said.

"Yeah, but this one traces back to here," Kim said.

Moon Dog frowned. "What are you telling me?"

"We confiscated three-and-a-half pounds of weed from a college kid who tried to sell it on the internet. As you see, it is stamped and tagged from a licensed dispensary. *Your* dispensary. Do you want to tell us how that could be?"

Moon Dog looked flustered. "Can you show me that again? Are there more photos?"

Kim held up the phone and swiped through a few more pictures.

"Whoa! Go back," Moon Dog said. "Back to the one showing the bag."

Kim raised an eyebrow but obliged him by swiping back. The picture was at a wider angle, showing the black canvas duffle bag and all its contents laid out on the table.

"That's a trip, man," said Moon Dog.

"What's 'a trip?'" Harold asked.

"Let me show you something," Moon Dog said, and he reached under the counter and came back with a white three-hole binder filled with pages. He laid the binder on the glass counter and spun it around for the detectives to see.

"Everything we sell is tracked, as you know. Every cannabis product has an RFID tag and is tracked in the state Inventory Tracking System, from seed to sale, as they say. My wife keeps up with the inventory on the computer, and she keeps this book as a double check. I can show you we are not missing any inventory."

"And yet we busted over three pounds of weed you're 'not missing' just a few hours ago," Kim replied.

"Yes, in one of these," he said. Reaching under the counter again, he came out with an empty black canvas duffle bag just like the one they had busted Ashok with.

"Yes, that's right," Kim said, her eyes narrowing. "So, what's with the bag?"

"We don't use these bags for our business. These are provided to us by a licensed transportation company. We buy cannabis in bulk, but it's not safe to store it here. Also, banks won't deal with us because weed is still illegal at the federal level, so they won't let us deposit the money we earn."

"Ok..." Kim said.

"So, we use this third-party company to transport and store the bulk of our weed and cash. They have armored cars, guys with guns, and a safe house where they keep everything."

"Are you saying this armored car company stole your cannabis?" Harold asked.

"They're the ones who provide us with these black bags. They come by every week to do pickups and drop-offs. When we need them to pick up cash or excess product, they have us put it in these bags. That way they can come in quickly, grab it and go. They're like Navy SEALS. Boom, boom, in and out. I'm not saying they stole it. But the fact that you found it in one of these black bags seems like a big coincidence. Especially because, as I said, you can check our inventory. We are square here."

"We just might do that," Kim said, thinking. "What's the name of the armored car service?"

"Green Zone Defense," Moon Dog said. "It's owned by the former Denver chief of police. Radford, or something like that, right?"

"The Colonel? Mack Radford has an armored car business moving marijuana now?" Harold asked in surprise.

"That's my understanding," Moon Dog said. "That's why we use them, because we figured he would do everything by the book. We don't want any trouble. We follow the law to the letter."

Kim drew a slow, deep breath.

"We appreciate your cooperation. We'll be back if we have any more questions," she said, and she and Harold turned and walked out. When they got in the car, Harold spoke first.

"No way The Colonel is dealing drugs. That man is a war hero," he said angrily.

"I know," Kim responded. "I was only there a few years while he was chief.

I think I spoke to him one time, but everyone knows who he is. Maybe it's not him. Maybe it's somebody who works for him, a janitor or something."

"What did he say the name of the business was?" Harold asked as they drove off.

"Green Zone Defense," Kim said, putting on her sunglasses. "I guess I better look them up."

5

Retribution

The passenger train clackety-clacked and swayed as the tree-filled landscape rushed past. A man with deep crevices covering his cheeks and thin wrinkles around his eyes shifted in his seat. He wore a blue pea coat. His pants were khaki and well-worn, and his shoes were brown leather.

The loudspeaker chirped and said, first in English, "Ladies and gentlemen, thank you for choosing Via Rail. We are now en route to Montreal. Please ensure your..."

Then again, in French, "Mesdames et Messieurs, merci d'avoir choisi Via Rail. Nous sommes maintenant en route vers Montréal. Veuillez vous..."

The elderly man slouched in his seat, sinking into his pea coat. He studied his reflection in the window. His eyes were sunken and shrouded by heavy lids. Wrinkles and spots adorned his cheeks. A gray beard billowed from his lower face, and strands of gray hair escaped his worn brown fedora.

There were only a few people on the train from Toronto to Montreal at 06:30. The train car's interior resembled a commercial airplane's, but with a row of two seats on the right and one seat on the left. Passengers stored their carry-on luggage in overhead bins, and there was a restroom and a coffee bar at the rear. Near the coffee bar, there were recessed areas where passengers stacked their oversized luggage, which were held in place behind cargo nets.

The elderly man sat on the right near the back of the car. A young woman with bleached blonde hair wearing a purple raincoat sat just in front and to the left of him. Other passengers were seated farther to the front. One was a large, bear-like man with a shaved head and a massive brown beard spilling down his black T-shirt. He wore heavy work boots with thick soles and mud caked along the heels. One hand rested on the armrest. It was muscular and veiny, adorned with silver rings on each finger.

About halfway up the car on the left side, two men wearing Toronto Maple Leafs jerseys were seated. One man was shorter than the other. He wore a black beanie over his ears. He had a thick, short brown beard and his eyes were shrouded in shadow. His brow bones protruded so that he looked primitive, almost Cro-Magnon. His taller friend was even more challenging to see, as he wore a hoodie over his head despite the heat. The shorter man was animated as he chattered about something to his associate, who sat quietly facing ahead.

The train shook and rumbled as it passed by rolling green corn, wheat, and soybean fields. A woman wearing blue nurse's scrubs sat towards the front of the car, her fingers tapping away at a laptop. Her bronze skin glowed in the overhead light, and her black hair was pulled into neat, small braids.

The train ride took over seven hours. Seated in his chair, the old man gripped the armrests, resisting the swaying of the rails. His khaki pants clung to his legs as he shifted about restlessly. As the train snaked through the countryside, the rolling hills of corn and wheat gradually morphed into streets lined with houses as they entered the outskirts of Montreal. Throughout the ride, the large, bearded man with the solid, ringed hands remained motionless like a tree trunk.

Close to 14:00, the Via train pulled into Montreal Central Station. As the locomotive decelerated, some passengers stood and took their belongings from the overhead bins. One of those travelers was the big, bearded man.

As the train arrived at the gate, the young blonde woman in the purple raincoat remained seated with her hands in her lap, gripping a cell phone tightly. The two men in the Maple Leafs jerseys stood up together. The shorter one became increasingly erratic. He was telling an animated story or reenacting a boxing match for his friend, swaying back and forth, pumping his fists and getting more and more excited. The old man's face flushed with heat, and he could feel sweat dripping down his sides under the coat. Shakily, he stood up as the train came to a stop.

He stumbled and caught himself on the blonde woman's seatback.

"Whoa there. Lost my balance," he said.

She flinched at his voice and glanced over her shoulder at him, her eyes wide. He scrutinized her. Her dyed hair was growing out, revealing dark roots underneath, and the sweet scent of her shampoo masked the scent of Chaat Masala. Her eye makeup was heavy, her lips plumped with color and gloss, but her cheeks were hollow and thin.

The Maple Leafs fans moved up the train, closer to the big, bearded man. The shorter hockey fan shadowboxed in an exaggerated display. His colleague in the hoodie stood stoically, hands jammed into his pockets. The excited fan tried to demonstrate a straight right punch and accidentally elbowed the great bearded man in the back.

With narrowed eyes and a clenched jaw, the big man turned. Puffing out his chest, the small hockey fan bravely stepped towards his challenger. Wide-eyed, the woman in braids and scrubs hastily folded her laptop and looked to escape from her seat. The shorter hockey fan stepped closer to the enormous bearded man. Spittle flew from his lips as he cursed in Quebecois French.

With two firm shoves, the giant drove the smaller man away. The shorter hockey fan reacted in a blur. His right foot shot forward in an explosive high kick, the heel of his boot smashing into the bigger man's chin, sending him stumbling backward and crashing into a seat. Within seconds, he was up again, lunging toward the shorter man just as the train doors opened. Punches flew, feet and elbows slammed into seats, and the big man's head crashed against an overhead bin. The bin door popped open, spilling luggage into the seats.

Passengers recoiled in terror. A woman screamed, and a man bellowed at the men to break it up. Amid it all, the young blonde woman in the purple raincoat sat frozen. She stared at the rapidly escalating fight, ten feet separating her from the open door. She looked towards the back of the train, the restroom, the coffee bar—and the cargo nets with the luggage.

The old man watched closely as she sat up in her seat, looking around in panic.

Abruptly, she stood and darted toward the back of the train and the cargo nets holding the luggage. She cast a frantic look toward the fight at the front of the car as she wrestled with a hard gray plastic suitcase stuck behind the net.

The old man shuffled toward the struggling woman. As he stepped behind her, he placed a hand on her shoulder and said, "Hey, don't worry, I can help."

With both hands on the suitcase's handle, she cast a frown at him over her shoulder.

"I'm OK," she said. "I don't need any help."

"Sure," he replied. Then his calming hand on her shoulder suddenly gripped a fistful of purple jacket and jerked her around.

"What the..." she protested.

The old man's gloved hand flicked from under his jacket and slashed upward, driving a ten-inch steel blade just behind her chin. Her teeth clacked together, and she whimpered. He drove the blade upward until he felt the tip strike the inside of her skull. Then he pressed a button on the knife's handle, releasing a hundred thousand volts of electricity directly into her brain. He held her arm with one gloved hand as she slumped in his arms, her life gone.

Looking around quickly, he leaned her body into the nearest seat and closed her eyes. There was no blood on her throat's pale skin, but a puff of smoke escaped her lips, and the smell of roasted flesh nauseated him.

The old man suddenly straightened. He stood tall, his movements lithe and catlike. Using the knife, he sliced through the cargo net and grabbed the handle of the gray suitcase. He pulled it from the net with ease, and it landed on the floor with a thunk. His gaze swept over the train car. The bald hockey fan was on top of the bigger man, pounding his face. The braided nurse, trapped in her seat, shrank in horror next to them, screaming.

No one noticed as the old man exited through the rear door of the train into Montreal Central Station, but the commotion on the train had alerted other people. Panicked shouts carried, and rubber-soled shoes squeaked on the polished floor. Glancing over his shoulder, he saw a teacher with a group of students clambering up steps to escape the fray.

He rolled the heavy suitcase across the open train station as fast as a hunched-over elderly man could, accidentally banging the luggage into the sliding door frame as he exited into the parking garage. He trotted a short distance up the garage ramp to a white van idling in a parking spot. As he approached, the rear doors flung open and a man wearing a black hoodie and ski mask jumped out. Together, they heaved the suitcase into the open back doors. The old man used the van's rear bumper to step up and into the vehicle.

"Everything good?" the ski-masked man asked.

"We're about to see," the old man responded, sitting on an upside-down milk crate on the van's floor.

At that instant, the glass door to the train station slid open, and the two Maple Leaf fans burst through, running at full tilt. The ski-masked man, stationed by the open rear doors of the van, waved them to hurry. They sprinted to the vehicle and jumped in through the back, both erupting hysterically.

The man with the ski mask closed the van's back doors and sprinted to the open driver's door. He jumped in, slammed it shut, and sped out of the parking spot, maneuvering the van sharply, tires squealing against the garage's concrete floor.

"Did you see that giant?" the shorter Maple Leafs fan exclaimed in Quebecois, slapping the old man on the knee. "He was colossal! But I dropped him like a sack of potatoes. You saw that, right?"

"Next time you're told to cause a distraction, pick someone your own size, you short bastard," the hooded Maple Leafs fan quipped. "What if that huge beast would have beaten you? I would've had to shoot him."

"No chance!" the shorter man said.

The van careened out of the parking garage and headed south on Route 136.

"Is that it?" the hooded man asked, gesturing with his chin toward the gray suitcase on the van's floor.

"That's it," the elderly man nodded.

"Well, let's see," he said as he tugged the suitcase towards himself. "Damn, it's heavy," he muttered. He fumbled briefly with the suitcase's locks before drawing a shiny hunting knife from under his jersey and prying them open. The latches popped. He unzipped the main pouch and opened the flap to reveal the contents. The suitcase was filled with rectangular brown packages, like loaves of bread, each meticulously wrapped in packing tape.

He plucked and scrutinized one package.

"Nice," he declared, holding it up. A white label with the black stamp of a lion's head adorned it. "Straight from Pakistan. Grade A dope."

The old man nodded. He removed his pea coat and fedora and ran his fingers through his few strands of gray hair. Then he pulled the brown leather gloves from his hands, revealing young pink flesh without a single liver spot. Reaching up to his weathered, wrinkled face, he grabbed his nose, and with a firm pull, the nose stretched, then tore away, finally ripping off completely. Large chunks of flesh peeled from his eyelids, cheeks, and forehead. Then he grabbed the long, gray beard and, with a tug, ripped off the lower half of the mask. He picked off the last bits of latex and glue, revealing Raison's gleaming blue eyes, straight nose, and broad, stubble-lined jaw. Under the mask, he wore a wig cap, which he removed, revealing his short brown hair.

As the van drove them away, the hooded man pulled a Glock 19 from his waistband and set it on the van's floor. He peeled his jersey and hoodie over his head, revealing a black Kevlar vest underneath. His pale-skinned latex mask was taut over his features, making him appear twenty years younger. He removed it with slow precision, revealing Bruno's swarthy features underneath.

"Damn, it's hot under all that shit," he spat in New York-tinged English.

Next, the shorter Maple Leaf's fan removed his mask, revealing Matheo's bald head. The bruises and cuts from his match at the Casino du Montreal were mostly healed.

"Throw me my phone," Raison told the driver, who tossed him a flip phone. Raison selected a number, dialed, and placed it to his ear.

"Everything's good," Raison said into the phone. "Time to exterminate the rats. Show no mercy."

He listened for a moment.

"Roulez comme si vous étiez déjà mort," Raison said, then closed the phone.

He reached down and retrieved one of the brown packages from the suitcase. He looked at Bruno and Matheo as he tossed the kilo of pure heroin up and down.

"Now, the wolf pack hunts," he said.

The van took the Route 10 bridge east over Nuns' Island, passed Brossard, and then turned onto Route 223. They continued until they turned down a dirt drive leading to a secluded fishing site on the Richelieu River. There, a green Ford Explorer was parked in the trees, waiting. They exited the van, took off their clothes, placed them near a fire pit, and changed into jeans and T-shirts from bags in the back of the Explorer. After they had changed, they pushed the van down the grassy embankment and into the river, where it floated and sank slowly into the fast-moving water, like a whale made of glass and steel.

Matheo built a fire at the campsite with split logs and lighter fluid. He placed their disguises into the flames one by one, hesitating only when he got to the Maple Leafs jerseys.

"Damn, bro," he said. "This is sacrilegious. I can't do it."

"Do you want life in prison? Huh? Maybe Mats Sundin will write to you there," Bruno laughed, then said sternly, "Make sure all that shit is burned up."

Bruno squirted lighter fluid into the fire just as Matheo tossed in the jersey. The flames leaped, singing Matheo's eyebrows. He jumped back, swatting his scorched face.

"Mother fucker!" he exclaimed.

Bruno roared with laughter. "Don't worry, Baldy. You can't burn your hair off if you don't have any."

Raison and Marky, the van's driver, dug through gear bags at the Ford Explorer.

"Hey, Marky," Raison said. "Good job today. Your dad would be proud."

Marky looked down into the canvas duffle he was rustling in. With his ski mask off, he appeared even younger than his 19 years.

"Thanks, man," Marky replied. "Dad taught me everything about driving." He continued rummaging. His arms, covered in black and red tattoos, appeared thinner than ever.

Raison hesitated, then laid a hand on Marky's shoulder. "He's watching over you. You make him proud."

Marky rummaged for a moment longer, then slammed his fist against the SUV.

"Fuck, man, I wish you would have let me go with Rage to kill those motherfuckers," he shouted.

Tears were streaming down Marky's face.

"All of us want revenge, and we're getting it. We all have to play our part, and we needed you to drive. That girl I just x-ed out on the train? She wasn't just a mule. That was the shooter's girlfriend. The girlfriend of the one who pulled the trigger on your dad. I melted her brain, bro."

Marky breathed heavily, his fists clenched tightly by his sides.

"Right now, as we speak," Raison continued. "Rage and our brothers are finishing off the rest of the assholes who killed your dad. Nothing will bring Wild Bill back, but today we're getting revenge, little brother, and that's as good as it gets. Those assholes are probably dead already."

Marky took a deep breath and let it slowly leak out.

"I hope they all suffer," he said.

"Me, too, little brother," Raison said. "Me, too."

Bruno and Matheo were thirty feet away at the campfire, horsing around, watching the disguises burn.

"Are you done yet?" Raison shouted at them.

"Depends how you like your laundry. Medium or well-done?" Bruno shouted back. Matheo doubled over in laughter.

Raison slipped a cell phone into his back pocket and a Glock 43 into his waistband. He pulled his hair back and secured it with a rubber band. He wore a yellow Molson Ice trucker hat and pulled a denim shirt over his muscular arms and shoulders.

The phone buzzed. Raison answered it.

"Go ahead," he instructed.

He listened for a moment.

"None of ours hurt? None of theirs left?" he asked.

He listened again.

"Good work. Everything is good here, brother. I'll see you tonight."

Raison clicked off the call. He walked to the water's edge, reached his arm back, and flung the phone far into the river, where it vanished with a splash. He strolled past Matheo and Bruno at the fire pit. Their polyester disguises had melted into a stringy blob of melted plastic. The black smoke smelled both sweet and acrid.

"Hurry up. Let's get out of here," Raison shouted as he climbed into the Explorer's passenger seat and closed the door.

He lit a Marlboro, took a deep drag, and blew it out the open window, then rested his hand on the windowsill. In the side mirror, he noticed it was shaking.

Meanwhile, in Montreal, a blue Jeep Grand Cherokee with tinted windows was parked at the curb near the intersection of Saint-Michel and Rue Deville with its engine running.

The street was lined with old, brick row houses on both sides. Rain had splattered the cracked concrete sidewalks. Trash cans overflowed with food wrappers, and TV sounds blared from open windows. The stench of boiled cabbage wafted out of droop-shouldered doors, past men smoking on doorsteps.

Four Dead Wolves sat inside the Jeep. Robeur was driving. Moose and Okwaho were in the backseat. Rage was in the front passenger seat. They wore tactical vests complete with body armor, extra magazines, knives, flashlights, and other gear. Each vest was constructed of Kevlar fabric and ceramic armor plates capable of stopping powerful rifle bullets. The two men in the back seat wore hard-knuckled combat gloves. Only their dark eyes gleamed through the narrow slits in their black balaclava masks. The men in the backseat held AK-47 rifles between their knees.

"Roger that," said Rage into a mobile phone. "Roulez comme si vous étiez déjà mort!"

He removed the cell phone from his ear and handed it to Robeur in the driver's seat. Then he lifted a small pair of binoculars and peered at one of the row houses halfway down the block on the right.

Rage sniffed twice, then forcefully blew his nose into his prosthetic left hand.

"Shit, Rage," Robeur said, "that's disgusting."

Rage lifted his left hand and inspected the dripping snot. The hand was stiff, unmoving. Using his right hand, he gave his mucus-covered prosthesis a sharp twist and detached it from its mount with a click.

"What's wrong, Robeur?" Rage asked, holding the hand towards Robeur. "Do bodily fluids frighten you?"

Robeur flinched away. "Fuck off, man! That's not fluid. That's straight up slime."

Okwaho laughed in the backseat. Rage pulled down the visor and used the mirror to glare at the men behind him.

"What about you, Okwaho? Are you also afraid of bodily fluids?"

"Well, there was this one time with your mom..." the smaller of the two men in the backseat joked. The larger man seated next to him, Moose, laughed.

"And you, Moose. Are you a moose or a mouse?" Rage challenged.

Moose stopped laughing. "There's no mouse back here," he growled.

"Good," Rage said and flipped the visor back up. "Because there's about to be a lot of bodily fluids, my brothers."

He retrieved a polished steel hand from a pouch on his vest. This prosthetic was shaped into a fist with a hole through it from top to bottom, as if it were gripping something invisible. He attached the new fist to his forearm with a firm twist and another click. Then, he retrieved a steel tomahawk from a pouch on his plate carrier. It was about a foot long and had a broad, polished steel blade. He slotted the small axe's handle into the prosthetic fist, where it rested on its hilt. He then secured it with a steel pin through a hole in the handle.

"C'est l'heure, mes loups," he said as he pulled the ski mask down his face. "It's go time, my wolves."

Taking a deep breath, the masked driver, Robeur, shifted the Jeep into drive and pressed the accelerator. The Jeep, powered by a growling V8 engine, sped down the neighborhood street. Rage held the door handle as they raced toward a red brick row house with peeling white shutters and green moss growing up the steps. As they neared, Robeur slammed the brakes, throwing the Jeep into a skid. It swerved, crashed into a chain-link fence, and bounced back, coming to a skidding halt at the red and green house's front stoop in a shower of dirt and rocks.

Rage quickly opened the passenger door and jumped out, pulling a CZ P-10 pistol from a vest holster with his right hand, his tomahawked left hand at his side. Simultaneously, the back doors opened, and Moose and Okwaho emerged, shouldering their Kalashnikovs. They dashed toward the house's peeling front door. Rage reached it first, but stepped aside.

Moose, the largest of them, delivered a front kick to the old wooden door. It cracked in protest. Rebounding, he delivered two more kicks. The jam splintered, and the door flung inwards with a bang. He shouldered his AK-47, crouched like a boxer, and entered the house.

Upon entry, the dimly lit hallway greeted Moose with the smells of Pakistani food. A cacophony of screams and shouts echoed from within.

A young black-haired man wearing jeans and white socks slipped on the linoleum floor in the hallway. Three bullets from Moose's AK-47 tore through his chest and stomach, spraying blood and tissue across the white baseboard. He curled into a fetal ball on the hallway floor, moaning.

Moose stepped over him and into the living room. A young man with long hair and a woman with dark hair and heavy eye shadow stood in front of the TV, frozen. The man started blabbering. Without hesitation, Moose fired.

Okwaho followed Moose. Together, they moved from the living room to the kitchen.

Rage, pistol at high ready and hatchet in a low defensive position, stalked carefully down the hallway, deeper into the house. Coming from the afternoon sun into the dimly lit hall, he waited for his eyes to adjust. From the back, he could hear confused shouting. He heard panicked feet thumping on the second floor. Listening, he crept down the hall.

A loud crash carried through the wall to his right as his brothers broke down a door, followed by shouting and four thunderous AK-47 shots. Then, a shout of, "Clear!"

Rage arrived at the stairs leading to the second floor. He slowly ascended the wooden steps, his eyes and the muzzle of his 9-millimeter aimed up the stairway.

The closer to the second floor he got, the clearer he could hear voices shouting in fear and confusion. He discerned two distinct male voices and one female. Rage found himself in an empty second-floor hallway with doors on either side. It reeked of cigarettes and marijuana. He stopped and considered the closed doors.

"Premier étage dégagé!" Moose shouted from downstairs. "First floor clear!"

"Deuxième étage! Deuxième étage!" "Second floor! Second floor!" Rage shouted back.

The rapid thud of boots on the stairs signaled the approach of his comrades. When they joined him on the landing, Rage gestured for silence with his tomahawk hand. Then he listened closely. The floor had gone silent. He motioned with his pistol for Moose and Okwaho to take positions on either side of the hall. Both men spread out while reloading their rifles with fresh magazines.

Rage waved his tomahawked hand, and both shooters unleashed a barrage of AK-47 fire, blasting high-powered rounds through doors and walls. The house erupted with flying bits of plaster and wood. Dust and smoke choked the air.

While the shooters reloaded, Rage kicked in the nearest door—a bathroom. A naked, bearded man, still wet from the shower, lay bloodied on the floor from a gut shot. He held up his hand in protest. Rage stepped into the bathroom, raised his tomahawk hand, and struck the wounded man in the top of the head. The blade stuck in the man's skull like an axe in a log. He gargled and convulsed. Rage kicked his chest and yanked his axe-hand free, blood splattering on his clothes.

Continuing down the hallway, the masked killers meticulously checked each room. They found two more victims in various states, dispatching them quickly with gunshots and tomahawk slashes. After the last room was clear, Rage listened. All was silent.

The men ransacked the second-floor rooms, scattering items across the wooden floor.

Once they had searched the last upstairs room, Rage ordered them back downstairs to the rear of the house. There, the yellow kitchen was outdated and dirty. Opening the refrigerator, Rage found Indian beer and to-go food containers. Next, he inspected the oven—empty.

"Check the cabinets," he shouted. "Let's go!"

Moose emptied the cabinets' contents onto the floor with a clatter while Okwaho opened a pantry door, revealing shelves of plastic containers. Leaning his rifle against the wall, he opened a container and peered inside.

"Found it!" he called out.

Rage walked over and checked the contents: small, blue baggies of white powder. He opened two other containers, finding bags of marijuana in one and colorful pills in another.

"Get all this," he ordered.

Okwaho removed a black trash bag from a pouch on his vest. He shook open the bag, took the containers from the shelves, and dropped them inside.

"Let's go!" Rage shouted as his companion shoved container after container into the bag.

"Shit, it's a lot. It won't all fit!" Okwaho exclaimed.

"Leave the rest. Let's move!" Rage replied.

Okwaho grabbed his Kalashnikov rifle with his right hand, then gathered the neck of the sack with his left and slung it over his shoulder like Santa Claus. They stormed through the hallway to the broken front door and stepped into the Montreal sun.

Tossing the trash bag of looted drugs through the Jeep's open door, Okwaho climbed into the vehicle. Moose came barreling out of the house, ran to the SUV, and jumped in.

Rage strolled casually behind. He scanned the deserted street, his eyes drawn to fluttering curtains and pale white faces in windows. Distant sirens grew louder. He walked to the Jeep and reached inside the open passenger door. From the cupholder, he retrieved a glass bottle filled with yellow liquid, a strip of white cloth dangling from its mouth.

"Come on!" Robeur yelled from the driver's seat.

Rage reached into his pocket, removed a silver lighter, and lit the cloth on fire. He reared back and threw the flaming Molotov cocktail through the open front door. The bottle shattered on the entryway floor, sending flames whooshing up the walls like crashing orange waves.

Rage jumped into the passenger seat. Before he could shut the door, Robeur pressed the accelerator, the sudden jerk slamming the door shut. The Jeep fish-tailed onto the street, its engine roaring. Robeur made a fast right turn at the intersection, causing the tires to squeal and the Jeep to rock.

"All right, slow down," Rage commanded, "and hand me my phone."

Robeur removed the phone from his jacket pocket and tossed it to Rage. He caught it with his right hand, tapped several buttons on the mobile device, then held it to his ear.

"It's done," he said into the phone. "Rat's nest exterminated."

Listening momentarily, he agreed, then set the phone in his lap.

He noticed that the tomahawk attachment, which was still fixed to his left forearm, was caked with blood and hair. He removed the steel pin, slid the hatchet out of its fist mount, and wiped the blade on his pants before sliding it back into its sheath on his plate carrier.

The men rode in silence, the only sound their heavy breathing. The Jeep continued south, out of the city, across the Honore Mercier Bridge, past the Kahnawake reservation, to a farmhouse near Russeltown Flats. There, they pulled the Jeep into a detached garage.

The men exited, and Moose pulled down the garage door. Inside, the men removed their clothing and threw them into a blue plastic barrel. They stacked their firearms on a workbench. Rage added his CZ pistol to the pile of weapons.

"Outside, let's go," Rage said.

Naked, they walked through a side door of the garage and into a fenced backyard, where a garden hose and bottle of dish soap waited. Each man took a handful of soap and smeared it over his head, face, and body while they took turns running the hose over themselves.

Once washed, the killers returned to the garage. Duffel bags of clothing awaited them on the floor. Each man quickly unzipped his bag and dressed in fresh jeans and T-shirts. Once dressed, Rage gestured toward the stack of weapons on the workbench.

"Moose," he said to the big man. "Cut those up with the torch."

Moose stood at a sturdy 6-feet 5-inches, and his broad frame was covered in tattoos and thick body hair. When he moved, his muscles flexed. His long, brown hair, woven into a braid down his back, matched his beard. Moose glanced behind him at an acetylene torch. Nodding, he walked to the stack of rifles, selected one, and proceeded to field strip it. He ejected the magazine and worked the bolt several times to ensure the chamber was empty before picking up the torch. Donning dark safety goggles and leather gloves, he unraveled the green and red lead from the bottles. He used a striker to light the torch, then adjusted the flame. Once it burned blue, he picked up the first AK-47 and, with slow precision, sliced it up like a block of cheese, sending sparks showering across the garage.

Okwaho put on a white T-shirt, black jeans, and black riding boots. His damp mohawk dripped water onto his shoulders.

The prospect, Robeur, was younger than the rest at barely 20. His arms were covered in tattoos. He was short and stoutly built, with a reddish buzz cut and a long, red goatee. He had scars on his eyebrows and wore a denim shirt over blue jeans and work boots.

Rage replaced the steel prosthetic fist with his usual plastic hand. Then, after dressing in black jeans and a T-shirt, he stepped to the barrel of clothing. He pulled a long, black rubber glove up to his elbow and picked up a bottle of sulfuric acid. He emptied it over the gear.

Once Moose had cut up the rifles and pistol, they placed the scrap metal into another barrel. Rage and Okwaho poured eight gallons of muriatic acid onto the scraps of steel. Then they added their vests and other gear to the steaming barrels, which bubbled as the contents dissolved. Using plastic lids, they sealed the barrels and loaded them into the back of the Jeep.

"Jim at the junkyard is going to come by later with a flatbed truck and take care of all this," Rage said. "Let's get out of here."

The men exited the garage, crossed the yard, and walked to the front of the house. There, four motorcycles sat in the driveway. The crew of Dead Wolves killers mounted their bikes, fired the engines, and roared onto the road back to Montreal.

6

Family

Detective Kim turned off the engine of her blue Lexus RX 350. The quiet of the Denver suburbs enveloped her as she sat in her driveway for a moment, gathering her thoughts. Then she grabbed her bag from the passenger seat and stepped out onto the driveway of her two-story home.

As she unlocked the door and stepped inside, the familiar smells of home greeted her—faint lavender from the air freshener and coffee from the kitchen.

"Kim, is that you?" Mike's voice came from the living room.

"Yeah, it's me," she called back, kicking off her shoes and heading toward the kitchen to drop her keys on the counter.

Mike appeared at the kitchen entryway, his tall frame filling the frame. At forty, his skin was a smooth, dark canvas that glowed in the low light of the hallway. He walked straight to her, his big smile and white teeth dazzling.

"Hey," he greeted, wrapping her in a warm embrace. "How was work?"

"Same old. Chasing shadows and hitting walls," Kim replied, allowing herself a moment to rest in the comfort of his arms. "How about you? How was your day off?"

"Good, good. I actually managed to relax for once. Took a long run, read a bit. And, of course, made sure there's enough food in the fridge for the next few days," Mike said, a twinkle in his eye.

Kim smiled, pulling back to look up at him. "You spoil me, you know that?"

"Only because you deserve it," Mike said, leaning down to kiss her forehead gently. "But I've got an early flight tomorrow. Six in the morning to New York."

"So early?" Kim frowned slightly.

"Yeah, but it's a quick turnaround. I'll be back before you know it," he assured her.

"I know. Just... be safe, okay?"

"Always am," Mike said, his voice firm yet gentle. He leaned in and kissed her.

"I better head to bed then. Got to be up at the crack of dawn," Mike said reluctantly, stepping back.

"Okay. Sleep well, love. I'll be in there later," Kim said, watching as he turned to head upstairs.

"Try not to stay up too late, alright?"

"I'll try," she promised, a soft smile on her lips as she watched him disappear around the corner.

She glanced at the clock, and with a resigned sigh, Kim made her way upstairs, her footsteps light on the carpeted steps. At the top, she paused, listening for a moment to the sounds emanating from Xavier's room.

Knocking gently on the door, she pushed it open to see her fourteen-year-old son, Xavier, engrossed in a video game. The glow from the screen illuminated his focused face, casting shadows that danced across his features as he tapped and shook the controller.

"Hey, Xavi," Kim said, leaning against the doorframe.

Xavier paused his game, a grin spreading across his face as he looked up. "Hey, Mom. You're home early." He was tall like his father, but medium complected like Kim. His hair was cut into an asymmetric flattop with wavy lines shaved into the sides. It wasn't Kim's favorite, but it's what kids were doing. Basketball posters lined the bedroom walls.

"Early enough to catch you still saving the world, I see," Kim teased, stepping into the room and glancing at the screen.

Xavier paused the game and looked up at her. "How was your day?"

"Long and complicated. The usual," Kim shrugged.

"I'm glad you're home," Xavier said, his smile genuine. "Do you need help with anything?"

She shook her head. "No, I'm good. I was thinking about making dinner. Any requests?"

"Um, is spaghetti okay?" he asked.

"Spaghetti it is," she affirmed with a smile. "Give me a few minutes to change, and I'll get started. You've got time to finish your game."

"Cool!" Xavier turned back to his game.

Kim lingered for a moment, watching him, a soft smile playing on her lips before closing the door gently and walking back downstairs.

Xavier waited a moment, then paused the game again. He turned his head and sat perfectly still, listening. Once assured his mother was gone, he stood up and stepped into his bathroom. There, a tripod was set up on the counter next to a bottle of rubbing alcohol.

Xavier checked his hair and his teeth in the mirror. Looking himself in the eyes, he smiled. Then, pulling his cell phone from his pocket, he clamped the device to the tripod, took in and blew out a deep breath, then tapped the record button.

"Yo, what's up? It's your boy Wavy Xavi coming at you from the Mile High City. That's right, I'm back at you with another insane fucking stunt. You'll never believe what you're about to see. I'm gonna need all the sexy ladies to pay close attention because this is something you're pussy ass boyfriend could never do."

He reached down and picked up the bottle of rubbing alcohol and a lighter.

"That's right, everybody, it's the motherfuckin' fire challenge. It's really about to go down live so tell your friends, your homegirls, your sisters, brothers, cousins—tell everybody—to come watch because this shit is about to be crazy."

Xavier pulled his T-shirt over his head, revealing his hairless chest and thin shoulders. He opened the bottle of alcohol and, tipping it over, squirted a stream of the cold, clear liquid across his chest where it ran down and soaked his shorts.

"Be sure to like and subscribe for more off-the-hook content," he said as he sparked the lighter for his invisible fans.

7

Drugs

Raison, Bruno, and Matheo rode their motorcycles through the vast Canadian wilderness. Sunlight streamed down, filtering through the trees and casting dappled patterns on the asphalt.

Raison's Harley Davidson Softail had an elongated frame. The glossy, obsidian-black paint was accented with silver flames trailing from the fuel tank to the rear fender. The handlebars were raised like the horns of a bull, and the Advanblack leather seat was meticulously stitched with silver thread. His leather jacket was crafted from the finest buffalo leather. It was dyed a deep black and had a rich, polished look. Its beaver fur collar ruffled in the wind. Sewn to the front right breast was a patch reading "President" in a blood-red font, and the back featured the MC's wolf's head colors.

Bruno's custom bagger was deep burgundy, punctuated by geometric patterns in muted gold. The front wheel was distinctly larger than the rear. His Z-shaped handlebars added an aggressive touch to the chopper's silhouette, and the seat was crafted from fine black leather. The powerful engine emitted a raw, guttural growl. His jacket was more rugged, the brown leather weathered and creased. A patch proudly declared his role as "Sgt. at Arms."

Matheo's Softail was a simple gunmetal gray. The handlebars were slightly bent forward, complemented by a low-hung seat upholstered in black leather. Chrome accents shimmered throughout, particularly on the engine, which produced a smooth, rhythmic purr. The front of his black leather riding jacket was adorned with genuine silver-gray wolf hide. Each strand of fur rippled in the wind, contrasting with the sleek black of his remaining attire.

The three riders rode in staggered formation, filling the lane from the centerline to the shoulder, with each rider in his appropriate position. At the front of the pack, Raison road in the righthand position, nearest the shoulder. Behind him, Bruno, as sergeant at arms, road in the lefthand position, near the road's centerline. Matheo, in the back of the pack, rode in the righthand lane, in line with Raison.

After a few hours' ride, they slowed and turned onto a single-lane crumbling blacktop road. The riders weaved through potholes as they traveled away from the highway and into the Canadian wilderness. After a few miles, they turned off the blacktop and onto a dusty caliche drive where they stopped. Each man tied a bandana over his face to protect from dust. Then they rode side-by-side, a cloud of dust behind them, until the dirt drive dead-ended at a dilapidated farm.

There was an aged double-wide mobile home teetering on stacks of cinder blocks surrounded by tall weeds. Several rotting outbuildings and a junk tractor sat in the back. A shiny white Ford pickup was parked next to three custom choppers in the front yard. The air was less oppressive than the city, and the occasional breeze brought the scent of manure.

The three Dead Wolves riders parked their bikes beside the others and stepped off. They hung their helmets on their handlebars and strode toward the mobile home. A green water hose coiled like a snake on the ground near the sagging wooden steps up to a deck. At the top, Raison knocked on the white front door.

Tommy Boy's bodyguard, Jester, opened it, his massive frame filling the doorway. He wore his Big Machine cut over a Metallica T-shirt and was holding a can of Coors Light beer.

"Well, if it ain't the fucking Paw Patrol," the big man bellowed.

Raison's jaw clenched.

"Jester, my boy," Raison said. "Haven't drank yourself to death yet? What's taking so long? You cutting back?"

"Shit," Jester said, stepping outside onto the deck, "they don't make enough beer to kill me."

Tilting his head back, he chugged the entire can, belched loudly, crushed it, tossed it into a mildew-covered garbage bin filled with more cans, then said, "Tommy's in the barn. Come on."

Jester lumbered across the backyard toward a large, old wooden barn, the Dead Wolves trailing behind.

Jester said over his shoulder, chuckling. "Get ready, 'cause they're about to go off."

"Who's about to go off?" Matheo asked, looking around.

When they were halfway across the yard, a single dog's deep, powerful bark came from a fenced kennel near the old barn. More dogs' heads appeared from shelter doorways behind the chain link. Then, all at once, the kennel roared to life, with six huge black dogs leaping and barking furiously.

"Holy shit!" Matheo exclaimed. "What breed are those?"

"Cane Corsos," Jester said. "They'll tear a man to pieces. Fucking brutal."

Raison stared through his Ray-Bans at the bellowing, slobbering dogs as they walked past.

The bikers approached the side door of the huge, dilapidated barn, its weathered wood peering through holes in the peeling red paint. Jester pounded on it with one beefy fist, then looked up into the shiny black eye of a security camera above the door.

"The Paw Patrol is here for Tommy Boy," Jester said. Raison gritted his teeth and ignored an annoyed glance from Bruno.

With a rattle and a ping, the barn door popped open with the release of an electric lock, and they walked inside.

Entering the old barn was like walking through a dream. The exterior of the barn, peeling and rotting as it appeared, was a façade. Inside was a state-of-the-art hydroponic greenhouse, masterfully camouflaged and hidden miles from civilization.

Within the vast room, a sea of verdant cannabis plants stretched as far as the eye could see, basking under the radiant glow of high-intensity lights. The air was thick with a humid, earthy aroma, punctuated by the gentle hum of the HVAC system and the soft gurgle of water circulating through hydroponic pumps. The plants were supported by overhead trellises and watered through drip irrigation systems placed between the rows. Amidst this jungle of green, monitoring devices blinked intermittently.

Through a steel door and into a side room, they went. There, they found Tommy Boy bathed in the soft luminescence of grow lights. He was leaning against a stainless-steel table covered in baby marijuana plants. His finger, adorned with a gold ring, toyed with a tiny plant in a small black pot. A rich golden mane cascaded down his back. He wore python skin cowboy boots, blue jeans, and his Big Machine cut over a white t-shirt. He had a lit cigar in his free hand and a pair of sunglasses perched on his head. The bottom rocker on Tommy Boy's cut no longer read "Toronto." Now, it read "Nomads."

"Raison!" Tommy Boy turned away from the clone table and smiled widely. "Good to see you, my man. I heard everything went well."

He reached out a dry, calloused hand as Raison approached. They shook, then clapped each other on their backs.

Raison's lips twitched upwards. "Everything went perfect, Tommy."

"Now, tell me if this is right," Tommy Boy said, stepping back and taking a drag from his cigar. "You shanked their mule, the girl, in the head with some kind of, uh, electric knife?"

"That's right," Raison nodded.

"Dropped her like a leaf, huh?" Tommy Boy asked. "And I heard there was no blood? Is that right?"

"The blade enters the skull," Bruno piped up. "Then you press a button to electrify the blade, like a powerful stun gun. The voltage fries the gray matter while heating the blade red hot, cauterizing the wound channel on the way out. The rubber hilt and handle save the user from getting shocked."

Tommy Boy squinted at Bruno. He took a languid drag from his cigar, the ember flaring bright, then exhaled slowly, the smoke billowing to the ceiling like a volcanic eruption.

"Far out, man," he said. "That's some real James Bond shit."

"Your man picked up the suitcase last night," Raison said. "Twelve bricks of pure Pakistani horse."

"Yes, he did," Tommy Boy said, turning to Raison. "I have to say, we were expecting more merchandise from the clubhouse. That stash didn't make its way to us."

Raison spoke evenly. "We delivered everything we got, Tommy."

Tommy Boy's response was a slow, thoughtful, "Hmmm." He stepped closer to Raison, his tall frame casting a shadow. Bruno stiffened, his leather jacket creaking, and Matheo shifted on his feet.

Tommy Boy nodded. "All right," he said, smiling. "Who knows, right?" He reached into his breast pocket under his cut and pulled out a thick manila envelope. He handed it to Raison.

Raison thanked him and slid the envelope inside his jacket.

"Is it true your brother, Rage, has an, uh, axe-hand?" he asked, holding up his left hand, fingers together like a karate chop.

Raison blinked. "Rage has made a few attachments for his prosthetic. The tomahawk is one."

Tommy Boy put the cigar into the corner of his mouth. He looked back and forth between the three Dead Wolves, taking them in as if for the first time.

"Far out," he said.

Suddenly, his face broke into a yellow grin. He clapped Raison on the shoulder. "Keep up the good work, boys. With your skills and drive, Quebec will be yours."

"What's next?" Raison asked.

"What do you mean? You got your revenge," Tommy Boy said.

"I'm talking about between us. Between the Dead Wolves and Big Machine. What's next for us?" Raison asked.

"You'll hear from me," Tommy Boy replied. "But the actual decision is yours, not ours. We made our offer. Now it's up to you men to have a vote, I believe."

"What happens if the vote is 'No'?" Raison asked.

Tommy Boy's smile widened. "Well, let's try to remain positive. We're all friends here."

He pointed with his cigar towards the manila envelope Raison had placed in his shirt pocket. "Now, don't spend that all in one place."

Tommy Boy turned back to the clone table. The three Dead Wolves MC members walked out of the clone room and back into the greenhouse, where Jester was waiting to escort them to their bikes.

As he led them across the yard, he spoke over his shoulder to Raison. "That shit at the clubhouse is all over the news. The fire took all night to put out, and they're still dragging bodies out. The heat will be on for that. The dead chick on the train hasn't made the news yet. No blood. That shit was slick, man," he said, shaking his head.

"The coroner is going to have fun with that one," Bruno replied.

They reached their motorcycles in the driveway next to the shabby double-wide trailer.

"Yeah, but y'all better lay low. Shit could get thick," Jester said, a fresh beer in his hand.

"Your gut is the only thing getting thick," Raison said.

Jester let out a huge belch. "My old lady loves it. So does yours. Tell her I'm coming by later."

Raison fired up his motorcycle, followed by Bruno, then Matheo. The engines rumbled and raged.

"It's the mother fuckin' Paw Patrol, everybody. Woo-hoo!" Jester shouted, throwing up his arms, beer foam sloshing.

Raison put his helmet on, then pulled his Ray-Bans over his eyes. He kicked up his kickstand, and the three Dead Wolves roared down the dusty drive. When they paused at the intersection with the main road, Matheo looked over at Raison.

"Paw Patrol," he spit. "I'd like to split that fat fucker's belly open and paw his guts out."

Raison ignored him.

"I know you noticed Tommy Boy's new bottom rocker," Bruno shouted over their rumbling engines.

"I did," Raison said. "If they promoted the president of the Toronto chapter to the Nomads chapter, meaning he has authority and support anywhere he goes, then Big Machine is expanding, and Tommy Boy is probably at the front of their plans. I would guess Big Machine is moving into Quebec—with us, over us, or through us."

Bruno snickered. "They could lose a hundred men for each one of ours and hardly notice a dent in their monthly dues."

"That's why we have to be smart," Matheo added. "I know Raison has the right plan for us."

Raison clenched his jaw and checked his watch.

"We better haul ass to get home before it gets too late," Raison said, and the trio revved their engines as they turned onto the blacktop back to Montreal.

Raison, Bruno, and Matheo arrived at the clubhouse after dark. They backed their bikes against the curb and dropped their kickstands, just as the Dead Wolves had for over fifty years. Several other bikes, including Rage's, were already parked there.

They climbed the wooden steps and walked inside, their boots thudding heavily on the wooden floor. Raison made his way to the back of the clubhouse, toward the president's office. The door squealed as he pushed it open. The sounds of the main room faded as he entered.

Inside, Rage and Okwaho were bent over a desk with lines of white powder arranged on the leather blotter. Empty blue baggies littered the table, and a few had fallen to the floor and lay scattered under their boots. The sharp, acrid scent of cocaine filled the room. The sight tightened Raison's jaw.

His eyes locked onto Rage. "You're playing with fire," Raison said, his voice low and steely. "We were supposed to deliver everything, all this, to Tommy Boy. You're risking our patch over and all our lives for this shit."

Rage straightened up defiantly, his nostrils flaring. His eyes were wide and black, his face thin and oily. He gritted his teeth and flexed his jaw. Veins protruded from his temples and neck. "'Risk our patch over?' We don't need a patch over," he snapped. "This is our territory. *They* need a fucking patch over."

"You don't get it," Raison shot back. "It's not about what we deserve or what we want. Big Machine doesn't play, Rage. They will either make us disband, patch us over, or wipe us out. They won't allow us to operate independently forever."

"*Allow us?*" Rage exploded, leaping to his feet, sending his wooden chair screeching across the floor. "Allow us? We just wiped out an entire pack of motherfuckers, but we're the ones who are scared?"

Rage's eyes glittered with cocaine and anger, but before he could respond, Raison's attention shifted.

"Where's Marky?" he asked, concern edging into his voice.

Okwaho pointed a thumb towards the back, then snorted another line. Raison's heart quickened as he walked down a narrow corridor. He pushed open the bedroom door and was hit by the putrid smell of human excrement. Marky lay sprawled on the bed, his skin pale and lips a deathly blue. Nearby, an empty syringe, a spoon, and a pile of blue plastic baggies lay on a table.

"Shit," Raison sighed.

"Ah, damn," Rage said from behind, shaking his head.

"Hey! Okwaho!" Rage shouted back at the office. "Fucking Marky OD'd back here, bro."

"What?" a voice called from the office.

"I said Marky fucking OD'd back here, motherfucker! Do you hear me? O-mother-fucking-D'd!"

"What the fuck?" came the reply, followed by boots rapidly thumping closer.

Okwaho came stumbling into the bedroom, his usually swarthy face pale.

"Fuck," he said, shocked. "Did y'all try to wake him up?"

Okwaho grabbed Marky by the arms and shook him.

"Marky! Yo, Marky! Wake up!" the Mohawk shouted.

Raison checked the pulse in Marky's neck.

"Shit, he's already cold," he said.

He used his fingertips to close Marky's eyes. The dead boy's pale, thin face looked skeletal.

"He's with his dad now," Okwaho said.

Raison's phone buzzed, and he removed it from his back pocket, checking the caller.

"It's Tommy Boy," he said. "Everybody shut up."

"Hello?" he answered the phone, then listened.

"Cool, man, I got it. It's all good," he assured Tommy Boy, then clicked off the call and stuck the phone back in his pocket.

Bruno and Matheo had silently joined Raison, Rage, and Okwaho in the bedroom. They stared at Marky's lifeless body, sprawled across the white bedsheets, shoeless, wearing jeans and a Nirvana t-shirt.

"I—we—don't have time for this shit. Do you know what that call was?" Raison asked his brother, Rage. "It was Tommy Boy telling me we've been called to a meeting with Pop."

Rage looked up quickly. "A meeting? For what?" his voice rose indignantly.

Raison glared at his younger brother. "He wants to borrow a cup of sugar. What the fuck do you think?"

Raison looked at Marky's body and sighed.

"Matheo, you and Robeur take Marky to the emergency room and drop him off. Rage and Okwaho, get your shit straight. We have work to do."

He looked around the messy room and at the dead body one last time before shaking his head, turning on his boot heel, and striding out.

Once again, Raison and Bruno cruised along a weathered, winding road through the Canadian countryside. The hum of their engines was the only sound for miles, accompanied by the rhythmic flapping of their leather cuts against the wind. Tall pine trees stood sentinel beside the road, their needles whispering secrets of the wild.

The two bikers pulled into the circle drive of a sprawling two-story white painted brick home. They dropped their kickstands, killed their engines, and walked to the front door. Three hard knocks and the wooden door swung open to reveal Tommy Boy. His eyes gave the two a once-over before nodding for them to follow him inside.

The house, once a fine estate, was now a dilapidated relic from another era. Inside, the dimly lit hallways were lined with boxes, the clutter of unopened deliveries and old memorabilia. The wallpaper was faded and stained, clinging desperately to the walls. The smell of stale cigarette smoke hung in the air. A television played a Tom and Jerry re-run in a carpeted and wood-paneled living room.

They passed through an open door leading to the garage. Several motorcycles, including a Honda Gold Wing and a custom black bagger, sat incongruously next to a sleek 2015 Ferrari 458 Italia, its bright red body untouched by the decay surrounding it. The sweet scent of engine exhaust and motor oil filled the air.

They finally reached Pop's office at the back of the house, its door slightly ajar. Inside, an overweight man with thick arms and a round belly sat behind an expansive desk. The flickering light from a muted TV cast irregular shadows on his face, highlighting his short gray buzz cut and matching handlebar mustache. Pop's sharp and calculating eyes remained fixed on the news broadcast, not budging when Tommy Boy and the others entered.

The room was filled with the combined scents of cigarette smoke and minty gum. Pop's cut was covered in patches, including a "Charter Member" patch and a "Mechanic" patch on his chest. His neck, wrists, and fingers were adorned with gold. He chewed his gum with an intensity that mirrored his gaze, occasionally bringing a lit cigarette to his lips, inhaling deeply, and then releasing a plume of smoke. Faded, bluish tattoos covered his fingers, hands, arms, and neck.

Pop finally acknowledged their presence, his voice gravelly from smoking. "Raison, sit," he said, exhaling another cloud of smoke. "But I don't know you," he gestured toward Bruno.

Tommy Boy held the door open for Bruno, and they both walked out, closing the door behind, leaving Raison alone with the founder and leader of the largest outlaw motorcycle club in the world.

Taking another long drag from his cigarette, Pop allowed the smoke to curl from his mouth as he stared directly into Raison's eyes. "You and your boys did some good work for us," he began.

Raison nodded, but remained silent.

Leaning forward, Pop's gold bracelets clinked on the desk. "One more mission, Raison. One more job," he said. "You do this for us, and I'll patch you and your boys over. All of you. You'll all ride under the Big Machine banner."

Raison sat motionless.

Pop continued, "This ain't just any job, Raison. We're talking millions in cash." He paused for emphasis, letting the magnitude of the sum sink in. "A *real* heist. The kind that'll set you and your boys up for life."

"And once it's done," he added, the corner of his mouth curling into a confident smirk, "you'll be leading the pack. President of Big Machine's new Quebec chapter. Your territory, under our flag, just as I promised you."

Pop leaned back in his leather chair, the worn-out springs creaking beneath his weight. The room was filled with the blue-gray haze of cigarette smoke.

"You know, Raison," he said, in a softer, more reflective tone, "in our business, people think it's the money that corrupts. That money is the root of all evil. But they're wrong." He took a deep drag from his cigarette, blowing it out. "You know what the root of all evil is, Raison? It's selfishness. Selfishness is the root of all evil. Do you believe that?"

"I'm no philosopher, but I can see what you're saying," Raison agreed.

"We don't do this for the money. That's why I don't care if a few packages from a raid don't make it back to us. We've always been about family here in the Big Machine," he continued, tapping ash into an overflowing dish. "Looking out for each other, sharing the wealth, the risk, the reward."

The low hum of the news played in the background.

Pop leaned in closer, his voice nearly a whisper, the smell of tobacco heavy on his breath. "You showed you're willing to do whatever it takes to protect your family when you helped us eliminate Max and Wild Bill. I know that was hard for you, turning against your own. But Max was a rat, and Bill should have known better. The Mounties were going to charge Max for murder and racketeering, so he was trying to pin it all on you guys—you, your brother, everyone but himself. I know it hurts, but we showed you the file. You did what was necessary for the greater good of your family. I respect that. Now, you and your Wolves served those Pakistani rats in Montreal up to me as a sacrifice. You keep telling your boys those were the assholes who killed Max and Bill. That way, their hunger for revenge is satisfied, you have a few dollars in your pockets, and a competitor of both of ours is out of business. That's what we call strategy, my boy. Alliances for mutual gain. That's how nations are conquered. And that's how you will become the outlaw king of

Quebec with a Big Machine army at your back. That's what you want, right?"

Raison's face was an unreadable mask except for the slightest twitch at the corner of his lips. His eyes were moist and glittered in the light.

"I do," he said.

Pop studied him, taking a drag from his cigarette.

The silence stretched on. Raison finally broke it. "So, about the job..."

Pop sat back and smiled. "Have you ever ridden through the Rocky Mountains, Raison? Let me tell you, it's quite a sight."

8

Meeting

Detectives Kim Wright and Harold Clarke pulled into the parking lot of the Green Zone Defense building. The commercial structure was mostly white with green trim, made partially of brick and partially of steel, and it had three tall rolling garage doors along one side of the front.

Kim looked around as she got out of the sedan. They were on the edge of town, in an industrial area filled with warehouses and commercial buildings.

"This used to be a city road maintenance building," Harold said. "They stored those big trucks they use to salt the roads in winter here. I guess The Colonel bought it because he needs the garage doors for the armored cars."

Harold looked around as they walked closer.

"It's just crazy to me. The Colonel was the police chief here for at least 10 years. I knew he left to start a security business, but I didn't realize it was, you know, *marijuana* related. I never would've dreamed."

"Does it seem odd to you?" Kim asked.

"A little out of character, yeah. He always struck me as a buttoned-up military type," Harold replied as he reached to open the building's front door.

"Cannabis is legal now," Kim said. "Get used to that. As long as he's following the law, he's not doing anything wrong."

"Yeah. 'Nothing wrong,' as long as you believe marijuana isn't the gateway drug," Harold said.

"I always thought of alcohol as the gateway drug," Kim replied.

Harold shrugged, and they walked inside. They found themselves inside a lobby featuring a sofa and guest chairs. Before they could sit, a petite brown-haired woman wearing blue slacks, a floral blouse, and a headset entered through another door and greeted them with a smile.

"Hi, I'm Rhonda. I'm the office manager, receptionist, dispatcher, and whatever else is needed around here," she said cheerfully.

"Detectives Wright and Clarke," Harold said, shaking her hand.

"The Colonel is expecting you. Come on, and I'll take you to his office. Can I get y'all something to drink? Coffee? Tea? Water?"

"No, thank you. I'm fine," Kim said.

"Me, too," Harold agreed.

Rhonda led the detectives through the mostly quiet office, down white hallways, past cubicles where uniformed employees lounged or typed.

After a few turns, they arrived at an open doorway. Rhonda knocked on the frame and a gruff voice answered. "Come in."

Rhonda smiled at Kim and Harold and beckoned them to follow. Inside, The Colonel's office was painted forest green with dark wood trim. Certificates and awards covered the walls. There were numerous framed photos of men in uniforms, both military and police. An American flag and a Colorado flag stood on poles in opposite corners framing a large, claw-footed wooden desk, behind which sat The Colonel.

The Colonel was stocky and broad-shouldered. His hair, jet black with gray at the temples, was cut into a precise flat top. His face was clean-shaven and tanned, and his arms bulged inside his crisp, dark green uniform. The name tag on his chest read "Radford," and he had Green Zone Defense patches on both shoulders.

He stood from behind the desk. "Detective Harold Clarke and...." he started, reaching out his hand with a beaming smile.

"Detective Kim Wright," she said, shaking his hand.

"Detectives Wright and Clarke, thank you for coming by," he said, shaking both of their hands heartily, then gesturing for them to sit. "Harold, how have you been? Still wearing a badge, I see."

"Eh," Harold said, leaning back in his chair. "The wife doesn't want me hanging around the house, so I guess I'll keep working until they find me dead in my cruiser."

"Hell, you'll outlast all of us. So, what can I do for you today?"

"We're here about a recent bust we made," Kim began. "Three pounds of legally grown marijuana was found in a black canvas duffel bag that seems to match the type used by Green Zone Defense for pickups. I'm interested in finding out more about these bags."

The Colonel listened, his expression unreadable. After a moment of contemplation, he responded, "If I remember right, those duffel bags we use are generic, Detective. We use them for transport because of their durability and size, but they are not unique to our company. They are not used for storage of any products, especially not for long-term."

Detective Wright nodded, taking mental notes. "Do you have records of how many bags were purchased and if any are unaccounted for?"

The Colonel leaned back in his chair, his gaze shifting to a corner of the room as if recalling the details. "It's been a year since we made that purchase. I can't say offhand how many are still in our inventory, but I assure you, I will have my team check it out. We keep meticulous records, so it shouldn't be hard to find."

"Thank you. That would be very helpful. If any of the bags are missing, or if you have any information about who might have access to them, that could be crucial to our investigation," Kim said.

The Colonel nodded. "Of course, Detective Wright. I understand the seriousness of this matter. Green Zone Defense operates within the confines of the law, and we have no interest in being inadvertently connected to illegal activities. I'll have the information sent to your office as soon as possible."

"That would be really helpful," Harold spoke up. "So, help me understand, as things have all changed so quickly. What is your business, Colonel?"

"I'm glad you asked, Harold. We are a licensed secure transport and storage service provider serving the legal cannabis industry. We pick up their cash and excess inventory and store it for them in a secure manner."

"There is a special license for this?" Harold asked.

"There are some state occupational licenses, along with Denver security guard licenses. Rhonda can pull copies of them for you as well."

"No, no," Harold said, holding up his hands, "we're not here for that. I'm just curious. Learning new stuff every day."

At that moment, a knock came from the doorway, and Kim could just see a uniformed guard standing outside.

"Mason," The Colonel said, "just in time. Come in here."

A tall man walked into the office. He was slim and walked in a fluid, cat-like manner. His brown hair was long enough to pull into a ponytail, and he had a scruffy brown beard. He wore sunglasses perched on top of his head. Kim noticed he had dirt caked on the soles of his boots and specks of sawdust on his pants.

The Colonel turned to Detective Wright, offering an introduction. "Detectives, meet Mason, one of our top guys. Mason, this is Detective Kim Wright and Detective Harold Clarke."

Mason extended a hand to Kim, who shook it firmly. "Pleasure to meet you, Detective," he said with a respectful nod. Then the same with Harold.

The Colonel turned the conversation toward the matter at hand. "Mason, the detectives are here investigating a matter that might involve one of our transport duffel bags. I've promised full cooperation. Could you show them the room where we store the excess cannabis for our customers? They may find it useful for their investigation."

"Of course, sir," Mason replied. He gestured to Kim and Harold. "If you'd follow me, detectives."

Kim and Harold bid goodbye to The Colonel and followed Mason out of the office. He led them through the corridors of Green Zone Defense. Kim studied Mason. She couldn't help but notice his disheveled appearance, untidy hair, and the rumple in his clothes.

"Mason, were you also a cop?" she asked as they walked.

"No, not me. Army," Mason said as they approached Rhonda's area. "Just a grunt."

Rhonda worked in an open space with various desks and counters covered with boxes, files, computers, and radio equipment.

"Just a grunt," Rhonda scoffed as she overheard. "Mason is being modest. He has more medals than anyone else in the building. Mason is our own Rambo."

Kim raised her eyebrows. "Spec Ops?" she asked.

"Hmmm," Mason said, inclining his head slightly. "And you? You were in the service?"

"Air Force," Kim said. "Harold was Army."

"Cool," Mason replied. "Rhonda, I need to show the Detectives the secure room."

"Go ahead," she pointed them towards a door next to her workspace. It was a steel door in a heavy steel frame, with a keypad next to it. Cameras covered the door and the hallway from all angles. Mason walked over and typed a code into the pad, and the door opened with a click.

Mason opened the door and said, "Come on in. Let me show you what we've got."

The door closed behind them with a click.

9

Deal

The thick cover of night enveloped Cornwall Island in a velvety darkness. A faint glow of distant city lights painted the horizon, but the remote end of the road remained covered in shadow. The rustling of tall trees in the wind mixed with the muffled sounds of water flowing in the nearby St. Lawrence River.

The plumbing company van, a nondescript white vehicle with faded logos on its sides, sat at the dark road's end. Inside, seven figures huddled. The scant light from a lone red flashlight revealed their faces smeared with black paint.

Bruno, Raison, Rage, Moose, Matheo, Okwaho, and Robeur, the last remaining members of the Dead Wolves Motorcycle Club, tried to find comfort on the van's hard metal floor, their dark clothes blending in with the shadows. Calm reigned, with only the occasional sniffle or muffled cough.

"Why do we have to sneak across the border like this?" Matheo broke the silence, the glint in his eyes betraying his restlessness. "I mean, why can't we just ride across?"

Raison chuckled. "Everybody in this van has a criminal record. The Americans would never let us in. They even have facial recognition cameras at the border now."

Okwaho nodded in agreement. "My kin on the Saint Regis Mohawk reservation have us covered," he assured. "We'll cross the border unnoticed and, by sunrise, be miles away. We're just waiting for my cousin to come get us. He said tonight is a good night because there's barely any moon, and it's supposed to be cloudy."

The group settled into a heavy silence again.

"Raison, I have a question," Robeur whispered. "If Tommy Boy is now the president of Big Machine's Nomads chapter, who is the head of all of Big Machine?"

"The short answer is Pop, but technically Big Machine doesn't work like that," Raison said. "They don't have a club or national president. They have chapters in every city, every state, almost every country. But most of those chapters used to be independent clubs. Pop formed them together under the Big Machine banner back in the '70s and '80s. Each club kept their members, but they patched-over—they traded their colors for Big Machine's and swore to Big Machine's constitution. Pop uses the Nomads chapter to travel around checking on everyone, making sure they stay in line."

"And only buying their dope from him," Rage piped up. "That's the thing with Big Machine. Once your club patches over with them, you have to get all your supply from them."

"Like a franchise," Bruno added. "Like McDonald's. If you buy a McDonald's franchise, you have to buy all your burgers, fries, napkins— everything—from McDonald's. With Big Machine, once your club patches over, you have to get all your dope from them and only them."

"They also send the Nomads to smoke you when you fuck up," Rage added. "That's why all those assholes have Mechanic patches. They're all killers. You can't join the Nomads without a few kills under your belt."

"So, by us doing these jobs, we're earning a patch over, right?" Robeur asked. "Even me? Even though I am just a prospect?"

"We're doing the job because it's a major score. We haven't had a vote about patching over yet. Think of this as our prospect period. If they like us and we like them..." Raison shrugged. "If we did patch over, you'd keep your status. Things wouldn't change much. We'd just have a solid supplier and major backup if we needed it."

"And our heads still attached," Bruno said. Rage snickered.

"That's what I don't get," Robeur said. "Are we joining Big Machine because we want to, or because we have to?"

"I just told you nothing has been decided," Raison said. "Now kick back before somebody hears us."

The gang returned to sitting in darkened silence.

Minutes later, the metallic creak of the van's back door pierced the silent night, revealing a man dressed entirely in black. He wore PV-14 night vision goggles, bathing his face in an eerie, greenish glow. Like the others, his face was smeared with black greasepaint. He surveyed the group inside the van.

"Let's go," he whispered.

The bikers exited the van individually, their boots thudding onto the ground. The night air was cool, carrying the earthy scents of the surrounding forest and the faint fishy smell of the river. Surrounded by shadows, they followed Okwaho's goggle-wearing cousin.

With him leading the way, the group weaved through the tall grass and underbrush. They stayed close, their figures mere silhouettes in the darkness. After a short walk along a trail through the brush, they reached the river's edge. The rippling water reflected the starry sky above, shimmering faintly in the dim light.

Four canoes sat by the riverbank, their forms sleek and low in the water. Black silhouettes of more men surrounded them. As Raison and his crew approached, Okwaho leaned in to whisper, "They use the canoes to smuggle cigarettes into New York," Okwaho whispered to Rage. "Sometimes, they bring back loads of coke. Sometimes people."

The canoes sat low in the water, their profiles barely breaking the surface. They were painted a dark blue-green that blended seamlessly with the waters of the Saint Lawrence. At a glance, they were practically indistinguishable from the shifting currents and ripples.

"Everybody get in and stay low," Okwaho's cousin said.

With that, the group loaded two each into the canoes, each man lying flat inside, their profiles disappearing into the boat's low silhouette. Each canoe was piloted by a smuggler wearing night-vision goggles. After the men loaded into the boats, the pilots covered them in dark blankets and shoved them off. Outfitted with electric trolling motors, the canoes moved quietly through the water.

Raison shared a canoe with Bruno. He lay still under the blanket, feeling the cold fiberglass against his back and the faint vibrations from the electric motor beneath. The night was silent as they glided across the water, broken only by the river lapping against the canoe's sides. From somewhere in the distance, he could hear the calls of nocturnal birds. The river smelled fresh with an earthy undertone of algae. Raison could feel Bruno's presence in the canoe—the slight movements as he adjusted his position, his nervous breathing. Then the canoes bumped against mud, and the Dead Wolves climbed out and kneeled on American soil.

A rustle of movement to his right alerted Raison. More silhouetted figures appeared from the wooded darkness, each wearing black clothing. The reflections from their PV-14 goggles gave them a predatory appearance. Each of the Mohawk mules carried two sizeable black duffel bags. They sprinted to the boats and, with practiced efficiency, tossed the bags inside. The electric motors hummed to life again, and the smugglers in their low-profile canoes vanished into the river, back across the Canadian border with their illicit cargo.

The ambient sounds of crickets chirping and water flowing filled the air as the Dead Wolves crew turned inland. They made their way along a narrow, trampled smuggler's path through the woods, leaves crunching softly underfoot. Within minutes, the looming silhouette of a Chevrolet Suburban materialized from the shadows, its engine purring, the glow from its dashboard lights faintly illuminating the interior. The driver was standing outside the vehicle, his face obscured by the surrounding darkness. Raison could barely discern his features.

"Tank?" Raison whispered from the dark woods.

"Yep," the man replied as they approached, gesturing to the SUV.

The gang loaded themselves into the vehicle as quietly as they could. The interior was awash with a muted blue light, revealing gray leather seats. The driver entered the Suburban, closed his door gently, and put the vehicle into gear. They took Highway 81 south, the world outside a blur of night.

"You got everything we need?" Raison asked the driver, Tank.

"Yep," he responded. "It's all packed up at my house in Syracuse, ready to go. I can fit everything in here. I'll be right behind you guys the whole way. When we get to the destination, I'll drop it off and head back to New York."

"You're not sticking around?" Raison asked.

"No, I guess not. Tommy told me to haul your gear and then get back here to move another load for him. You know Tommy moves more loads than Freightliner."

They rode for a while longer, then Raison asked, "How long have you been a prospect for Big Machine?"

"About a year," Tank responded. He was young, with dark shaggy hair and a black spear-like piercing through his septum. His chin was tattooed with tribal designs, and his arms were covered in biker ink. "I think I'm getting close to getting patched, though. Especially after this job."

"Yeah? How the hell did you get Tommy Boy to sponsor you? I've never heard of him having a prospect."

"Yeah, no shit," Tank chuckled, one hand on the wheel and another casually holding a cigarette. "My dad was with Big Machine. He was good friends with Tommy Boy back in the day. They rode together and did a lot of crazy shit in the '90s. Dad's dead now, but Tommy is like an uncle to me."

Raison lit a cigarette and cracked his window. Tank turned on the radio, and they listened to classic rock for the rest of the drive.

Tank lived in a small brick house on the edge of Syracuse, New York.

"There are a couple of beds in the back, the couch folds out, and there are air mattresses and comforters in here," Tank said, flipping on a light switch, illuminating an otherwise empty living room. The carpeted floor was stained, and the couch was worn and smelled of medicine. The men selected their sleeping arrangements, and soon, the house fell dark and quiet except for Moose's rhythmic snoring.

The following day, inside the honking urban sprawl of Syracuse, under a bright blue sky, stood a one-story brick motorcycle dealership named Frank's Motor Sports. Its exterior walls were stained with graffiti and age.

The windows were blurred by time and dirt. Stepping through the door, the scent of exhaust and fresh leather mixed in the air. Rows of polished motorcycles gleamed under the overhead fluorescent lights, their chrome finishes reflecting distorted images of the Dead Wolves as they crossed the showroom floor. Bruno and Raison walked at the front of the pack.

Behind the cluttered counter, the owner, a stoutly built man wearing a gray and black flannel shirt and a black ball cap, came quickly from behind his desk. "Bruno! What's up, my man?"

"Frankie, what's up, brother?" Bruno said, removing his Ray-Bans and clasping Frank's hand.

"It's all good," Frank said. "Did you know, my youngest graduated last month, and he's off to college. He got into Berkley. Can you believe it? Who would've ever thought, after the shit you and I used to get into, that I would have a kid going to a fucking ivy league school. You know what I mean?"

"No, shit! Frank, that's amazing," Bruno gushed, clasping his old friend around the shoulders. "I told you back then you were smart to leave Brooklyn and come out here. You've done real good for yourself and your family. I'm proud of you."

Bruno turned to Raison.

"Frank, this is Raison, who I told you about," Bruno said.

"Nice to meet you, sir," Frank said. "Why don't you's guys come back and let me blow your fucking minds? Did Bruno warn you? I cause my customer's heads to explode."

"Oh, yeah?" Raison said in accented English. "Let's see what you've got."

Frank led Raison and his gang through swinging double doors into the service garage. On one side, there was a rolling bay door that was locked with a padlock. Frank used a key to unlock it and then rolled up the door.

"Feast your eyes, gentlemen," Frank said proudly.

Behind the door was a brick warehouse space about twenty feet wide and thirty feet deep. Inside, an array of sparkling motorcycles was arranged side-by-side, in neat rows, each one appearing as if brand new. A fleet of bikes sporting custom paint jobs in every shade of red, blue, green, black, and white stretched before them.

97

"Holy shit!" Okwaho gasped.

"Motherfucker! It's heaven," Matheo agreed.

The men spread out through the sea of glittering chrome and smooth leather, excitedly touching handlebars, examining engines, and pointing out fine details in paint and upholstery.

Frank leaned into Raison and said quietly, "Look, I believe in being transparent with everybody. If you want to buy from me, you should know what you're getting. So, I won't lie to you. The scooters are all hot. I get them from a guy who jacks bikes from all over the U.S. He only brings me the cream of the crop. I strip them down and sell the parts or use them for my other customers. We sandblast, prep, and repaint the frames right here. My paint and body guy is top-notch. We strip the bikes to the frame and completely change their profile. If it had a fancy embroidered seat, we swap it for a simple one. We change the wheels, forks, tanks, handlebars, everything. Once we're done rebuilding a bike, the owner would never recognize it."

Raison's eyes settled on a sleek black chopper. Its raw steel frame contrasted with a matte black fuel tank and silver accents. He ran his fingers down the seat, then the gas tank, then the handle bars.

"What about tags?" Raison asked.

"Check this out," Frank said, waving Raison to look at the back of the bike where there was a New York state motorcycle license plate. "Check out this plate. The steel is the same thickness as the official plates. The colors are flawless. The paint even has the correct amount of reflectivity. My paint and body guy makes them. He's a genuine artist, this guy. When I'm at biker rallies, I take photos and videos of all the bikes and their license plates. Then, when we need to clone a plate, I go through and find a tag for a bike of the same make, model, and year, and my guy makes an exact copy of it. Nobody realizes there are two bikes riding around with the same tags. Then you carry a paper bill of sale from the original owner and if you get jammed, you claim you're the victim of a scam. But do you know what the best part is? Even with the fresh paint and mostly new parts, I can still let them go for half the price you would pay even for used. I am politically neutral. I sell to several outlaw clubs, and my reputation is everything to me. One of the bikes gives you trouble within the first year. You have my word, I will make it right. So, what do you say?"

"My brother needs a right-hand clutch," Raison pointed out.

"Tommy Boy called me directly and told me to give you guys VIP treatment, and I am here to deliver. I have a Dual-Lever right-hand clutch system in stock. Tell your brother to pick the bike he wants, and we'll install it right now," Frank said.

Raison listened as he walked around the motorcycle, inspecting every detail. The other wolves admired the bikes. Raison chose a glossy black Softail. Beside that was a blood-red custom build, which Rage gravitated to. Bruno was drawn to a gleaming green and chrome bagger. The reflection of the overhead lights danced on its polished surface. Moose chose a hulking V-twin chopper that looked like it was made from salvaged tank parts. Its dark green frame bulged with raw power. Matheo sat on a bike with chaotic graphics resembling flames and tribal tattoos. It seemed restless even when stationary. Okwaho chose an imposing V-Rod in matte-gray, like the hide of a timber wolf. Last, Robeur, chose a deep blue chopper with chrome pipes.

Reaching in his jacket pocket, Raison produced a thick manila envelope and asked, "Where do we settle up?"

Frank smiled and beckoned to a workbench. "We can count it right over here."

Afterward, the Dead Wolves ate at a nearby diner while the shop mechanics prepared their new bikes. Once complete, they helped roll the newly purchased motorcycles out of the garage and into the parking lot. The scent of new leather, grease, and gasoline was heavy in the air, mixed with the woosh and hum of nearby traffic.

Bruno smirked, rubbing a clean rag over his bike. "Frank never lets me down."

"Yeah, man," Matheo said, "that was a sick deal. I'm ready to ride."

Moose piped up, "So where are we headed?"

Raison put on his sunglasses and said, "Bring it in, wolves."

The men circled close around him in the middle of the parking lot.

"We're going to Denver, Colorado. We've got a robbery to pull," he said.

"Who are we jacking? Another MC?" Matheo asked, leaning in.

"No. Here's the deal," Raison replied, lighting a cigarette. "They just legalized pot in Colorado, but the shit is still illegal federally. That means, the people growing and selling weed there can't take credit cards or have bank accounts because those are federally regulated. So, these new dispensaries are rolling in cash with no banks to store it in because the feds would just seize it."

"So, are we robbing a dispensary?" Robeur asked.

"Nope," Raison replied, blowing out smoke. "There's a private security company called Green Zone Defense. They go around to the dispensaries and grow houses, pick up the cash, and store it in some kind of facility. That's who we're jacking."

"What's the facility like?" Okwaho asked.

"That's something we have to figure out, because right now, we don't know for sure."

"So, we're robbing a building nobody knows about? In the U.S., where they bury robbers in Super Max prisons for hundreds of lifetimes?" Rage spat.

The others shifted nervously. Raison clenched his jaw.

"What do we always say? 'Do everything ourselves so we know it's done right,' yeah? Would we do a job using somebody else's plan, or would we do it ourselves? Think! This is what we do. It's another job, and when we're done, we can decide whether to patch over with Big Machine or not. If we do, when Big Machine rolls into Quebec, we would be the home chapter."

"And you would be chapter president," Rage said under his breath.

"And you would be the vice president, just like now. Everyone keeps their rank," Raison growled back.

"The Big Machine is coming, and we can't stop it," Bruno agreed. "But where were we just a few months ago? Max and Wild Bill got killed. We lost our leadership, our direction, and our pride. Now look. We avenged Max and Bill. We took back our pride. And we came up with some real money and some real connections. Look at these fucking bikes. If we patch over, we'll be unstoppable. We could go wherever, and nobody would fuck with us."

Some men nodded in agreement. Rage squinted and stared into the distance.

"That's right," Raison agreed. "Make no mistake, Big Machine is rolling into Quebec. Nothing will stop them. Shit, we wiped out their last real competition, other than us. One thing I know is that when Big Machine offers you a patch, it's either take the patch or take a bullet."

"Shit, I say let's get rich," Robeur added eagerly.

"Let's go get rich," Raison agreed.

The other men cheered, except for Rage. The men put on their new helmets, mounted their bikes, and Raison waved to Tank, who was waiting nearby in his Suburban.

Bruno revved his engine, pulling beside Raison. "Colorado's going to be a hell of a ride."

Raison nodded, his eyes on the road ahead. "You only live once, brother."

Behind them, Matheo and Okwaho shouted in excitement.

"Wolves!" Raison shouted above everyone. "What do we say?"

"Roulez comme si vous étiez déjà mort!" the men shouted in unison. "Ride like you're already dead!"

The Dead Wolves MC roared out of the parking lot, their new bikes rumbling like thunder, kicking up dust in the summer heat. Tank followed a distance behind, his Suburban loaded with gear. The fresh smell of asphalt mixed with gasoline fumes bid them farewell as the pack rolled out and headed west.

10

Work

Thrash metal roared from an old cassette deck, the demonic shrieks and growls and staccato pounding of the double kick drum vibrated the dusty workbench. The bright Colorado sun beat down, scorching and baking the dusty construction site. Mason, shirtless and covered in dirt and sawdust, held a board to be nailed. He wore black wrap-around sunglasses. The muscles in his tanned shoulders rippled as he hammered a nail. Dirt clung to his sweat-streaked face, sticking to the whiskers of his beard as he banged a wooden window header into place. The rhythmic thud of his pounding echoed through the structure. With one final bump, the header was in. He hung the hammer on his tool belt and looked around the soon-to-be completed Green Zone Defense Training Center. Steel frames outlined what would become classrooms and offices, while stud-framed walls gave hints of interior hallways and rooms being built into a sprawling kill house.

Mason walked over to the bench, unclasped his tool belt, and let it fall with a crash to the cement floor. He plucked a cold Budweiser from an orange Home Depot bucket filled with ice, cracked it open, and took a long pull. He reached into the bucket, scooped ice water with his hands, and used it to wash the sawdust from his face. Reaching over, water dripping from his beard, he clicked off the cassette player and the construction site went quiet except for the passing big rigs on the nearby highway. He took another cold beer from the bucket for the short walk to the travel trailer where he lived.

The interior of Mason's RV was cramped. Plastic storage bins and camouflage rucksacks were neatly stacked in the living area. The small kitchen table was littered with papers and beer bottles, and the linoleum floor was covered in dirt tracked in from the construction site.

Water rained down on him from a shower head in the cramped bathroom, sluicing away the grime. Each droplet raced down his tanned skin, creating a muddy rivulet. After his shower, still naked, he stepped into the tiny kitchenette. The sizzle of eggs and sausage filled the small living space as he cooked an omelet in a scorched skillet, the rich smell temporarily overpowering the scent of dirty towels. He dumped the completed omelet onto a paper plate from a stack beside the sink where he stood and ate with his bare hands. When he was done, he threw the paper plate into a plastic trash can.

In his crowded bedroom, Mason pulled on boxers, then thick socks, before pulling up dark green uniform trousers and stepping into the same worn and dirty combat boots he'd been wearing. Next, he donned a white cotton undershirt, followed by a black Kevlar vest. He lifted a starched green uniform shirt from a hook on the bedroom door and shrugged into it. He tucked it in, buttoned it, and put on a belt. Lastly, he strapped a digital watch to his wrist and wrapped a nylon duty belt around his waist. From atop the dresser, he picked up his SIG Sauer P226 MK25 pistol and slid it into the polymer holster on his right hip.

In the dresser mirror, he noted his shoulder-length brown hair was still dripping from the shower, so he combed it back with his fingers. Then he opened the dresser's top drawer, reached in, and pulled out a half-empty bottle of Tito's vodka. He unscrewed the cap and took a swig, feeling its familiar burn coursing through his veins. From the same drawer, he retrieved a bottle of green spearmint mouthwash. He took a mouthful and swished it around as he walked through the trailer, switching off lights as he went. He opened the creaky front door and spit the mouthwash next to the steps.

He slid into his lifted Bronco, and the engine roared to life. He drove to work that morning with the window down to dry his hair and blow away the smell of booze.

The Green Zone Defense building was mostly inconspicuous. It did not have a sign announcing its purpose, and its stark white walls, broken by green trim around the doors and windows, blended in with the other warehouses and commercial buildings in the area. The three tall garage doors lining the south end made the building appear similar to a fire station.

Mason pulled into the dirt-and-rock parking lot in the back of the building and killed the Bronco's engine. Stepping into the bright sunshine, he retrieved a gear bag from the passenger seat and walked through the dust to the back entrance. He swiped a key card at a terminal next to the back door, and it buzzed to allow him entry. Inside, he strode down a white rubber tiled hallway until he came to an open office door. A deep voice boomed from inside.

"I understand, and none of us are happy about cost overages," The Colonel was saying into the phone. "We had to make choices, and the secure storage facility was paramount. We have enough to complete the shoot house, but my contractor is telling me it's going to cost 30% more to finish the classrooms, and the current credit line will not stretch that far."

He listened, then responded, "We are already doing some of the building ourselves to save money," he said, staring disappointingly at Mason's dirty boots.

The Colonel listened to the other person on the line momentarily, then said, "Email me a list of what you need from me, and we'll get started on it. Thanks, Bill. Take care."

He hung up the phone and looked Mason up and down.

"Glad you took time to clean your boots this morning, Mason. I am sure the cleaner won't mind your dirty footprints in her hallway."

"Sorry, Colonel. My butler didn't have time to brush them off," Mason replied.

The Colonel threw up his hands. "Listen, the investors are looking for more money for us. Until then, I need you to keep doing what you're doing at the training center. The electrician will be out there next week to install the wiring for the lights in the kill house, but I need you to hang the cans. Oorah?"

"Hooah, Colonel. Not a problem," Mason responded.

"Do you realize," The Colonel said, standing and walking around to the front of his desk, "that we are about to open the most high-tech shooting range—and the longest indoor shooting range—in the U.S.? They just opened a new place in Manassas, Virginia, with 42 shooting bays and the longest indoor bay on record at 100 yards. Ours will have 50 shooting bays at 25 yards and four at 125. And not just indoor but underground and climate controlled. With our automated target system, we will be a global destination for top shooters. With you as our lead trainer, a real-life special operator with over 16 years' experience, and how many deployments?"

"Nine," Mason answered. "Three for OEF, four for OIF, and two I can't talk about."

"Nine," The Colonel said, standing face to face with Mason. He let out a sigh and relaxed his shoulders.

He looked Mason in the eyes. "Mason, there are huge contracts available at every level of policing for the kind of tactical training we can provide. After the Marines, when I was in charge of Denver PD, we spent millions on that kind of training, and it wasn't half as good as what we're going to offer. And a lot of that is because of you."

The Colonel stepped close, his eyes darting around Mason's face, searching.

"I will do my best, sir," Mason said, his hands beginning to fidget.

"Good," The Colonel said, clasping Mason's shoulder. "You can start by cleaning your boots before you climb into one of my vehicles. Now, get squared away. We roll out in five."

Mason left The Colonel's office and strolled to the locker room where he was greeted by the familiar clatter of guards dressing mixed with the aroma of Irish Spring soap. Matt Anderson, the tall blonde-haired SWAT officer who now worked at GZD, looked amused at Mason's shaggy appearance, and remarked, "Looks like our war hero rolled out of a bush, not a bed. Did I miss the party last night?"

There was a chuckle from the other guards, except for one. Mason's old friend, Benito, continued buttoning his uniform shirt.

"What's good, Mason?" he asked as Mason walked to his locker, setting his black nylon duffel bag on the bench.

"It's all good, Benito," Mason said as he shrugged into a black armor plate carrier. The bullet-proof ceramic plates hanging heavily on his shoulders.

"Those guys," Benito nodded toward the ex-cops, "especially Matt, love acting like they're the shit. But you know, not that long ago, they were kicking in doors, arresting dudes for having a little bit of weed. And now?" He raised his eyebrows. "Now, they're here, guarding the weed."

"Yeah, but like you told me once, it's legal now," Mason responded.

"Yeah, I know," Benito continued. "But imagine being locked up in some Colorado prison for a weed charge from a few years ago, and now you hear weed has been legalized, but you still can't get out because it's an old charge. Man, that's messed up."

"Yeah, no shit," Mason replied.

"OK, are you ready, Rambo? Let's go get this bread," Benito said to Mason, slamming his locker. They both exited the locker room and walked down the white hallway to the garage.

In the garage, they took turns standing at the plexiglass window of the armory. They scanned their employee IDs and checked out their weapons. When it was Mason's turn, he retrieved his short-barreled FN 15 rifle. He inserted fresh magazines into the pouches on the front of his plate carrier, then slammed one into the FN's magazine well.

"Let me get the EBR, too, would you, Mike?" Mason asked the armorer.

"Sure thing," the middle-aged armorer, Big Mike, said. The overweight, silver-haired man waddled back to a rack of rifles and, from a table, retrieved a long, black plastic gun case. He slid it across the counter to Mason, who opened it. Inside was an MK14 Mod 0 EBR, the Designated Marksman Rifle favored by Navy SEALS and Delta Force. It had a black alloy frame, stock with an adjustable cheek rest, and a Leupold 3.5–10X scope. He closed the case, thanked Big Mike, slung the FN 15 over his shoulder, and strolled to a staging area inside the garage.

Three dark blue 2007 Chevrolet 2500 HD Suburbans were lined up side-by-side behind the garage doors. Instead of tailgates, the older models featured barn-style double back doors, allowing quick access to the rear cargo spaces.

At the lead Suburban, farthest to the right, Mason noticed another guard standing on the sill of the open rear door. He was mounting a black object to the roof using a drill. Mason strolled over and stopped next to him, watching him work.

"Caleb, what the hell is that?" Mason asked.

"This is what I've been working on," Caleb, The Colonel's son, said. He was in his early twenties, had an average build and a dark brown buzz cut. His face was smooth, and he wore black sunglasses on top of his head. His uniform was crisp and starched, his boots gleamed, as did his brown eyes.

"This," he said, pointing to a matte black panel attached to the roof of the Suburban, "is the port I designed. And this," he said, placing a small black quadcopter drone onto the panel, "is the drone that works with it."

Caleb stepped down from the doorsill and lifted his left arm. A touchscreen smartphone was attached to his wrist. He tapped the screen twice, and with a sudden whir, the drone lifted away from the port and hovered above the Suburban. With another tap, the drone descended, landed on the roof port, and shut off its rotors. A beep chimed from Caleb's wrist-mounted device.

"The drone attaches to the port with magnets. While it's attached, it recharges its battery and uploads data at the same time. I control the whole thing from inside the Suburban with this phone, safe behind NIJ III rated vehicle armor. I don't even have to open the door to launch it. I can livestream as well as record. I can even put the system in autonomous mode, and it will launch itself, circle overhead, and record everything. I'm testing it on Longhorn 1, but the plan is to sell them to police departments one day. It's like a dash cam or badge cam, but with a bird's-eye view."

"Sounds solid to me," Mason said, clapping Caleb on the shoulder.

Just then, The Colonel strolled into the garage wearing a black plate carrier and black gloves over his green uniform. He wore his wrap-around sunglasses on top of his salt-and-pepper flat top and carried a Benelli M4 shotgun with a dozen red shells strung along its bandolier sling.

"All right, gentlemen," The Colonel began as he strode into the staging area. "Bring it in. I've got a few words," his gravelly voice commanded the room. "It's Monday, our busiest day of the week. After the weekend is when our clients are holding the most cash. That is why we roll with all three Suburbans today. Caleb has been working hard on a new drone system, which I know he is excited to test in the field, and that could be a real asset for us. Eyes in the sky can never be a bad thing, right?"

The men clapped and murmured their support.

The Colonel continued, "Listen up. We switch routes, we change schedules, and we try to make the bad guy look left while we slip right, but we don't truly know what the bad guy knows until he acts on it. Maybe we move smoothly, and nobody knows what we're up to. Or maybe they have an ambush waiting for us. We just don't know. Therefore, we conduct ourselves at every moment as if danger is imminent. We move as a team, we communicate as a team, and if needed, we shoot as a team. Oorah?"

The garage erupted with a mix of Oorahs! and Hooahs!

"Remember, we're not just moving money and merchandise," he continued. "We're delivering trust. The way we carry ourselves reflects the quality of service we provide. Let's keep it professional and look sharp. Frazier and Caleb, with me in Longhorn 1. Carver and Mason, Longhorn 2. Anderson and Mink, Longhorn 3. Load up. We go to work in two minutes."

Doors slammed as green-uniformed security officers loaded into their assigned Suburbans.

Mason loaded into the passenger seat of Longhorn 2, a stock Suburban with tinted windows. A tall, powerfully built Black man with dark skin, a low beard, and a fade haircut climbed into the driver's seat.

"Ali, what's up? You ready to do it again?" Mason asked.

"What's up, Mason?" Ali Carver replied, his voice deep and rumbling. "You know I stay ready."

"You look like you stay at the gym. What, your wife doesn't want you at home?" Mason replied.

Ali laughed. "You should get your ass down to the gym with me. My 12-year-old has more meat on his arms than you."

"That's because his father is a drill instructor with a PT addiction. I bet you make your kids run a mile before school," Mason said.

"What? That's child abuse. I don't abuse my children," Ali said as he stuck the key into the ignition. "I let them run *after* school."

Mason laughed, and the garage rumbled to life as the big SUVs ignited their engines. The overhead doors rolled open, and the morning light spilled in. In quick succession, the Suburbans pulled out of the garage, crossed the parking lot, and entered the street. After several turns, they merged onto Highway 70 and headed east into downtown Denver.

The stops were quick. As soon as the convoy pulled up to a dispensary, the passengers of Longhorns 2 and 3 jumped out to provide overwatch. Then the convoy commander, The Colonel that day, exited Longhorn 1 and supervised the pickup or drop off. As soon as the load was stored or delivered and everyone loaded back up, the convoy pulled off and headed to the next stop.

Pull up. Stop. Load up. Pull off.

Denver's streets were a mosaic of ages, the old brick city blocks rubbing against the sharp lines and steel of polished skyscrapers. Gleaming SUVs and sedans glided past buildings, honking horns, engines rumbling loudly as lights changed from red to green. Each dispensary stop was a carefully orchestrated dance. The exchanges were brief and uneventful: a short greeting, a handshake, and duffel bags transferred from the shops to the vehicles.

Pull up. Stop. Load up. Pull off.

Inside those bags, the distinct, spicy aroma of legal cannabis was almost overpowering. Neatly sealed packages of various strains, from Purple Haze to Denver Diesel, rested next to stacks of cash. Some bags were filled to overflowing with bundles of bills.

Pull up. Stop. Load up. Pull off.

They moved from one part of the city to another—from the upscale locales of Cherry Creek, where chic dispensaries resembled Apple stores, to the more laid-back establishments in neighborhoods like Five Points, where the scent of weed mingled freely with the notes of jazz music in the air.

Pull up. Stop. Load up. Pull off.

The GZD convoy rolled into the parking lot of a small dispensary in the River North Art District. The building was a box of gray brick. Its entire front was covered in a mural depicting a herd of green elephants. A neon "Open" sign and a marijuana leaf sticker on the window invited customers in.

Once the convoy stopped, Mason and Mink exited their Suburbans and looked around. Caleb's drone was already somewhere high overhead, circling the property, searching for threats. Mason and Mink both carried their rifles on slings. The parking lot only had two parked cars in it, and there did not appear to be any threats. Mason opened the door of The Green Elephant dispensary and, with the clang of a bell, strolled in.

The inside of the weed shop was a square space ringed with glass display cabinets filled with legal cannabis products. There was a cash register and a flat-screen TV with the day's menu and prices. Bongs and posters of Bob Marley covered the walls. The single room smelled of fresh pot and burning incense. Mason focused on the sole budtender, a young woman with bright green hair. Her skin was inked with multiple tattoos. She returned Mason's gaze with a frown. He ignored it, leaned out the door, and gave a wave toward Longhorn 1.

The Colonel opened the passenger door and stepped out. He carried only a clipboard and his Colt 1911 in a holster on his black leather Sam Brown belt. He strolled through the front door and into The Green Elephant.

Mason remained at the front door as security. The FN 15 hung vertically, muzzle down, along his chest, his hand resting on the pistol grip. He watched the parking lot while The Colonel announced their business.

"Hello, ma'am. Green Zone Defense. I believe you have a load for us," he said to the green-haired budtender as he held out the clipboard. He noticed her nose wrinkling with distaste.

"Do you really need to bring that in here?" she asked, pointing one long, white finger toward Mason.

The Colonel looked back at Mason, confused. "I'm sorry. Which 'that' do you mean?"

"That enormous gun. There's like all of three people in here, but it looks like Baghdad with all these guns," she frowned.

The Colonel turned to face her, his gaze unwavering. "Those guns ensure that your business and mine can run safely. The world outside isn't as friendly as the one you've created here," he replied calmly, waving the clipboard toward a shelf of ceramic Buddha statues.

She crossed her arms defensively. "This is a place of peace and healing. Those guns bring negativity."

He took a deep breath, weighing his words. "Listen," he began, "I respect what you've built here. But our job is to ensure everyone's safety. The world can be unpredictable, dangerous even. These firearms aren't for aggression, but protection."

She paused for a moment. "I just don't understand why you need them inside here," she murmured.

The Colonel remained calm. "We must expect and prevent threats. That's what we're here for. We're not here to disrupt your peace, but to safeguard it. Next time, we'll leave the big guns in the truck. Now, about that load?"

The budtender waved toward a black duffle bag on the floor. Mason slung his rifle over his shoulder, picked up the duffle bag, and walked out the door. He opened the back door of Longhorn 2 and tossed the bag on top of the pile from earlier stops. The Colonel exited the dispensary just as Mason walked from the rear of the vehicle to the passenger door. The two men exchanged weary glances before loading up and continuing to the next stop.

That night, Mason parked his Bronco next to his travel trailer and climbed out into the dusty driveway. He walked around and opened the rear door. From inside, he removed his personal gear bag and another, larger black duffle. After slamming the door, he walked to the trailer, where he changed into jeans and a T-shirt. He tucked his pistol into his waistband and walked down to the construction site, carrying the large black bag.

An hour later, amidst the hum of nocturnal insects and the pops and pings of sun-heated steel cooling on the construction site, Mason was at his workbench, meticulously measuring and marking trim boards. The Colonel's leather-soled cowboy boots crunched the earth as he approached. Mason didn't look up, but he sensed the familiar presence. After a moment, he set down his tools and dusted off his hands. "Evening, Colonel," he greeted.

The Colonel surveyed the job site. "You've got a knack for this, you know? I never took you for an artisan," he trailed off, tapping a newly assembled wooden frame. "It's in you though. Precision. In shooting and building. Impressive."

Mason smiled. "The Army taught me a lot, but I learned carpentry from my old man. Helps me focus, gets me away from my head, I suppose."

The Colonel's gaze rested on the orange Home Depot bucket. The ice had melted, and it was filled with dirty, tepid water. A few beer cans rested on the bottom. There was a heavy pause. "Talent is a gift from your ancestors, Mason. Don't waste it."

Mason dragged the tape measure down another board and marked it.

"You went through a lot overseas. You served your nation above what most others could even imagine, and your reward was what? Nightmares? Anger? Busted knees? But warriors aren't the only people to face hardship. Every creature on God's green earth must struggle to survive. Life has to be earned every day through work and sacrifice."

The Colonel looked around, taking in all the framing, electrical boxes, light fixtures, and other work Mason had done.

"Ultimately, the measure of a man's life is what he has built, not what he has torn down. We are building something here, Mason. Something to be proud of. Stay focused." He clapped Mason on the back, then turned and walked out.

Mason waited until he heard The Colonel's pickup truck drive away before he set his tape measure down, walked to his Bronco, and headed to town.

The Black Horn Saloon sat nestled in an old corner of Denver's downtown, a forgotten dive bar. Its neon sign flickered intermittently, the buzzing sound blending with the muted chatter. Inside, dim yellow bulbs smeared with years of nicotine and grime cast a somber glow over the wooden surfaces. Peeling faux leather booths lined the walls, while cracked stools sat in a haphazard line before the bar. The air was thick, saturated with the scent of old beer, stale smoke, and worn-out memories.

Mason pushed open the heavy wooden door, the hinges protesting with a groan. A few heads turned, glancing at the newcomer, before resuming their whispered conversations or lonely musings. He chose a stool at the far end of the bar, away from the smattering of patrons. The bartender, a woman with steel gray hair and lines mapping her face, slid over and wiped the bar in front of Mason with a wet rag.

"Shot of Buffalo Trace and a Coors Light," Mason said, settling onto his stool.

He sipped the liquor, letting the alcohol burn its way down his throat. The first drinks were soon followed by more. A jukebox in the corner played old Hank Williams ballads.

Hours passed. As the night wore on, Mason's eyes grew heavy.

He paid cash, then staggered out of the bar, the door thudding shut behind him. He fumbled for his keys, eventually finding them in his pocket, and clumsily unlocked his Bronco. As soon as he turned the ignition, the roaring strains of heavy metal music blasted from the speakers, swallowing him in its furious embrace. The frantic beats of double bass pedals and guttural growls filled his screaming head. Denver's dark streets blurred past as Mason laid on the gas pedal. The Bronco's headlights sliced through the night, briefly illuminating the desolate sidewalks, scattered trash, and occasional night wanderer.

He took turns too fast, tires squealing in protest against the asphalt. Each twist and turn seemed to blur into the next, the urban landscape melting into a series of lights and shadows. His reflection in the rearview mirror was a disheveled, wild-eyed specter. The heavy chug of the guitars and the relentless pounding of the drums filled every inch of the vehicle.

But as he neared the construction site, his adrenaline waned. He parked haphazardly next to his trailer and switched off the music. The Bronco's engine rumbled for a few moments as he sat collecting himself before stumbling out of the Bronco and to his RV, where he passed out fully dressed on the sofa.

The next day at work, Mason loaded his gear bag through Longhorn 2's back doors. When he slammed them closed, he caught his reflection in the dark-tinted windows. His uniform shirt was wrinkled, and his collar hung like limp dog ears, one point flopping while the other was trapped under his vest.

Strands of hair hung in his face.

Ali appeared with the pickup schedule on a clipboard. He was strong, with a barrel chest and thick arms.

"All good, Mason?" he asked, eyeing Mason up and down.

"Yep," Mason replied, not meeting Ali's gaze as they loaded into Longhorn 2's front seats.

Ali started the engine, and the garage door opened. The sun's rays passed through Mason's sunglasses like a 5.56mm round through butter. He squinted and felt his stomach churn. He burped up bile, and his throat burned.

Ali looked at Mason hard. "You sure you're good?"

"I'll be good when we get this day over, my man, so let's roll out."

"Nothing but a word," Ali said as he dropped the SUV into drive and pulled out.

They drove for a while, and then Ali leaned in, lowering his voice to a hushed whisper. "I got what you've been looking for," he murmured. "Marissa had to sneak it out of the vet's office, but she managed. Swing by tonight. You're going to love it."

Mason's head perked up, and he nodded slowly. "I'll be by tonight then," he replied.

Back at the office that evening, the fluorescent lights in the locker room cast a dim hue over the shiny green lockers and wooden benches. Mason peeled off his uniform.

Caleb walked up. "Mason," he started, a hint of hesitation in his voice, "do you think you'll have time this week to show me some stuff at the range?"

Mason glanced up, his gaze meeting Caleb's eager eyes.

"The kill house isn't done yet," he replied.

"But the underground range is," Caleb fired back.

Mason sighed, his head throbbing. "Tomorrow. We'll do it tomorrow."

Caleb's face brightened instantly. "Thanks, Mason," he said earnestly. "I won't let you down."

"Cool," he responded as he lifted his gear bag and walked out.

The evening sun was setting, casting long shadows over the suburban houses, as Mason pulled up to Ali's home. It was a one-story gray brick house in a neighborhood with mature English oak trees and big, grassy front yards. There was a child's bicycle on the front porch. Dogs' barking echoed from inside. Mason rang the front doorbell, and Ali opened it with a big smile. He wore a gray T-shirt with Marines across the front, black jogging pants, and white sneakers.

"Mason, come on in," he said, and the men clasped hands. Ali welcomed Mason inside, where he was met by a little girl of about six who peered up at him with enormous eyes, her hair dangling in braids with pink and red barrettes.

"Kayla!" Mason exclaimed to the gleaming little face looking up at him.

"Come see, Mason!" she said, tugging his hand.

Ali's Colombian wife, Marissa, entered from a back hallway. Marissa was tiny compared to her hulking husband. She still wore blue work scrubs, her hair was in a messy bun, and she was holding a chew toy. A flurry of wagging, yapping dogs trailed behind her. There were two Cocker Spaniels, a dachshund, a Yorkie, and two or three Mason couldn't identify.

"Hi, Mason," Marissa said, giving him a peck on the cheek. "Come back here, and I'll show you."

She waved for him to follow, and little Kayla almost tugged Mason off his feet. The gang of dogs fell in, their nails clicking on the tile floor as the procession crossed the kitchen, down the hall, and into the garage.

The two-car garage smelled of animals and dog food. Cardboard moving boxes were stacked neatly in a corner beside a washer and dryer, and ten-speed bicycles hung from hooks in the ceiling. Beneath that, a row of white plastic kennels with mesh doors lined the wall.

As soon as they entered the garage, Marissa's gang of terriers and spaniels exploded in a barrage of barking. One of the plastic kennels burst to life, barking and shaking violently in response.

"Hey! Hey!" Ali yelled over the din. "Take them back inside," he ordered.

"Yes, sir," Kayla said dutifully, and tried to use her little arms to shepherd the dog pack back into the house. "Let's go, you guys. You misbehaved, so you have to go back inside," she scolded them.

Marissa rolled her eyes. "Kayla, close the door!" she shouted.

Once the gang was gone, Marissa, Ali, and Mason turned their attention to the lone occupied dog carrier. Mason squatted down and peered inside. Just behind the mesh gate, he saw the soft, liquid eyes and sniffing black nose of a young Dalmatian, its white face dotted with black spots. It watched Mason with curious eyes.

Marissa stepped forward. "This is Bud," she introduced. "He is a full-blooded Dalmatian. Dalmatians are known for their protectiveness. They were bred and trained to guard the king's carriage. They stick closely with their owners and love to protect vehicles. That's why they are associated with firefighters. In the old days, they used them to protect fire wagons and their horses."

Mason held a finger up to the cage, allowing Bud to sniff.

"Why Bud?" Mason asked.

Ali laughed. "Years ago, Budweiser used Dalmatians in their commercials."

Mason chuckled. "Makes sense."

"He's almost two years old. He bit his last owner. Not badly, but the owner didn't want to deal with him, so they brought him to the clinic. The vet told me to put him down, which, of course, I did. I did not secretly bring him home, not at all."

"No, not at all," Mason and Ali said in unison, laughing.

Marissa picked up a coiled blue leash from the top of the kennel. She opened the kennel's door, and as the young dog tried to escape, deftly grabbed his chain collar and hooked the leash.

"He is house and leash trained, and I think deep down he's a sweetheart," she said. "His owner was an asshole. He just needs love and affection, like all of us."

She held out the leash. "Here," she said.

Mason took the leash. Bud was nervous, pacing around the garage, sniffing. Mason tugged the leash a little, and the black-and-white dog looked up at him curiously.

"That's what you wanted, right?" Ali asked. "Full-blooded Dalmatian?"

Mason reached out his hand and scratched Bud on the head. The dog instantly stopped sniffing the concrete and trotted close to him. He looked into the pup's sparkling eyes, its pink tongue hanging out.

"Can he ride in the Bronco like this?" he asked, holding up the leash.

Under the dark of night, Mason and Bud drove to the trailer in Mason's old Bronco. Struggling to carry a bag of dog food, his dry cleaning, and the dog's leash, Mason led Bud to the travel trailer, allowing the dog to sniff here and there as they walked. He unlocked the door, and the two went up the steps and inside.

Mason opened the kitchen cabinet, and a rainbow of glass bottles glinted in the dim light. He grabbed one and brought it to his lips, taking a big swig. The vodka burned its way down his throat. He glanced down to see Bud staring up at him, the blue leash dragging from his collar across the linoleum floor.

"I suppose you want room and board," Mason said.

He took another swig from the bottle, laid a paper plate on the floor, and used his Spyderco folding knife to slice the dog food bag. He poured a pile onto the paper plate. Bud looked at him quizzically, not moving.

"Oh, a foodie, huh? You should be thankful. In Afghanistan, dogs eat out of the dirt."

Mason filled a cereal bowl with water from the sink and placed it next to the plate of food. Bud walked over and lapped it up.

"Enjoy that. Tomorrow, you start your new job. Everybody earns their keep in this outfit."

Mason chuckled as he watched the dog eat, scattering kibbles across the floor. He grabbed a glass and sat with the bottle at the small dining table. The kitchen light was warm. Outside, crickets chirped. Mason drained the glass. He refilled it. Drained it again. He promised he would slow down as he refilled it again.

The last thing he remembered was Bud's soft whine before everything faded into nothingness.

11

Colorado

Meanwhile, on a Local Road just miles from Mason's trailer, seven motorcycle headlights followed by an SUV's dual beams pulled off the blacktop road onto a private dirt track leading into the woods. They drove slowly through the dark into the rocky forest.

The rumble of the motorcycles gradually quieted as the gang pulled into a hidden clearing surrounded by old pine trees. A split-log cabin with a roofed patio and a barn, rough from years in the weather, was there, hidden away. On the horizon, the Rocky Mountains kept watch in the moonlight.

Raison killed his engine and stepped off his bike. After surveying the surroundings, his eyes lingered on the moonlit peaks above. He stepped onto the porch, reached up, and felt around a beam in the ceiling, where he retrieved a key ring. He unlocked the front door, walked inside, and searched for a light switch. Once the lights were on, he saw a rustic but comfortably furnished vacation cottage. A massive stone fireplace and buckskin sofas dominated the living area. There were prints of bighorn sheep and fly fishers on the walls, colorful rugs in Native American patterns covering the floor, and a high ceiling spanned by log beams. The walls were exposed wood throughout, and the entire house smelled of cedar.

Raison's boots clonked on the wood floor as he strolled through the living area into the kitchen. There was ample counter space, a double porcelain sink, and an old white refrigerator. He continued his inspection of the cabin as he heard the voices and boots of his brothers enter behind him. Down the hallway, there were four bedrooms. One room had four bunk beds against the walls. There were colorful quilts on the beds, and the bathrooms were hotel-clean and guest-ready. Satisfied, Raison returned to the living room. Rage, Bruno, Matheo, Okwaho, and Moose set their gear bags on the floor.

"This is it, wolves. Our home for the next while. The owner is a friend, and they've been paid well, so we have it to ourselves. Grab a room and get unpacked."

Moose grunted in agreement, already heaving his duffel bag. "Place is isolated. Good choice, boss."

Matheo, crossing the living room, grinned. "No neighbors to complain about the noise. What's out back?" he asked as he opened the back door from the kitchen and exited into the night.

The backyard was landscaped with crushed granite paths and a flagstone patio dominated by a rock fire pit. There were stone and wooden benches, rocking chairs, and a hammock. Several chords of split wood were stacked near the back door next to a stainless-steel grill. A large, abandoned horse barn stood a hundred feet to the left of the cabin. Under a carport, an old blue Toyota Land Cruiser was parked.

Walking to the center of the yard, Matheo stretched his arms to the sky, tilted his head back, and sent his best wolf howl echoing through the mountains.

"Owoooooooo!"

12

Back to Work

The sun's harsh rays pierced the blinds of the RV, making the dust particles dance in the air. Mason, disoriented and dizzy, woke up face down on the kitchen floor. He groaned and blinked hard. As his blurry vision cleared, he met the liquid eyes of Bud, his new Dalmatian, watching him with a mix of concern and curiosity from the sofa.

Grunting with effort, Mason pushed himself upright, his head throbbing. He winced as he touched his cheek, feeling a sharp and unexpected sting. Using the dinner table's edge for support, he pulled himself up from the floor and stumbled towards the bathroom. His reflection in the mirror revealed a swollen bruise, dark and angry, on his left cheekbone. The eye was blackening, too. For a moment, Mason stared at himself. Then Bud's whimper broke his reverie, and he looked down at the dog.

"Damn it," he muttered, rubbing the sore spot on his face. "What happened, Bud? Did I black out and take a dive last night?"

Bud tilted his head curiously.

Mason lifted the toilet seat, stuck his finger down his throat, and, with a series of gags and retches, emptied his stomach. The liquid burned, leaving Mason's eyes watering. He climbed into the shower, rested his head against the fiberglass wall, and let the water pour down his back until it ran cold.

The sun was already up. Mason struggled into his uniform and holstered his pistol. Bud jumped up when he entered the kitchen, his tail wagging furiously.

"Son of a bitch," Mason trailed off.

In the night, the dog had shredded his running shoes. Bits of rubber and white stuffing mixed with wet dog food were strewn across the floor.

He opened the freezer, removed a plastic ice tray, and dumped it into a dish towel. He whacked it hard against the counter to shatter the ice, then stood at the sink holding it to his swollen cheekbone while he ate his usual omelet breakfast from a paper plate. Bud watched him eagerly. Mason continued eating for a moment, thinking. Finally, he set the plate down and wiped his mouth. Reaching into the cabinet, he found a partially full bottle of Beefeater gin. He raised the bottle to the dog.

"May bronze and medals not be the only reward of the brave," he recited.

He drained the bottle, winced, then retched into the sink. He tossed the empty bottle into the white trash can, where it thonked heavily. Bud laid back down and chewed a rubber shoe sole. Mason found the blue leash on top of a pizza box near the trailer's front door.

"If I leave you here, there won't be anything left when I get back, so I guess you're coming with me," he said and clicked the leash onto Bud's collar. They walked out into the cool Colorado morning. Mason opened the back door of the Bronco and, with a pat on the seat, Bud loaded up. Mason climbed into the front seat, placed black sunglasses over his bruised face, tuned the radio to classic Country music, and the duo headed back to work.

At the GZD office, Mason parked the Bronco in the rear employee parking lot and opened the passenger door. Out jumped Bud, his tail wagging. As he crossed the gravel lot toward the office building, the dog trotted by his side, casting long shadows under the morning sun.

Around the back of the building, Mason found a shaded spot where he set up a makeshift space for the dog. He looped a sturdy chain around a tree, attaching it to Bud's collar, ensuring ample slack for the dog to walk around. Beside the tree, he placed a bowl of fresh water and another with some dry food, patting the dog's head affectionately.

"Stay, Bud," Mason instructed.

As he walked to the office's backdoor, Bud tried to follow, until he reached the end of the chain. There he stood, watching as Mason disappeared into the building.

The GZD office was a hive of activity, but Mason was distant. He walked in, sunglasses on, the glossy frames hiding the evidence of the previous night's fall. In the locker room, Mink nudged Benito, tilting his head towards Mason. "Rough night?" he whispered. Benito shrugged and turned away.

Mason went to his locker and slid into his body armor without a word. He checked his sidearm, holstered it, slammed the locker door, and headed to the break room. In the sterile ambiance of the GZD coffee bar, he filled an oversized travel mug with black coffee and grabbed a water bottle from the refrigerator. He sat at a round table just as Caleb walked in.

"Hey, Mason," Caleb said. "How's it going?"

Mason smoothed some hair out of his face. "It's going."

"You know, about that range time..." Caleb started.

"What about it?" Mason asked, rubbing his left temple.

"Well," Caleb shifted on his feet, "I was hoping we might go today. After work?"

Mason slumped in his chair.

"Uh," Mason said. "Man, tonight. I don't know. I have to get this dog set up."

"Dog? You got a dog?" Caleb was surprised.

"Yeah, he's out back." Mason pointed toward the rear exit.

"No shit?" Caleb spun around and walked out.

Mason remained seated at the table, drinking coffee and rubbing his temples.

His cell phone vibrated in his pocket. He removed it and read a text message.

"Turn on the news," it read.

He picked up the remote to the break room TV and changed the channel. There were images of U.S. soldiers in Iraq, dust, smoke, military vehicles, shouting men, and the fluttering black flag of the Islamic State.

The screen changed to a portrait of a soldier in front of a U.S. flag. His head was shaved smooth, his face chiseled granite. He wore a blue Army

122

Service Uniform covered in patches, pins, and emblems. Mason saw pins for Airborne and Rangers, plus the long, blue Combat Infantryman Badge. But most importantly, he saw the emblem on the soldier's epaulets—the red arrowhead inlaid with a black dagger of America's most secret combat unit, Delta Force.

Mason turned up the volume as the newscaster spoke from behind her desk.

"In Iraq, in a tragic turn of events during Operation Inherent Resolve, Master Sergeant Joshua Lloyd Wheeler of the elite Delta Force has been confirmed as the first American service member killed by enemy fire in action against Islamic State militants. This sad incident marks the first loss of an American in combat operations in Iraq since November 2011. Master Sergeant Wheeler leaves behind a legacy of courage and dedication, reflected in the 11 Bronze Star Medals he earned throughout his service, four of which were adorned with Valor Devices. Our thoughts are with his family, comrades, and all those who knew and respected this decorated hero."

Mason watched the screen, his hungover head pounding, the self-inflicted black eye throbbing. He removed his sunglasses, and in the break room, held a solitary moment of silence. When he was done, he followed Caleb's path down the hallway and outside.

Caleb was in the parking lot on one knee. Bud, still tied to the pole, was at the end of his tether, wagging his tail at full tilt like an Apache gunship's tail rotor, almost knocking Caleb over. Caleb scratched Bud hard behind the ears and smiled when he saw Mason approach.

"Cool dog," Caleb said. "I always liked Dalmatians. They can be hard-headed, though."

"Yeah, well, so can I," Mason said. "About the range. Come by tonight at about 19:00. We'll run some drills. Sound good?"

"What about this guy?" Caleb asked, shaking Bud's head playfully.

"I'll get him set up," Mason assured.

"OK, then," Caleb smiled. "See you tonight."

13

Crime

A family of four passed through the glass doors leading into Denver's Cherry Creek Shopping Center right as three 14 year old boys shoved their way through. It was midafternoon, and the luxury shopping mall buzzed with shoppers. Xavier and his two friends, Kenan and Liam, weaved through the milling throng. Xavier, a green backpack slung over his shoulders, winced and stopped to pull his hooded sweatshirt away from his chest.

"Come on, Xavi!" Liam, a pale, skinny kid, exclaimed.

"Hang on, damn," Xavier said, removing the backpack and setting it on the white-tiled floor. His eyes squinted in pain. "This shit still hurts."

"That's because you're not supposed to light your pubes on fire," the other friend, a light-skinned boy with a short Afro named Kenan, laughed. "It's the fire challenge, not the burn-your-dick-off challenge."

Kenan and Liam laughed and traded punches.

"Man, y'all are dumb as fuck," Xavier said, adjusting his shirt. "I didn't burn my dick. I barely burned my stomach. It just hurts when something touches it."

"What, like this?" Kenan said, slapping Xavier on the chest.

"Ow, motherfucker!" Xavier yelped and swung at the other boy. Kenan jumped behind Liam, the two laughing and nearly tumbling over each other. "Damn, you play too much!"

Irritated, Xavier yanked the backpack from the ground. "Here, stupid ass boy. Take this and go upstairs where we talked about," he said, pushing the backpack into Kenan's chest.

Kenan took the bag, then looked around. "Man, I don't know. There's a lot of people here right now. This shit is kind of bananas."

"Man, I knew you were a pussy. I don't even know why I bring you," Xavier said, reaching for the backpack. "Don't ask me to tag you in the video or nothing, man."

Kenan snatched the bag away. "Chill, damn. I didn't say I wasn't gonna do it."

Both boys had a grip on the bag.

"Well, are you or are you not?" Xavier demanded.

"Yes, damn," Kenan replied. "Chill, you're making the rich people nervous, bro."

"Ok then," Xavier said, releasing the bag. "You two go upstairs, and I'm going to the Grand Court. But when you see me, act like you don't. Got it?"

"Yeah, man," Kenan replied.

"This shit is going to be wild," Liam said with a big smile.

Slinging the backpack over his shoulder, Kenan took off to an escalator with Liam by his side.

His scorched chest stinging, Xavier walked through the mall past stores like The North Face and Kay Jewelers. Noisy people of all shapes and colors passed him, the cacophony of voices blending into a single, indistinct hum.

At the center of the mall was the Grand Court, an open space featuring a coffee kiosk and numerous arm chairs in shades of brown. The irregularly shaped area was carpeted in gray and surrounded on all sides by a second-floor balcony with a railing of glass and steel. Xavier felt his heart thumping as he approached. The smell of coffee was overpowering, and adults sat here and there in the armchairs sipping their brews and studying their phones or laptops. Xavier strolled around, taking in the scene. His eyes flicked upwards, and he caught sight of his friends on the balcony above. Liam, staring right at him, waved to get Xavier's attention.

"Stupid idiot," Xavier mumbled under his breath, turning away to act like he hadn't noticed. Pulling out his phone, he dialed. On the balcony, Kenan answered.

"What's up, fam?" Kenan asked.

"Tell your boy to stop giving me away like a newb and get ready," Xavier said.

"We been ready, Xavi baby. I got this," Kenan said.

"Bet," Xavier replied, and clicked off the call.

Looking around cautiously, Xavier turned on his phone's self-facing camera. He checked his hair and teeth on the screen, then tapped the record button.

"What up, what up, everybody? It's your boy, Wavy Xavi with more drip than the Navy coming right at you once again. That's right, you know it's time for another crazy video from your boy and the Mile High Hit Squad."

"As you see," he said, spinning around to display the setting, "we're out here in Cherry Creek Center doing what we do—making history, you know what I'm saying, doing what others won't. This may be our craziest stunt yet, so you're going to want to stick around for this one. As usual, tell your friends to get on this because they will not want to miss it. We've got pure craziness coming right up, so hit that subscribe button and hang tight."

Xavier looked up at his friends, who were now rummaging through the backpack. As Liam held the bag, Kenan reached in and cautiously removed two latex condoms, each filled to the brim with water and tied shut, their surfaces stretched and glossy. The boys held them carefully, like delicate babies. They both looked down at Xavier, their eyes wide with excitement.

Shoppers passed through the open court unaware. Xavier watched as a mother with two children walked under Kenan and Liam. Then an elderly couple, the man with a cane, passed in the other direction. Xavier watched and waited. Kenan and Liam were anxiously posted on the balcony above, trying to be inconspicuous but fidgeting and giggling.

"Idiots," Xavier whispered.

Next, a man in khakis passed under the balcony, then a teenage girl in a work uniform. Finally, in the distance, Xavier saw a group of teens approaching. There were three boys and two girls, all high school aged. Xavier looked up at his friends and tapped the top of his head. Liam and

Kenan flinched in excitement, almost dropping the water-filled condoms.

Xavier tapped the record button on his phone again. Smiling to himself, he pointed the camera at the oncoming teens. It was a mixed group of kids, just a little older than Xavier and his friends. The girls wore short shorts and long T-shirts, and the boys were all wearing basketball shorts and T-shirts, and they were holding drink cups from the food court. As they got closer, Xavier could see their smiles and hear their laughs. They poked and played with each other as they walked directly under the pranksters.

As they passed under, Xavier tapped his head again, and right on cue, Kenan and Liam released the water-filled condoms. The first balloon landed directly on one of the boy's heads, a tall kid with dark hair. Instead of breaking on impact, the condom stretched, elongated, and completely enveloped the boy's head. He barely had time to react when the second condom came hurtling down, missing its mark, and smashed onto the tile floor, an eruption of water dashing the teens with spray.

Startled and soaked, the kids first scattered, then stopped and studied themselves in wide-eyed confusion. Shocked and enraged, the girls were flicking water off themselves and flinging their hair about.

"What the fuck?" one of the boys began, then he saw his panicked friend remove the condom from his head, and he looked up. There he saw Kenan and Liam leering over the balcony, howling with laughter.

"Are you fucking serious?" he said, his face morphing into a snarl. His friends looked up, too, then around the court. One of them spotted Xavier laughing and recording.

"Oh, is that funny to you?" the tallest kid said. He started towards Xavier, and his friends started to follow.

"Oh shit, everybody," Xavier said to his viewers. "Here they come."

"Are you fucking recording this shit?" the kid said as he closed the distance.

"Yo, chill it's just a prank," Xavier said, and the kid lunged at him. He smacked the phone out of Xavier's hand, then swung a wild haymaker at his head.

"Yo, chill!" Xavier said again, but the angry teen was on him.

The two boys exchanged rapid blows to the face and head, then tumbled across a group of armchairs. Xavier tried to stand, but the other kid dove into him, knocking him over a planter and spilling soil across the carpet.

Customers started to yell, but Xavier was disoriented on the ground, his hoodie partially pulled over his head. He struggled and fought to free himself. Just then, a strong hand grabbed him by the upper arm and lifted him easily to his feet. He flailed, but another powerful hand grabbed his other arm and held him tightly. He heard the deep base of men's voices, then somebody pulled his sweatshirt down from his eyes. In the light, he saw two big, uniformed police officers had him and the other kid tightly restrained.

"Cut that out," a big black officer said sternly to Xavier, "before I put my boot up your narrow ass."

"They attacked us," the tall kid protested, but the officers were already dragging both boys away. As they passed under the balcony, through the puddle of water, past the soaked, angry victims, Xavier looked up for his friends, but they were gone.

Kim was at her desk when a uniformed officer came by and whispered into her ear. Kim looked at him, her face scrunched.

"Are you serious?" she asked incredulously.

"He's downstairs in the lobby now," the officer said, shrugging.

The walk to the lobby slipped by in a flash, and then Kim was standing in front of her son. Xavier was sitting in an armchair, his shoulders hunched and his lip swollen.

"Let me see," Kim said, grabbing his face and turning it up to her, but he pulled away.

"I didn't even do anything," he explained. "I was just chilling, and those dudes jumped me."

Kim studied the boy's face calmly, then stood up and stared at him. Xavier looked away.

"That's enough. I know what you and your little buddies get up to with your pranks. I hoped it wouldn't go this far, that you'd have enough sense not to bring other people into your little circus, but I guess that was too much to hope for."

"It was just a joke. Nobody got hurt until dude swung on me," he continued.

"Shush," Kim said, shutting him down. "I don't want to hear it. Not here, and not now. I don't get off until 6:00, so you'll have to sit here until then. Boy, wait until your father gets home."

Xavier started to speak, then looked down and waited.

"Hand over the phone," she said, holding out her hand.

"But Mom!" Xavier protested. "I told you. I didn't do anything!"

"Xavier," Kim said, her eyes narrowing. "Give me the phone."

The boy relented and handed over his smart phone. Kim sighed, then turned to walk back to her office.

"Don't you even think about moving from that chair," she warned as she passed back through the security door. Then she was gone. Xavier slouched in his seat and tucked his hands in his pockets.

14

Preparations

Rain drenched the narrow dirt track leading to the cabin. The thick and eerily silent surrounding woods pressed in from all sides. A lone black BMW with dark-tinted windows made its way through the fog-laden trail to the clearing with the cabin. Pulling to a halt, the car door swung open, and a middle-aged man wearing khaki pants, a green raincoat, and white tennis shoes climbed out. His hair was gray and thin, and he wore rimless glasses. Bruno watched him through the curtains as he opened the BMW's trunk and removed a gray plastic tub. Without a word, he walked to the cabin's front porch and set the tub down. Then he returned to the car, closed the trunk, climbed into the driver's seat, and drove away.

Bruno watched him leave, then stepped out onto the porch dressed in black jeans, black cowboy boots, and a gray flannel over a black T-shirt. His dark hair was in a ponytail. He carried the tub into the kitchen and placed it on the wooden dining table. Inside were many small boxes. It took a few minutes to open them all and arrange the contents across the table. As he finished unpacking, Raison entered the kitchen.

"That was the guy? Did he bring everything?" he asked.

"Yeah, he brought it all," Bruno confirmed.

They both stood for a moment, taking in the table's contents.

"Ten cell phones and chargers and ten SIM cards," Bruno listed. "Two tracking devices with matching weatherproof cases and two more SIM cards for those. The SIM cards are set up on cloned cellular accounts. They will be good for maybe 30 days, but once the account owners get their bills, they'll call their carriers, and the cards will probably get deactivated."

"This," he said, holding up a device, "is the latest wireless trail camera. It has motion detection, night vision, everything. You can mount this anywhere and it'll record HD video both day and night."

"And this," Bruno continued, lifting a black nylon tool bag, "is a professional locksmith set. We can use it to duplicate keys."

"Is that the hard shit?" Raison asked, pointing at a long cardboard box with several red plastic tubes inside. The tubes were threaded on each end as if to screw together.

With a big grin, Bruno reached into the box and plucked out one of the red tubes.

"It sure is. Gel dynamite. They use it for seismic surveying. If you put a few of these together with the right ignition source, it'll open any door we need."

"We'll have to test all this. Store the dynamite in the barn so we don't get blown up," Raison said. "Help me gather the wolves. It's time to get to work."

Later that night, an old, blue Toyota Land Cruiser cut its headlights before turning into an industrial park. The off-road vehicle pulled down an alley and parked close to a metal building's back wall. Matheo and Okwaho rolled the windows down and waited a few moments, listening.

After a while, Okwaho said, "Alright, let's get this camera setup."

Both men donned black balaclava masks before exiting the SUV. Matheo climbed onto the hood and then the roof of the Land Cruiser. Okwaho, carrying a black bag across his back, followed him. But when he stepped on the vehicle's roof, the sheet metal flexed under his weight with a metallic clonk. He froze, closed his eyes, and cursed through tight lips.

"Shit!" Matheo hissed, instinctively crouching as he looked up and down the alley. Everything appeared calm.

"Fuck it," he said. "Come on."

Facing the wall, Matheo squatted, allowing Okwaho to climb up his back.

On his powerful fighter's legs, Matheo stood to his full height with Okwaho on his shoulders, allowing him to reach the roof's edge and hoist himself up. Once atop the building, crouching low, Okwaho scurried toward the front. There, he laid flat and slowly inched on his belly until he could peer over the edge and confirm his target. Removing the bag from his back, he unzipped it and retrieved one of the digital trail cameras. He inserted a memory card into a slot near the charging port and switched the camera on. Careful to trap the screen's light with his gloved hand, he opened the wireless camera app on his smartphone. Once he verified the feed was active, he retrieved a plastic weatherproof case, inserted the camera, and sealed the case shut with a latch.

His Bluetooth earpiece crackled.

"The guard is moving," Moose's voice carried over the microphone. Okwaho froze.

Moose was sitting on his motorcycle a hundred meters down the street from the industrial park. He had a clear view of a small white pickup truck with yellow rotating lights on the roof and a security company logo on the door.

"The security truck is driving in your direction," Moose said into his headset.

"Shit!" Matheo cursed, still on top of the Land Cruiser.

"Robeur, fire it up," Raison's voice came over the headsets.

"Roger that," Robeur replied.

Robeur was seated on his own motorcycle in the industrial park's back parking lot, between the guard and the alley where Matheo and Okwaho were working. On Raison's order, he cranked his motorcycle and revved the engine hard and loud. Smoke billowed from the rear tire as the rubber shrieked against the pavement. He cut the wheel and let the backend slide, showering bits of sand and rock as he burned a black donut onto the cement.

The scream of Robeur's engine carried all the way to Moose, who watched the security truck closely. It continued slowly on the same path, yellow lights flicking around lazily.

"Moose," Okwaho called over the line, "what's the guard doing?"

"Still heading your way," he replied.

Okwaho took a deep breath, then hurriedly returned to his task. There was an HVAC unit that provided enough height for a precise angle on the building across the street. Using strong double-sided tape, Okwaho mounted the camera's case to the HVAC unit, hoping nobody would notice. Watching the live feed on his phone, he adjusted the camera's swivel mount until the target building was entirely in view. Once satisfied, he slung the bag over his back and crawled to the rear of the building, where Matheo waited. There, he peered over the edge. Matheo had jumped down from the Land Cruiser's roof and was on the ground watching for the guard.

"Hey, dummy! How am I supposed to get down?" Okwaho hissed.

Matheo looked up at him, sweat beading on his forehead.

"You stay there. I'm going to take off. I'll come back for you later," Matheo said.

"Hell, no! Don't you fucking leave me up here," Okwaho spat.

Matheo opened the driver's door, cast a hesitant glance at Okwaho, and climbed inside as if to leave. Just as he was about to crank the engine and drive off, Moose came over the headset.

"It worked," Moose said. "The guard turned around. He's heading to the back parking lot."

Okwaho exhaled hard. "Come get me down, you idiot!" he whispered harshly.

"OK, damn!" Matheo called back.

Once Okwaho was down from the roof, the two climbed into the Land Cruiser, closed the doors, and slowly rolled out of the parking lot. They headed back up the alley, only removing their masks and turning on the headlights once they reached the main road. From the intersection, they saw the security guard try to chase Robeur, who simply gunned the throttle and left the truck behind.

As they turned the corner at the end of the block, Okwaho watched the target building in the rearview mirror. A white building with green trim and three tall garage doors along the front faded into the distance.

Kenny's Wheelhouse was a tire shop built of red brick and trimmed with peeling blue paint. The sun-faded sign creaked in the wind, and there were stacks of glossy new tires in the front parking lot. Inside, the scent of rubber permeated everything. Fluorescent lights hummed overhead, casting a sterile glow over the grimy tile floor. The waiting area, positioned off to the side, had four cracked faux leather chairs, a coffee machine that gurgled periodically, and stacks of outdated magazines. The main working area was an expansive open garage with multiple service bays. Hydraulic lifts stood in each bay, and tool chests on wheels were scattered about, stickers and decals displaying years of different brands. The clang of metal on metal, punctuated by the occasional hiss of an air compressor or the buzz of an impact wrench, filled the atmosphere. Old automotive signs and promotional posters decorated the walls, and the front counter was a chaotic mix of paperwork, greasy parts, and a ringing landline.

The bell above the door jingled, announcing Robeur's entry. An older man with a silvering beard and grimy hands looked up from his counter, peering at Robeur over a pair of smudged reading glasses.

"Morning. Whatcha need?" His voice was rough.

Robeur approached the counter, noting the chaos of invoices, scattered tools, and a half-eaten sandwich. "Hey there, I saw you might be hiring. I've got experience in tire changes and some basic mechanical work. My name is Tom. Tom Wallin."

Kenny leaned back, scrutinizing Robeur for a moment. "Yeah? Where'd you work before?"

Robeur didn't skip a beat. "Down at Martinez Auto in Pueblo. But moved up here recently. Looking for something local."

Kenny raised an eyebrow. "Martinez, huh? Ever change a tire on a semi?"

"Yes, sir. Did a bit of everything down there."

Kenny nodded, mulling it over. "Alright. Let's see how you handle a wrench. Mitchell!" he shouted, causing a younger mechanic in the back to look up. "Show this young man the F-250 with the rear blowout. Let's give our friend here a test."

With an amused smirk, Mitchell led Robeur to a Ford truck with a shredded tire dangling from a back rim. "Have at it," he said.

Mitchell rolled a replacement tire to the truck and let it fall over to the floor, then walked away. Robeur pushed up his sleeves. Looking around, he found the tools he needed. The rhythm of the task was familiar—break the lug nuts, jack up the vehicle, remove the lug nuts, remove the wheel, replace the tire, mount and balance the tire, remount the wheel, replace the lug nuts. His movements were swift and precise, honed from years of similar tasks.

Once done, Robeur wiped his hands on a rag and walked back into the lobby. "All set," he said.

Kenny walked around the counter and into the garage to inspect the vehicle. He bent over, checked the tire, and nodded appreciatively. "OK, Tom. That was almost fast enough. The job pays $14-an-hour, paid in cash every Friday. Can you start tomorrow?"

"Absolutely," Robeur replied with a smile. "See you bright and early."

15

Team

Bright fluorescent lights clicked on in the concrete stairwell. Mason and Caleb descended a wide steel staircase, the echo of their boots dulled by the soundproofed walls. Each man carried a rifle case and a gear bag. The stairs descended twenty feet underground into a basement under what would be the Green Zone Defense Training Center. A door at the foot of the stairs opened into a vast, subterranean expanse. Rows of well-lit shooting lanes stretched into the distance. Reinforced with thick concrete, the walls were dotted with innovative acoustic panels. Ultramodern ventilation systems hummed softly overhead, and the floor was covered with anti-fatigue mats.

Caleb whistled. "Man, this place has come a long way."

"Yes, it has," Mason agreed. "The range is segmented. Those are movable ballistic partitions, which allow for creating various shooting scenarios. The automated target system can mimic advancing enemies, pop out from side lanes, or swing across the shooter's field of view. It's all state-of-the-art."

Mason looked around, the dim blue light casting an ethereal glow over everything.

"Let's set up on lanes 1 and 2," he told Caleb.

Caleb set his gear bag on a table behind the shooting lanes. He pulled out his pistol, a Glock 19 with an underslung flashlight and red dot sight dovetailed onto the slide. Opening his gun case, he retrieved a SIG Sauer SIGM400 rifle with an ACOG sight.

Mason asked to inspect the rifle. Caleb handed it over, and Mason placed it to his shoulder, careful to keep the muzzle downrange. He peeked through the sight.

"You like the stock adjusted in close like this? I like mine extended out," Mason said.

"It works for me," Caleb shrugged.

Mason returned the rifle to Caleb, then picked up a large remote control. He pressed a few buttons and lights clicked on down the range. A few more clicks and motorized targets sprung to life, whizzing here and there as Mason programmed the drills.

"All right," he said, "get your eyes and ears on and let's get to work."

Both men donned eye and ear protection, and Caleb loaded magazines into his rifle and pistol.

In the half-lit underground expanse, a white silhouette-style target stood forty feet from the shooters.

Mason barked. "Box Drill!"

Caleb gripped his holstered pistol—a faint bead of sweat on his brow.

"Draw. Aim. Top left. Two shots. Top right. Two. Bottom right. Again, two. Finish bottom left. Two." Mason's voice was measured and instructive.

"Grip properly, extend toward the target, line up the sites, focus on the front site, front site covers the target, squeeze the trigger with the pad of your finger, not the crook."

Caleb inhaled. Exhaled. Began.

The sharp reports filled the air, echoing off the concrete walls as the bullets found their targets. After several tries, Mason congratulated Caleb on his hits.

"Israeli Wall Drill, next."

With the push of a button and the whir of motors, a target now stood menacingly close, just an arm's reach away.

Caleb felt the closeness, his heart thudding.

"Lean. Draw. Fire." Mason instructed. "No sights. Point like you would with your index finger. Use your instincts."

The shot was deafening.

After a few reps, the challenge escalated.

"Rolling Thunder," Mason said.

Targets were now spread out, scattered across the range in a chaotic mix of near and far.

"Put the two drills together. Close targets? Hit them fast. Point and shoot. Distant ones? Take them slow. Mind your breathing. Aim. Squeeze."

Caleb raised his pistol. Rapid fire, then slow deliberation. His breathing matched the rhythm, controlled chaos.

"Final drill. El Presidente."

Three targets. Side by side.

"Turn. Draw. Two shots each. Reload. Repeat."

Caleb's silhouette, backlit by the muzzle flashes, danced to the deadly rhythm. The reload was swift, competent, and then it was over.

"Good work," Mason said honestly. "The kill house is not complete, but the first couple of rooms are. Let's go check it out."

They collected their brass, packed their gear, and walked back up the steps. Together, they strode to a large, metal warehouse door with a sign that read, "Shoot House," followed by "DANGER! Live Ammo!" along with graphics of safety glasses and ear protection.

"This," he said, turning to an eager Caleb, "is where we train for real-world scenarios. Are you ready?"

"Hell, yeah!" Caleb exclaimed.

The shoot house echoed like a plane hangar. Darkened hallways, ominous doorways. Shadows played tricks. The men set their rifle bags on a table and unpacked them. Each man loaded his rifle with a fresh magazine.

Mason pointed to the first door. "Let's talk Slicing the Pie."

"You approach the doorway, always exposing minimal body parts. Clear each segment step by step, like slicing pieces off a pie, as you wrap around the corner."

Caleb took a breath. He moved smoothly, every inch calculated. His gun followed his gaze. Left. Right. Up. Down. The corners of the room became visible slowly and deliberately.

"Sweep the arcs and predict. Engage targets from outside the room when possible.”

Just as Mason said it, a silhouette came into view at the back of the room. The character was brandishing a revolver, so Caleb pulled the trigger twice, double tapping the target in the face and chest.

“Good!” Mason exclaimed. “Moving on.”

Another door.

“Dynamic Entry.” Mason’s voice was grave. “We want to be explosive, rapid, dominant. We breach together. Simultaneous entry by crisscrossing. First man, first corner. Second man, opposite corner.”

Caleb set himself, with Mason just behind.

Three.

Two.

One.

The door burst open. Caleb led, crossing right, gun up. Mason, at his six, moved quickly left. They flowed into the room, fluid, synchronized, transitioning from one point to another, eyes scanning, fingers tensed on triggers. The room was cleared in heartbeats.

Mason set up for the next drill. “Remember, you clear threats as they appear. Prioritize.”

Rifles up, they approached a Y-Hallway.

“Synchronized sweep.”

Together, they stepped, guns ready, clearing each angle, each potential threat zone, constantly aware of each other’s position.

Mason explained the particular issues when clearing an L-shaped room and finished with a lesson on gaining dominant angles by changing your perception.

“Every door, every corner, can hide a threat. The drills? They prepare you. But always, always be ready to adapt.”

The men bumped fists, then began breaking down their gear.

Under the dim glow of the parking lot lights outside the kill house, the chill of the Colorado evening set in. Mason and Caleb loaded their gear bags into their trucks. The sounds of zippers and metallic clicks of gun cases added to the night's chorus. A maroon pickup truck pulled into the lot and stopped. Benito climbed out wearing sweaty exercise clothing.

"What's the dealio?" he said, clasping each man's hand. He was drinking from a protein shaker bottle. "I was passing by here on my way home from the gym, and I saw your trucks," he said. "When is it finally gonna be done? I heard there were problems with the contractor or the investors or something. But the underground range is done, right?"

Mason nodded. "There's no problem. We might have to wait on some of the classrooms, but the range and the kill house are basically done."

Mason removed his shooting glasses. Benito noted his bruised face, his eyes narrowing.

"Damn, Mason," he began, his voice filled with genuine concern, "are you good, bro? Took a nasty hit on your cheek there."

Mason didn't meet Benito's gaze. Instead, he focused on securing his gear. "I'm fine," was all he offered.

Benito, undeterred, continued, "You know, if something's going on, we're here for you. The team's a family, after all."

Mason paused, finally turning to face Benito. "I said, I'm fine," Mason reiterated.

He lifted his rifle case, bid the men goodnight, then walked to his RV.

"That dude is a trip," Benito said, shaking his head. "Always solo. Always on edge. But deadly. Like a mountain lion."

Caleb nodded. "Yeah, I guess you're right," he agreed. "But you? You're like a skunk. At least you smell like one."

"What?" Benito shouted. "I'll make you smell this skunk."

He grabbed Caleb in a headlock and smashed his face into his armpit as the younger, smaller man shouted in protest and fought in the dust to escape.

The next day, in the bright, oil-scented ambiance of the Green Zone Defense garage, Mason and Caleb examined the fleet of dark blue Suburbans. Mason knocked on the side of Longhorn 1, feeling the thick, reinforced steel beneath the paint.

"This one," Mason began, "is fully armored. Bulletproof glass, run-flat tires, the works."

"It cost about a quarter million bucks, too," Caleb added. "Dad, uh, The Colonel complains about the price of Longhorn 1 almost daily."

Mason nodded and continued.

"These other two are bone stock—just regular factory Suburbans. Virtually any pistol, rifle, or shotgun round will penetrate these soft quarter panels, not to mention the glass windows. But in OIF, we didn't wait for the DOD to send us armor kits for our Humvees. If we had waited, soldiers would have died. So, we up-armored them ourselves."

Caleb's eyes widened. "What did you use?"

Mason chuckled. "Anything we could get our hands on. Scrap armor, scrap steel, hell, even sandbags. We used it if it could add an extra layer between us and the outside world. But here at home, we can do better. Today, my boy, I teach you how to make your own composite armor."

"Let's get to it," Caleb said, clapping his hands together.

In a spacious corner of the garage, both men set out the materials they would need: rolls of fiberglass, sheets of plexiglass, rolls of plastic, and containers of epoxy resin.

With Caleb's help, Mason spread a large plastic drop cloth on the floor. Then Mason grabbed his toolkit and walked to Longhorn 2 with Caleb trailing behind. He opened the driver's door and unscrewed the Suburban's inner door panel with an electric screwdriver. The interior panel detached, revealing the door's mechanics—a web of wires, insulation, and steel. Mason disconnected the wiring harness, and the door panel fell free.

"Take this over and lay it on the plastic," Mason said, handing the panel to Caleb.

They repeated this procedure around the Suburban until all four door panels were lying on the drop cloth. Then, with Caleb's help, Mason wrapped each panel with plastic wrap. Laying the panels face down, he sprayed the backs with a detaching agent.

"Next," Mason said, "put on your PPE because fiberglass is hell. Gloves, goggles, and long sleeves. Cover everything. Then put on your painter's mask because you don't want to inhale the fibers either."

They both donned protective gear. Unfurling a fiberglass roll onto a table, Mason continued. "We need to cut the fiberglass to just a little bigger than the panels."

He demonstrated how to cut one layer of fiberglass fabric.

"The magic is in the layering. Fiberglass by itself? Not much protection. But once you layer it and add epoxy, it becomes a different beast. So, what you want to do is fold this long sheet of fiberglass back and forth on itself to make a bunch of layers—as many as the shears can cut at once. That way, you cut 4 or 5 layers at a time. We need a lot of layers, so start cutting," Mason said, handing the shears to Caleb.

After Caleb had cut sufficient layers, he stacked them up. Mason laid a single fiberglass sheet onto the plastic-wrapped door panel.

"We're not going to put the old door panels back. They would never fit with the armor, anyway. Basically, we are replacing the stock door panels with laminate armor panels. We're going to use the back of the old panels as a sort of mold or template. We covered them in plastic, so now we can form our armor to the surface the plastic creates. If all goes well, with some trimming, we'll be able to remove these armor panels from their molds and mount them nice and clean where the old panels used to be."

Taking a brush, Mason coated the fiberglass with a generous layer of epoxy resin, ensuring every inch was covered. The noxious scent filled the air.

"Next," he said, layering another fiberglass sheet over the wet first layer. "Press it down. Make sure it makes full contact. Then, add another layer of epoxy."

Caleb nodded. "So, we're just stacking them up?"

"Like bulletproof lasagna," Mason replied. "Be sure there are no bubbles or gaps. Each layer needs to be perfect. Bullets and shrapnel have a way of finding weak spots, so we can't have any. We'll layer the sheets and add weight to press them while they dry. Once cured, the panels will be hard as a rock but flexible enough to absorb and distribute force."

Once they had built up about an inch of fiberglass and epoxy, Mason and Caleb laid a piece of plastic wrap over the still-wet laminate armor, then they set a piece of plywood on top. Finally, they put various heavy objects from around the garage—spare parts, a wheel, tools—on top of the board to press the fibers below.

"We'll leave this panel to cure for a while," Mason said.

"So, this protects the doors. But what about the windows?" Caleb asked.

"I have another trick for those. Let's get these other door panels layered up and set to cure."

Once they were done cutting and layering fiberglass on the other door panels, they switched to the windows. First, Mason showed Caleb how to trace the shape of Longhorn 2's windows around the inside of the frame using painter's masking paper and a marker. Then, they cut out the traced shape and placed it on a sheet of quarter-inch Lexan. Mason then traced the paper shape onto the bullet-resistant plastic.

"Lexan is a polycarbonate," Mason said. "Nearly 250 times stronger than glass, but with only half the weight."

Donning his eye protection, he used a rotary tool to cut the Lexan perfectly to size.

Handing the paper template to Caleb, he said, "Now, your turn. Cut another one the same as the one I just cut."

Caleb obliged, carefully following Mason's instructions. Once they had two pieces of Lexan cut, they carried them to the Suburban. Caleb passed a tube of superglue to Mason. He twisted the cap off, the pungent aroma of the adhesive hitting the air. Working methodically, he applied a generous layer of glue around the edges of a Lexan sheet. The clear adhesive shimmered in the overhead garage lights. Holding the Lexan by its edges, he carefully aligned it with the inside of the window. Then, with a firm press, the Lexan adhered to the glass. He held it while Caleb put clamps around to hold the plastic sheet in place while the glue cured. Stepping back, Mason wiped away the excess adhesive with a cloth. The added interior layer was invisible from the outside.

"So, now you've got a layer of laminated auto glass, then another layer of Lexan. That could save your life," Mason said.

"Yeah, but how do you roll the window down?" Caleb asked.

"You don't," Mason replied. "Let's go check the panels."

The men worked through the day, removing door panels, cutting Lexan, and layering fiberglass sheets. After removing the heavy garage parts from the tops of the boards, the two men broke the freshly cured armor away from the door panels. The fiberglass was rough, but Mason showed Caleb how to trim them with a saber saw and sand down the rough edges. Once the presses were all disassembled and the armor panels trimmed, they wiped them off and sprayed them with a rubberized undercoating to seal in the glass fibers. Once dry, they carried the new ballistic panels to the SUV.

With Caleb's help, Mason aligned the first door panel with the door, adjusting to ensure that all the points matched. Reaching for his electric screwdriver, he fastened the panel. Once it was secured, Mason retrieved a reciprocating saw from the workbench. Caleb watched intently as Mason skillfully cut an opening into the laminate armor, ensuring the door handle from the other side could operate without obstruction. Despite the chattering and vibrating of the saw, the cut was clean, almost surgical. As the saw's noise subsided, Mason wiped the surface clean with a rag and checked the door handle's function. Smooth. He stepped back, admiring his work.

"We've just added another layer of defense," Mason remarked. "This wouldn't do shit in Iraq or Afghanistan where IEDs are the problem. But it will help against bullets. Even then, there's still a glaring weak point. What is it?" he quizzed Caleb.

Caleb realized what Mason was referring to. "The windshield."

Mason nodded, "Exactly. Our laminate armor and Lexan are makeshift solutions for flanking or oblique fire, but that windshield is a vulnerability. A big one."

Caleb pondered for a moment. "Can't we just add Lexan to the windshield, too?"

Mason shook his head. "It's not that simple. The windshield's curvature and the optical clarity needed for driving make it impossible. If we compromise the driver's visibility, we're just trading one danger for another."

Caleb sighed. "So, what do we do?"

"Simple. We don't drive toward people shooting at us."

Caleb laughed.

144

"Oh, one last thing," Mason said. "Follow me. This is the best part."

He led Caleb through the back door of the garage to the yard where the city once stored piles of sand and salt for de-icing the roads. Caleb noticed a shovel and a bundle of woven polypropylene bags next to a sand pile eight feet tall.

"One of the oldest, cheapest, and still best protections known to man is dirt. Dirt is our friend. You're going to shovel this sand into those bags."

Caleb looked confused. "What for?" Caleb asked.

"We—or rather you—are then going to stack them behind the rear seats of Longhorns 2 and 3. I think ten bags per truck should do it. That gives us some protection from attacks from the rear."

"Are you serious?" Caleb looked back at the sand pile.

"Yep." Mason clapped him on the shoulder and walked back inside.

The sun had set long ago, and everyone else had left for the day. Mason straightened up the garage, showered in the locker room, and got dressed in jeans and a denim shirt. He stuffed his pistol in a leather holster inside his waistband, then walked down the hallway to The Colonel's office. The door was closed. He removed a jingling key chain from his pocket and unlocked the office door. Just inside, on the floor, were two black nylon duffle bags. He grabbed both by the handles and lifted them. He locked the office door behind him, then carried the bags out the back door to the employee parking lot.

Outside, it was dark. Mason scanned the parking lot, making sure he recognized every vehicle. He looked closely for shadows behind cars and reflections in windows and mirrors. Once he was sure the parking lot was clear, he continued walking to his Bronco. He was parked next to an oak tree bordering the rear parking lot. Bud stuck his head out from under the vehicle and, upon seeing Mason, dashed towards him. The tie-out attaching his collar to the tree brought him up short, so he waited eagerly, tail wagging, for Mason to come within petting distance.

"How you doing, boy?" Mason asked. "Have a rough day laying under the truck? See any hot chicks?"

At the Bronco, Mason loaded both duffels into the back. Then he swapped

Bud's tie-out for a leash and loaded the dog into the passenger seat. He climbed in the driver's seat, handed Bud a treat from a bag in the cupholder, and drove home. At the RV, Mason unloaded the black duffle bags and tied Bud's leash to the trailer's hitch. Bud looked up at him eagerly.

"You wait here," he said. "I'll be right back."

Lifting the black bags, Mason walked down the path toward the construction site. He returned empty-handed a few minutes later.

Exhausted, he grabbed a beer from the refrigerator and collapsed onto the small, worn sofa. He kicked off his boots and turned on the TV. An old movie channel was playing "The Green Berets" starring John Wayne. Without taking a sip of beer, Mason fell asleep with Bud's head in his lap.

The RV was still. The only sound was crickets chirping from the surrounding fields. Mason was in a light sleep, the day's exertions lingering in his muscles. Outside, a faint rustling blended with the noises of the night. A figure silhouetted by the moonlight stealthily approached Mason's Bronco parked outside the trailer. The figure wore a black mask, and his gloved hands carried a tool. He lowered himself and began inching under the Bronco's underbelly.

Suddenly, a low growl broke the quiet. Bud's ears perked up inside the trailer and his nostrils flared. In a flash, the Dalmatian bolted through the doggy door, his white and black body a streak against the night. The intruder barely had time to look up before Bud lunged under the Bronco, teeth bared and snarling. The man in black yelped, taken off-guard, dropping his tool with a clatter. Bud bore him down, the dog's jaws clamping onto the trespasser's forearm.

Mason was jolted awake by the sudden commotion. He sat up quickly, listening. In two steps, he was at the trailer's door. He flicked on the exterior lights. Bud stood protectively near the truck, barking furiously while a man wearing all black scrambled backward, clutching an injured arm.

Mason reached for his pistol on the couch and threw the RV's door open, the metallic creak slicing through the silence. He cleared the steps and covered the man with his muzzle, the pistol steady in his hand.

"Show me your hands! Show me your hands now!" he bellowed.

Bud was leaping and barking, growling furiously at the injured man. The intruder was frozen on the ground, his eyes darting between Bud's thrashing teeth and the cold steel of Mason's pistol. His breathing was rapid and shallow.

"Show me your hands, or I will shoot!" Mason barked again. "Last warning!"

The man flinched and threw his hands up, still trying to fend off the dog and cover his bleeding arm at the same time.

"Do you have a weapon?" Mason barked, his muzzle never leaving the intruder's body.

The man, panting heavily from pain and fear, shook his head rapidly. "No, no, man! I... I just wanted the catalytic converter. I'm just... I'm just trying to score." His voice quivered as he gripped his bleeding arm.

Mason aimed his gun, seeing the man's filthy attire and twitching movements.

"Lay out flat on your stomach and stretch your arms above your head. Don't reach for shit. I'll blow your head off and go watch 'The Wheel of Fortune' like nothing. Now, roll over," Mason ordered.

The injured man complied. As soon as he was on his stomach, Mason was on him. He placed a knee in the center of the man's back. Keeping his muzzle aimed at the man's head, Mason quickly patted him down. He felt something in his pocket.

"What's that?" he asked.

The man didn't respond.

"Huh? What is in your pocket? Is it a weapon?" Mason grabbed the man by the ski mask and yanked it off. He was hit with the smell of unwashed human body and sweat.

"It's just my pipe and shit, man. It's just my fucking pipe," he said. His body relaxed, and he laid his head on the ground in exhausted surrender.

Mason retrieved the object from the man's pocket. It was a glass pipe, caked with burned drug residue.

Mason sighed deeply, lowering his weapon slightly. "Damn tweaker," he muttered.

Gingerly, the intruder grabbed his injured arm, a mixture of blood and saliva smeared across it. "Please, man... I'm really hurt. Please, just let me go."

Mason glanced at his truck, then back to the junkie.

"Shut the hell up and lay there," he said.

Mason retrieved his cell phone from his pocket and dialed 9-1-1.

Mason put Bud on a leash and tied him to the trailer. He made the tweaker lie on the ground while he scratched Bud behind the ears. After a few minutes, a white Denver PD Tahoe pulled into the parking area, and a large officer climbed out. Mason explained the situation, and the officer handcuffed the thief before taking Mason's statement on a clipboard. As they were wrapping up, a white Chevrolet Caprice pulled next to the Tahoe, parked, and out stepped Detective Kim Wright.

As she walked toward them, her hand rested instinctively on her service weapon. "Mason?" she asked.

"Yes, that's me. Detective Wright, nice to see you. Caught this guy trying to steal from my truck."

Detective Wright's eyes briefly flicked to the injured man on the ground, noting the blood and fear in his eyes. "When I heard the call from here at the GZD construction site, I decided to come see."

"This one looks like a wrap. How's your other investigation going, with the missing cannabis?" Mason asked.

"I spoke to Rhonda earlier today, in fact. She informed me that there are 14 black duffle bags missing from the original order."

"Hm," Mason said. "What does that mean for Green Zone?"

"Not much," Kim shrugged. "The bags are generic, sold by various distributors all over the U.S. You can even buy them directly from China. So, tracking the bags as a lead won't get far."

Mason looked at her. "So, what does that mean for you?"

"It means I am still interested in how three pounds of weed made it from secure storage to the Dark Web. Do you have any theories, Mason?"

"Not a clue," Mason responded. "I'm busy enough trying to keep the crackheads away from my catalytic converter."

Kim stared Mason in the eyes without blinking.

"Are you ok, Mason? You seem a little unsteady, and you're stammering a bit. Have you had a bit to drink tonight? Maybe smoke a little bit?"

"No and no," Mason replied. "And you know, it's late and I'm tired. Are we done here?"

Kim watched him a moment longer.

"Sure. As for this," she gestured to the man on the ground, "we'll process him. Somebody may call you to follow up."

She then took a step closer to Mason, her eyes locking onto his. "I'll be around to make sure things are straight."

"I look forward to it," he replied.

Mason watched her leave, then took the leashed dog inside. He sat on the couch, wide awake, then looked at Bud, who was lying on the floor chewing the rubber sole of his former running shoes. The dog had a red scratch on his muzzle from his fight with the thief.

"Good boy," Mason chuckled. "You earned yourself a steak."

The TV was playing reruns of "I Love Lucy." Mason resisted the urge for almost half an hour before retrieving a bottle of Smirnoff and a shot glass from the kitchen.

16

Trap

The first glow of the morning sun lit the sky as the rumble of engines echoed loudly down the street, lined with warehouses and other businesses. Moose and Okwaho, riding their motorcycles side by side, turned onto the road leading to the GZD office, the tinted visors of their helmet's masking their faces.

Moose's fingers twitched, readying. Right as they passed the driveway into the GZD lot, he pulled a clenched fist from his pocket filled with dull gray, broad-headed, roofing nails. With a nonchalant swing of his arm, he scattered them onto the asphalt. Okwaho followed Moose's lead, dropping his own handful of nails right in front of the Green Zone Defense's main driveway. Then, without stopping, they rode on.

Later, after the sun had risen, the overhead doors rolled up, and Ali eased Longhorn 2 out of the garage. He adjusted the rearview mirror and checked his pickup list. Matt Anderson rode shotgun, an M4 carbine next to his leg. They exited the GZD parking lot, took a right, and headed out for their pickups. As Ali guided them on their route for almost two blocks, the tire pressure monitoring system set off a warning light on the dash. A rear tire was losing air rapidly.

"Looks like we have a flat," Ali said.

"Yeah? Damn. Ok, I'll call it in," Matt replied.

Reaching for the radio handset, Matt pressed the comm button. "Base, I've got dropping pressure on the rear driver's-side tire. Looks like we've got a flat."

There was a brief pause before Rhonda replied. "Head to Kenny's Wheelhouse. It's the tire shop we use a couple of blocks down from the office. Do you know it?"

"Roger that. Longhorn 2 is en route to Kenny's Wheelhouse," Matt said and set the handset down.

Ali turned the vehicle around and headed back, driving slowly on the deflated tire. Pulling into Kenny's Wheelhouse, Ali maneuvered the Suburban into an open bay and stepped out. Both guards strolled through the shop's lobby door, a bell jingling with their entry. Kenny looked up from the counter.

"Good morning," Ali greeted. "We've got a flat. Think I might've run over something."

Kenny nodded, taking the vehicle keys. "Alright. Parked it in the bay?"

Ali confirmed with a nod. "Yes. Rear driver's-side."

"OK," Kenny said. He walked out from behind the counter, through a swinging door, and into the garage area.

From another bay, Robeur's eyes tracked the exchange. Leaning against a tire rack and wearing blue workman's coveralls, he wiped his greasy hands on a rag. He could see one of the Suburban's back tires was a dead flat. He set the rag down, picked up a canvas tool bag, and walked over.

"These gentlemen look important," Robeur said as he approached Kenny. "I can handle this. What size tire is that?"

Kenny squinted at the tire, then at Robeur. "You get down there and see. You're the one with young knees."

Robeur squatted and read the numbers printed on the tire.

"I think we have these in stock, boss," Robeur said.

"Well, then knock this out. They probably need to get back to work," Kenny said, and he waddled back inside the air-conditioned office.

Behind the cover of the Suburban, Robeur crouched low. His canvas tool bag sat on the ground near him. Through the glass partition, he could see Kenny talking to the GZD guards—a big black man who looked like he could lift the

Suburban overhead, and a balding white man with wrap-around sunglasses and a serious expression. Both men wore body armor and carried pistols on their hips. He tried not to stare as he broke the lug nuts loose and jacked the SUV up. Kenny spoke to the guards briefly, then walked back behind his desk. The white guard leaned against the wall, pulled out his cell phone, and started swiping. The black guard sat in one of the waiting chairs, looking at the lobby TV.

With nobody watching, Robeur unzipped his tool bag, revealing a long package. Four red sticks of gel dynamite were bundled together with electrical tape. There was a touchscreen cell phone and a battery pack taped to the bomb.

Inside the waiting room, Matt Anderson suddenly stood up, his attention focused on the Suburban. Robeur froze, leaving the device inside the bag. Matt leaned over to Ali and said something as Robeur watched. Both of them peered through the glass partition into the garage, their eyes fixed on the Suburban. Ali nodded and pointed through the glass. With that, Matt walked briskly through the swinging door into the garage and headed straight towards him. Robeur, crouching beside the vehicle, felt his heart race.

Matt walked through the garage, around the front of the Suburban, and directly to the driver's side where Robeur was working. As he rounded the front of the vehicle, he stopped and looked Robeur in the eyes.

"How's it going?" Matt asked.

"Huh?" Robeur stammered. "Good, good. Uh, got the wheel off. Just checking the wheel bearing and the wheel well per, uh, policy."

"Yeah?" Matt asked, tipping his head, his eyes searching around Robeur's tools. "Are you always that thorough?"

"I actually just started here, so I couldn't say," Robeur deflected.

"Oh?" Matt said, his gaze fixed piercingly on Robeur. "You know what you're doing, though?"

"Oh, yes sir," Robeur said. "It's not my first rodeo."

"Good, good," Matt said, his eyes lingering a moment longer.

Robeur felt a bead of sweat run all the way from his armpit, down his ribs, to his waistband.

Matt placed his hand on the driver's door handle, then opened it, reached inside, and pulled out the end of a cellphone charging cable.

"Phone died. Have to plug it up," he said as he connected his phone to the charger.

Robeur, still crouched by the tire, said, "Yeah, I hate when that happens. This won't take much longer," he replied, swallowing hard, his hands shaking.

Matt gave him a brief nod and walked back towards the lobby. Once Matt was out of sight, Robeur let out a quiet sigh of relief. After a quick glance around to make sure no one was watching, he retrieved the bomb from his tool bag. He closed his eyes and said a silent prayer. Holding his breath, he powered on the mobile phone connected to the battery pack and detonator.

The phone's screen flashed, beeped, then went dark. Robeur exhaled in relief.

Sounds from the shop were loud: the pneumatic hiss of air wrenches, Kenny shouting at someone, a radio playing somewhere. Nobody noticed as Robeur popped out the retainer clips and pried open a section of the plastic wheel well liner. Nobody noticed when he carefully placed the bomb behind the rear driver's-side wheel well and secured it to the vehicle with tie wire. Nobody saw his hands shaking as he replaced the clips, or the sweat dripping down his face as he worked the tire changer and wheel balancer despite the cool temperature.

Once the wheel was replaced, Robeur wiped the area clean of fingerprints. He pressed the button for the lift to lower the Suburban, then backed it out of the bay and into the parking lot, parking it near the front door. The guards came out of the tire shop just as Robeur put the Suburban in park. Ali walked around the front and waited for Robeur to get out.

"You're good to go," Robeur said, climbing out the driver's door, wiping his hands on a yellow rag, aiming his biggest smile into the guard's face.

The guard smiled back. "Thanks a lot. Take it easy now."

Ali climbed in, and Robeur closed the door for him, making sure he only touched it with the rag. Once Matt was in the passenger seat, they drove off. Robeur grinned and waved as he watched them go, soaked in sweat, an icy fist squeezing his stomach.

The dim light inside the cabin pooled over the worktable Bruno had set up in the living room. It was covered in electronic gear: a laptop computer, soldering iron, clamps and vices, a swing arm magnifying glass, and numerous gadgets. Bruno was seated on a stool at the table, wearing a flannel shirt and black jeans. He wore a pair of reading glasses low on his nose.

Okwaho was seated on the couch, staring into space. Raison was standing in front of the fireplace wearing black cowboy boots, black jeans, and a black T-shirt. He was holding a water bottle and only half listening to Matheo, who was animatedly talking about something. A white sheet was nailed to the wall over the fireplace.

The cabin's front door opened, and in walked Rage and Robeur. Robeur was wearing his blue overalls from Kenny's Wheelhouse, his face still showing streaks of dirt and grease. Rage walked through the living room to the kitchen, opened a bottle of Jamison, and poured some into a glass. He cracked two ice cubes from the plastic tray, returned it to the freezer, and joined the rest of the Dead Wolves MC in the living room. He sat on the sofa next to Okwaho and kicked his booted heel onto the coffee table next to a digital projector.

"All right, let's get to it," Raison said. "This is a club business meeting now. That means no bullshitting."

The room turned somber. Everyone watched Raison closely.

"Robeur, cut the lights," Raison instructed.

The room dimmed save for the late afternoon sunlight filtering through the closed curtains.

"Go ahead, Bruno," Raison said.

Bruno tapped a computer key, and the digital projector flashed a square of light onto the white bed sheet stretched over the fireplace. A video played. It was daytime and appeared to be a high-angle view of a commercial building. The building was white with green trim and had three large bay doors on one side. The garage doors all opened, and in sequence, three dark blue suburbans rolled out. The convoy paused momentarily, then turned right out of the driveway and vanished off the edge of the screen.

Another clip played. The sun was at about the same angle, but there were more clouds in the sky that day. Again, the garage doors rolled up, and the suburbans rolled out. This time, however, they took a left turn out of the parking lot.

Bruno doubled the playback speed. Another clip played, this time twice as fast. Another day, same Suburbans. Again-and-again the clips played. Sometimes the Suburbans turned right, sometimes left. Sometimes it was one suburban, sometimes all three.

Raison took a sip of water. "Let's talk about Green Zone Defense, or GZD, as they are called. Based out of Denver, the company was started last year by a former military officer and police chief. They collect green from a lot of dispensaries around town. And by green, I mean both weed and cash. They collect and store cash for the growers and dispensaries. The banks won't touch the drug money, and sometimes sellers have hundreds of thousands of dollars invested in inventory. Men with evil intent know this, so the dispensaries hire GZD to store their bulk inventory for them."

The image on the projector changed to a demonstration video of a man firing an AK-47 at an armored Suburban. The windshield shattered, but the bullets did not penetrate. Same with the quarter panels. The rounds left deep dents but did not pierce the armor plating.

"GZD's setup involves three Chevy Suburbans," Raison continued. "One is a fully decked-out armored beast, like you see here. But the other two wagons don't appear to be armored."

The men watched closely, the light from the projector flickering across their faces.

"Let's talk more about GZD's head honcho," Raison said, motioning to Bruno.

Bruno tapped a computer key and the image on the bed sheet changed to the picture of a stern, middle-aged man in a police uniform.

"This is Mack Radford, known to his people as 'The Colonel.' Retired marine officer and former Denver police chief. He saw heavy action in Iraq where he led U.S. Marines in Nasiriyah and Fallujah. After retiring from the military, he was a cop in Denver for about ten years. He quit to start GZD last year. Now he's making big money in the legal weed business."

Taking a sip of water, Raison continued. "He's not just a businessman. Radford is hands-on. He even suits up and rides with his crew on pickups sometimes. The rest of the guards are ex-cops and ex-soldiers. There is no way of knowing how good they are at their jobs. But you have to wonder about guys who were busting weed dealers a year ago and are now trafficking weed themselves."

The men chuckled and shook their heads. The image on the bed sheet changed to blueprints.

"We pulled the engineering drawings for the GZD office from the city. The city built this building in the '90s for snowplows and salt trucks, but they stopped using it. The Colonel bought it last year and renovated it. We also learned he's building a new office and training center outside of Golden. It's not open yet, but that shows you how much money this guy is raking in."

Matheo and the others nodded.

"For now, they're in this old snowplow building. That must be where they store the cash and the weed. Through process of elimination, we believe they are storing the money in this room," Raison said, pointing at the blueprints.

"All this money we keep hearing about," Rage leaned forward, "and you're telling me it's just inside this regular building? Do they have a vault in there?"

"City plans don't show a vault," Bruno said.

Raison shrugged. "Might not be a vault. They could use safes."

Rage frowned and leaned back on the sofa.

"When we hit the GZD office, we need as much time as possible. They have every type of security they can get in this place. It may not be a bank, but it's still locked down tight," Raison said.

"When they renovated," Bruno interjected, "they added security cameras everywhere. There are keypads to enter certain areas, steel doors with steel frames, motion sensors, all that."

"Damn," Moose said.

"Relax. This isn't impossible," Raison said. "We have a plan to defeat everything they've got. Here's what we know. Every day, GZD sends out one of their Suburbans for regular cash pickups from specific dispensaries.

That's their daily grind, running just one truck."

He paused, letting the information sink in before he added, "But every Monday, it's a different story. On Mondays, they roll out with a full caravan of all three wagons. It's their big haul day, collecting from a wide network of dispensaries. So, all day Monday, most of their workforce is out on the streets and away from the office."

He locked eyes with each man, ensuring he had their undivided attention. "Our best move? Distract the local police, then ambush the Suburbans during Monday pickups. Hit them hard, hit them fast. If we do it right, we cripple their response team. They won't be able to rally and reinforce the GZD office in time, which will give us time and space to breach the office and crack the vault or safes or whatever they've got in there."

He leaned forward, his voice dropping an octave. "We don't want a firefight at the GZD office. We want them scrambling, out in the open, away from their stronghold."

"Wait," Rage piped up again. "So, we ambush their convoy in the streets, and we hit their building to raid their safes or whatever at the same time?"

Raison lifted his head and challenged his younger brother with a piercing look. "You act like we haven't run dual missions before. We just did it in Toronto, remember?"

Rage shook his head. "Toronto was different. Those were clowns. This is a fucking bank robbery *and* an armored car robbery at the same time. Look at our numbers. We can't be in two places at once. It's too crazy, even for you."

The room was silent.

"You are correct," Raison said. "That's why Tommy Boy is sending reinforcements."

Matheo's eyebrows raised. "Big Machine is sending backup?"

"Well," Rage said, turning up his whiskey glass and draining it. "Now it's a fucking party."

17

Punishment

Kim, her husband, Mike, and their son, Xavier, sat at the kitchen table.

"Xavier, what happened the other day at the mall was not just a mistake. It was dangerous and irresponsible. You could have hurt someone, or gotten seriously hurt yourself," Kim began.

Xavier shifted uncomfortably in his chair. "I know, Mom. I just thought it would be funny."

"Hush," Mike said sternly, and Xavier looked at the table.

"That's exactly the problem. You don't think about the consequences. Actions have repercussions, and you need to learn that," Kim said, her decision weighing heavily on her heart. "Which is why we've decided you're going to spend the rest of the summer at your grandfather's place in Arkansas."

Xavier's head shot up, disbelief and panic crossing his face. "What? No, you can't send me to the country. There's no internet there. How will I talk to my friends? How will I... how will I do anything?"

"Maybe doing 'anything' is the problem," Mike spoke up. "You need time away from all these distractions, away from the internet and this need to impress others with dangerous stunts."

"But it's the middle of nowhere. And Grandpa's idea of fun is waking up at dawn to fix fences. That's not fair." Xavier protested, his voice rising in desperation.

"Fair would have been facing legal consequences for your actions today, Xavier. This is a chance for you to reset, to think about the decisions you make and who you want to be. Your grandfather has a lot to teach you, about responsibility, about hard work, and about being part of something bigger than yourself," Kim countered.

Xavier slumped in his chair, the fight draining out of him. "It's going to be so boring, Mom. I don't see how this is going to help."

"It's not about being entertained every minute of every day, Xavier. It's about learning and growing. You might not see it now, but this experience will change you for the better. I believe in you, and I believe this is what you need right now," Kim said.

"I guess I don't have a choice, do I?"

"No, you don't. But how you choose to approach this experience, that's entirely up to you," Mike replied.

With that, Mike and Kim dismissed the boy to start packing.

After Xavier left the table, the room was filled with a heavy silence. Mike and Kim exchanged glances. Kim let out a sigh, her gaze following Xavier's retreat.

"Do you think he'll hate us?" Kim finally broke the silence, her voice laced with worry and second-guessing.

Mike squeezed her hand reassuringly. "He's a smart kid, Kim. He's going to come out of this stronger and more mature. It's just going to take some time for him to see the bigger picture. And his grandpa? He's the best kind of teacher for what Xavier needs right now."

"I hope you're right," Kim murmured, leaning into Mike's embrace.

18

Mentorship

At the end of his Friday shift, Mason dressed in the locker room in jeans and a Carhart hunting jacket. He had a flask of peppermint schnapps in his gym bag. After a quick look around, he took a swig, tucked the bottle into his inside coat pocket, and clocked out. As he left, he passed The Colonel's office, unlocked the door, and retrieved a black duffle bag, which he brought with him. He walked outside and found Bud in his usual spot, in the dirt under the Bronco. He swapped the wire lead for a leash and opened the passenger door for the dog to load up.

Captain Doug Frazier, a tall and formidable man with salt-and-pepper hair, a cowboy hat, and a permanent furrow in his brow, was standing at his crew cab pickup parked next to Mason. He opened the rear door and hung a garment bag inside. Then he turned and watched as Mason loaded the dog and shut the Bronco's door.

"People already think this is a firehouse, Mason," Doug said. "The Dalmatian isn't helping. Folks are going to think we're in the kitten-saving business."

"I promise to never save a kitten, Captain," Mason said.

"Hell, no," Doug replied. "Only Superman can save kittens *and* fight bad guys. The rest of us have to be mean sons-of-bitches. I'm sure they taught you that in the Army."

Mason laughed, and the captain smiled.

"Have a great weekend, Mason. We need to go hunting soon. Maybe The Colonel will let us hunt his place this year."

"He just might. Have a great weekend, sir," Mason tipped his ball cap toward the captain, then walked around to the Bronco's driver's side. He got in and closed the door. Bud was restless, climbing in Mason's lap, tail thumping back and forth against the seat and dash.

"Whoa, Bud, whoa!" Mason said, trying to fend off the licking, nuzzling ball of black and white.

He petted and scratched the dog until he calmed down, feeding him treats from his palm. As he was petting Bud, he took a few swigs from the flask of schnapps. The parking lot was mostly empty, everyone having gone home for the weekend. But across the lot, Mason saw Caleb sitting in his truck. Feeling loose from the schnapps, Mason climbed out of his Bronco and started walking.

The idling engine of Caleb's trick thrummed as he approached. Through the window, Mason saw Caleb studying his phone closely, not paying attention. He crept up and rapped on Caleb's window sharply with his knuckles. Through the glass, he saw Caleb jump so suddenly he dropped his phone. Mason laughed and pointed for Caleb to roll his window down. Caleb hesitated.

"Roll it down," Mason said out loud.

There was a moment's hesitation, but finally, the window lowered.

"What's up, Mason?" Caleb asked. Mason noticed a slight tensing of his jaw.

"Just checking in," Mason said, leaning into the window gap, his nostrils flaring at a familiar scent. "What's up with you? How was your day? Any issues on your runs?"

Caleb shifted in his seat, eyes darting momentarily around before refocusing on Mason. "Nah, everything was smooth. Same old, same old."

Mason hummed in acknowledgment, "Good, good. We need to maintain that consistency. You know, it's not just about the pickups. It's about building trust with the dispensaries."

Caleb nodded. "Yeah, I get that. Every link in the chain matters."

There was a beat of silence, then Mason's gaze sharpened, his nose twitching. "Hey, you mind telling me why your truck smells like a dispensary right now? Did you fall into a pile of weed or something?"

Caleb's face drained of color and his eyes widened as he stammered for an answer. Mason's sharp eyes quickly zeroed in on a bulky black duffel in the backseat.

Pointing a finger to the bag, Mason's voice took on a harder edge. "What's that?"

Caleb avoided Mason's gaze, the panic clear on his face. "That? Oh, it's just some gear. Y'know, personal stuff."

"Personal stuff? Hm, smells like it." He leaned in closer and sniffed, his eyes never leaving Caleb's. "I really hope that's not what I think it is, kid."

Caleb licked his dry lips, trying to muster an explanation. "Look, Mason, it's just some personal stash, okay? For the weekend."

Mason's eyebrows knitted together. "Personal stash? You think I don't recognize one of our duffel bags? Unlock the doors."

Caleb's voice wavered. "Man, come on. We can talk about this, right?"

"No talking. Unlock the doors. Now!"

Caleb started to protest, then let out a slow sigh. The click of the doors unlocking was as loud as a gunshot. Mason pulled the rear door open and reached in to pull the black bag out into the dull light of the overcast afternoon. The zipper slid open easily, revealing tightly packed bags of cannabis, their aromatic potency slicing through the crisp air. Mason inspected the contents, his face stony and impassive.

"Personal stash? This is, what, five pounds?" Mason said.

The words seemed stuck in Caleb's throat, but he choked them out, "Mason, I... I'm sorry."

"Out. Now," Mason's voice was icy as he opened Caleb's door.

Caleb hesitated momentarily, then complied, pushing the door open. He took a shaky step out onto the dirt.

"Take it," Mason said, thrusting the duffel at Caleb, waiting for the younger man's fingers to grip the handles. Caleb took the bag and let his arms hang down.

He spoke, his voice quivering, "Look, Mason, I can explain—"

Without warning, Mason swung. Three hooks, right-left-right, precise and brutal, landed in quick succession on Caleb's ribs. Before the third sting could fully register, an open-handed slap caught Caleb square on the side of his face. The force sent him stumbling into the side of the truck.

Gazing up from the asphalt, eyes glassy, Caleb looked at Mason, stunned. The duffel bag, momentarily forgotten, lay between them. Mason stood over Caleb panting, jaw clenched, fingernails digging into his palms. All Mason could hear was his heart thudding like the blades of a distant helicopter. He stood towering over Caleb. His eyes blazed with rage when he grabbed the younger man by the collar, yanking him hard.

"You think this is a game?" Mason shouted into his face.

Caleb, still dazed, shook his head, a red welt forming on his cheek.

"Your father gives you a chance to be a man, and you steal from him? You're the reason the cops are coming around. He barely gets the business going and you're already trying to tear it down, you little shitheel."

Caleb stuttered and tried to respond, his head spinning, barely able to breathe from the pain in his ribs.

"Get up," Mason said, grabbing the younger man by the shirt and pulling him to his feet.

"Go home," Mason ordered, pointing sternly to the driveway. "Get the fuck out of here before I kick your selfish ass back to the ungrateful place you came from."

Bent over in pain and panting, trying to catch his breath, Caleb climbed back into his truck, started the engine, and drove off. As he pulled away, Mason saw tears running down his cheeks.

He stood for a few moments, catching his breath, trying to relax. Clutching the duffel bag tightly, his chest heaving, Mason walked to the office's back door. With a swipe of his key card, he was back inside. He walked down the hall to the steel door behind Rhonda's work area, where he punched his code into the keypad and entered with the stolen duffel bag, closing the door behind himself.

19

Brothers

Denver's autumn night was alive under the glow of streetlights. The sidewalks in the older part of the city, with its combination of vintage brick townhouses and newer steel construction, were filled with people out for a good time. Here and there, an old neon sign buzzed, illuminating the entrance of a long-standing tavern or a late-night diner. Tree branches, their leaves turning yellow and red, rustled gently in the breeze. People, in pairs or small groups, walked about. Some stepped out of establishments, laughter trailing them. Others walked dogs, the animals occasionally sniffing at something before being gently tugged away.

The activity made it difficult for Bruno and Raison to do their work with no one noticing. They strolled along the sidewalk, allowing people to pass, absorbed in their conversations. Both men wore jackets and blue jeans. Raison wore a ball cap pulled low, while Bruno wore a blue knitted beanie and a black hoodie.

They strolled to a corner and paused. Raison leaned against a brick wall and lit a cigarette. Bruno, hands in his jacket pockets, glanced around as if people-watching on a Saturday night. When no one was near, he removed his hands from his pocket, coming out with a handheld device the size of a camera. Placing it to his eye, he scanned from building to building, the digital range finder capturing distances, while his eyes noted specific architectural features and potential cover points. Raison pulled a GPS device from his back pocket and began marking points, occasionally glancing up to match reality with the device's digital display. As they walked, Bruno also used his cell phone to take photos of the surrounding street. They photographed doorways, windows, and alleys.

A blue and white RTD bus trundled past, its windows reflecting the neon lights as the men quietly surveyed the street, mixing in with the evening revelers. Once they were done, they walked back to the parked Toyota Land Cruiser they had borrowed from the cabin. Raison climbed into the driver's seat while Bruno entered the passenger side, and they drove away slowly, allowing drunken pedestrians to cross.

"Raison, can I ask you something?" Bruno began. "Why is it you and Rage don't get along? You're blood brothers, after all."

Raison exhaled a stream of cigarette smoke, his gaze fixed on the passing people. "Rage," he started, his voice tinged with a mix of frustration and fondness. "He's brave as a wolverine, and loyal as a sled dog. I've never doubted that. But his way of seeing things... it's too narrow, too impulsive. He doesn't always grasp the bigger picture."

Bruno nodded, understanding. "But you grew up together. That's got to count for something, right?"

"It does," Raison replied, his eyes reflecting a distant memory. "We've been through thick and thin. We have different fathers, you know. My father rode with the Devil Hounds. He died when a truck pulled out in front of him. I was still a baby. It messed my mom up. She was just about 19. She always said my dad was her true love. After he died, mom decided she liked getting high more than being a mom. She was running around all over with any club who would take her in. So, Rage... she never would tell us who his dad was. Could have been any biker in Quebec, or a hundred others just passing through. Rage and I are built differently, having different dads. It's not that I dislike him. It's just that he acts first and thinks later. I wish he'd weigh his choices better, since his decisions affect not just him, but all of us."

"Well," Bruno said, "I guess that's what he's got you for."

Raison sighed, and both men rode in silence from the city back to the cabin.

Meanwhile, across town, The Temptress Lounge came alive with vibrating bass and a dazzle of lights. The exterior was plain white stucco with a neon sign featuring the silhouette of a dancing woman. Inside, plush velvet seats lined the main stage where dancers displayed their bodies, moving fluidly with the rhythm of the music. There were elevated booths draped in red curtains along the back wall, and a long bar to the left.

Five Dead Wolves entered rudely and loudly. The bouncers let them through with a weary look. Rage led the way, wearing his black leather cut with the Dead Wolves MC patch emblazoned on the back. Okwaho followed, laughing at something Moose had said. Robeur took in the scene with an appreciative smirk while Matheo, sunglasses still on despite the dim lighting, headed straight to the bar.

Rage strolled through the club, strutting towards the stage. In one swift move, he tossed a handful of cash onto a table, catching the attention of several dancers. One of them, a slim blonde wearing a lime green fishnet body suit, glided over and whispered in his ear, trailing her long fingernails down his neck. He threw his head back and laughed.

Okwaho and Moose were soon in a heated drinking battle, shot for shot. They cackled hugely as they challenged each other to out-drink the other. Robeur, the youngest, got dragged away by a feisty Latina with a thigh tattoo to a private booth.

Matheo joined Rage and the blonde at the table near the main stage.

"Hi, I'm Margot," the blonde stripper said, holding her hand up to Matheo.

With an exaggerated grin, he took her hand and kissed it. "Oh, yeah? Margot, like the chick in Wolf of Wall Street?"

"That's right! She's so pretty," she said excitedly. "And Wolf, like on your jackets."

"That's right. But Matheo there is no Leonardo DiCaprio, I hate to tell you," Rage said, pulling her squealing into his lap.

"So," she asked, sitting on Rage's lap, poking the patches on his chest, "what's up with the Dead Wolves? Are you, like, outlaws?"

Rage gave a slow nod, taking a swig of his whiskey. "You could say that."

"How did you lose your hand?" she asked bluntly, tapping the plastic prosthesis with her nails.

"Well, shit," Rage chuckled, the sound rough and gritty, and took a sip. "Back when my brother, Raison, and I were kids—I was 12, so he was 14 or 15—we tried to steal this guy's bike. But this was no regular sled. It was a '91 Fat Boy, just like Arnold rode in Terminator 2."

He took another sip.

"My brother always has a plan. One of his favorite's is creating a distraction. He loves that one. Probably learned it from a movie."

A waitress in a black miniskirt and a red corset brought more drinks. Margot took a sip from a cosmopolitan.

"He says that to jack the bike from the back of the house, we have to create a distraction at the front. So, you know what I did?" Rage raised his eyebrows.

"What?" she asked.

"I lit the entire front of the house on fire," Rage said.

Margot's eyes bulged. "What? Damn!"

"Yeah, but that's not the craziest part," Rage continued. "So, it's nighttime. I'm hiding in the bushes in this guy's front yard, and Raison is in the back. I throw this fucking flaming Molotov cocktail—it's a beer bottle filled with gasoline, and you light it like a torch and throw it," Raison explained, "And I throw it, right? I throw this shit, and—woosh! — the porch goes up in a fireball. It's way more fire than I expected, and it's all on the front window, up the wall, the patio furniture. There's fire everywhere. Well, then the dude who lives there opens the front door, and he's like, 'What the fuck is going on?'"

He took a long drag on his cigarette. A bit of smoke went into his eye, and it squinted involuntarily.

"Well, he had this massive dog. More wolf than dog, really. As soon as he opened the door, this beast came straight at me like it could see in the fucking dark. It could smell me, I guess. But, no shit, it charged me like a grizzly bear."

Margot's eyes widened in anticipation. "Holy shit!"

"It rushed me and bit hard onto my hand, all teeth. Then it started shaking and pulling at me. It pulled me right out of the bushes, right in the open. But the homeowner..." Rage chuckled, "the homeowner was busy trying to put out the fire, so he didn't notice what was happening to me..."

Her mouth dropped open. "Holy shit!" she shouted. "A dog bit your fucking hand off?"

"Chewed it up so bad they had to amputate what was left."

"Oh, my god!" the exotic dancer declared. "So, did your brother come to help you, or what?"

Rage looked into the distance. He sighed, then took a sip from his drink and a drag from his cigarette.

"My brother said he didn't hear me screaming at the front of the house, because he was at the back, you know, cranking the bike up."

"Oh, my god," Margot whispered.

"Raison got the bike to crank and eventually came around to the front to get me. I was all fucked up. He drove into the yard and tried to hit the dog with the bike. It finally let go and we took off. The man was screaming and shit, it was wild. But we were screwed. My hand was basically hanging off and bleeding everywhere. My fingers were gone. We couldn't exactly go home, so Raison took me to the hospital. We got arrested there. "

"So, did y'all get in a bunch of trouble?"

Rage chuckled. "Two years each in Shawbridge Boys Farm for theft and arson."

"Damn," Margot said, still wide-eyed. "That's crazy. So, are you guys, like, cool now?"

"Me and my brother?" Rage asked, staring into space, lost somewhere in old memories. "Sure. We're cool."

Later that night, the neon lights of the gentlemen's club faded as Rage's motorcycle roared down the dark highway. The cool air was bracing. Behind him, Margot the stripper clung tight, her cheek buried against his back. Okwaho, Moose, Matheo, and Robeur followed on their bikes. They drove down Route 6 towards the mountains, the city fading as they followed their single headlight beams into the wilderness.

In time, the cabin appeared, its wooden porch glowing softly from a single bare bulb. They parked and dismounted. When they entered, Robeur lit the fireplace, its orange flames dancing and casting flickering shadows on the walls. The room smelled of old wood and cigarettes.

Margot noticed Bruno's gadget-covered workbench.

"Do you guys fix computers or something?" she asked.

Rage glanced up from taking off his jacket. "Yeah, my buddy. Always tinkering with computers and shit. But that's boring," he said, grabbing Margot by the arm and turning her away from the table and toward him. He pulled a plastic bag from his jacket pocket. "Ever tried shrooms?" he asked, holding up the bag of dried psychedelic mushrooms.

"Sure," she smiled, "I like to trip."

Rage smiled and took her by the hand. He led her down the hall, through the kitchen, and out the back door. Okwaho, Matheo, and Moose were already in the backyard, building a fire in the rock pit. The campfire's flames lapped hungrily at the air, sending tendrils of smoke spiraling upward, where they vanished into the inky fabric of the night sky. The fire cast a shifting orange glow over the yard, causing the shadows of the trees to elongate and contract as if in rhythm to a cosmic dance. Okwaho handed Rage and Margot each a beer, and they sat next to each other on a bench near the fire. Rage's face reflected the vibrant flames as he plucked a few of the long-dried mushrooms from the bag. He looked Margot in the eyes as he shoved them in his mouth and started chewing.

"Ew! I could never do that," she recoiled. "Aren't they so gross?"

Rage crunched them, then took a long swig of his beer and smacked his lips.

"Delicious!" he exclaimed. "Now, your turn." He held a handful of mushrooms up to Margot.

"Oh, no!" she laughed, taking them. "I can't just eat them like that."

"Yeah, you can. Hold your nose, shove them in, and chase them with the beer," Rage said, pushing her hand towards her face.

"Not all at once," she protested, turning away and fending off his hand.

"Come on, you can do it," he insisted. "Don't make me trip alone."

"I won't," she assured, "I just have to take them a little at a time."

She broke a piece off. Then, pinching her nose, she tossed it into her mouth, chewing quickly, then washing the fungi down with beer.

Rage passed the bag to Okwaho, who cried, "Ah, shit! It's on now."

He and Matheo whooped and hollered as they chomped down the magic mushrooms. Moose grabbed the bag and turned it upside down into his mouth. They all three howled at the moon. Margot laughed and snuggled closer to Rage.

They chatted for a while, waiting for the drugs to take effect, laughing at Matheo's and Okwaho's antics. Margot ran her finger along Rage's chest. The psychedelics eventually kicked in. Rage felt a wave of tingles wash over him. Sparks floating in the updraft over the fire turned into long streaks of orange neon against the night sky. The stars grew bigger, brighter. Each ember in the rock fire pit became a story, a fleeting moment of life. He watched ancient warriors in battle and demons dancing in the flames. Even in the cold of night, sweat beaded on his forehead.

Under the canopy of the night sky, the moon cast a milky glow over the backyard, its luminescent rays playing upon the trees and shrubs. Across from him, Margot, her green eyes shimmering with reflected starlight, was captivated by the sky. As the psilocybin took hold, the once mundane night sounds became an orchestral symphony of nature. The chirping of crickets was no longer just a sound but a series of colorful waves, each note splashing a different hue before her eyes. The rustle of leaves transformed into whispers of long-forgotten tales. Reaching out, Margot cupped her hands and watched liquid starlight run together and pool into them, dripping through her fingers in luminescent streams.

Rage stood shirtless, with a bottle of whiskey in his hand. He moved, his silhouette a writhing shadow against the bright moonlight. His feet thudded against the ground, each step an echoing beat synchronizing with the thrumming in his chest. The sweat on his thin tattooed torso caught the moonlight, turning him into a shimmering, ethereal figure. He drank from the bottle. His voice, raw and feral, melded with the whispers of the night as he howled at the stars.

Then the bottle was empty, so he threw it into the woods. He noticed his hands. In a moment of clarity, he realized the prosthetic hand was no longer a mere replacement. Instead, it had been transformed into a mystical artifact with supernatural powers. He held the rigid polymer to the sky and watched billions of stars flow down from the heavens and fill it with blinding white light. He couldn't believe his eyes.

Captivated, Margot sat on the bench, laughing and watching Rage lurch around, her eyes wide and filled with the reflected glow of the campfire. The flickering flames painted her face in a warm, orange hue, illuminating her features in a soft, dreamy light.

Rage spun around and stared at her. Drawing himself to his full height, he stalked directly to her, his intense gaze never wandering. As he stood before her, she smiled up at him.

"Woman!" he shouted. "I have been chosen to give you the eternal power that courses through me."

Margot smiled up at him, intoxicated, barely able to understand his words.

"Do you accept this gift of eternal power?" he asked officiously.

"Yes!" she said, her youthful face brimming with joy at their game.

"So be it!" Rage declared.

With that, he raised his prosthetic hand high and, with the force of all the stars in the sky, slammed it into the top of Margot's head. She shrieked, but a punch to the side of her jaw silenced her. Her long hair flew as he followed her over the bench and to the ground, both screaming, where he hammered her face with his magical hand. His hair stuck to his sweaty, blood-splattered chest as he hunched over her limp body, pounding and sweating.

"Have you been saved?" Rage screamed repeatedly. "Have you been freed now?"

"Oh, shit!" Matheo said when he saw what was happening.

He rushed over with Okwaho, and the two men fought to pull their screaming brother off the mangled young woman.

"I am free!" he screamed, spit flying as he fought against the other men. "We are all free!"

The rugged terrain surrounding the cabin lightened as the morning sun rose, cutting through the mist that settled in the valleys below. Birds chirped their sunrise serenades, and the stillness of the forest was occasionally interrupted by the distant sound of a creek bubbling along its course. Raison and Bruno drove their motorcycles up to the cabin and parked their bikes next to the others.

"I think we got what we need," Bruno said as the two men walked up the steps. "Give me your GPS device, and I'll get all the waypoints and ranges compiled."

Raison pulled off his leather riding gloves and hung his Ray-Ban sunglasses on the collar of his T-shirt. He handed the device to Bruno, and the two walked into the cabin. Stepping inside, the scene was in disarray. Empty beer bottles littered the floor. A haze of cigarette smoke hung in the air.

"Where are the others?" Bruno asked.

Raison continued walking through the cabin, checking the bedrooms. He found Robeur asleep in a bunk bed in the bedroom he shared with Moose, but Moose was not there.

Bruno smirked. "Looks like they had one hell of a party."

Raison heard a sound from another bedroom, so he walked down the hall to investigate.

Rage and Okwaho shared a bedroom. Okwaho was lying on one bed, flat on his back, shirtless, snoring. Matheo was on the other bed, fully dressed. Moose was naked on the floor, his head on Okwaho's riding boots, an Indian blanket barely covering his massive torso. Raison noticed red-brown splatters, like mud, on Moose's arms. Okwaho's clothes were filthy, and the room stank of booze and sour sweat. Raison walked over to Okwaho and shook him by the arm.

"Hey," he said, tugging it. "Okwaho, wake up!"

The sleeping Mohawk jerked awake suddenly, his eyes wild. Raison noticed how wide and black his pupils were.

"What the hell did y'all get into last night?" Raison asked.

Okwaho blinked and rubbed his eyes before sitting up and turning to put his feet on the ground. Raison watched patiently as his old friend took a moment to clear his groggy thoughts. Finally, with a big inhale, Okwaho stood up. He looked down at Moose's sleeping figure on the floor, then back at Matheo snoring on the other bed. Then he looked down at his hands and arms. His hands were primarily clean where he had washed them, but his forearms were streaked with crusty dried blood.

"Hey! Snap out of it," Raison insisted. "Where the fuck is Rage? Where is my brother?"

"Shit, I don't know, man," Okwaho said. "If he's not in here, then maybe outside."

Raison left the bedroom and stomped down the hall. The back door squealed as he stepped from the kitchen onto the rear steps, then down to the crushed granite and flagstone path leading to the stone fire pit. A wispy column of gray smoke drifted up from charred logs, and the distinct smell of campfire lingered in the morning air. The ground was damp with dew.

Raison could see Rage. He was sitting on the ground, leaning against a bench with his back to the cabin. He was shirtless, and as still as a statue. As Raison approached, he saw a cigarette burning between his brother's blood-crusted fingers.

"Bro, what the fuck?" Raison asked, stepping around to look him in the face.

Rage was awake, arms outstretched on the bench, legs extended, ankles crossed, casually smoking. Dried blood was splattered across his face and chest and down his jeans.

Rage stirred, groggily looking up at Raison. "Wha—?" he began, but Raison's fury cut him off.

"What happened? What is all this blood?" Raison shouted. He saw discarded clothes and empty beer cans scattered about. There was a jacket and some lacy undergarments in a wad near a bench. The clothes were covered in blood. Raison walked to them.

"What is this? Whose shit is this?" Raison demanded.

Rage continued staring into the smoking ashes. He took a drag from his cigarette, then stood up and looked around the yard, wavering on his feet. He looked at the ground, then patted his pocket to make sure he had his cigarettes.

"I never knew people put freezers inside barns," he said before flicking his cigarette into the fire pit and walking unsteadily past Raison and into the cabin.

Raison's eyes darted to the barn. He crossed the yard quickly, opened the barn's main door, then a smaller door inside leading to a feed room. The room was made of rough wood and smelled of dust and alfalfa. A white chest freezer sat humming against the far wall. As he walked to it, he could see bloody handprints on its glossy surface. The bottles and vials of veterinary medicine that had been inside were scattered haphazardly on the floor. With a knot forming in his throat, Raison pulled on a leather riding glove and opened the freezer.

Inside was the naked, bloodied, blue-gray body of a young woman. She was petite and thin. They had folded her corpse into the fetal position so she would fit. Her long blonde hair was matted with blood. She had colorful tattoos on her arm and thigh. Her face was pulverized, the blood and torn tissue crusted with ice.

Raison let the freezer's lid drop with a thump. Nostrils flaring, he stormed out of the barn, across the yard, and up the cabin steps. He was in the kitchen and in Rage's face in a blur.

The brothers were chest-to-chest, screaming, spit flying. Raison swung a left hook and caught his younger brother with a glancing blow to the side of the head. Rage swung, clocking Raison in the temple with his prosthetic hand. Raison staggered back, colliding with the refrigerator. He returned at Rage with a one-two punch combo, the straight right connecting with Rage's teeth, busting his bottom lip. Rage staggered against the kitchen table, where he picked up a screwdriver.

In a flash, Raison drew the Glock from his waistband, pointing it at the ground between them. The two brothers stared furiously across the kitchen.

Okwaho stumbled in. "Whoa! Shit! Chill out," he pleaded with the warring brothers.

Rage glared across the room. Shirtless, chest heaving, fresh red blood dripping from a split lip.

"Who the fuck is that in the freezer?" Raison demanded, pointing toward the barn with his gun.

"Some chick from last night," Okwaho spoke up. "A stripper from the Temptress. She came back to party. The shrooms were strong, man, like too strong. Raison, bro, please put the gun down."

"Why did you kill her, though?" Raison demanded.

"Whoa, whoa," Okwaho protested. "I didn't kill anybody, man. Hell, no." With that, he turned and walked out of the room, shaking his head.

Alone again, Raison stared at his brother. Rage was still holding the screwdriver.

"It was you. You killed her."

Rage smirked under his furrowed brow. "The stars killed her, motherfucker. What the fuck do you care?"

Gritting his teeth, Raison hissed, "You idiot! If the Americans catch you, they'll either execute you or throw you into a hole so deep you'll forget what the stars even looks like. And if Big Machine finds out what you've done in the middle of a job, it won't just be you they come for. It'll be all of us. What part of that do you not fucking understand?"

"Wait, wait, wait," Rage said, waving the screwdriver back and forth. "You think you can tell me who I can and can't kill, after what you did?"

Raison glared.

Rage stood up straight and licked his bleeding lip. "You think I don't know, brother? You think I don't know what you will do for power? What you've already done. You know exactly what I'm talking about. You gave me the vice president patch to shut me up. To distract me. That way I don't ask questions," Rage said, his eyelids lowering, "because you know how much Max and Bill meant to me. To all of us. And I know you had them killed."

Raison flinched. He stepped to the kitchen door and peaked down the hallway. Then he stepped close to Rage, their noses almost touching.

"Shut the fuck up," Raison said under his breath.

The brothers glared into each other's eyes, unblinking.

"Yeah, motherfucker," Rage finally said. "I knew it. I knew you set them up. It's the only thing that made sense. Now I know for sure. You got Max and Bill killed, you piece of shit."

"Max was snitching," Raison growled, his face turning purple. "Big Machine has members inside the Mounties. They showed me the file. He was trying to pin me and you for everything."

Rage sneered. "Bullshit! And Wild Bill? What did he do?"

Raison broke his stare and stepped away to the middle of the kitchen. He took several deep breaths, looked at the pistol in his hand, then looked out the kitchen window.

"Get rid of that body and clean up the yard," Raison commanded, his voice steely. "Pop sent backup, and they're supposed to be here soon. If they roll in here and see any hint of this, any sign of what went down last night, you'll probably be in the freezer next to her. We all will."

"They can sure fucking try," Rage snapped back.

Raison looked at his brother again. Then he put his sunglasses over his eyes, stuck the pistol into his waistband, and shouldered Rage hard as he passed on his way out of the kitchen.

"How did it feel? Seeing Marky overdose because his dad got killed, knowing you're the one who set him up? Huh? Did it make you feel like a king, brother?" Rage shouted, his voice chasing Raison down the hall. "Do you feel like a fucking king now?"

Outside, Bruno was leaning on the front porch, smoking. He stared at Raison as he stormed past, his heavy boots echoing on the wooden deck. The roar of Raison's motorcycle shattered the early morning stillness as he tore down the dirt path, scattering birds and rocks behind.

20

Strength

That same night, Mason drove the hundred feet from his travel trailer to the training center construction site, the hum of the Bronco a familiar background to his thoughts. The back of his SUV was piled with electrical boxes, tools, and spools of wire. As he opened the door to step out, Bud jumped ahead, tail wagging, surveying the surroundings quickly before settling in the shadows and watching his master.

Balancing himself on a ladder, Mason nailed light cans to the ceiling joists. His movements were methodical initially, carefully measuring the distances and ensuring everything was flush. As the night wore on, however, the fluid level in the bottle of Tito's he'd brought got lower and lower.

As he wired up the lights, the world tilted. Stepping down from the ladder, he winced in pain. His right knuckles ached from punching Caleb. Sitting on the bench, he removed the bottle of vodka from the Home Depot ice bucket and plunged his swollen hand into its place. He drained the last from the bottle, then let it fall to the ground with a loud clank. His hand went icy numb as he stared out into the night. He pulled it out and couldn't feel a thing.

Suddenly, in a rage, he swung his arm, knocking over a pile of electrical supplies. The metal boxes crashed loudly, echoing into the night, but he felt nothing with his numbed hand. He stormed into the kill house, picked up a crowbar, and swung it at a freshly hung light fixture, letting it shatter upon the ground, shards flying in all directions.

Bud jumped up and barked, startled by the sudden chaos. His ears lay flat as he backed away.

Mason flung the crowbar far across the room, sending it clanging along the concrete floor. He kicked over a sawhorse, causing a stack of lumber to fall, a stray board rapping him soundly on the shin. He cried out and fell to the ground. Rolling on his back, he cussed and held his stinging shin to his chest. Then he noticed blood. He held up his injured right hand. The already swollen knuckles were now cut and bleeding, too.

Mason curled into a ball on the concrete floor, sawdust in his hair, and cried. Eventually, Bud walked over and sniffed his face, licked his tears, and laid down beside him. The two remained on the floor together as the night hours passed.

The next morning, Mason's eyes fluttered open. He gripped his bruised and cut hand and winced. Dried blood crusted on his skinned knuckles. Pushing himself upright, he looked around. Bud was not there. Mason's body ached from sleeping on the concrete, and a chill had seeped into him. He saw the dangling, busted light fixtures and the scattered lumber. He stood up slowly, dusting himself off. Then he limped out of the kill house and started across the construction site towards the trailer. He breathed the fresh fall air as the morning sun peaked over the hills.

As he walked along the dusty path toward the RV, he saw animal tracks. Two sets. One was clearly Bud's, but the other set was different. Mason paused and took a knee to examine them closer. There were no claw marks, and the heel print showed three distinct lobes. The edges of the tracks were crisp, with little crumbling, meaning they were fresh.

Mason stood up and looked around. The wind was in his face, and the tracks followed the trail to the RV, so he followed them, walking slowly and quietly. As the RV came into view, so did Bud. The dog was standing perfectly still and at full alert. He was staring toward the trailer. Mason followed the dog's gaze. There, on the front porch, laid a full-grown mountain lion. It was lying peacefully, eyes squinted shut, ears twitching occasionally.

Mason slowly took a knee, his eyes never leaving the cougar. For a moment, the three creatures—man, dog, and panther—shared the morning in peace. Then something changed. A shift in the wind, or the sound of a joint popping. Bud looked over and saw Mason, which set the dog to barking protectively at the cougar. The lion flinched and jumped up. It glared at the barking dog, then noticed Mason. It hunched its back and bared its teeth. Mason watched in silence. Bud's barking became even more frantic, more threatening, and the Dalmatian began closing the distance with the big cat. The lion hissed, then lashed out with its paws in a threatening display. Bud never backed down. Finally, after a brief standoff with the determined Dalmatian, the lion broke contact and sauntered off the porch, trotting around the back and heading back to the tree-covered hills and soaring mountains beyond.

"Bud!" Mason yelled once the cougar was gone, and the dog stopped barking. He trotted to the front porch, where he immediately began sniffing all over. Mason strolled the rest of the way to the cabin.

"You know he would've kicked your ass, right?" Mason said to the dog as he walked inside.

In that moment, as he looked around the dirty trailer, as he felt the throbbing in his hand, as the thrill of seeing the cougar up close filled him, Mason remembered who he was. He remembered once being as brave and strong and dangerous as a mountain lion, and in that moment, as clear as the Colorado sky, he wanted to be that man again.

In the bathroom, he showered and wrapped his knuckles with gauze and medical tape. Then he got dressed in jeans and a sweatshirt. In the kitchen, he opened the cabinet. Inside were green, brown, and clear bottles of gin, vodka, rum, and whiskey. He pulled them all out and arranged them on the counter. Then he went to the refrigerator and took out a handful of beer bottles. In the bedroom, he opened dresser drawers and retrieved even more bottles. Gathering them all in the kitchen, he emptied an olive-green duffle bag onto the floor and placed the bottles inside.

Bud was lying on the front porch, in the same spot as the cougar, when the screen door banged behind Mason. Bud hopped up, tail wagging, and the two walked back down the trail to the shooting range. Mason's boots echoed on the steps leading to the underground range, and the bottles clanked inside the bag. He flipped on the lights, then grabbed a folding table and, hanging the bag of bottles over his shoulder, carried the items down one of the shooting lanes. At about twenty-five feet, he set the bag down and set up the table. Then he opened the bag and placed each of the bottles on the table in a row. Afterward, he walked back to the firing line.

Securing his protective earmuffs and eyewear, Mason drew his pistol from inside his waistband, feeling the familiar cold metal against his skin. Then he pressed the remote to light up the bottles.

The first shot resonated with a loud blast, and a bottle of Budweiser exploded downrange. Bullet after bullet, he fired, watching as they burst each bottle with showers of liquid and glass. He reloaded with a steady hand, extended toward the target, and fired again. The loud cracks of each round echoed through the room, and his breathing grew deeper in rhythm with each shot, his concentration unbroken. Once the last round had left the barrel and the last bottle was vaporized, he watched the smoke drift away. His injured hand ached and throbbed from the recoil.

He swept the shattered glass into a dustpan, then collected his brass, reloaded his magazines, and climbed up the steps into the morning light, arising from the submerged range into a brand-new day.

The voices of Clay Walker and Travis Tritt serenaded him as he drove to work. In his office cubicle, he could see dust motes dancing in a patch of sunlight slanting between the blinds. Outside, cars passed noisily. As he sorted through the paperwork, his right hand wrapped in fresh gauze, he felt a presence near his desk. Looking up, he found Caleb standing uneasily before him, eyes on his fidgeting hands.

"Hey, Mason," he began. "I wanted to say..."

Mason leaned back in his chair, patiently studying Caleb. The young man's temple was bruised and swollen.

"I'm... I'm sorry," he continued, swallowing hard. "I was thinking about money to launch my drone business, and... I messed up. Big time. It was stupid. The last thing I'd want to do is hurt my dad. Or you."

"What the hell got into you?" Mason asked. "What even gave you the dumbass idea to steal from your own family's business?"

Caleb took a deep breath. "I was going through the contract we use with the dispensaries, and I found out there was a spoilage clause. It covers us if a certain percentage of the cannabis goes bad and has to be destroyed, you know, like mold."

"So, you figured nobody would notice if you stole just a little," Mason said.

"More or less, yes," Caleb said.

"But you got busted, anyway. Didn't expect that, did you?"

"No, I didn't," Caleb said.

Mason took a deep breath, staring hard at Caleb's bowed head.

After a brief pause, Mason spoke, his voice firm. "I hear your apology. Meet me behind the office at the sand pile after work. Be in your PT gear."

Caleb's eyes widened. "Um, okay. I'll be there," he responded and backed out of the office slowly.

The workday crawled by, and as the office emptied, Mason found Caleb waiting outside as instructed, wearing gray sweatpants and a white T-shirt.

"You want to make things right? Then you need to make amends. The employee parking lot floods when it rains because of runoff from the hill behind the office. You are going to fix that. First, you're going to shovel that sand into those bags. I know you remember how to do that," Mason said, pointing to the big pile of sand and bundles of empty sandbags next to it.

"Then you will carry those filled sandbags to the back parking lot. There, you will stack them at four high along the entire back of the lot as a retaining wall."

Caleb looked at the pile of sand and took a deep breath.

"And there's more," Mason continued. "You're going to work nights and weekends at the training center with me. We need trenches for water and septic lines dug. I was planning to rent a trenching machine, but since I know you're a good and remorseful son and therefore eager to help your dad save money, you are now my trenching machine."

Caleb swallowed hard.

"This is your chance to show your father, and me, that you are more than your mistakes."

With that, Mason turned and walked away, leaving Caleb to his thoughts and his shovel.

21

Missing

The phone rang.

Click.

"911, what's your emergency?"

"Hi, um, my name is Lacey Shaw. My roommate has been missing for three days. Her name is Angelina Spencer. She's a stripper, uh, entertainer, at The Temptress Lounge. She uses the name 'Margot' sometimes."

"Ok, ma'am. 9-1-1 is for emergency calls only. There is a separate number for missing persons."

"OK, but I talked to her friends at work, and they said she left Friday night with some bikers, and nobody has heard from her since. Her phone is off, but I have her last location. We always shared locations with each other. But nobody has heard anything from her. She's not just missing. Something bad has happened."

"Ma'am, I understand, but unless you have specific knowledge of something happening, you're going to have to hang up and call the missing person's number."

"Just, please, listen. She was a witness in a case a few years ago. Her ex was a big drug dealer, and she testified against him. She told me if she vanishes or anything to call you guys and ask for Detective Clarke. Please."

A pause.

"Ok, ma'am. Please hold on the line."

Detective Harold Clarke wandered through the cubicles to Detective Kim Wright's desk.

"Kim, got a minute?" he asked.

She looked up from her computer screen. "What's up, Harold?"

"Well, I've got a special case. It's a missing person. A stripper from The Temptress Lounge. Her roommate says the girl left the club with some bikers last Friday and nobody has heard from her since."

"So, a stripper ran off with some bikers. Sounds like a match made in heaven," Kim said, turning back to her computer. "And you are bothering me with this because..."

"Because the girl, Angelina, was a CI for me," Harold explained. "A couple years ago, she helped me put her boyfriend away for a long time. He was the big meth dealer around town and an all-around shitbag. She stuck her neck out for months and helped us take him down and his associates. I want to look out for her."

"We're narcotics detectives. That's missing persons," Kim pointed out.

"Kim, Angelina put it all on the line. Plenty of people know she testified against her man, and I'm sure a lot of them aren't happy about it. Somebody he's connected with could have decided to take action against her. I want to...No, I have to find her."

Kim looked at Harold. She saw the eagerness in his posture and felt the intensity of his gaze.

"OK," Kim said, swiveling in her chair to face him. "You have my attention. What do you need from me?"

"Good, thank you. The roommate says she has Angelina's last location from her cell phone. Something about sharing locations. You know as soon as I hear 'cell phone' I come see you," Harold explained.

"Lord, Harold," Kim said, exasperated. "Can't you watch a YouTube tutorial or something?"

"A what tutorial?" Harold asked.

Kim rolled her eyes. "You have got to be kidding me. This is why you should've had kids. They'd make sure you knew how to use technology."

"But that's what I have you for, my dear," Harold said. "Care for a drive?"

Kim sighed, then stood and grabbed her jacket and phone. "Come on, dad. Lead the way."

Harold grinned. "I enjoy our time together so much."

Detectives Wright and Clarke arrived at the apartment Margot shared with her roommate. The building had three stories of tan stucco and vinyl siding. Each unit had a little balcony with a black railing. A young woman with brown hair cut to shoulder length answered the door, her eyes red from crying.

"I'm Detective Harold Clarke. This is Detective Wright. Did you call about a missing person?" Harold asked.

"Yes, I'm Lacey. Please, come in," she replied, ushering them into the living room.

The apartment was modest, but fashionably decorated in black and white. Photos of Margot and Lacey, smiling and posing at various locations, adorned the walls. A Siamese cat walked across the back of the white leather sofa. Lacey tapped the screen of her cell phone to open an app, then handed it to Harold, who quickly passed the device to Kim.

"That was her last known location from Friday night," she said, her voice trembling. "It's a motel. I already went over there and looked. I got out and walked around, but I can't tell which room she could be in, or even if she's still there."

"Did she drive herself?" Kim asked.

"No, she doesn't have a car. I have one, so sometimes I drive her, but sometimes she works all night, especially on Fridays, so she takes an Uber or whatever to work so, like, I don't have to come get her."

"Do you also work at the Temptress?" Harold asked.

"No, sir," Lacey said, holding up her fingertips. "I do nails."

"How long have you known Lacey?" he asked.

"Like, 6 years. Since high school. She never stays out without texting me. I asked her work friend, this girl Keisha, the next day, and she told me she left with some bikers. Right then, I knew something was wrong," Lacey explained, her voice breaking.

"We'll do everything we can to find her," Kim said. "Can you tell us anything about the bikers she left with?"

Lacey shook her head. "Not much. Nobody knew them. They were from somewhere else. Maybe France or Canada or something is what Keisha said."

"Could she describe them?" Harold asked. "What they were driving or wearing?"

"She said they drove off on motorcycles. I know that's why Angelina wanted to go with them, just to ride on one."

Tears ran down Lacey's cheeks.

"I also have her location from before the motel. I looked it up on Google Earth and it looks like a cabin in the woods outside of town," she continued. "Look, I took a screenshot. She was there until early Saturday morning, and then she went to the motel, and then her phone went off."

"How long has her phone been off?" Kim asked.

"Um," Lacey thought, "two days."

"Maybe a biker swept her off her feet," Kim said. "She is an adult. She can leave if she wants to."

"She could, but she wouldn't," Lacey said.

"How can you be sure?" Harold asked.

"Because of him," Lacey said, pointing at the Siamese cat. "She would never leave him. She cares more about that cat than herself."

Kim and Harold thanked Lacey and assured her they would check out the two last known locations. As they walked down the apartment's stairs and back to Harold's blue Caprice, Kim asked, "Was the ex-boyfriend a biker?"

"No, but he was tied in with a lot of bad dudes, so anything is possible," Harold said. "The cabin is a drive, but the motel isn't far. Want to ride with me?"

"Why, Harold. What would your wife say if she knew you were accompanying a younger woman to a seedy motel?" Kim joked.

"Ha! She'd probably say, 'Keep him, so I don't have to hear him snore anymore.'"

Kim laughed as they drove away.

The motel was a two-story Comfort Inn just off the highway in an area filled with hotels. Kim and Harold parked, entered the lobby, and approached the front desk, flashing their badges to the clerk.

"We're investigating a missing person and believe she may have been here recently. Have you seen this woman?" Kim asked, showing a photo of Margot on her cell phone.

The clerk, a young African American man with glasses, short dreadlocks, and a name tag bearing "Christopher," shook his head. "I don't recognize her. Do you know what day she was supposed to be here?"

"Last Friday," Kim said.

"Ah, I was off Friday. My manager isn't here right now, but I know they don't mind if you guys check the video," Christopher offered.

"Let's do that," Kim said.

They moved to a small office where a bank of six monitors displayed different angles of the motel.

"These hard drives keep the last 30 days of video, so we can zoom back and pull up Friday's footage easily," the clerk said as he sat at the bank of monitors.

He clicked the mouse to bring up footage from Friday.

"Do you know about what time?" he asked.

"No, we don't," Kim answered.

"No worries," Christopher said. "We can zoom through this and see if we spot her real quick. I'm going to run through all cameras at the same time, so if you'll help me watch the monitors, maybe one of us will spot her. OK, here we go."

Video began streaming across all six monitors at several times normal speed. The footage started in the quiet early morning darkness, then proceeded through sunrise, when people and vehicles started moving about the property. Christopher fast-forwarded through hours of footage in a few minutes as they watched closely for any sign of Margot.

Suddenly, Kim said, "Stop. Go back."

Harold leaned in. "Did you see her?"

"No, I don't think so. But go back."

Christopher rewound the footage until Kim told him to stop again. She pointed at one of the monitors.

"Look right there," she said.

The footage was from a camera covering the back of the building, away from the front office and most eyes. It captured not just the parking lot, but also a back driveway from the road into the lot. As they watched intently, they could see an object coming up the road. It was a small black blob at first, smaller than the cars it passed. It was coming right at them. The blob turned as it approached the back driveway and they could see clearly then a dark motorcycle and rider.

"Can you zoom in on that motorcycle?" she asked.

"Yeah, sure," the clerk said. He used the mouse to drag a box around the subject, and the image was magnified. The rider was wearing black from head to toe, including a black helmet with the visor down.

He pulled into the parking lot and stopped, setting his feet down. He looked around for a moment, then reached into his leather jacket, where he retrieved something small and rectangular from his pocket. He reached his arm back and hurled the object high over the motel.

"Whoa!" said Christopher, his brow furrowing as he leaned in closer. "What did he just throw?"

"I think I know," Kim said, pointing at the monitor. "Can you show me where this is?"

"Yeah," said the clerk. "It's in the back. I'll show you."

As they walked through the lobby, the clerk set a "Back Soon" sign on the main desk. He led the detectives along the sidewalk around the back of the two-story building. Once there, he pointed up to the camera mounted on the exterior wall.

"That's the camera we were looking at, so he was about right there when he threw whatever it was that he threw," said the clerk, pointing.

Kim and Harold looked up at the second-floor balcony.

"Anybody turn in any cell phones?" Kim asked.

"No, we don't have any phones in the lost-and-found right now."

"Could be on the roof," Harold said.

Kim thought for a moment, then smiled. "Wow! Look at you, Harold. You do get this technology thing."

Harold waved her off.

"Christopher, do you have a tall ladder?"

A few minutes later, the motel maintenance man leaned a ladder against the building. After a brief explanation, he climbed up to the roof line and peered over.

"¡Oh sí! Hay un teléfono celular aquí arriba," he called down from the roof.

"Interesting," Kim said. "The biker threw her phone on the roof to make it look like she was here on GPS, since the satellites can't tell the signal is coming from the roof and not from the room beneath."

"So, she was probably never here, and we have a biker distracting anyone who might come looking for her," Harold said.

"Exactly," Kim replied.

Kim squinted up at the roof.

"I know your old ass ain't climbing that ladder, but we'll need the phone for evidence. Let me get some gloves and I'll climb up there," Kim said.

"Detective Wright," Harold said with a grin, "you are a truly remarkable woman."

22

Reinforcements

The late afternoon sun filtered through the dense canopy of the forest, casting dappled shadows on the trail as Raison pulled up to the cabin on his motorcycle. The air was cool, the scent of pine and earth rich in his nostrils. He killed the engine. Dismounting, he walked up the steps and into the living room.

Inside, Bruno was hunched over his workbench, absorbed in his task. He looked up as Raison entered, a serious expression on his face. "Raison, we need to talk. Outside."

"OK, after you, brother," Raison agreed, waving to the back door.

Bruno stood from his workbench, set his glasses down, and led Raison outside. They walked across the yard to the edge of the forest. There, they came to a trail lined with tall Ponderosa pines and Blue Spruce, their branches swaying gently in the breeze. The ground beneath their feet was a tapestry of pine needles and soft earth, muffling their footsteps as they walked.

After walking for a few minutes, Bruno broke the silence. "Raison, I have to ask you straight up. Who were those people we hit in Montreal, on the train and in that house? I can't shake the feeling that they weren't the ones behind Max and Wild Bill's deaths."

The forest seemed to listen, the usual chatter of birds and rustling leaves falling silent. Raison stopped walking and turned to face Bruno. His face was etched with lines of stress. "Bruno, you're listening to too much of my brother's crazy shit. What happened in Montreal was necessary. You saw how much dope they were moving in our city. We could never let that be. It was them or us," Raison replied, his voice tinged with frustration.

Bruno furrowed his brow. "I've known you for years, Raison, but something about this doesn't sit right. I need to know we didn't just massacre innocent people."

Raison breathed deeply and scratched his beard, his gaze shifting around. "Look, Bruno, I did what I had to do to protect the club. Rage, he doesn't always see the big picture. Don't make his same mistake."

Bruno glanced away, his eyes tracing the path that disappeared into the thick foliage. "Shit, man. It's not just about what Rage thinks," he said, his voice stern. "It's about doing what's right."

The forest around Raison and Bruno was serene. Then there was a distant rumble from the direction of the cabin. Raison held up his hand, his ears attuned to the sound. "Do you hear that?" he asked, his eyes narrowing.

Bruno stopped as well, listening. The deep, throaty rumbles of motorcycle engines were growing louder. "Yeah, I hear it. Sounds like someone's at the cabin."

"Better head back," Raison said. "And bro, I am counting on you to keep your shit together. We are too close to this job to start falling apart now."

Bruno sighed and looked away.

Quickly, they retraced their steps along the forest trail. The tranquility of the woods fell away with each step as they neared the cabin. The sound of the engines became clearer, more pronounced. As they emerged from the cover of the trees, the cabin came into view, and they were greeted by the sight of three motorcycles pulling up, dust swirling around their tires as they slowed to a stop. Clad in black leather, the riders parked and dismounted.

The first of the three bikers was an average-sized older man with a billowing gray beard and a long gray ponytail. He wore black sunglasses and a camouflage headband. Blue tattoos of Viking runes trailed down his cheeks and neck.

The second man was in his thirties. He was short and powerfully built, with a bald head and a long brown beard. Broad gauges stretched his earlobes.

Like the first man, he also had rune tattoos on his face and head.

The third man appeared to be a younger version of the first. They were the same general height and weight, but the younger man's beard was brown rather than gray, and it had a braid with beads in it. Like the others, he had Norse runes tattooed on his face and the sides of his partially shaved head. The rest of his hair was woven into a thick braid down his back.

The older man pulled off his leather riding gloves.

"I'm looking for a man about a wolf," he said in a deep, gravelly voice. "Would you know anybody like that?"

"I would. I am Raison," he replied in English, reaching out to shake hands.

"And I am Gunnar Odonson," said the older man as he clasped Raison's hand. His eyes were as pale and silver as his beard, and his black leather jacket was dusty and weathered. Each finger bore a large ring.

"This is my son, Ragnar," Gunnar said, motioning to the younger man with the braid, "and our brother-in-arms, Reaper," he said, gesturing toward the stocky bald man.

The men all shook hands.

"Let's talk more inside," Raison said and led the men into the cabin.

Bruno was back at his table in the living room, glasses on, working on his laptop. He stared under his eyebrows as Raison entered. Moose was on the couch watching hockey reruns on TV. Matheo and Okwaho were in the kitchen eating hamburgers. Rage and Robeur came in from the backyard where they had been smoking. The men of the Dead Wolves Motorcycle Club gathered to greet the newcomers. Once everyone was in the living room, Raison addressed the group.

"Tommy Boy sent these men from the Nomads chapter to help out. Gunnar, why don't you tell us about yourself?" Raison said.

Gunnar smoothed his gray beard down and looked around the room.

"Well, we were once like you," Gunnar began. "We had our own club out of Salt Lake City. I returned from Nam in '75 on one of the last transports. Myself and some other Marine buddies started riding together, getting into fights, fucking shit up throughout the West. This was in the late '70s and early '80s. That's when Big Machine first exploded out of So Cal and then spread to Vegas. They were at war with the Desperadoes for a long time. In those days, if you weren't with Big Machine or Desperadoes, you could not ride west of the Rockies. They would blow you off your bike with a sawed-off shotgun if they didn't know you. Luckily, I knew Pop from prison. We both did time in Soledad. He was also a Marine. Did you know that?"

Raison shook his head.

"Many people think Pop is Canadian. He's not. He's American. He's just been in Toronto so long he's adapted. But he won't come back to the U.S. because the feds will bury him under a mountain."

Raison nodded.

"Anyway, I'm a dinosaur, so I take a while to get to the point," Gunnar said. "We patched over in '87. We were Big Machine's Utah chapter for twelve years after that. My son here, Ragnar, prospected and joined. Then I got three years in the feds for guns. The Utah chapter was too small to run itself, and the Mormons wanted us gone anyway, so we got absorbed into the Nomads."

"But even amongst the Nomads, our clan, is unique," Gunnar continued. "In Nam, I was a scout sniper with 34 confirmed kills. From an early age, I embraced war and the warrior ethos. After Nam, I traced my Scandinavian roots and reconnected with the lost Viking tradition of raiding. I reconnected with the gods of my Norse ancestors and, through my studies, became a gothi, or high priest."

Matheo and Okwaho cast each other a glance.

"Within the Nomads, some call us the Raiders, or the Vikings. We are the only members allowed to wear the Skeggøx, or battleaxe, patch. Anyone you see with the battle axe patch must also earn a Mechanic patch."

"To become a Raider," Ragnar explained, "first you have to be a killer."

He trailed his finger down the blue runes tattooed on his cheek.

"We document our raids with runes," Gunnar continued. "Ragnar and Reaper are both veterans of many raids."

"What do you mean by 'raids'?" Matheo asked.

Reaper spoke up. His voice was deep, and his expression cold. "Banks, armored cars, check cashing stores, pharmacies, dope dealers, jewelry stores. We specialize in armed takeovers. We can take down a bank in two minutes, no problem."

Matheo nodded.

"Sometimes," Gunnar said, "it's just 'Mechanic work.' When Tommy Boy wants somebody's lights cut off, quietly or loudly, he calls us. I train every Raider to shoot like a Marine. Every Raider is familiar with all aspects of Marine Corps combat doctrine, and every one of my Vikings is trained in multiple weapons systems and team tactics."

"What about gear?" Raison asked.

"It's on the way," Ragnar said. "We never travel with heat. Someone will deliver it."

"It's good to have you and your Raiders here, Gunnar. Robeur, get them settled in," Raison said. "We start preparations tomorrow. We've got a raid to plan."

Gunnar grinned even wider, revealing brown teeth.

"How else will we to get to Valhalla, brother?" he said, laughing and clapping Raison on the back.

Later, Raison, Okwaho, and Matheo walked into the backyard to find Gunnar sitting on a bench, smoking. Seated on a rock not far away was Reaper. He appeared lost in a trance, mumbling incantations.

Raison stopped and watched. Reaper was shirtless, his body covered in lightning bolts, swastikas, and other neo-Nazi prison tattoos. A braid of herbs, tied up with twine, was burning on the stone before him, and a trail of pungent-smelling smoke drifted up.

"He's preparing for the calling," Gunnar explained. "He wants to walk the path of the Berserker. Claims the All-Father whispered it to him."

Raison arched an eyebrow. "Berserker?"

Gunnar nodded. "Ancient Norse warriors. They used psychedelic mush-rooms to enter a trance before battle. They were fearless, powerful, unstop-pable. Today, he prepares by recaning—smoke cleansing. He burns juniper and mugwort to cleanse his spirit and connect with his ancestors."

He turned to Raison. "You know, our people found North America long before Columbus. Landed close to where you're from, in Newfoundland."

The gray-bearded man took a drag on his cigarette and inclined his head at Okwaho. "But they had some... disagreements with the natives."

Okwaho held his stare. The musky smoke from Reaper's spiritual cleansing hung thickly in the air.

Gunnar held up his hands in mock surrender. "Just history, my friend. No hard feelings."

He laughed and smiled, baring his stained and crooked teeth.

Okwaho held Raison's eyes, then walked away.

Raison entered the cabin through the back door and found Bruno working at his table. He held a car key under a magnifying glass. Next to it, clamped in a vice, was a key blank. With a thin needle file, he copied the peaks and valleys of the original key onto the blank.

Raison watched him work. "How's it going?" he asked.

Bruno lifted his head and lowered his bifocals.

"Almost done," he said, blowing metal filings off the table. "Once I'm finished with this one, we'll have keys for all three vehicles."

He held up several key rings.

"Over the last few weeks, Robeur swiped keys and owner addresses from the tire shop for a '90s model Jeep and a big truck. I already copied the door and ignition keys for those. The one I'm making now is for the van you wanted."

"Good," Raison said, clasping Bruno on the shoulder. "We need to get wheels tonight. The sooner we get this over and return to Quebec, the better."

That night, the suburban neighborhood was blanketed in peaceful silence, broken only by the distant barking of dogs, the gentle whispers of the wind, and the muffled footsteps of a black-clad man creeping up the sidewalk.

Okwaho slipped through the shadows, his face covered with a black mask. He crept towards a blue Jeep Grand Cherokee parked along the curb. Using a copy of the Jeep's keys, he slowly opened the driver's door and slid in. One more turn of a key and the engine roared to life. With the headlights off, he drove down the block to the main road and headed out of town.

Meanwhile, on the south side, Robeur walked up to an older model white Ford work van parked outside an apartment. Confidently, he strolled to the driver's door, inserted the key, opened it, and hopped in. He cranked the engine, backed out of the parking spot, and drove away.

On the outskirts of Denver, wearing all black, Moose crept up the driveway of a two-story house toward a silver Dodge Ram 2500 pickup. As he got closer, he could hear a television playing inside the home. He struggled to crouch his huge frame low and to step carefully. He made it to the truck, placed his hands on the door handle, and suddenly, a motion detector security light clicked on.

Moose froze, then quickly fumbled for the keys. Suddenly, the front door swung open. A man stood in the doorway, his figure illuminated against the backdrop of the brightly lit interior. His face, a mix of confusion and dawning realization, quickly turned to alarm as he spotted the shadowy figure near his truck.

"Hey!" he bellowed, his voice cutting through the quiet night. "What are you doing?"

Moose opened the driver's side door, slid into the seat, and turned the ignition. The truck's engine roared to life, shattering the silence of the neighborhood. The homeowner, now fully aware of what was happening, ran towards him, shouting at the top of his lungs. "Help! He's stealing my truck!"

Moose put the truck into gear and accelerated, slinging grass and dirt as he gunned it across the front yard and jumped the curb. The homeowner reached the end of his driveway just as the truck sped off, his shouts fading into the distance.

23

Leadership

The foot of the Rocky Mountains was alive with the sounds of nature. Two figures moved silently through the tall grass like lions on the Serengeti. Mason and The Colonel cradled their hunting rifles and scanned the terrain. As they trekked further into the wilderness, the quiet was punctuated only by the occasional chirp of a bird or the distant rustle of a breeze.

After a prolonged silence, The Colonel turned to Mason. "I wanted to thank you for the training you've been giving Caleb," he began, the age lines on his face deepening in the waning sunlight. "He looks up to you like a hero, you know."

"Caleb's a good kid. He's got a lot of potential," Mason replied, watching the horizon.

They paused for a moment, letting the serenity of nature envelop them. The Colonel continued, his gaze distant but thoughtful. "Caleb is smart, but he's disappointed in himself. That's my fault, I suppose. I raised him to be the only kind of man I knew to be—a Marine. He was good at sports. Always listened. Maybe he played too many video games while I was away, but he always made his grades and respected his mother."

Mason listened as they walked through the tall grass.

"He did everything he was supposed to. Graduated with honors. We were all proud when he enlisted. They sent him to MCRD San Diego for basic training."

The Colonel exhaled heavily and adjusted the brim of his cowboy hat.

"They sent him home after three weeks. Medical discharge for sleepwalk-ing. Sleepwalking. We had no idea."

He stopped and adjusted the leather rifle sling over his shoulder. He wore a brown cowboy hat and a camel hunting jacket with patches on the elbows. Mason could see the late afternoon sun reflecting in The Colonel's shooting glasses.

"I was disappointed when he came home. I didn't see his life going that way. His mother and I felt like we'd failed him. He drifted from us after that. Started hanging out with his loser high school buddies—drinking and smoking dope. I was the chief of police at that time, and I knew that if I didn't do something, I would see my son in the back of a cruiser one day. Then they legalized cannabis, and it all hit me. I didn't start this company to make a bunch of money or to help the damn weed dealers. I started it to give my son something to live for. Something to build and be proud of. It's another chance for him. Now, he's got a business idea of his own, with the roof-mounted drone, and I see hope in his eyes again."

The two men scanned the horizon. Bending down, the Colonel gathered dried grass, then released it, noting which direction the breeze took it. The pair started slowly walking again, noses into the wind.

"I guess nothing ever really goes as planned, Mason. But from the ashes of the old plan, we must make a new one. My son is no longer a Marine, and you are no longer in Delta Force. But you are still alive to build something new for yourself. Do you see that?"

Mason chewed the end of a dried strand of grass.

The Colonel continued. "You've seen and done things most can't imagine. But there comes a time when the gunfights fade, and the body yearns for peace. Just like Green Zone Defense is not just a security company to me, our training center is not just another business. It's your legacy. It's where you pass your knowledge to the next generation."

Mason stared towards the sprawling mountains.

The Colonel patted his shoulder reassuringly. "Remember: Glory is fleeting but building something and teaching others to carry it forward, that's the kind of legacy that endures. Teaching Caleb to shoot beer cans is just the start."

Mason chuckled.

The distant howl of a coyote interrupted them. Both men stopped dead in their tracks, listening. The sun painted the landscape in golden hues, warming the terrain as the men stalked their prey. Eventually, they came to a creek crossing. They waded through the shallow water and climbed the opposite bank, staying low and silent. Once they reached the top and peered over, Mason saw a broad pasture of golden grass waving in the sun.

The Colonel reached into his pocket and retrieved a mouth call, worn from years of use. He put it to his lips and mimicked a wounded rabbit's high-pitched yips and howls. The seconds ticked by. Mason's grip tightened around his rifle, his eyes scanning the field ahead. The decoy calls echoed through the silence. After a few moments, a lone coyote emerged from the western tree line, its ears perked, nose sniffing the air. Cautiously, it stepped into the open, head darting around as it tried to follow the sound.

With a deep breath, Mason steadied his aim. It trotted along, sniffing the ground here and there. Mason waited patiently. Eventually, the coyote stopped on a small crest, sniffing the wind, its body turned broadside to their position. Mason placed his crosshairs 2 inches above the animal's heart.

The world slowed, every detail magnified. Mason clicked off the safety and eased the slack from the trigger. Then, with a silent exhale and a gentle squeeze, the shot rang out. The coyote flopped back and crumpled, its body tumbling across the ground.

"Good shot," The Colonel commended.

The land was silent and still as Mason and The Colonel crossed the field to the limp carcass. As the sun descended, painting the Rockies in deep oranges and purples, Mason skinned the coyote, its blood flowing and pooling in the grass and the dirt.

24

Investigation

Detective Harold Clarke steered his blue Caprice Classic west on I-70 through the pine-covered hills. Kim Wright rode in the passenger seat, her hair pulled into her signature bun. She wore a white blouse under a navy pantsuit with dark red lipstick.

"The cabin was listed on a website for short-term vacation rentals. I called the number on the web page, but nobody answered," Kim said.

"We'll see if anyone is there today," Harold replied.

After a while of driving, Harold turned off the highway onto a blacktop road that wandered through the hills. They wound their way through the trees, across culverts with streams running through them, until they came to a dirt turnoff. Kim checked the GPS map on her cell phone.

"This looks like the only way to get to the cabin where Angelina's phone was pinged the night she went missing," she said.

"OK, here we go," Harold said and steered the car onto the bumpy, potholed dirt drive. They drove on through dense trees, past jagged boulders. After a few minutes' drive, the dirt track opened to a clearing of long dry grass blowing in the breeze. At the back of the clearing was a log cabin. There were four motorcycles parked in the front. One of them had a rider on it wearing a New York Yankees ball cap who appeared to be leaving.

Inside the cabin, Bruno was sitting at his worktable in the living room, surrounded by electronic parts, when his laptop signaled a motion alert from the remote game camera he had placed on the entry drive. He opened the camera viewer on the laptop's screen. As soon as he saw the clip of the Chevrolet Caprice driving toward the cabin, he snatched the bifocals from his face and leaped to his feet. Looking around, he grabbed a leather jacket from the couch and, in near panic, snatched a ball cap from a hook by the front door. He pulled on the jacket and stuffed his ponytail under the hat, pulling it down tightly. He took a deep breath, then dashed onto the porch and hurried down the steps. Quickly, he sat on his motorcycle, kicked up the stand, and started to walk the bike backwards just as the unmarked police car pulled into the clearing.

Harold and Kim parked the Caprice and stepped out. The air smelled strongly of pine. They strolled toward the motorcyclist wearing a leather jacket and ball cap.

"Hello, sir," Kim said as they walked up. "Detective Wright and Detective Clarke with the Denver Police Department. Can we speak to you for a moment?"

"Sure," Bruno said, lowering his kickstand and climbing off the bike.

Kim looked around. She studied the bikes, studied Bruno, then smiled.

"About to go for a ride? We didn't mean to interrupt you," she said.

"No worries, Detective. What's this about?" Bruno replied.

"We're investigating the disappearance of a young woman, an entertainer who went by 'Margot.' She was last seen at The Temptress Lounge. Her phone was pinged in this area. Is she here now?"

Bruno's brows furrowed, and his eyes were raised in shock. "No, there's nobody here now but me. A missing stripper? I can assure you, I know nothing about that. There's nobody here except my lawyer buddies for our annual ride. Usually, we just stay on the East Coast, but this year we were like, 'Eh, Rocky Mountains, why not?' So, when did this, uh, young lady turn up missing?"

"Friday night," Kim replied.

"Ah," Bruno said, stroking his goatee. "We just got here on Sunday afternoon, so we missed her. I know there were some people here before us, but you'd have to talk to the owner or property manager about that."

"Yeah, funny you should mention that," Harold said. "Who is your contact there? How do you get in touch with the rental people?"

Bruno scratched his head and sucked his teeth. "I actually don't know. My buddy took care of booking all that..."

"What's your buddy's name?" Harold asked.

"Roger," Bruno said.

"Is that his first or last name?" Kim asked.

"Uh, first. Roger Daniels is his name," Bruno said.

"OK," Kim said. "Is Mr. Daniels here now?"

"No, I'm sorry. Everyone went into town in the rental van to get supplies and groceries," Bruno said. "I was here all alone and bored, so I thought I'd go for a ride."

"How many people are staying with you here?" Harold asked.

"Just the four of us," Bruno answered.

"Have there been any other guests here since you've been here? Any visitors or friends stopping by?" Kim asked.

"Nope," Bruno said. "Just us Staten Island boys. I don't think any of us know anyone west of Philly, you know?" He smiled again.

Bruno looked back at his bike. "Look, detectives, with all due respect, I've answered your questions. Now, if I'm not being detained, I'd like to get on with my ride."

"Sure," Kim said. "Here's my card."

Harold handed Bruno his card as well, and the two detectives started to walk back to Harold's car, but then Kim turned back.

"These are some nice bikes," she commented. "Mind if I snap a photo or two? I have a friend who's crazy about motorcycles."

Bruno managed a strained smile. "Sure," he said, his teeth clenched.

Kim pulled out her cellphone and took her time photographing each motorcycle, capturing every detail—paint, license plates, unique markings—from every angle. When she was done, she put her phone in her pocket.

"Margot was last seen leaving the club with some bikers. We also have a report of a man on a motorcycle at a motel where her phone was later found," she said, watching Bruno's reaction.

He kept smiling.

"Could be anyone," he said. "It's summer. Bikes are common around here. Plus, why would one of us go to a motel when we have this cabin?"

"I can think of a few reasons a middle-aged man 1,800 miles from his family might take a stripper to a motel," Harold said.

"Oh, well," Bruno waved him off, "none of my guys would do that."

"Sure. Let us know if you hear anything," Kim said, and she and Harold turned and walked to his car.

As they drove away, Harold asked, "What do you think?"

"He said he was going for a ride. Have you ever seen someone ride a motorcycle with a ball cap on? Wouldn't it blow right off?"

Harold chuckled. "Good point. So, he's hiding something. His face? His hair?"

"And he was trying to keep us away from the cabin. Make it seem like nobody's in there when there is," she replied. "The photos I took of the bikes might give us something more. I'll run the plates. Something is up at that cabin."

The car merged back onto the main road, leaving the seclusion of the forest behind.

At the cabin, Bruno released a chestful of air, then the front door opened, and out walked Ragnar.

"Those were cops, right?" he said, his eyes bulging. "What the hell were the cops doing here?"

Bruno walked up the steps. "They were asking about a missing girl. Nothing to do with you," he said as he walked past Ragnar and into the living room.

Ragnar stormed in behind him, the veins bulging in his temples and neck. "Nothing to do with me? Are you fucking nuts?" he shouted at Bruno's back.

Just then, Gunnar stepped into the living room.

"Hey, hey, what's all this about?" he demanded. His eyes glittered within his tanned and wrinkled face.

Ragnar looked at his father. "The cops were here," he shouted, pointing toward the front of the cabin. "They just left. They were asking questions."

Gunnar's eyebrows shot up and he looked at Bruno. "Cops? Questions? Who did they talk to?" he demanded.

Raison came in through the back door wearing a dirty T-shirt and jeans, wiping his greasy hands with a rag. "Everyone, chill out! Ragnar and Gunnar, let me talk to my man really quick. Bruno, come with me." Raison waved for Bruno to follow him outside. Bruno walked toward him, and Gunnar started to follow. Raison looked him in the eyes.

"In private, Gunnar," Raison said.

"I don't think so," Gunnar replied, and pushed past Raison. "There were cops here, and I will know why."

Raison gritted his teeth and nodded his head for Bruno to follow Gunnar outside. In the backyard, Raison pointed toward the barn and the three men walked to the building. Raison opened the main barn door, and they entered. The rest of the motorcycles were arranged inside, away from view. Gunnar walked to the feed room door and opened it. Bruno and Raison exchanged a knowing look as they followed him inside.

The room smelled of horse feed. Raison cast his eyes around the dusty room with its bare wooden walls. Against one wall, where there had once been a freezer covered in bloody handprints, there was now a stack of old wooden crates, saddle blankets, and a cobweb covered chair.

"I was back here in the barn working on my bike," Raison began. "Why is everybody talking about cops?"

"A couple of cops came by," Bruno said. "They're looking for somebody who went missing recently. Some lady. They said she might have been in this area, but they also said something about a hotel in Denver, miles away. It sounded to me like they were just asking everyone around if they had seen her."

"What, like a hiker?" Raison asked.

"They didn't say, and I didn't ask," Bruno answered. "I was just trying to get them out of here."

Gunnar's eyes were fixed on Bruno's face.

"Well," Raison said after a moment of reflection. "I guess people go missing out here sometimes. Hiking, camping. What did you tell them about the bikes? Good thing most of them are in the barn."

"I told them we were a group of lawyers from Staten Island on our annual ride. No big deal. They bought the story." Bruno shrugged it off.

Gunnar never blinked.

Raison scratched his chin. "Well, shit. I don't like it, but it sounds like a coincidence. They didn't see much but a couple of bikes. We'll keep an eye open, but we're only a few days out. We can't let this upset us now. Let's get back to work."

Raison and Bruno started to walk away when Gunnar spoke up.

"Hold on now," he said. "Just hang on there."

The Dead Wolves stopped.

"This story about the cops... it doesn't sit right with me," Gunnar said. His blue-gray eyes glowed with icy intensity.

Raison turned to face him. "I know how it sounds, but it's nothing to do with us."

Gunnar folded his arms across his chest, his gaze unyielding. "And you're sure about that? Because in my experience, cops don't just wander into the woods for no reason. They had a lead, a reason to come all the way out here."

Bruno shifted uncomfortably, the unease clear in his posture. "They also mentioned a motel in Denver, Gunnar. They're casting a wide net. We just got caught in it."

Gunnar's expression didn't waver. "And this missing lady... No one here knows anything about her. She just goes missing, and the cops show up at our doorstep?"

Raison met Gunnar's gaze. "It's a coincidence, Gunnar. A bad one, I'll give you that. But we stick to the story, and we keep our heads down. We're close to finishing what we've started here. We can't get rattled over some cops on a wild goose chase."

Gunnar looked from Raison to Bruno, his eyes lingering on each man. The floorboards creaked under their feet, and dust motes floated in a stream of sunlight beaming through a crack in the shutters.

"OK," Gunnar finally said. "We have just a few more days to get this job done. If the cops come sniffing around again, or if anything else out of the ordinary happens, I want to know immediately."

Raison and Bruno nodded in agreement.

"Let's get back to work then," Gunnar said finally, turning to leave the feed room. Bruno walked out after him. Raison cast a glance at where the freezer once sat and noticed the drag marks on the floor. With a deep breath, he turned away and followed Bruno out.

25

Monday

The gritty streets of Denver took on a sheen in the early morning light. It was Monday again. As the city's heart throbbed with life, Mason guided his lifted Bronco through a traffic jam toward the office. Bud sat next to him on the front seat, occasionally letting out a short bark at passing vehicles, his Dalmatian spots stark against the worn leather seat.

Pulling up to the Green Zone office, Mason parked in his regular spot by the tree. He killed the engine, the sudden silence amplifying the distant murmurs of the city. Opening the passenger door, he attached the leash to Bud's collar with a click, led the dog to the tree, and swapped the leash for the cable tie out.

Ali exited his Toyota 4Runner parked nearby and greeted Mason with a shout.

"Mason! You ready for some Monday madness?" Ali asked.

"Our favorite day," Mason replied.

He squatted and scratched Bud's black and white spotted head.

"Today's the long day," Mason explained to the dog. "So, I'll see you later tonight."

He used a key to lock the Bronco, then walked with Ali to the building's back door, where he swiped his key card to enter. In the locker room, Benito and Mink continued their usual morning banter, their laughter echoing against the concrete floor and steel lockers. Mason dressed out in his dark green uniform. He strapped his webbing belt around his waist and holstered his nine-millimeter. Two spare magazines went in sleeves on his belt. He lowered his plate carrier over his head and attached the front to the back with hook-and-loop straps, then picked up a Motorola two-way radio with a hand mic from a table on the way out.

In the garage, he waited behind Ali to retrieve his FN 15 from Big Mike, the armorer, as well as the MK14 Mod 0 precision rifle in its case. He loaded one thirty-round magazine into the FN 15 and placed three more into sleeves at the front of his plate carrier. Walking to the middle of the garage, he hung the rifle muzzle down from its sling. He placed the Motorola radio into a pouch on the flank of his plate carrier, ran the hand mic's coiled remote line up his chest, and attached it to his body armor near his left shoulder. Benito and Matt followed behind him, carrying their rifles.

Mason's watch read 09:01 when Captain Doug Frazier entered the garage carrying the shift clipboard.

"The Colonel is busy, so I'm Longhorn 1 today," Doug said.

He flipped through the clipboard, checking closely.

"It's the fourth Monday of the month, so we run... Route D, which means we start in the South and work our way up. We have twenty-four stops on the list, so let's get moving. Anderson, you're driving Longhorn 1 with me. Mendez, you're driving Longhorn 2 with Mason on shotgun. Carver, you're driving Longhorn 3 with Mink in the passenger seat."

He lowered the clipboard to his side and looked around at the group of men.

"Keep it sharp, play safe, and if you see something, say something. Let's make all our infils and exfils clean. Watch your background. Clean shots only. Let's get home safe. Bring it in for a prayer."

The team gathered, everyone reaching out their hands, some with gloves, some without, to form a circle.

"Dear Heavenly Father," Doug began, "we thank you for the opportunity to serve our fellow men and women and to feed our families. We ask that you watch over us as we do our work today. We ask that you help us to make the best choices to protect lives. Above all, we ask that for those who feel the call of evil today, Lord, that you fill their hearts and minds with love and peace, so we don't have to fill them with lead. Amen."

"Amen," the team chuckled.

"Load up, gentlemen," Doug said, swinging his hand overhead.

The garage doors rolled up as Mason opened Longhorn 2's passenger door.

"Mason, what's up, homie?" Benito asked. "You ready to get this paper?"

Mason laughed. "Let's do this."

Through the open garage doors, he saw a hawk gliding in the clear blue sky above, searching for prey.

"Here we go," Benito said as he shifted Longhorn 2 into drive. He followed closely behind Longhorn 1 as they pulled out of the garage and turned onto the blacktop to begin another routine Monday.

The morning sun crept over Denver's skyline, casting the streets in muted gold. The city was awake, and drive-thru lines at coffee shops were filled up while joggers took on the day's first miles.

Longhorn 1 rolled out first, its armored body heavy and solid like a tank. Behind its tinted windows, Matt Anderson had a grip on the wheel. Captain Doug Frazier sat shotgun, occasionally giving short, clipped instructions over the radio. In the back, Caleb had his world of gadgets—drones, radios, and screens. His fingers moved with precision, eyes darting from one screen to another.

Longhorn 2 followed with its homemade armor. Benito drove, his hands drumming a rhythm on the steering wheel. Mason was next to him, the early morning light catching the edges of his beard, his eyes hidden under his black sunglasses, silently watching every alleyway, every car, every pedestrian. He had been sober for many days, and his eyes were clearer than they'd been in years.

Longhorn 3 brought up the tail. Ali Carver navigated the big SUV with ease while Park Mink-kyu scanned for threats.

The three Suburbans, dark against the brightening city, made their way through the city's streets to a ramp onto Highway I-25. They drove south across the city as the sun climbed. Denver stretched out under the morning haze, a maze of brick and steel, with fresh coffee wafting through the air and the hum and honks of traffic.

The GZD caravan smoothly transitioned from one stop to the next. The Suburbans slowed as they exited the highway, passing onto a frontage road that hugged a strip mall. Once inside the parking lot, the caravan stopped, and Mason and Mink exited the passenger seats of Longhorn 2 and Longhorn 3, respectively. Once they determined the area was secure, Captain Frazier exited Longhorn 1 and entered the store. The door chime hardly finished ringing before the cash, products, or both were loaded into the SUVs, the doors slammed, and off they went.

Pull up. Stop. Load up. Pull off.

Denver watched as the GZD caravan wound its way through its streets, collecting their treasures. Around 11:30, the caravan eased into the parking lot of a dispensary with a green mural covering the front. Mason stepped out of Longhorn 2 and placed his rifle back inside the truck. After casting Benito a weary look, he opened the dispensary's door and walked in.

The Green Elephant was alive with the vibrant energy of customers, music, and conversation. Aromas of sandalwood and sage wafted through the air, mixing with the heady fragrance of cannabis. The glass display case along the wall was filled with colorful edibles. Customers laughed and chatted as they perused the shelves of marijuana under the enthusiastic guidance of budtenders.

The green-haired lady was behind the counter. Her vibrant hair shimmered under the store's lighting, but her face contorted into an unmistakable expression of distaste as Mason stepped inside.

"Morning," Mason said.

Her eyes narrowed. "Yay," she responded, "it's my fav guys again." Her eyes darted disdainfully toward his holstered pistol.

Mason motioned through the door, and Captain Frazier exited Longhorn 1 and walked into the shop. With a few words, he asked the budtender about the pickup and filled in blanks on his clipboard. Once their business was concluded, she pointed to a black canvas duffle bag on the floor behind the counter. Mason walked over, lifted the bag by its straps, and walked out the door.

Pull up. Stop. Load up. Pull off.

The noise of the Denver streets filled the air. Pedestrians and shoppers walked purposefully by. Taxis honked and buses hissed. On the western side of the street, just south of The Green Elephant, a 90s-model four-door Jeep Cherokee sat idling at the curb. Tinted windows dimmed the interior. Ragnar sat in the driver's seat, while Rage sat in the front passenger's seat and Matheo sat in the rear. All three men wore black balaclava masks, so the only parts of them exposed were their eyes. Over their clothes, they wore armored plate carriers, the heavy vests pressing against their chests. Matheo had a rifle nestled between his knees, his fingers indexed close to the trigger. All three men's eyes were riveted on the caravan of dark blue suburbans idling at the Green Elephant dispensary about fifty meters north of their position.

Rage lifted his phone and dialed a number.

"I'm looking at three fat birds ready to get plucked," he said.

Rage clicked off his phone. He sat low in his seat with just enough of his eyes above the dash to peer through the windshield. He had a clear view of the GZD Suburbans. The bright Colorado sun glinted off their navy-blue paint.

With a ripping sound of hook-and-loop opening, Rage retrieved his stainless-steel tomahawk from a pouch on his vest. He slotted the handle into the hole in his prosthetic hand and secured it with the retention pin. In his lap, he held a CZ Scorpion submachine gun.

He watched as the GZD guards exited The Green Elephant dispensary, loaded a duffel bag into the back of a Suburban, and entered their vehicles to leave. The three Suburbans started rolling together across the parking lot toward the exit, where they had to wait for a line of cars to pass. Once traffic cleared, the convoy slowly turned right out of the lot, heading north on the two-lane city street to the traffic light at a four-way intersection.

Across town, Raison tapped his smart phone's screen. Two rings and an automated system answered.

"9-1-1, what is your emergency?"

"Listen closely," Raison's voice was icy and calm. "I am a soldier of al-Dawlah al-Islāmīyah fī al-'Irāq wa Al-Sham—the caliphate that your government calls ISIS—and if our demands are not met, I will detonate bombs across your city. You might think this is a threat, but I will now prove otherwise. I will call back once I have your full attention."

Raison disconnected the call. His finger hovered momentarily over the screen, then dialed another number. After two rings, the line beeped. There was static, and the call disconnected.

Across town, in the Central Business District, the still morning was shattered by an explosion. Flames shot up from a trashcan on a curb. Windows of nearby offices shattered by the shockwave, alarms blared, and the haunting silhouette of thick black smoke climbed into the sky.

Raison tapped an icon on the smartphone's screen. A thrum of chaos emanated from a police scanner app playing through the phone's speaker. He listened for a moment. Eventually, an urgent call went out for first responders to converge on the bomb site.

Raison redialed 911. "Do you believe me now?" he snarled. "Now, listen. There are bombs in your schools. Every child is at risk. Meet my demands, or the next explosion won't be harmless. I will call you back in 30 minutes. Do not miss it."

He clicked off and dialed another number.

"The fire is lit. Let's roast some birds," he said, then hung up.

As they turned onto the street, Mason looked out his passenger side window at a homeless man lying on the sidewalk. He was curled on his side, his body concealed under a filthy blanket. He appeared asleep despite the bright sun and loud cars just feet away, a hood covering his face and head. The caravan pulled up to the intersection and stopped at the red light.

"Benito, how's life treating you outside the force? Do you miss being a cop?" Mason asked.

Benito, reclining slightly in his seat, chuckled. "You know, it's different. Less adrenaline, but I can't complain. My wife's happy I'm not working on the streets anymore. How about you? Are you adjusting to the civilian grind?"

Mason nodded. "Yeah, it's a change of pace, but a good one. I don't miss the bullets flying past my head, that's for sure. And this gig with Green Zone is solid. Keeps me busy enough. Just pushing to get the training center complete and open before winter."

"Will you still do pickups with us in the Longhorns, or are you going to work at the training center full time?" Benito asked.

"The idea is for me to run the training center full time, but that depends on getting enough students and training contracts. I guess we'll see," Mason replied.

Benito smirked, tapping his fingers on the steering wheel. "I never thought I'd see Mason, the tough-as-nails operator, settling into the security life. We're getting old already, bro. You ever miss the action?"

Mason paused, reflecting for a moment. "Sometimes, I guess. The rush, the intensity. But then I remember the quieter moments, the simple things. I don't miss the chaos, but I miss the guys, the brotherhood."

Benito nodded in understanding. "Yeah, that's the part that sticks with you, bro. It's hard to find that kind of camaraderie anywhere else." He glanced out the window at the peaceful street. "But I have to admit, chill days like these are a nice change."

"Yes, they are," Mason agreed

The two men returned to silence as they waited for the light to change.

On the street behind them, inside the Jeep Cherokee, Rage lifted the phone from his lap, never taking his eyes from the GZD caravan waiting at the red light.

Seconds ticked by.

"Are you gonna do it?" Ragnar asked, staring at Rage.

Rage waited, his thumb hovering over the call button.

"Do it, man, before they take off," Ragnar became more insistent.

Rage didn't move.

"Man, if you don't..."

Ragnar reached for the phone, but just then Rage pressed the call button. Instantly, a violent burst of orange and red erupted from Longhorn 2, followed by a deafening boom as Rage detonated the gel dynamite Robeur had planted inside the Suburban at Kenny's Wheelhouse. Smoke and dust billowed up and out, engulfing the Suburban, which bucked and lurched to the side. Its rear driver's side wheel was blown completely off and sent bouncing across the street and over a fence. The back doors blew open, and several windows shattered. Pedestrians screamed. Some scrambled for cover, while others ducked or froze in shock. Car alarms wailed, and bits of rock and dirt rained down.

Inside Longhorn 2, the world turned upside down. The force of the blast lifted the vehicle's left rear off the ground. Glass shattered, spraying the interior with shards. Still gripping the wheel, Benito felt an intense, burning sensation across his left side. His seat belt dug into him, the sudden force jerking his body. He cried out, feeling the heat and force from the blast.

From his spot in the passenger seat, Mason was thrown violently against his seat belt as the explosion erupted behind him. A high-pitched ring screamed in his ears. Sand and smoke choked him, and the world was a blur of dust and noise. He blinked hard, trying to clear his vision. The ringing in his ears persisted, and the taste of metal filled his mouth.

"Benito!" he shouted, though the words felt distant, as if he were underwater. Turning to his left, he saw Benito clutching his face.

"Benito! Talk to me!"

Coughing, Benito cried out, "Shit!" Blood began to pool and soak into his uniform, starkly contrasting the dark green fabric.

Mason pulled a knife from his vest and cut away his seat belt. His body burned and stung from the explosion. He leaned across the console to check on Benito when, through the haze of his ringing ears, he heard a thunderous, penetrating thump. A split second later, the hood of Longhorn 1, just ahead of them in the convoy, erupted into a shower of sparks. The lead vehicle jerked violently, steam and smoke pouring from the decimated engine block.

Precisely 210 meters north of the kill zone, Gunnar lay prone on the tar roof of a two-story commercial building. He scanned the scene below through the scope mounted on his Armalite AR-50 sniper rifle. He smoothly worked the bolt action of the black .50 caliber rifle, his eye never leaving the eyepiece of the Nightforce NXS 8-32x56mm scope. The spent shell of a Raufoss Mk 211 armor-piercing incendiary round ejected onto the asphalt roof with a heavy thud. The morning sun, beaming from the east, cast the shadow of a taller building over his position. He was wearing black and lying on a dirty blanket, his silhouette blending into the roof. The rifle was supported by a bipod and had a long flash suppressor attached to its muzzle.

The lead vehicle's engine was destroyed. Through the scope, Gunnar spotted movement behind the windshield. The silhouette of the driver was visible. Gunnar's heart remained steady as he adjusted his aim. He considered the movement of the vehicle, which was still rolling forward slowly, its momentum unchecked by the destroyed engine. A slow, deliberate exhale, a minute trigger squeeze, and the .50-caliber boomed. The bullet punched through the thick, armored windshield with a plume of glass shards.

Mason looked up just as Longhorn 1 took another direct hit from the front. The damaged SUV rolled forward aimlessly, smoke billowing from its hood. He cursed, then returned his focus to Benito.

"Hang on!" he said. "I'm getting you out of here."

Mason opened the passenger door and exited when suddenly a cacophony of ear-splitting explosions rang from the passenger side sidewalk. Mason dove back into the SUV and closed the door as machine gun-like booms rang out. Impacts thudded along the side of Longhorn 2—one, two, five, ten. Bits of fiberglass and plastic shrapnel scattered about the cabin like deadly confetti as the rounds penetrated through the Suburbans body panels and impacted the make-shift laminate armor Mason and Caleb had installed.

Benito covered his head with his arms. Through the window, in the side rearview mirror, Mason noticed movement, sound, and a muzzle flash from their 5 o'clock position. He focused his gaze and was shocked. The homeless man he had seen sleeping on the sidewalk was on his feet, a long gun of some sort to his shoulder, strafing the convoy with heavy rounds from a drum magazine, the solid projectiles punching holes right through the vehicles.

Psychedelic mushrooms coursed through Reaper. The berserker rage filled him with an energy he had never felt. As soon as the bomb blew the middle Suburban's back wheel off, he leaped to his feet, flinging off the dirty blanket he had been hiding under. The Saiga12 semiautomatic shotgun in his armored grasp looked like a harbinger of doom, its massive cylindrical drum magazine brimming with one-ounce, 12-gauge slugs.

Reaper's first shots were methodical. He worked the trigger as fast as he could, sending slug after slug tearing through the air, colliding with the side of Longhorn 3, leaving ragged holes in its wake. He pivoted and pumped a line of slugs into the already-damaged Longhorn 2, causing a guard to dive back into the vehicle. Each slug punctured steel skin with rhythmic cruelty. Glass shattered, and the thud of heavy metal meeting an unstoppable force was deafening.

He roared a battle cry and let the fury of war take him.

Just south of the kill zone, inside the stolen Jeep Cherokee, Rage, Matheo, and Ragnar watched the ambush unfold. In the back seat, Matheo kept one hand on his AR-15, nervous energy causing his knee to bob up and down. He stared at the scene, his body tense with anticipation. Rage's fingers curled around his cell phone's cold, sleek surface. He dialed and brought the phone to his mouth.

"The birds are on the grill," he said.

Then he set the phone down and licked his lips, watching the carnage in the street intently.

26

Raid

A white van sat idling on the curb one block south of the Green Zone Defense office. Inside, the atmosphere was thick with tension as Raison, Bruno, and Robeur waited. The dull hum of the idling engine vibrated softly beneath them. Raison, sitting in the rear, sat upright, his foot tapping rapidly on the van's floor. In the front, Bruno gripped the steering wheel, his knuckles white. He took slow, deliberate breaths. Robeur, squatting in the back of the van, fidgeted and watched Raison. Every few seconds, his gaze darted outside, surveying the streets.

The light from Raison's phone screen cast a dim glow on his face when he answered it. He listened, then said, "We're moving on the chicken coop now."

His fingers swiftly tapped to dial another preset number. The faint sound of a ring echoed in the confined space, followed by the voice of Okwaho.

"Go!" Raison growled into the mouthpiece. "Go!"

Just up the street from the white van idling at the curb, Moose held the steering wheel of the silver Dodge Ram 2500 HD. The massive pickup truck had a steel brush guard wrapped around the front like a bulldozer blade. He looked at Okwaho, whose face was taut.

The vibration of a phone cut through the quiet. Okwaho quickly answered.

"Hello," he said, then listened.

Moose could hear Raison's gruff shout through the speaker. "Go! Go!"

Okwaho hung up the phone, then he met Moose's eyes and nodded. "It's on, bro. Hit the gas, and don't let up."

Both men fastened their seat belts and inserted boxing mouth guards between their teeth. Moose pressed down hard on the accelerator. The powerful truck roared to life, gaining speed as it surged down the street, the world blurring past as the asphalt whipped by underneath.

The driveway into the GZD parking lot rushed at them. Without hesitation, Moose veered sharply, sending the truck careening onto the property. The parking lot passed in a blur. Ahead, the three garage doors on the front of the building stood side-by-side. Moose focused on the center one, floored the accelerator, and both men braced for impact.

With a resounding crash, the reinforced steel brush guard of the Dodge Ram met the middle garage door. The door's sheet metal buckled, then ripped apart as the force of the truck tore through. On impact, Moose slammed the brakes, the tires squealing on the polished concrete floor inside the garage. Dust and debris filled the air as the truck smashed into a tool bench, sending tools flying across the spacious room.

When Moose and Okwaho quickly clambered out of the Dodge truck, pieces of debris were still falling and clanging around the garage. Okwaho circled around the front of the truck and gave Moose a quick nod. Together, they shouldered their rifles and bounded across the garage toward the side door into the main building. Moose grabbed the door handle and prepared to open it. Okwaho set up on the other side of the door, flat against the wall. He nodded, and Moose yanked it open. Okwaho whipped his rifle up and entered the hallway in a rush, finger on the trigger, walking in a heal-toe manner to keep his muzzle steady. The dimly lit hallway stretched ahead, the insect-like hum of fluorescent lights above mixing with their soft footfalls.

Suddenly, a figure loomed ahead—a large man, both in height and girth. The armorer, Big Mike, was walking toward them, a confused and concerned look on his face. When he saw the black-masked men, his mouth froze open, and his eyes widened. Okwaho squeezed the trigger of his AR-15 twice. The sharp cracks echoed in the corridor, and Big Mike crumpled to the floor.

Okwaho and Moose continued their advance up the hallway, stepping over the man's body, quickly checking offices as they stalked into the interior of the building.

Through the windshield of the van parked up the road, Raison watched the silver pickup truck smash into the office and disappear inside, the shattered garage door crumpling to the pavement behind. Moments later, the dull crackle of gunfire echoed up the street. Raison slapped the seat hard.

"Bruno! Go!" he ordered.

Bruno pressed the gas, accelerating the van towards the Green Zone Defense office. The tires screeched against the asphalt when he turned into the parking lot and brought the van to a skidding halt just outside the front door. The moment the vehicle stopped, the sliding door rolled open, and Raison and Robeur leaped out, boots hitting the ground in quick succession. Each man wore a mask and body armor. Robeur carried a backpack filled with breaching tools, dynamite, and detonators. Each man had their rifle shouldered and ready when they quickly stepped to the front door, where they stacked up and waited to enter.

A loud crash jolted The Colonel from his computer screen, causing his chair to scrape sharply against the floor. He quickly stood to investigate. Then he heard the unmistakable bang–bang of a rifle double tap from the direction of the garage. In two rapid steps, The Colonel made a beeline to the corner of his office where his Benelli M4 stood. Grasping the gun, he instinctively reached down to feel the cold steel of the 1911 .45 caliber pistol holstered on his hip. Quickly, he left the sanctuary of his office and raced down the hall. The smooth tiles underfoot reflected the overhead lights, creating brief gleams that danced as he moved. His steps were sure and swift, but his heart thundered as he charged toward the unknown threat.

27

Casualties

Smoke and chaos filled the air. Mason pushed the persistent buzz in his ears and throbbing in his head out of his mind. Grasping the door handle, he swung the passenger-side door open and jumped out again. On the pavement, he instantly dropped to one knee, shouldered his rifle, and peered through the sight. With both eyes open and squinting, he scanned toward the rear of the convoy, finger poised on the trigger.

The street was enveloped in the staccato rhythm of gunfire and the sharp tang of spent powder. Mason, pulse racing, quickly locked onto Reaper's silhouette on the sidewalk. He fired his FN 15—two loud cracks—hitting Reaper squarely in the torso. Astonishingly, Reaper barely faltered. The plates on his armor absorbed the impact, and, with a grimace of annoyance, he turned and hoisted his Saiga12.

Mason's instincts took over. Anticipating Reaper's next move, he rolled backward under the open door and dove in front of the Suburban, aiming to place the dense engine block between himself and the impending return fire. The fierce roar of the Saiga12 filled the air. Slugs tore into the Suburban's side quarter panel, leaving gaping holes in their wake. Mason felt the vibrations of the impacts and the sting of flying metal shards. Dirt and tiny stones pelted Mason's skin as he slid into a squat in front of the Suburban, grit clinging to his cheeks and the skunky scent of burning rubber clouding around him. Amidst the chaos, the radiator's heat wafted against his skin. His fingers, coated in sweat and grime, curled tightly around his rifle, his muscles tensed in anticipation.

Mason canted his rifle to the right, twisting the weapon horizontally to clear the Suburban's hood. With a subtle inhale, he surged upwards and dispatched two more rounds with clinical precision toward Reaper. He saw the dirty, ragged figure of the shooter stagger back and heard the shotgun clatter to the sidewalk.

From inside Longhorn 2, he heard Benito groaning in pain, but Mason kept his focus. He scanned toward Longhorn 1, which had been hit but continued rolling forward 20 more meters before stopping against a telephone pole on the right side of the road, smoke and steam drifting from its hood. The passenger door of Longhorn 1 opened, and Captain Doug Frazier spilled out backward like a scuba diver. Straining, he pulled Matt's limp body with him as they both crashed to the ground. Climbing to his feet, Doug drew his pistol from its belt holster. With his other hand, he grabbed the nylon drag handle behind Matt's neck and dragged him over the curb, across the sidewalk, and behind a nearby building, pistol pointed up the street toward the shooter. Matt's limp body left a trail of blood behind.

Another volley of gunfire erupted from the direction of Longhorn 3. Squatting low, Mason peered around Longhorn 2's front bumper toward the convoy's rear, but he couldn't see anything. Mason extended his right leg for balance and leaned down to peek through his holographic sight under the Suburban, scanning for threats. At that moment, a thunderous explosion blew Mason to the ground. A high velocity round impacted Longhorn 2's grill mere inches from his head. He was sprayed with shards of plastic and glass as the .50 caliber round punched a hole through the Suburban's engine.

"Contact front! Sniper, 12 o'clock! Sniper 12 o'clock!" Mason bellowed.

He went flat on the pavement, then jumped up and raced around to yank open the driver's door.

"Benito!" Mason screamed, fearing he had been hit again. "Benito! Talk to me!"

Mason's ears were ringing, and gunshots reverberated from the direction of Longhorn 3, but he could see Benito's mouth moving in agony.

"Come on! We have to get out of here!" he said, grabbing Benito by the vest and pulling him from the vehicle. With his rifle to his shoulder and the muzzle aimed up the street in the sniper's direction, Mason dragged Benito to his feet and helped him limp to the ditch on the left side of the road.

28

Invasion

Back inside the dimly lit GZD office, The Colonel trotted down the hallway, his cowboy boots tapping on the floor, the Benelli M4 tight against his shoulder. At a corner, he crept up quietly, then paused to listen.

He heard a scuffle, maybe a whisper, from around the corner. He held his breath. He heard the piercing squeak of rubber-soled shoes. He took two steps back, raised the shotgun, flipped off the safety, and waited.

Slowly, the jagged black muzzle brake of a rifle peeked around the corner. Moose was just feet away, silently wrapping around the corner, little by little. The Colonel waited a split second for the lead hand supporting the rifle to appear, then fired. One close-range blast of 12-gauge buckshot blew Moose's hand apart, sending the rifle clattering to the floor. Moose roared in shock and pain as he crumpled, clutching his destroyed hand. Another load of buckshot to Moose's exposed belly liquefied his internal organs, the force sending him sliding against the wall, blood splattering across the floor.

Okwaho whipped the muzzle of his AR-15 up and fired round after round into the corner wall, blasting holes through the sheetrock toward The Colonel. Dust filled the hall as he emptied the magazine, then released his rifle and smoothly drew a Glock 17 from a drop leg holster, aiming it at the unseen defender around the corner.

There was silence except for Moose's last ragged breaths as he gurgled and twitched on the floor. Okwaho wiped the gypsum dust from his eyes, then looked over his shoulder, down the hallway where they had come. It was a long way back to the garage and escape. Gritting his teeth, he eased forward. As he inched toward the corner, he raised his pistol to a high chest-ready position, took a deep breath, dropped to one knee, and quickly peaked around the corner. He instantly pulled his head back. Nothing. Extending his pistol, he slowly wrapped around the corner, exposing as little of himself as possible while keeping his muzzle pointed ahead. The hall was empty, but there was a trail of blood spots leading away. Okwaho inched down the hall, muzzle up, checking each doorway. He noticed the blood spots got bigger as he followed the trail deeper into the building.

29

Shooters

Longhorn 1 shuddered from the chaos, but Caleb's concentration remained unshaken. Above him, nestled securely on the vehicle's roof, was the drone on its mounting dock. Caleb toggled the drone's release mechanism via his controller, and the quadcopter sprang to life, its propellers spinning into a blur as it disengaged from its roof mount. The drone soared vertically into the urban sky. Caleb's fingers deftly navigated the controls, his eyes glued to the screen that mirrored the drone's aerial vantage, scanning the patchwork of black and gray rooftops. Through the high-resolution optics, he searched for subtle out-of-place details—the subdued glint of metal, a patch of mismatched color on a roof.

Something caught his eye, so he hovered in position. Using the touchscreen on his wrist, he zoomed the camera. From the high angle, he could just make out the shape of a prone figure behind the elongated silhouette of a rifle. Caleb tapped on his digital map interface to tag the sniper's position.

Through the ringing in his ears, Mason's hand mic crackled. Caleb's voice cut through the din of the ambush.

"Mason! Sniper, 12 o'clock, gray building, second from the left corner, rooftop. He's prone and has a view of the entire street."

Amidst the chaos, the blurred world of smoke and shattered glass, Mason tucked himself tightly against the rugged tire of Longhorn 2, adrenaline pulsing in his veins. His eyes darted upward, tracing the skyline to the north,

225

locating the building Caleb had described. His fingers tightened around his rifle. He whispered into his mic a quiet acknowledgment, "Copy that, Caleb. Keep your head down. He's got a .50 cal."

Mason's eyes flicked upwards, scanning the distant rooftops, calculating the sniper's line of sight. Ducking low to avoid being silhouetted, he sprinted around to the back of Longhorn 2. He reached inside the shattered rear door and found a rifle case covered in sand and glass. Popping open the latches, he pulled out the MK 14 Mod 0 Designated Marksman Rifle. He yanked the rubber lens covers off the scope and jacked a round into the chamber, then grabbed an M18 smoke grenade from a gear bag.

With a deep breath, Mason yelled, "Popping smoke!"

He yanked the pin from the M-18 and hurled it over Longhorn 2 toward Longhorn 1 and the distant sniper. Billowing white smoke from the fizzing cylinder filled the street, obscuring everything.

"Moving!" he called again and darted from behind the vehicle.

Gunnar saw the smoke cloud form. He peered intently through the rifle's scope, searching for movement, but finding none.

Mason sprinted down an alleyway to the right. Halfway down, he found the backdoor of an office building. Looking up, he counted four stories. He tried pulling the door, but it was locked. The lock was a basic pin and tumbler model. He leaned the MK 14 against the wall, retrieved a palm-sized packet from a vest pocket, and took a knee in front of the door. He opened the pouch and removed a lock pick set. Selecting a rake and tension wrench, he went to work on the lock. In just seconds, the tumbler spun, and the door swung open. Mason grabbed his rifle and dashed inside. Just inside the building's back door, he found an entry to a stairwell. He ran up the steps—second floor, third floor, fourth floor—to the roof. Bursting onto the tar roof, he crouched low and stalked to the front of the building. When he got close, he laid down and belly crawled until the enemy sniper's rooftop perch was in view.

He brought the rifle to his shoulder and peered through the scope. About 100 meters out, he could just make out the sniper's head and shoulders. The rest of his body was obscured by another building. Mason timed his breathing, inhaling and exhaling slowly, watching the heat mirage shift and leaves blow as he gauged his adjustments. Then Mason squeezed the trigger.

A single shot echoed across the rooftops. Gunnar's head exploded like a water balloon, showering liquid and skull fragments across the roof.

Mason closed his eyes and released his breath. He picked up the DMR, ran back across the rooftop, and down the stairs. He burst into the first-floor hallway, colliding with a man in a white-collared shirt and khakis. The man staggered back.

"What's going on?" he pleaded.

"Stay away from the windows," Mason barked. "Gather people into interior offices and have them lie down. Do not go outside. Call 9-1-1. Do you understand?"

The man looked Mason up and down, blinking.

"Do you read me?" Mason yelled.

"Yes! OK!" the man replied and began edging down the hallway backwards, away from Mason.

Mason pushed the back door open. Gunfire continued to hammer from the south, where Longhorn 3 was engaged with the sidewalk shooter. Back in the alley behind the offices, he grabbed his hand mic.

"Caleb! The 12 o'clock sniper is down," he called over the radio as he ran. "There is another shooter to the east of Longhorn 3. Find him for me!"

"Roger!" Caleb responded. Working the drone's controller, he maneuvered it over the ambush site in search of Reaper.

Back at the street, Mason peeked through the scope toward the gunfire, but he had no visual. Longhorn 2 sat smoking and leaking fluid on the curb near the alleyway. Mason tossed the DMR into the open rear doors and retrieved his FN 15 SBR. He positioned himself at the front of Longhorn 2, aiming towards Reaper as he keyed his hand mic.

"Caleb! What's the deal?" Mason called.

In the back of Longhorn 1, on his screen, Caleb could see that Reaper was pinned down by gunfire from two shooters using Longhorn 3 for cover.

"It looks like Ali and Mink are still in the fight," Caleb called over the radio. "The shooter is using a dumpster for cover, 4 o'clock, 20 meters east of Longhorn 3. He's got one arm down by his side and might be wounded."

Reaper was behind a dumpster, his right arm shattered. He couldn't raise the Saiga12, so he had dropped it to the ground. Under his filthy disguise, he carried a Draco AK-style pistol attached to a single-point sling. Using his left hand, he held the Draco over the dumpster and blindly fired a burst at Longhorn 3.

Ali and Mink were both crouched on the driver's side of Longhorn 3, Mink behind the front wheels while Ali kneeled behind the rear. Both returned fire at Reaper with their AR-15s. Ali fired under the rear of the vehicle while Mink sagged back a few feet from the front quarter panel to avoid rounds skipping off the hood when he popped up to return fire.

"Mink! What have you got?" Ali yelled.

"One shooter wearing body armor. About 20 meters out. He keeps popping out from behind the dumpster," Mink yelled back.

"When I say 'Now,' I need you to suppress the hell out of that motherfucker, OK? I'm moving up. I'm gonna try to flank him," Ali said, peeking under the Suburban, searching for a shot.

"Where are you moving to?" Mink asked.

"It's about 15 yards to that white Benz parked on the curb. From there I can see about flanking him on the right. Just keep his attention," Ali barked back.

"Fuck, bro," Mink said. He tightened his rifle into his shoulder and focused through his sight. "Say when."

Ali gathered himself up and looked around the back of the Suburban, making sure the path was clear. He looked at his destination, a white Mercedes Benz sedan. Sweat ran down his face as he leaned into a sprinter's stance.

"Now!" he said, and Mink began firing toward Reaper. The blasts from his rifle echoed through the streets like a starting pistol as Ali rocketed from behind Longhorn 3 and across the street, bent low, his legs pumping. He crossed the opening in a blur, and his shoulder slammed into the Mercedes as he skidded to a halt. Immediately, he raised his rifle and prepared to return fire, but none came. Cautiously, he crept around the back of the sedan, searching for a clear shot at the dumpster where Reaper was hiding.

Mink fired until his magazine ran dry. As soon as he paused to reload, Reaper popped out and fired back. Ali watched closely from the Benz's rear bumper. He could hear the Draco firing, but his view of the shooter was obstructed by the dumpster, so he watched and waited for a clean shot.

Mink reloaded and fired on the dumpster again. Rounds ricocheted and whizzed overhead. Sweat ran into Ali's eyes, and he wiped it away with his fingertips. His breathing was steady, his rifle a feather in his grip. Just then, he saw a flash of movement from behind the dumpster. The shooter had exposed part of himself. Ali watched, waiting for him to step back into view, finger tight on the trigger, cheek welded firmly to the stock.

Just then, part of the shooter flashed from behind the dumpster again, and Ali fired. The 5.56 mm bullet bored a hole through Reaper's left hamstring at 3,000 feet per second, from left to right, burrowing through his thigh and causing his leg to buckle. The hot round burned like a trail of fire through his muscle. Reaper fell to his knee and bellowed in pain. But then rage took over. He climbed to his feet and limped to the dumpster, the wounded leg unable to support his weight. Growling in pain, he ejected the spent magazine from his AK pistol, reloaded it with a fresh magazine from under his dirty disguise, and spun around, blasting shots wildly into the street.

30

Snatch

From their parked SUV just behind the ambush, Rage, Matheo, and Ragnar watched as Ali and Mink battled with Reaper in the street. Reaching into his vest, Rage pulled out a spent 7.62x39mm shell casing. It was packed to the top with cocaine. He pulled the bottom of his balaclava mask down beneath his chin. Putting it first to his right nostril, then his left, Rage took two powerful snorts. He passed the casing back to Matheo, who dumped some of the flaky crystalline powder onto his glove and snorted it clean, wiping the residue on his gums. He offered the bullet to Ragnar, who didn't notice.

"Let's do this, man," Ragnar said in frustration, pounding the steering wheel. "Come on! We can't leave Reaper out there alone. It's time to move."

Rage sat motionless, watching through the windshield for another moment before finally sitting up in his seat. He raised the CZ Skorpion and cocked it using his tomahawk hand.

"I think you're right," Rage said. "Matheo, get ready."

From the backseat, there was a clack-clack as Matheo cocked his AK-47. "I'm ready," he said.

"Good," Rage replied.

In a flash, Rage slashed his prosthetic left hand toward Ragnar, the tomahawk's steel blade slicing deep across the driver's throat. Ragnar yelped, his eyes bulging in shock, then burbled and gripped his throat as blood sprayed between his fingers. From the backseat, Matheo quickly looped a

Shemagh scarf over Ragnar's neck like a garrote and tugged tightly, choking the man while keeping blood from spraying everywhere. The dying man struggled at first, but within seconds, fell still. Matheo released his grip on the length of cloth, allowing Ragnar's limp body to fall against the steering wheel.

"Viking," Rage snorted. He turned the rearview mirror to look back at Matheo. "Listen. Our bikes are parked in the lot on the other side of the dispensary. We each grab a bag of cash from the Suburbans, and we fucking take off. No unnecessary bullshit. Slip in, grab some cash, get out. The rest of whatever happens here has nothing to do with us. I'm not giving up my life for Big Machine or my traitor brother. We grab a stash for ourselves, and we fucking vanish, just like we planned. Are you ready?"

"Fuck yeah, bro," Matheo said. "I'm right with you."

Matheo's hand was already on the door when Rage said, "It's time to roll. Let's fucking do this!"

The two outlaws exited the passenger side of the Jeep and raised their rifles. Matheo moved up online with Rage as both men sighted through their red dot sights. Rage could see Ali and Mink were not paying attention to their approach from the south. As soon as Rage and Matheo were lined up, they opened fire.

Behind the Mercedes, dust kicked up around Ali as rounds impacted the surrounding pavement. Exposed to the new attackers from the rear, he ducked as bullets blew holes in the car, shattering a rear taillight. He spun with his rifle to face the new threat, ready to pull the trigger. Then his head snapped, and blood sprayed in a mist onto the Benz's white paint. He went limp, like a marionette with its string cut, his rifle still cradled in his arms.

Mink turned right, whipping his muzzle down the street toward two masked shooters who had suddenly appeared. The bright orange flowers of their muzzle brakes flashed, sending bullets whistling and zipping past his head. He dumped his magazine at the newcomers, the recoil of each shot rattling his teeth. He felt light as air. With extreme focus, he placed his sight on the left side shooter, registering a dark silhouette in the reticle. Bang! Bang! Bang! His rifle cycled and ejected brass until the bolt locked, the magazine spent. Without lowering the weapon, Mink released the empty magazine, tore a fresh one from a pouch on his chest, and slammed it into the receiver. He stretched his left thumb out and depressed the bolt release. The clack of steel-on-steel carried through his jawbone as a new round was driven into the chamber.

Mink pulled the trigger just as three rounds impacted his bulletproof vest. The bullets smacked the ceramic armor plate protecting his chest like mule kicks, knocking Mink from his squatting position to his back. He grunted and flailed on the ground. More rounds whistled and zipped overhead. Gathering himself quickly, he dove in front of Longhorn 3, landing hard on the concrete, the force to his already bruised chest knocking the wind from him. Panting for air, he rolled over, worked his way up to his knees, and checked the street.

The shooting had stopped.

Mink reached up and keyed his hand mic. "Longhorn 3 to Longhorn 1! I am holding at the front of my vehicle. There are two shooters on our 6 and one shooter on my 3. Ali is down. I need back up now!"

Mink let go of the hand mic and, wrapping his rifle sling around his lead hand for stability, scanned to the rear of the Suburbans for the newest two shooters. He couldn't see anyone. Just then, he heard boots scraping on gravel from the rear of Longhorn 3. Then he heard the back doors open and felt the vehicle shake. There were voices coming from the rear.

Outnumbered, Mink decided on a tactical retreat. He darted from the front of Longhorn 3 up the street to the front of Longhorn 2, which was nothing more than a mangled heap of smoking steel at the intersection. He prayed as he ran, expecting the burn of hot bullets in his back with each step. He slid into position at the front grill of Longhorn 2 and aimed his rifle back towards the men hidden behind Longhorn 3. Looking over, he was surprised to see Mason standing in front of the Suburban, sighting down his rifle toward the rear of the convoy.

"How's it going?" Mason asked nonchalantly.

"What?" Mink yelled and blinked at him.

Mason gave a thumbs up. "You're doing great."

Mink's face squinched with incredulity. "Are you serious right now?"

Just then, he saw movement at the last Suburban's rear driver's side. A rifle muzzle was sweeping around, searching for targets. Mink aimed at the vehicle glass where he assumed the shooter's head would be and squeezed the trigger as fast as he could, the AR-15 lurching with each shot.

Rage lost sight of the GZD guard as he and Matheo sprinted to the back of Longhorn 3.

"Cover us!" he barked at Matheo, who scanned the area through his rifle sight while Rage opened the double back doors. Inside was a pile of black canvas duffle bags. He unzipped the first bag. It was mostly filled with vacuum sealed bags of cannabis, so he discarded it. He unzipped another bag. It was filled with bundles of cash. He pulled the bag out and threw it to the asphalt street behind the Suburban, then he searched for another bag filled with cash.

Suddenly, rounds smashed into the Suburban's rear side windows with jolting whacks. Rage and Matheo ducked.

"Shoot back!" Rage yelled.

Matheo, not seeing where the shooter was, fired randomly up the street.

"Here, take this and go!" Rage yelled, handing Matheo the bag from the ground. "Get to your bike and get the fuck out of here."

Matheo turned away from his rifle sight to look over his shoulder at Rage. "Where's your bag?" he shouted.

"I'm looking for one. But there's no use in both of us staying here. I'm right behind you, bro. Take this and run!" Rage ordered.

Matheo hesitated, then grabbed the duffle of cash by the handles and took off in a sprint toward the Green Elephant dispensary.

Mason remained vigilant at the passenger side of Longhorn 2. Aiming down his rifle, he could see movement at the rear of Longhorn 3. Just then, a figure sprinted from the back of the Suburban and ran across the street carrying one of their cash bags. Mason popped a shot at the fleeing robber but missed.

"We've got one squirted east. Headed to the dispensary," Mason called out.

Mink reached up to his hand mic.

"Longhorn 1, this is Longhorn 3. They're going after the cash bags," he called into the mic. "One of the 6 o'clock shooters just ran east."

The radio crackled.

"Longhorn 3, this is Longhorn 1. I'm sending the drone to your position. Stand by," Caleb's voice said. Within seconds, Mink heard the buzzing of the drone's rotors as it passed overhead and took a position hovering over Longhorn 3. He watched it as it spun around in space, searching. Caleb's voice came over the radio again.

"Longhorn 3, the rear of your vehicle is clear. There is nobody there. I am proceeding east to find the runner."

"Uh, there were two shooters at Longhorn 3's rear. Do you have visual on the other shooter?" Mink called back.

After a moment, Caleb responded, "Negative. There's nobody else around."

Frowning, Mink licked his lips and focused his mind.

"Mason, cover me, I'm moving. I'm about to push up and check Longhorn 3."

"I've got you," Mason said, peering through his sight toward the last Suburban.

With his rifle tight against his shoulder, Mink sprinted down the driver's side of the wrecked Suburbans towards the rear of Longhorn 3, his muzzle fixed on the rear of the vehicle. His blood pumped and his head pounded. His body ached with each step, but adrenaline fueled him. He reached Longhorn 3 and wrapped around the rear, ready to shoot anyone or anything there—but there was no one. The rear doors were shut and there were bags of cannabis strewn along the ground, but both robbers had slipped away somehow. Just then, he heard shots and a scream from the Green Elephant 75 meters away. Instinctively, Mink ran toward the sound.

Caleb watched everything unfold from the sky. He could just make out the black figure fleeing across the parking lot carrying a duffle bag and an AK-47. The robber ran across the dispensary's parking lot to the entrance, where he grabbed the front door handle and jerked it open. He was hardly inside the small shop before Caleb heard muffled claps of gunfire through the drone's audio-video feed.

"Shooter just entered the Green Elephant dispensary and appears to be firing on civilians," Caleb called over the radio. He guided the quadcopter drone to the front of the building and lowered its altitude so he could see through the windows, but they were covered.

"I'm on it," Mink called back through his radio as he ran from Longhorn 3 toward the Green Elephant. He crossed the parking lot, ears pounding and heart racing. The dispensary's front door loomed ahead as his legs and arms pumped, his rifle feeling heavier by the breath. Once he arrived at the front door, he listened. The drone's whirring blades grew louder as it descended to head height.

"I've got the front. Go around and watch the back," Mink barked at the drone. Caleb heard the instructions through the drone's microphone, and he complied. Using the touchscreen control on his wrist, he guided the drone up and over the top of the Green Elephant to an alley that ran along the back of the store. The narrow passage had several blue trashcans and a green dumpster in it. There were two cars parked there as well. Caleb spotted the back door, a solid steel panel covered in peeling green paint. He positioned the drone high above and waited.

Meanwhile, Mink was paused at the front door, listening. He could hear shouting and screaming from inside, both male and female voices. Another gunshot boomed from behind the door.

"Shit!" he cursed under his breath, then keyed his mic.

"Longhorn 1, I am making entry now," Mink said. Caleb heard the transmission, and a chill went up his spine. He leaned in closer to his screen, watching for any movement.

Mink let his rifle hang from its sling and drew his Springfield Armory XD-M .45 caliber pistol. He took a deep breath, placed his hand on the metal door, and yanked it open. With all the speed and force he could muster, Mink leaped into the room, his pistol up and scanning instantly. In less than a second, he spotted a civilian body bleeding on the ground, and two more figures struggling behind the counter. One figure had bright green hair, while the other was wearing all black. They were grappling and shoving at each other as the robber was trying to escape through the store. When Mink made his entry, the doorbell chimed. The figure in all black turned his head just in time to see the flash from Mink's muzzle. One shot caught Matheo in the arm, spinning him around. He reflexively fired a round from the hip back at Mink, but the shot went wild, shattering a store display. The green-haired lady screamed and jumped away as Mink covered the distance from the front door to the counter, both men firing at each other. Bullets whizzed centimeters from Mink's face, forcing him to duck, while bongs and display cases shattered. He heard the squeak of rubber soles on the waxed floor and looked up to see the robber fleeing into the store's back room.

Mink leaped to his feet and jumped over the counter in pursuit. The back room was separated by a green curtain still swaying from the robber's passage as Mink darted through. The back room was dim, causing him to stop short as his eyes tried to adjust. A thunderous gunshot and muzzle flash from ahead caused him to dive behind a shelf.

Then the storeroom went quiet. Mink couldn't hear anything over the sound of his own breathing. Sweat poured down his face, and his vision was blurred from lack of oxygen. He took big, deep breaths, then dropped the magazine from his pistol and loaded a fresh one.

"Drop the gun!" he yelled.

"Va te faire enculer," Matheo yelled back.

"I don't know what that means," Mink returned.

"It means, 'Go fuck yourself', stupid Yankee," Matheo yelled from the back of the storeroom. Mink could not detect his exact location through the forest of shelves and boxes. He scanned around from left to right across the room.

Just then, he heard a metallic clack-clack followed by a thud, and suddenly, light poured into the room as the robber shoved open the back door and fled the building.

"Shit!" Mink cursed. "He ran out the back," he called into his radio as he jumped up and began pursuit. Ducking and dodging packages and shelves, Mink dashed through the storeroom to the back door. He burst into the daylight, pistol up and ready. Looking left, then right, he just saw the back of the robber running away.

"Longhorn 3 in foot pursuit!" Mink called, all his police training kicking in.

"Mink! Don't do it. Let the cops get him," Caleb called back over the radio.

"Send backup," Mink replied, but from the drone's vantage point above the scene, Caleb could see that Mink had not stopped chasing the robber.

"Damn it, Mink. Stop the chase. It's not your job," Caleb pleaded over the radio. Still, he could see Mink running full tilt after one of the men who had killed Matt, Ali, and maybe others. Caleb gritted his teeth, knowing Mink wouldn't stop until either he or the robber were down.

Caleb thought for a moment, then decided to enact a plan he had rehearsed in his head many times. Looking closely at the screen, he raced the drone ahead, focusing on the fleeing robber. His black clothing stood out against the gray pavement below, and Caleb had no trouble following him from a high altitude. He watched the fleeing man as he struggled to carry the cash bag and his rifle while also wearing body armor. From above, Caleb could see the masked robber was slowing, his energy draining as the chase hit an open parking lot. Mink was narrowing the distance as the two weaved through alleys, across sidewalks, and eventually into another parking lot filled with cars. Out of breath, the robber ducked behind a black SUV, where he crouched in ambush.

"Mink! The shooter is waiting behind the black SUV at your 11 o'clock, about 10 meters in front of you. Do you see it?" Caleb called over the radio.

"Affirmative, I see it," Mink called back as he slowed to a walk. Caleb could hear him panting for breath.

"Catch your breath and get ready to rush the SUV," Caleb said into his radio.

Mink had just enough time to wonder what Caleb meant when he heard the drone's buzzing blades grow louder. He looked up in time to see the little quadcopter swoop down from above like a diving hawk. It vanished behind the black SUV. Mink heard a shout and a scuffle. Realization hit him, and he took off at a full sprint. He crossed the distance in a blink, running as fast as he could between the parked cars. He ran down the side of the shiny black

SUV until he wrapped around the back of the vehicle, his pistol up.

The shooter was bent over, holding his face and groaning in pain. The drone was whirring and flopping around on the ground next to him, one of its rotors broken from the impact with his head. Matheo looked up, and Mink saw blood dripping into one eyehole of his mask. He took half a breath, then unloaded his pistol into Matheo's head and neck, the heavy .45 rounds blowing his skull to pieces across the dirty pavement.

"Suspect... is... down," Mink called over the radio, panting and wheezing. "Nice... move... Longhorn 1..."

He bent over to catch his breath, then called Caleb again.

"Caleb, where is the other 6 o'clock shooter?" he asked.

"I don't know, Longhorn 3," Caleb called back. "Eye in the sky is out of business. I have no visual on any other shooters."

Panting, Mink slumped to the ground, trying to catch his breath. Matheo's AK-47 and the bag of money lay at his feet in a spreading pool of blood.

31

Oil

The GZD office smelled faintly of printer ink and fresh coffee. Raison led the way, each step precise on the pale tile floor, the patterns reflecting the fluorescent overhead lights. Robeur followed a step behind, his steps echoing Raison's. The two men moved like a single shadow, rifles shouldered and pointed ahead as they crept down the hall. They passed a row of cubicles on the right, each desk neatly organized with sticky notes, calendars, and family photos pinned to fabric dividers.

They arrived at an office door with frosted glass. Using his gloved hand, Raison gently turned the metal knob and nudged the door with his boot. Inside, an empty leather chair sat behind an oak desk. To its side, a potted plant drooped, thirsty for water. The computer screensaver displayed a serene mountain scene. Robeur entered next, sweeping the space with his rifle's muzzle, past an open filing cabinet, its drawers revealing rows of neatly labeled manila folders. The scent of old paper and ink filled his nostrils.

Exiting the room, Raison gave a hand signal showing two more rooms to go. They continued methodically clearing their path. The muted hum of the office air conditioning was interrupted by a soft whimper. In a dimly lit corner of a break room, just beside the blue and white water cooler, a woman sat hunched, clutching a headset. Her mascara was smudged with tears. Raison locked eyes with her, and in one swift motion, he was upon her. Grasping her arm, he pulled her up, her slight frame quivering with fear.

"What's your name?" Raison demanded.

"Rhonda," the terrified dispatcher responded. She was much smaller than Raison with shoulder-length brown hair. She was wearing a white blouse, navy slacks, and pumps.

"Rhonda, I need you to take us to the money," Raison growled into her ear, his voice muffled by his mask.

Rhonda hesitated, her hazel eyes darting between the two armed figures, settling on the glinting muzzle of Robeur's AR-15.

"Now!" Raison's voice echoed.

Tears welled in her eyes, yet she found the strength to speak, her voice barely above a whisper. "There's no money here."

Raison tightened his grip, fingernails digging through the thin fabric of her blouse. "Don't lie. The secure room. Take us there!"

"I'm telling you, there's no money here," she insisted.

"Which way?" Raison shoved her. "Let's go!"

The trio made their way down a series of corridors. Each footstep on the tile seemed magnified tenfold. They arrived at a steel door with a keypad to its right. Rhonda's hand trembled as she entered a series of numbers. A magnetic lock thumped open, and Raison opened the door and pushed Rhonda to her knees.

"Watch her," he told Robeur, who stepped forward and took a fist of Rhonda's brunette hair. She winced. Raison walked into the storeroom. It was about twenty feet deep and fifteen feet wide, and, overhead, LEDs brightly lit the space. Lining the walls and stacked neatly on industrial shelves were massive plastic bags bursting with green, freshly trimmed cannabis buds. An intense skunky aroma filled the space. He hurried around the room, checking each shelf, spilling marijuana across the floor.

Raison's pulse raced. Every shelf was covered with weed and only weed. Turning suddenly, he leaned down and grabbed Rhonda by the collar. "Where is the money?" he hissed, only his eyes visible through the mask.

Rhonda's eyes welled up with tears, and her voice cracked. "I don't know. I really don't. I have never seen any money here."

Two gunshots echoed down the hallway, deep and loud. Raison and Robeur froze, listening.

Robeur, glancing uneasily at the door they had entered through. "We don't have time for this."

With a final, frustrated look around the storage room, Raison released Rhonda and nodded at Robeur. They exited hastily, back into the hallway. Raison's face was contorted in anger and desperation, his eyes wide and searching. Their rapid footsteps echoed, and their gear clattered as they ran. Raison's pulse pounded in his ears as he and Robeur hurtled down the corridor, back to the front door.

On the other side of the GZD office, Okwaho came to a T-intersection in the hallways. There, the blood trail ended. He looked left and right. He listened carefully. Nothing. Looking at his watch, then back down the hall where he had come, he calculated. He could not tell which way the wounded defender had gone, and every step could be a trap. He cursed, then turned and ran back down the hallway toward the garage.

Running full speed, he jumped over Moose's body. He could see the hall door to the garage directly ahead. He glanced behind one last time as he turned the corner, his heart racing as he passed Big Mike's body. At the garage door, he twisted the shiny steel knob and shoved it open. The door swung ahead of him as he stepped into the bay. The silver Dodge pickup was where they had left it, the engine still running inside the shattered space. Okwaho stepped through the doorway, releasing the door handle, and immediately felt his feet fly out from under him. He fell backward—hard—smacking the back of his head on the concrete. He tried to catch himself, but his hands slipped away. Rolling over, he looked at his palm. It was covered in fresh motor oil.

In that instant, the door he had entered through swung closed, and from behind it stepped The Colonel. He stood over Okwaho as he flopped on the ground. The Colonel held out his hand holding a quart bottle of motor oil. He turned it over, spilling the last drops onto Okwaho's head. Then he shot him in the face with the Colt 1911 in his other hand, sending Okwaho's brains splattering into the syrupy puddle.

The Colonel stepped back and looked around. He spotted a box of blue shop towels on a table. Staggering to them, he pulled out a handful of cotton rags. Looking down, he saw his shirt and pants were soaked with blood. He lifted his shirt and saw a ragged bullet hole through his rib cage. Dark fluid was pumping out of it. Groaning in pain, he stuffed the wound with blue shop towels. Sweat poured from his face as he clenched his eyes and felt his body getting weak.

32

Regroup

Meanwhile, at the ambush site, smoke lingered, and gunshots echoed off nearby buildings. With sporadic bursts of his Draco leaving streaks of gun smoke in the air, Reaper paced behind the dumpster, arm outstretched before him, taking potshots at anything that moved, bellowing a hoarse war cry. He dropped a spent magazine, then fumbled under his dirty rags for another. He patted his chest rig, but all the pouches were empty, all the ammunition spent.

Reaper lowered the gun. He looked around at the destruction. Bullet holes pockmarked every surface around him, and his arm was covered in blood. He was mostly deaf from all the gunfire, and his ears felt full of cement. He looked up at the sky, at the clouds floating past. He could still feel the psychedelic mushrooms tickling his brain, and he thought he saw a great bearded war god in the clouds, looking down at him.

Suddenly, Captain Doug Frazier rose from a low wall behind the dumpster where he had slowly crawled, a black pistol clenched in his grip. With a steely focus, Doug aimed, exhaling slowly as his finger tightened around the trigger. The first shot boomed like a cannon. Reaper, caught off-guard, felt a punch to the back of his neck, then his body went numb. The bullet's force thrust his head to the side, blood spattering onto the sun-heated asphalt below. He couldn't hold himself up, so he collapsed onto the pavement, his legs and arms paralyzed.

Doug, his stance solid, watched as the shooter crumpled. He took a moment, steadying himself, then emptied the magazine of his HK45 into the head and torso of the downed attacker. He quickly dropped the spent magazine and reloaded, crossing the distance to the crazed enemy. The smell of burning plastic and gunpowder wafted through the air. From afar, the shrill wail of sirens grew louder.

Doug, his face a mixture of determination and weariness, grabbed his hand mic.

"This is Longhorn 1 actual. Rally on me at the back of Longhorn 3," he transmitted.

From his overwatch position at the front of Longhorn 2, Mason turned and looked toward the lead suburban. The rear passenger door opened, and Caleb climbed out, crouching, looking around uneasily. Mason scanned the street through his sight as Caleb, bent low at the waist, sprinted towards him, carrying his rifle.

"Let's move," Mason said. Both men trotted to the rear of the convoy, where they joined Doug at the back of the battered Longhorn 3. Mink came jogging up from the east, sweat pouring down his face.

Caleb spoke up. "I got an alarm ping from the office." He wiped the smoke from his eyes.

"They hit the office, too? Shit!" Doug exclaimed. "What are our casualties? Matt is dead."

"So is Ali," Mink said, his jaw clenching.

"Benito is wounded over there," Mason said, pointing. "He needs medical immediately."

Mink exploded, "Where the hell is Denver PD?"

Doug, with traces of soot on his face, said, "I don't know what is going on here. Something is definitely fucked. If these assholes hit the office, then The Colonel needs our help. But we can't all leave here. We need to split up. Mink and I will stay to help Benito and the first responders. Mink, get the med kit out of Longhorn 1 and go to work on Mendez."

"On it," Mink said and took off at a sprint.

"Mason, you and Caleb, go help at the office."

"Roger," Mason said. Then to Caleb, "Longhorns 1 and 2 are busted. Let's check Longhorn 3. Move!"

Mason and Caleb hoisted their rifles and ran to the last Suburban. Mason opened the driver's door and climbed in, leaving the door open. The keys were in the ignition. He cranked it. The engine turned over, hesitated, then finally started. Caleb opened the passenger door and set his rifle on the floorboard. Mason got out to check the tires. He set his rifle on the seat and looked towards the front of the Suburban. The windows were shattered but still in place because of the Lexan he and Caleb had applied. The front driver's side tire was still good. He walked toward the back of the SUV. The rear tire was good. He walked around the rear of the Suburban to check the other side when one of the back barn doors suddenly burst open, and a shadow sprung at him from within.

Rage, his face twisted in a maniac's snarl, kicked the back doors open and lunged toward Mason from inside Longhorn 3 where he had been hiding. He swung his prosthetic tomahawk in an overhead arch. Mason reflexively threw up his arm to block, and the razor-sharp blade sliced into his right biceps. Mason let out an agonized cry, pain exploding down his arm as the polished edge chopped through his muscle and struck bone. He reached across with his left hand and grabbed the handle as Rage grasped Mason's plate carrier, spun him around, and slammed him against the rear of the Suburban.

Reaching down, Rage pulled a pistol and aimed it at Mason's face. Mason ducked and yanked Rage's arm just as he pulled the trigger, sending the shot wild. He grabbed Rage's other arm, pulled him in, and kneed him in the groin. Then he smashed his forehead into Rage's nose. Rage grunted in pain and tried to angle his pistol to fire again. He pulled the trigger at point blank, the ear-shattering shot passing millimeters from Mason's head. Setting his feet apart, Mason tightened his grip on both of Rage's arms, then thrust his hip into Rage's while twisting and dropping his knee, hurling Rage's body up and over in a judo throw.

Rage slammed to the ground. Mason instantly put Rage's gun arm in a lock and twisted the pistol out of his grip. It skittered away on the pavement.

Mason drew his own pistol from his hip, his right hand weak and tingling from his cut biceps. Just as the pistol cleared the holster, Rage's left hand bearing the tomahawk swung up from the ground, smacking the gun to the pavement. Then he swung at Mason's face, forcing Mason to dodge and release his arm.

Freed, Rage sprung to his feet, slashing at Mason with his tomahawk hand. Mason jumped back and drew a double-edged fighting knife from a belt sheath. The men squared off in the street. Mason bent his knees and held the knife in front like a sword fighter. Rage led with his left, his hands in an open guard position. He lunged and slashed at Mason, who sidestepped and pivoted, slashing Rage on the arm as he passed, like a matador passing a bull. Rage spun around, slashing relentlessly. Mason danced away and slashed back, blood pouring from his arm. In the distance, sirens could be heard closing in. Mason and Rage circled each other in the street, then onto the sidewalk, trading jabs and lunges as they tried to cut or stab the other.

The sirens grew even louder. Mason scored a slice on Rage's thigh just as the first Denver PD Tahoe came barreling up the street from the south. With a screech of tire rubber, it slid to a stop about 20 meters behind Longhorn 3. The young officer jumped out, a shotgun in his hands. He shouldered the shotgun, yelled an order, then fired toward Mason and Rage.

The buckshot hit Mason's ceramic back plate and sent him tumbling to the ground. The second boom was deafening but missed. Rage jumped out of the way, falling and rolling across the pavement.

"Whoa! Whoa!" Mason yelled from the ground.

"Drop your weapon! Drop it!" the cop yelled.

The wind knocked out of him, Mason panted as he scanned around. Rage was gone.

"Drop the knife! Drop it!" the officer yelled.

Mason looked all around, but Rage was nowhere to be seen.

"Drop the knife now!"

Mason complied, tossing the knife away.

"Hands on your head! Do not reach for anything!"

Mason started to put his hands on his head when suddenly Longhorn 3's engine roared to life. The reverse lights came on and the battered-but-functional Suburban backed up quickly, tires squealing, putting itself directly between Mason and the shotgun-wielding cop. Through the shattered passenger window, Mason saw Caleb in the driver's seat.

"We don't have time for this. We have to get to the office now," Caleb yelled through the busted window.

Mason jumped to his feet in a flash and sprinted to the passenger door. He yanked it open and jumped in.

"Go! Go! Go!" he yelled as Caleb threw it into drive and mashed the accelerator. They raced through the intersection and away from the oncoming sirens.

Longhorn 3's engine growled, echoing off the surrounding buildings as they raced toward the home office. Caleb drove at top speed with both hands on the wheel, eyes glued to the road. Wind whistled and hissed through the bullet holes, and the battered vehicle shuttered and rattled.

"I hope this baby can make it," Caleb said, leaning into the steering wheel.

In the passenger seat, Mason tore the sleeve from his injured arm. Blood ran profusely from the chop into his biceps. His arm would not bend anymore, and he could feel the traumatized muscle spasming in shock. He opened the center console and removed a first aid kit. Tearing open packages with his teeth, he placed a big wad of gauze on the gash and wrapped it heavily with a bandage. He removed his belt and used it to improvise a sling, strapping his right arm tight across his chest.

The exterior of Longhorn 3 was riddled with bullet holes. The tires, however, still held firm, and the engine responded without hesitation. Once they made it onto the highway, Caleb floored the accelerator, sending the vehicle surging forward, tires squealing against the asphalt.

"Did you get any details about the office?" Mason asked.

"No," Caleb said, "just the alert from the alarm system. It's still going off."

Mason gritted his teeth. "Don't stop for shit," he said, and Caleb made the engine roar.

33

The Law

The Denver Police Department was in a state of high alert, with officers and staff scrambling in response to the bomb threat called in by Raison. Detectives Kim Wright and Harold Clarke were at Denver Police Department headquarters on Cherokee Street near the State Capitol. They were gathered in a conference room with about thirty other detectives and ranking officers. Phones, radios, and laptops covered the expansive conference room table as the officers coordinated the city's response. Kim was speaking with an FBI bomb specialist when she heard a crackle over the radio.

"Attention all units, shots fired on Larimer Street in the River North Art District. Multiple reports coming in," a female dispatcher said.

Before Kim could process this development, another report came in.

"Shots fired at the Green Zone Defense office, north edge of town. Need immediate response. Address to follow."

Kim looked at Harold, who was standing beside her drinking a Dr. Pepper.

"The Business District, the schools, River North Art District, and now Green Zone Defense? What the hell is going on?" she asked. "Is this a terrorist attack?"

Harold took a sip from his canned soda. "Since when do terrorists attack marijuana businesses?"

"That's my point..." Kim said, furrowing her brow.

He shrugged. "A few years ago in Stockholm, a gang robbed a cash depot using a helicopter. They roped in from the top, loaded up, and lifted the cash out. Meanwhile, the SWAT team was banging on the front door with a battering ram, trying to get inside the depot to stop them, but they couldn't get in. But you know what was even smarter? Before the gang launched their raid, they placed a bag labeled 'Bomb' at the police helicopter's hangar. The cops couldn't launch their chopper because it was being held hostage by a fake bomb." Harold took another sip from his Dr. Pepper. "I watched a documentary about it on YouTube."

Kim's mouth fell open. "Since when do you know about YouTube?"

"Since you told me about it," he shrugged. "What can I say? I listened."

Kim shook it off. "So, you're saying all this bomb shit is a decoy to throw us off from a robbery?"

Harold shrugged. "Maybe somebody else watched the same documentary. It was free, after all."

Kim stared at Harold in awe. "I can't even argue with that. So, what do you think we should do, wise man?"

Harold swished his soda around casually. "If there is any real money to be had, it would be at the Green Zone building. Plus, The Colonel is there, and cop or no cop, he's one of us. I think we should go there."

"Let's do it," Kim said.

Harold smiled. "Kim, you are a good cop, but you are young. If you were my age, you would know: this old fart is staying right here. Nobody needs me and my glaucoma out there playing cowboy in the streets. But I will be here when you return."

"Fair enough," Kim said as she grabbed her keys.

"Be safe out there, Detective," Harold called after her as she ran out of the room, down the stairs, and into the parking garage where a marked Tahoe waited. Most of the department's officers were out securing the local schools, but still the garage was busy with cruisers coming and going. She ran to the vehicle and opened the back door. From the rear, she removed a plate carrier, which she slid over her head. She slipped a ceramic plate into the front pouch, then reached in and removed an M4 carbine with an ACOG site and a vertical fore grip. She checked the magazine and checked the safety, then slid two more magazines into pouches on her plate carrier. She slammed the doors and raced around to the driver's seat. Inside, she set the rifle next to her seat and cranked the engine. The tires squealed on the concrete as she sped out of the garage and headed north on Cherokee Street until she ran onto Highway 70, which she took west.

"This is 4118, Detective Wright, en route to the Green Zone Defense office. Requesting backup and an update on the situation."

As she drove, updates came over the radio. "Multiple units en route to Larimer Street and Green Zone Defense building. No casualties reported. Ambulances on standby."

She took a ramp onto Interstate 25 and headed north. The engine of her cruiser roared as she flicked on the sirens and lights, weaving through traffic.

At the Green Zone Defense building, Longhorn 3 slid into the driveway at full speed. Caleb mashed the brakes and swerved the heavy SUV, gravel showering like wake from a speedboat. Mason noticed the gaping hole where a garage door had been. The Suburban skidded to a stop at the front door, and both men instantly opened their doors and sprung out. As they ran to the front door, a white van parked along the curb suddenly revved its engine. Mason and Caleb looked up just as the van's tires screeched against the pavement, kicking up a cloud of dust and gravel as it sped away.

"Shit, what was that?" Caleb asked.

Both men watched as the van roared across the parking lot and careened onto the main road, almost colliding with a honking sedan. It straightened itself and accelerated away, when suddenly a white Denver PD Tahoe came blazing up the street. The cruiser instantly hit its overhead lights and siren and gave chase.

"Fuck yeah!" Caleb yelled as they watched the Tahoe chase the speeding van down the street and out of sight.

"Give me your sidearm," Mason said, his right arm still bound to his chest with his belt. Caleb could see the gauze around Mason's biceps were soaked with blood. He quickly drew his Glock 19 from a drop leg holster and handed it to Mason.

"Get ready, we're going inside," Mason said, and they both lined up next to the front door, prepared to make entry.

Kim Wright turned off the overhead lights and siren as she neared Green Zone Defense in order to maintain stealth, but as soon as she arrived at the scene, she saw a white van exit the GZD parking lot like a loose bull, swerving into traffic and nearly causing a wreck. Without hesitation, she hit the cruiser's lights and siren. The van sped up, so Kim followed, the Tahoe's powerful engine responding with a throaty growl as she chased the fleeing van.

Inside the van, Bruno gripped the steering wheel and glanced in the rearview mirror at the persistent police SUV on his tail. His heart pounded in his chest like a drum as he saw the flashing lights. The roar of the van's engine filled his ears as he pushed the accelerator to the floor, the vehicle lurching forward with a sudden burst of speed. His hands gripped the wheel tightly, knuckles white with tension.

The streets of Denver blurred past as Bruno weaved the van through traffic. Cars honked and swerved to avoid collisions, their drivers shouting curses that were lost in a flash. The van's tires squealed with each sharp turn, the scent of burning rubber seeping into the cabin.

Ahead, a four-way traffic light turned red. Bruno's heart skipped a beat. He gritted his teeth and barreled through the intersection, narrowly missing a crossing car. The sound of horns and screeching brakes filled the air, but he didn't slow. The chase continued, the van and cruiser barreling up the street. Bruno's breathing was ragged, his mind frantic for an escape. He took a sharp right, tires skidding, and sped down a narrow alley. Trash cans and debris clattered in his wake, but the cruiser followed relentlessly, never losing ground. Emerging from the alley, Bruno's eyes searched wildly for an out. The cityscape was a blur of buildings and lights, but no clear path to freedom presented itself. He glanced at the fuel gauge—less than a quarter tank remained.

Kim kept a steady distance and radioed for backup, her voice calm and collected despite the adrenaline pumping through her veins.

"4418 in pursuit of a suspect in a white van heading north from the GZD office. Requesting backup and roadblock assistance."

As the van barreled down the streets, narrowly avoiding other vehicles, Kim remained in hot pursuit. The chase escalated when they merged onto a freeway. The traffic was lighter here, allowing both vehicles to pick up speed. Kim kept a safe distance, her eyes calculating the best moment to act. As they weaved through the freeway traffic, Kim waited for the perfect opportunity.

Spotting an opening, she sped up, her cruiser closing in on the van. With precision and control, she bumped into the rear corner of Bruno's van with the front corner of her cruiser. The PIT maneuver caused the van to fishtail, its tires losing grip as it spun out of control. Bruno fought the wheel, but it was too late. The van skidded across three lanes, tipped, and then slammed sideways against a concrete highway divider with a shower of sparks and dust.

Kim didn't waste a moment. She slammed her cruiser to a stop, flung the door open, and, in a swift motion, drew her Glock 17, aiming it directly at the van's driver-side window.

"Hands up! Get out of the vehicle now!" she shouted.

Bruno, his face a mask of shock and defeat, raised his hands in surrender. Slowly, he opened the van's door and stepped out, his movements cautious under Kim's watchful eye.

Kim kept her weapon trained on him as she approached. "On the ground, now!"

Bruno complied, lying face down on the pavement.

"Who else is in the van?" she yelled at Bruno.

"Nobody," he said calmly. "It's just me."

"Lie down with your arms extended and don't fucking move," she barked at him. Then, cautiously, she approached the van, her pistol outstretched in front of her. She peeked through the open driver's door, then climbed inside and confirmed it was empty. Then she turned back to Bruno.

"One at a time, I want you to put your hands behind your back, starting with your right hand," she said.

After she had cuffed Bruno, she called over her radio.

"4418, I have suspect in custody on the side of Highway 36 north, northbound near Sheridan."

She jerked Bruno up to his feet and frisked his waistband and pockets.

"Lawyer from Staten Island, my ass. Why were you at Green Zone? Why did you run? Are you part of this terrorist group that's attacking us today?" Kim asked.

"No," Bruno said. "I'm not a terrorist."

"Then what are you?" Kim asked, spinning Bruno around, her face close to his. "Because that building back there has friends of mine in it. Why were you there?"

Bruno let out a deep sigh. "You'll have to ask my lawyer. I plead the fifth."

Kim glared at Bruno, her fists clenched.

"You piece of shit. Get your ass in the car," she ordered through clenched teeth as she shoved Bruno toward the Tahoe.

34

Loss

Back at the Green Zone Defense building, Mason and Caleb made their entry through the front door, Caleb with his carbine up and ready, and Mason carrying a pistol, his right arm bandaged and useless. The overhead lights cast a dim glow on the polished tile floors as they crept inside.

They swept through the maze of hallways silently and fluidly, bounding until they came to an office. There, they posted on either side of the door, weapons ready. When Mason gave the nod, Caleb opened the door quickly. Mason entered first, crossing the threshold from right to left, with Caleb following just behind, crossing from left to right.

They cleared two offices quickly, one after another, then returned to the hallway and began making their way deeper into the building. The office was quiet except for the hum of the air conditioning. But, as they approached a corner, Mason heard approaching footsteps. He froze, his pistol aimed down the hall. A few seconds later, a figure turned the corner dressed in all black, wearing a mask, and holding a rifle.

"Contact front!" he yelled as he squeezed the trigger. The 9mm Glock worked smoothly in his left hand, popping five rounds accurately down the hallway, each shot a direct hit. The bullets struck the attacker's body armor with loud cracks, and the victim let out a brief squeal. Mason dropped to one knee, and Caleb opened up with his SIGM400. The overpressure of the shots battered Mason's eardrums. Still, he watched as the black-clad attacker was chewed up with high-velocity rounds.

Silently, cautiously, Mason and Caleb crept down the hallway, ears ringing. They passed Robeur's bloodied corpse close enough to see his red beard and neck tattoos from under the mask. Both men kept their weapons trained toward the blind corner from where the attacker had come.

Muffled female screams from ahead pierced the silence. The men increased their pace. Offices blurred past as their boots pounded the tiles. Approaching the back of the building, Mason heard the loud clang of the back door slam, so they followed.

Sunlight filtered through the trees over the employee parking lot behind the building, illuminating Mason as he stepped through the back door. He swept the scene with the pistol as he and Caleb spilled out. In the middle of the parking lot, another black-clad bandit was dragging Rhonda by the neck.

Raison clutched Rhonda tightly. His arm was coiled around her throat while the other hand pressed a pistol to her temple. Her eyes, swollen and rimmed with fear, locked onto Mason. Her breaths came in panicked, irregular rasps, each exhale shuddering her frame.

Mason pointed his pistol at Raison's face, every synapse firing with cold, clinical analysis. His mind cycled through options, evaluating the geometry of every shot. Raison's eyes flicked frantically around the parking lot, his grip on Rhonda quivering.

"Whoa!" Raison barked frantically. "No farther!"

Mason's voice was level. "Let her go. It's over."

Rhonda's whimpers threaded through the tension as seconds dragged on. Amid the shifting shadows and the hazy remnants of dust kicked up from the commotion, Raison and Mason stood facing each other. Raison's face was a collage of desperation and calculation. The pistol pressed into Rhonda's temple, her frantic heartbeat visible in her throat where Raison's fingers tightened.

Mason stood steadily, his pistol trained. "You want to get away? I can help with that."

He slowly, deliberately, reached into his pocket, producing a ring of car keys. "It's the Bronco," he said calmly, pointing toward his SUV. "Take it.

Just let her go."

Raison glanced at the Bronco, then back at Mason.

"Throw me the keys, or I will blow her brains out!" Raison yelled. "Now!"

Without hesitation, Mason tossed the keys to Raison, who released Rhonda just long enough to catch them. She started to escape, moving inches away, but Raison quickly grabbed her hair and yanked her back. Then, he started walking backward, dragging the sobbing Rhonda with him. Mason and Caleb followed, guns up, matching his pace. They slowly crossed the dusty parking lot while Rhonda sobbed and begged to be let go.

They reached the Bronco. Raison cast a wary look at Mason.

"I want you to stand right here," he said into Rhonda's ear. "If you try to run, if you move one inch, before I drive off, I will shoot you in the back. Do you understand?"

Rhonda whimpered.

"Do you understand?" Raison screamed at her.

"She won't move," Mason said calmly. "Rhonda, just stand still. It's ok. Do what he says. Just stand still."

"Ok!" Rhonda said through tears. "Yes, I understand."

Slowly, Raison removed his arm from around her neck. Keeping the pistol aimed at her, he backed away a few inches. He watched Mason and Caleb cautiously before raising the keyring to his eye level and looking at it quizzically.

"The round key is for the door. The square one is for the ignition. Go ahead," Mason assured him.

Raison looked at Mason skeptically, then slowly inserted the round key into the door lock, never taking the pistol from Rhonda's back. The driver's door swung open.

Suddenly, a growling, black-spotted white blur erupted from underneath the Bronco. Bud the Dalmatian lunged from under the vehicle, snarling ferociously, sinking his sharp teeth into Raison's thigh. The outlaw jumped and cried out as the dog's powerful jaws ripped through his pants. He stumbled back and fell against the neighboring pickup truck just as Caleb squeezed the trigger twice—Bang! Bang!—placing two .223 caliber bullets into Raison's head.

Rhonda screamed and dove to the ground. Caleb and Mason raced forward. Caleb grabbed Rhonda and pulled her clear as Mason fired more shots into Raison's fallen body with his pistol. Bud scampered under the Bronco, baring his teeth and growling.

"Are you hurt?" Caleb asked Rhonda.

"No, no, I don't think so," she sobbed, hanging onto Caleb's arm.

Mason kicked Raison's pistol from his dead hand, then stood for a while, watching the blood leak from the outlaw's head.

Inside the office, beneath the stark, unyielding light of the overhead fluorescents, The Colonel staggered down the hallway, each step a symphony of agony and sheer will. His breathing was tight and ragged. Blood bubbled from his mouth. His elongated and trembling shadow etched a dark silhouette against the pristine tile, now tarnished with marks of chaos and conflict.

A raspy breath escaped him as he leaned heavily against the wall, streaking it with a dreadful pattern of red. Glazed but unyielding, his eyes traced along the familiar path towards his office. Mustering his last shreds of strength, The Colonel eased the door open, the creaking hinge singing a melancholy duet with his labored breaths.

With an agonizing effort, he sank into his chair and set his Colt 1911 on the desk with a solid thunk. His hands, trembling, slid along the chair's arms, fingers tracing over the aged, softened leather. He heard gunshots and a dog barking from the back parking lot. His gaze shifted upward, past the accolades and memories framed on the walls, landing on a photograph—he and his son, Caleb, holding up a coyote Caleb had killed on a hunt together.

His lips twitched into a faint, pained smile. A soft exhale, almost a sigh of relief, passed through him, his body slackening, releasing.

35

Aftermath

Under a cloudy gray sky, a solemn assembly formed on the well-maintained grounds of the town's community center. Neat rows of white chairs, meticulously arranged, hosted the survivors of the harrowing encounter: Mason, Doug, Caleb, Mink, Benito, and Rhonda. Benito wore a neck brace and bandages on much of his face and body. Mason, also dressed in black, carried his right arm in a sling. The seats were filled with family and community members. Ali's widow, Marissa, sat with their daughter, Kayla, her tiny head lying in her mother's lap. A contingent of Marines in dress uniforms, including several of high rank, as well as a throng of Denver police officers, surrounded the memorial.

Kim Wright, wearing a black pantsuit and black sunglasses, her hair pulled tightly into a neat bun, stood with Mike and Xavier, her hands clasped before her. Her bottom lip trembled slightly, and she looked down for a moment before raising her chin and facing the photographs of the deceased.

The backdrop to the gathering was a series of portraits on easels, flanked by elaborate floral arrangements of white and green. First was a portrait of Matt Anderson as a rookie cop, with a full head of blonde hair, smiling in his Denver PD uniform. The second portrait was Ali in Marine BDUs, his smile lighting up the day. The third portrait was of Big Mike sitting on a couch at Christmastime, surrounded by his smiling children. In the center was a portrait of The Colonel wearing Marine Corps Officer Dress Blues. The silver eagle insignia of his rank gleamed on his shoulder boards. His face was rugged and stern, but there was a slight upward curve to his lips.

Behind black sunglasses, Mason stared at the memorial in somber reflection. By his side, Doug sat stoically, his eyes puffy and his nose red. Caleb sat on Mason's other side, next to his mother, holding her hand as she cried.

An icy breeze rustled through the gathering, carrying a chill down from the mountains.

Under the amber glow of a deer antler chandelier, Pop and Tommy Boy relaxed in a living room. Pop sprawled in a brown recliner smoking and chewing gum, while Tommy Boy sat casually on a plush leather sofa. A crackling fireplace illuminated the ornate woodwork of the luxury cabin. A plasma TV above the fireplace played live coverage of a failed robbery and shootout in Colorado. As images of the tattered Green Zone Defense office and smoking, bullet-riddled Suburbans played, an anchor passionately debated with a three-person panel of commentators.

"Police are still not saying whether the bombing in downtown Denver was tied to the ambush and assault on Green Zone Defense or not," the male anchor said.

"That's not a coincidence," a panel member responded. "None of this is a coincidence, Bill. This was not Benghazi. This was not Bogota or Kabul. This was Denver, Colorado. We experienced an ambush and shoot-out in the middle of our city like nobody has seen since the days of the Dillinger Gang. I mean, this was a real Wild West shootout, and it was not a coincidence that it happened here, in Colorado, where we just legalized marijuana."

"The target of what police are calling a robbery gone wrong was a security firm dedicated to protecting cannabis enterprises," the anchor agreed.

"Exactly! These criminals came to our city with high-powered weapons of war, with every intent to destroy lives, and it's because we have legalized marijuana."

"We legalized marijuana," another panel member chimed in, "and just as so many of us feared, criminals are coming here to target these cannabis businesses. We were assured it would all be manageable, but this does not look manageable to me."

Pop watched intently, his eyes reflecting the flicker of the TV screen.

"You see that, Tommy Boy?" he said, thumping his ash into a plastic ashtray. "This changes the entire game. After this, no other U.S. state will touch weed legalization."

Tommy Boy sat on the sofa, one cowboy-booted ankle crossed over his knee. He took a deep drag from his cigar, then exhaled slowly, creating a hazy cloud that drifted across the room.

Pop chuckled, his hearty laugh echoing through the cabin. "It's always about the bigger picture. It's not just about dispensaries in Colorado or pulling off some fucking robbery. It's about a message. Welcome to the jungle, motherfuckers. We let America taste the chaos. Now watch as they back away from legalization like it has teeth. No more legal markets. No more medical this and recreational that. There will only be us. Our production, our shipments. The Big Machine rolls on, untouched."

Tommy Boy nodded slowly. "So, Raison, Rage, the robbery," he waved his cigar toward the TV, "all this was just a chess move, huh?"

Pop chuckled. "Always stay two moves ahead, Tommy Boy. That's how we stay on top. That, my boy, is how we conquer Quebec and the rest of the world."

Tommy Boy sat calmly, his fingers tapping against the armrest. "You know, Pop, I never liked Raison. Too ambitious. You can't trust a man who sold his leaders to their enemy."

Pop nodded thoughtfully, "True. But, as much as I didn't trust him, Raison and his boys were useful in their own way. In this game, you need pawns. Crash dummies."

Tommy Boy smirked. "And they played their part well, didn't they?"

Pop laughed. "Like they were born for it."

"The one they arrested, the Yank, Bruno. They're still holding him in isolation in the Denver County Jail. We don't know if he's cooperating or not. And they still haven't caught the psychotic brother, Rage," Tommy Boy added.

Pop waved his hand. "We can take care of Bruno anytime. Behind bars, not behind bars, we can touch him. As for Rage, either the cops find him, or we will," he said, standing up from the recliner. "It's just a matter of time. Now, go put on your new cut, and then let's get a steak. I'm starving."

Tommy Boy stood and walked to the bar. Sitting on the glossy wooden counter was a denim vest. The front patches said "Tommy Boy" and "President". He turned it over. The back featured a grinning skeleton riding a massive chopper in red, white, and black. Above the center patch, the top rocker read "Big Machine." Below it, the bottom rocker read, "Quebec."

36

The Builder

The construction site was silent in the twilight. Mason parked the Bronco and got out. Bud hopped out and trotted along beside him. Mason walked around to the back of the SUV, opened the tailgate, and pulled out two large black duffle bags. They were full, and Mason strained to lift them.

He carried the heavy bags past the RV, down the worn, dusty path to the range. The soft hum of overhead lights greeted Mason and Bud as they descended into the underground shooting range, the muted echo of their steps resonating off the concrete walls.

They walked down the aisle of shooting lanes to the far side of the subterranean room. There was a plain steel door marked "Mechanical". Mason opened it and stepped inside, closing the door behind himself. The walls were mostly covered with electrical panels, wiring, and blinking lights. Mason stopped before a plain, bare section of block wall and set the bags down. He pressed his hand flat against the wall. The wall glowed momentarily around his hand, first red, then green, then an electronic beep sounded. There was a faint mechanical whirr before the wall section slowly retracted and slid open, revealing an entrance to a hidden chamber. The cool, metallic scent of the room filled his nostrils as Mason carried the bags through the secret doorway.

Inside, a seven-foot-tall vault door covering most of the back wall greeted him. Mason punched a code into the keypad, pressed his thumb against a reader, and looked up into a facial recognition camera. The vault door hummed and rattled, then slowly opened.

Within the vault, shelves lined the walls and ran in rows across the interior, each stacked high with neat bundles of U.S. currency. The faint glow from overhead lights illuminated the vast wealth, casting shimmering highlights on the transparent plastic wrappings. For a moment, he stood, taking in the sight. Then he looked down at Bud, who was cautiously sniffing the strange bundles. Mason set the bags on a stainless-steel table and unzipped them. They were filled with money. He reached in and pulled out a stack. The top bill, a $20, had burn marks on it, and the bag smelled of smoke.

"This is the pickup from Monday. What's left of it, anyway. This is what my friends died for. Stacks of paper," Mason said out loud to the dog, throwing the bundle of bills back into the bag. "I would burn it all to get them back."

He walked out, closed the vault door, passed through the secret doorway, and shut off the lights before climbing up the stairs with Bud by his side, back into the chilly night air. They plodded to the trailer. A stillness hung over the construction site, the training ground's skeletal framework bathed in the moon's soft glow. Mason sat on a creaky chair under the front porch awning, gazing out into the expanse. His left hand, rough from years of labor and combat, clenched tightly around the chair's arms. Stitches and staples held his biceps together inside the sling. Bud lay quietly on the ground beside his feet.

Suddenly, Mason surged up from his seat, muscles taut, veins pulsating in his neck, and roared into the sky. A bellow erupted from the depths of his soul, tearing through the silent evening like an artillery barrage or the roar of a furious lion. He screamed his rage into the night and let his pain wash over the construction site, the hidden money, the city below, and the mountains above.

Jolted, Bud leaped to his feet, ears perked. The cry echoed across the barren construction site, bouncing off the structures, dissipating into the infinite sky above, leaving behind a piercing silence. Mason's arms slowly fell back to his sides, his body hunched.

He collapsed back into the weathered chair on his porch and buried his face in his hands. Sobs overtook him, racking his body. Finally, he gasped for air, sat up straight, and fell silent.

Mason and Bud sat together on the porch together for some time.

The next day, as the sun climbed in the Colorado sky, Detective Kim Wright pulled up to the construction site in a police Tahoe and parked next to Mason's Bronco. She climbed out and walked toward the sprawling, half-built structures. The sun shining through the openings cast long shadows across the dirt and gravel. Her eyes scanned the area before settling on Mason, who was sitting on a chair in the open watching Caleb dig a ditch with a Mattock.

As Detective Wright walked toward them, Caleb, noticing her arrival, paused his digging and wiped the sweat from his brow.

"Keep going, Caleb," Mason said. "Unless you're under arrest, we need this trench dug before the plumber gets here tomorrow." His voice was firm, but not unkind. Caleb nodded and resumed his work. The sound of his pick biting into the earth filled the air.

Kim sat in an empty chair next to Mason, her gaze lingering on Caleb for a moment. "Hard work can be an excellent teacher," she commented.

Mason nodded, his eyes not leaving Caleb. "It teaches more than just the value of a dollar," he said. "It teaches about consequences, responsibility."

The detective looked back at Mason. "And what about you, Mason? What have you learned from all this?"

Mason's gaze drifted off into the distance. "That's a good question, Detective. I've been asking myself the same thing."

"Well, I could tell you what I've learned then," she continued. "The whole thing was a robbery. Canadian bikers. Came all the way from Montreal to do this...."

Mason stared through his black sunglasses. There was a bit of sand on his beard, and his face was tanned from being outside. "The one you caught. He's talking, huh?"

Kim looked around. "That I can't say, but just know that we have it on good authority that it was the Big Machine biker gang behind all this. The robbers who died were Big Machine members, or members of another club who wanted to join them. Real bad actors, all of them. We searched their cabin and found bomb making parts. It's amazing you and Mendez survived the IED attack. You know they might give you a civilian medal for this? My partner thinks the president will want to meet you."

Mason didn't budge. "Well, I don't know about that. Caleb and I have to finish up here, and I'm down one arm," he said.

Kim leaned forward, her elbows on her knees. "You've got a lot on your plate. GZD, this construction site, and whatever else you're not telling me. You're a man with secrets, Mason."

"Aren't we all, Detective? But you're right. There's a lot going on, and I'm trying to figure out my next move."

Mason took a long drink from a water bottle.

"The right move," Kim corrected gently.

"Yeah, the right move," Mason echoed. He glanced at Caleb again, then back at Kim. "It's not just about what I do next. It's about making sure it counts, making it mean something. I know that I've seen too much, done too much, and lost too many friends to let it all go to waste. How can we give up on life when so many others gave up their lives so we can have ours?"

Kim nodded. "And what about Caleb? How is he handling this?"

Mason's expression softened. "I could never be the man his father was, but Caleb won't be alone."

The detective stood up, brushing off her pants. "Well, I'll leave you to your teaching, Mason. Just remember, if you need help, you have friends."

Mason looked up at her, a hint of gratitude in his eyes. "I appreciate that, Detective."

Kim turned to walk away, then turned back.

"Did you guys ever find out what happened to the missing weed?" Kim asked.

"It's been handled," Mason replied, his eyes returning to Caleb. "There won't be any more mysterious bags of pot appearing out of place. I guarantee you that."

Kim followed his gaze to Caleb, sweating in the dirt. She nodded knowingly.

"Well, after everything, I think that's good enough for me. Take care of yourself, Mason."

As Kim walked back to her cruiser, she took one last look at the construction site. Mason sat there with his dog, watching over Caleb, a silent guardian building a better man.

The End

About the Author

Rex Holloway writes crime thrillers shaped by a life that has seen both darkness and redemption.

His Mason Origins Trilogy (*The Wolf and the Lion*, *Gladiator Farm*, and *A Fire Devours*) plunges readers into a brutal world of outlaw bikers, crime syndicates, cartel violence, and elite security operators. Known for gritty realism and relentless pacing, Holloway's stories explore the thin line between justice and vengeance, loyalty and betrayal, survival and faith.

Before becoming an author and entrepreneur, Holloway lived a life far removed from the world of publishing. As a young man he became involved in gangs and the outlaw lifestyle that surrounds them. Those choices eventually led to prison, where he spent years in solitary confinement. It was during that time that he rebuilt his life through discipline, faith, and an unrelenting commitment to change.

After his release, Holloway went on to build successful businesses and begin writing the stories that had been forming in his mind for years. Today he writes stories about violence, consequence, and redemption for crime thriller readers who crave authenticity.

When he's not writing, he lifts weights, draws portraits, and spends time with his wife.

You can connect with me on:

🌐 https://rexhollowaywriter.com/home-1

Also by Rex Holloway

Thank you so much for reading this book! It is my sincere pleasure to share my thoughts with you.

I hope you will take a moment to leave this book a review on Amazon. Reviews are crucial for new authors.

Also, please visit my website rexhollowaywriter.com to keep up with my latest plans and maybe read a blog post or two.

Gladiator Farm: Mason Origins Book Two
Zane, a young, fame-hungry influencer boxer is seduced into a Houston crime empire rooted in prison violence, while Mason, now sober, must rescue him from a world that feeds men to hogs and brokers death through sports and fentanyl.

A Fire Devours: Mason Origins Book Three
When coordinated cartel attacks ignite oil fields and cripple refineries across South Texas, private security operator Mason is pulled into a fast-moving war that is far more organized and personal than it appears. As the violence escalates, he uncovers a ruthless adversary who knows his past and is orchestrating the chaos to draw him in, forcing Mason to confront an enemy who is always one step ahead—or lose everything in the fire.

Executive Powerbuilding

In a world engineered for comfort and excess, modern professionals have become biologically mismatched to their environment—trading strength, resilience, and mental clarity for convenience and decline. *Executive Powerbuilding* equips readers with a top-down system to reclaim control, combining decades of real-world training insight into simple, actionable strategies for building muscle, optimizing nutrition, and operating their body like a high-performance enterprise.

www.ingramcontent.com/pod-product-compliance
Lightning Source LLC
Chambersburg PA
CBHW061321200626
46813CB00016B/2605